# COLOSSUS RISING

# COLOSSUS RISING

## TORTH BOOK TWO

ABBY GOLDSMITH

Podium

Podium

# COLOSSUS RISING

# PART ONE

*Jonathan Stead freed a thousand slaves and brought them to paradise, where they and their children are free. He created a deadly storm which slew a thousand Torth. The Torth hunted him and murdered him, but with his dying breath, he promised to come back and free us all. We await his return.*

—Legend among urban slaves

# A CHOICE OF WORLDS

Ariock lounged across a row of cushions. He had earned this rest, these cushions, after months of gladiatorial fights and suffering.

But he kept thinking that his mother deserved rest, too. She should be here. Instead, her body was buried beneath rubble back on the planet Umdalkdul. That was her reward for sacrificing a lot of her own happiness in order to keep her son hidden and shielded. She had done her best.

"Ariock," Thomas called from the control deck on the far side of the room. "I've narrowed down our options. Come here."

Ariock made a lazy gesture. He could see the holographs from where he lay. Five semitransparent spheres glowed against the eternal nighttime of outer space, each sphere larger than Thomas's hoverchair. They lit up the ship's cushy interior. Each ghostly sphere swirled with clouds and continents.

"Our first option." Thomas floated near the first globe in the lineup. Its greenish glow added to his unhealthy skin tone. "Are you paying attention?"

"I can see fine," Ariock said, uncaring. He wouldn't feel at home on a random alien planet, no matter how nice it was. He had no family.

And how could he enjoy safety, with Earth under threat of being invaded and conquered?

Vy perched on an armrest nearby. "If you found those planets in a Torth database," she said to Thomas, "then the Torth know about them. Right? Won't they be searched?"

Thomas rolled his eyes. "Sorry, but I don't have a magical power to discover undiscovered planets. I just weighted the odds heavily in favor of planets where we have a chance to survive and hide for more than a decade." He pointed to the greenish globe. "It's chilly. Lots of tundra. Pretty much a wild frontier, with lots of herbivores and plants we can eat. The Torth figured they didn't need a pristine wilderness that's in dangerous proximity to a supernova. Its solar system is predicted to be annihilated within the next thousand years."

The villagers of Duin had dubbed Thomas their "Teacher," and Thomas looked like one, despite his prepubescent age. He spoke in a dry, lecturing tone. Dark circles underlined his eyes, and his chin jutted from his sallow face.

With his skeletal limbs and the yellow irises the Torth Empire had given him, Thomas looked more like a wizened android than a child.

His condition was due to a neuromuscular disease. He floated in a hoverchair, too weak to stand up. But he could soak up knowledge. Apparently, Thomas had absorbed hundreds of thousands of Torth lifetimes before severing himself from the collective network known as the Megacosm. Not only had he quit the Megacosm, but he'd quit owning slaves, and he'd given up his Torth privileges. Bloodstains marred his golden robes.

But although Thomas had rescued everyone in the starship, they didn't show him much sympathy. Ariock supposed he understood why. As a Yellow Rank, Thomas had mistreated his friends, and he had yet to express any remorse. His former best friend, Cherise, refused to go within his telepathic range. She wouldn't speak to him.

To make matters worse, Thomas seemed to consider himself a Torth. A renegade, but still a Torth. He never mentioned the human half of his heritage. Whatever human nature he had seemed to be buried inside the grim teacher he'd become.

To Ariock, those were all minor personality flaws. Thomas deserved respect. No one else among them had risked so much to escape. Besides, Thomas had once empathized with Ariock's crippling fear of the world outside his mansion.

"Supernova planet." Thomas pointed again. "Any questions?"

"Yes," Kessa said.

Like all the midget-size aliens known as ummins, Kessa had a fleshy beak and brow ridges. Her gray skin was extra wrinkled and papery. A custom-cut cloth covered the bald dome of her head, pinned into crisp folds and pleats, vaguely Egyptian in style.

"What is a supernova?" Kessa asked.

"It's a sun that explodes." Thomas could have translated his simplistic reply to the slave language, since the ummin refugees—there were over a hundred of them, perhaps one hundred and fifty—must be curious. They gazed at the holograph in awe.

But they had to rely on Kessa for translations. Thomas ignored them entirely, treating them like nothing. He might even consider them to still be slaves.

"What is a thousand years?" Kessa asked before Thomas could launch into his next spiel.

Thomas looked as if he'd rather answer questions from anyone else, preferably someone who was not an ummin elder. Slaves in the Torth Empire were forbidden access to calendars and clocks, so their concept of time was shaky.

"The supernova could consume the planet anywhere within five to fifty generations from now," Thomas said. "Everyone here will probably be dead by the time it happens."

He made that sound like a good thing.

"So our descendants would be doomed," Vy said.

Descendants. Did she assume that she would have descendants?

With Ariock?

He glanced down the length of his lanky body. He was the only man in the starship, but he was well over nine feet tall, and he had to duck through most doorways. He didn't fit on normal-size furniture. He used to cringe at the idea of being seen by the public. Why wasn't Vy repulsed by him, or afraid of him?

She had actually hugged him.

Ariock knew it was only an innocent hug meant to celebrate their escape from the planet ruled by Torth. They'd all been celebrating. But even so, he basked in the memory of her arms around his shoulders and her chest pressed against his.

"Right," Thomas said in a bland voice. "Well, we have four other options."

He pointed to the next holographic globe.

"Option two. All plate tectonics have ceased, and most of the surface is frozen. We can survive in unpleasant conditions if we're very careful with resources. And we'd have to become vegans. There aren't any meat animals. Just swarms of unpleasant bugs."

Vy scrunched up her face in horror.

"It is clear why the Torth never colonized these worlds," Kessa said. "They are dangerous."

"They're known as reject planets," Thomas said. "And yes. The Torth have settlements on all the best planets in the galaxy. Still, there are plenty of second-rate worlds that they've pretty much ignored."

"You mean crappy worlds?" Vy asked.

Thomas gave her a patronizing yellow stare. "I factored in survivability, accessibility, and security. These are our best options." He did not say that he had worked through astronomical calculations in a matter of minutes, but it was implied.

"Won't the Torth send Red Ranks to wait for us on each planet?" Kessa asked.

"Reject planets are pretty much outside the galactic infrastructure," Thomas explained. "The Torth can and will send troops, but their resources will be limited to whatever they bring. The Torth Empire hasn't fought a serious enemy for more than ten thousand years. Most of their outposts are demilitarized. What this means for us is that the Torth will take a surveillance approach instead of an aggressive approach. They'll want to locate us before committing all their military resources."

"They'll see us fly in, though, right?" Vy asked worriedly.

"We have two advantages," Thomas said. "One, a supergenius pilot." He gestured to himself. "Two, a Yeresunsa stormbringer with an incredibly long reach." He indicated Ariock. "Our goal is to blind their sensors or kill them before they see where we land."

"But they'll know what planet we're on," Vy pointed out.

"It depends," Thomas said. "If it's just one Torth in a jumper shuttle, I'm sure Ariock can introduce some problem—an asteroid or whatever—to distract them while we jaunt in some unpredictable direction and land, unseen. If we're unlucky and the Torth detect us with certainty? We'll have to decide whether we want to risk staying on that reject planet or try our luck elsewhere."

"Can the Torth not search these planets?" Kessa asked.

"They can try," Thomas said. "But a planet isn't just a collection of mountains and oceans and deserts. It's an entire world. We could hide in dense forests, or caves, or in habitats with animals that will register like us on orbital scans. Even if the Torth pinpoint what planet we choose, it might take them several lifetimes to track us down."

Finished with his lecture, he began to move on.

"Might?" Kessa asked. "This word expresses uncertainty."

Thomas gave her a look. "Yes. The Torth might capture us in a matter of centuries, or in a matter of hours after we land. Obviously, centuries will allow you time to grow old and die. Then the Torth would find your bones, and maybe the free descendants of ummins."

Kessa looked fascinated. Ariock felt the same awe and uncertainty. He had never imagined that he would grow old and die on an uninhabited alien world, isolated from Earth and the rest of the universe.

"Next," Thomas said without a trace of emotion. He pointed to the third sphere. "Think *Jurassic Park* on steroids. We can probably avoid the twelve-ton predators. If not, I'm sure Ariock can handle them."

Ariock drummed his fingers on the floor. He wanted to test his powers, to find out what his limits were—if he even had limits—but that was insanity. His mother's dead body flashed through his mind, white-haired and bloody. She'd been severed in half by a scrap of metal.

Her death could just as easily have been Vy's or Thomas's.

"Maybe you can handle them," Ariock suggested, studying Thomas. The boy might be able to protect everyone by brainwashing herds of wild megafauna.

"No." Thomas gave him a scathing glare. "My power has a severe distance limitation. Also, this planet has another significant danger. Its orbit passes through an asteroid belt, so we'd need you to destroy any incoming meteorites. I can't handle things like that."

"But—" Ariock wanted to argue, but Thomas floated to the fourth globe, a pretty turquoise color, and cut him off.

"This one has some nice tropical islands. The downside is an atmosphere that isn't well suited for our type of life. There's heavy air pressure. We'd be wheezing and exhausted all the time, except for Ariock, who inherited some heavy-G strength and endurance. On the other hand, the unpredictable seasons would make it difficult for the Torth to ascertain whether or not there's a Yeresunsa hidden on this world."

Ariock had nearly forgotten that the Torth could detect his sphere of influence, which supposedly engulfed an area the size of a solar system. His presence was said to cause unseasonable weather and disrupt animal migrations.

"So that's probably our safest hideout," Thomas said, "although it's problematic for long-term survival." He floated to the last globe in the lineup. "And the fifth. This planet was used as a testing ground for mass bionomic modification and chemical warfare during the early beginnings of the Torth Empire. The results have spawned some mutant strains of disease and wildlife that wouldn't normally arise in nature. We might catch an unknown plague if we go there. But—" He gestured toward Ariock. "We have a healer. So it should be fine—as long as Ariock doesn't get infected with something fatal."

Vy and Kessa exchanged doubtful looks.

"I'd also be concerned about undocumented variants of predators with bioengineered powers," Thomas said. "There are reports of telepathic packs of hyena-like predators there."

"Telepathic hyenas?" Vy drew out the words in a doubtful tone.

"According to ancient Torth lore," Thomas said, "the Torth species evolved from similar experimentation on Ice Age humans."

"Oh," Vy said, and Ariock inwardly agreed with her tone of realization. He had wondered why the Torth resembled humans.

"The Torth no longer allow bioengineering or genetic modification," Thomas said.

"What if we go to Earth?" The question slipped out of Ariock before he could contain it.

"Earth." Thomas made the word sound alien. "The wilderness planet the Torth are planning to invade and conquer. We can hope the Majority votes to delay that invasion, but all cards are off the table if we show up. We are a major target. Anywhere we go, if the Torth find us, they won't hesitate to go into destruction mode."

Vy looked conflicted.

"If you care about Earth," Thomas said, "it's the last place we should go."

Ariock clenched his fists, helpless, hating the Torth. They were genetically modified humans, yet they had become monsters without emotions or empathy.

He even hated his own shameful ancestry. Torth had watched Earth for untold millennia, like distant Olympian gods, and when they had come down to interfere with humans, Ariock and Thomas were born. Now the Torth were using them—their own hybrid offspring—as an excuse to speed up the enslavement of humanity.

The Torth thought they were entitled to own Earth, just like they owned everything else.

"They value logic." Ariock's voice was so cold and dark, the ummins stopped their soft chattering and watched him with owlish eyes. "Is it possible to offer them logical reasons to leave Earth alone?"

The suggestion seemed to catch Thomas off guard. He looked almost startled, and thoughtful. Then his face settled back to its usual dourness. "That's a nice little fantasy. You're wasting time thinking about it."

"Why not?" Vy demanded. She slid off her chair and began to pace. "Ariock is a threat to the Torth Empire. Maybe if they leave Earth alone, he'll leave them alone. Otherwise?" She hammered her fist into her palm in a crushing motion. "He'll come after them."

Ariock tried to look willing to hunt down Torth armies. He sat up, but inwardly, he knew that he wasn't going to seek ways to terrorize people, or to wreck spaceships and cities. Innocent people had died in that spaceport battle. It wasn't worth doing again.

Thomas leaned back in his hoverchair, studying Vy and Ariock. "You're dreaming. There are thirty-eight trillion Torth. They can command kamikaze slaves, and they have all the resources and knowledge in the known universe." He gestured around the ship. "We have enough food to last three days. We are not in any position to negotiate."

"But we can make threats," Vy said.

"I've killed a lot of Torth," Ariock added, reluctant. "If they keep hunting us, more Torth will die." That should be enough to make Red Ranks listen. "I can offer them peace."

He would even offer to surrender his own life, if it meant he could trust the Torth to leave Earth alone.

Thomas shook his head. "Honor means everything to a Torth. It's the basic economy of the Empire. Serving the Torth Majority is the most honorable thing a Torth can do. For the military ranks, that includes sacrificing their lives in service." He made an awkward shrug, impeded by his hunched spine. "A heroic death ensures that they'll be remembered in the Megacosm. They want to die heroically, and that means they want to take you down."

The Torth sounded painfully single-minded to Ariock. Honor was supposed to be a good thing, but they'd twisted it into something oppressive.

"The Torth sense of honor is what enabled them to conquer the galaxy," Thomas said. "And Ariock, you have your own single-minded sense of honor, so don't get too judgmental."

Maybe he had a point. Ariock did share some traits with the Torth.

They were his relatives, after all.

"Anyway," Thomas went on, "even if we were in an amazing position to negotiate, the Torth won't haggle with a nontelepath. They consider all other species to be inferior." He gave Ariock a level look. "You're inherently untrustworthy to them."

"That's idiotic," Vy said accusingly. "They can read minds and know if Ariock is lying or not."

"Slave species have volatile emotions," Thomas said. "Ariock might agree to a peace treaty, then get outraged for some reason and decide to wreck things."

Ariock began to defend himself. "I would never—"

"I know," Thomas cut in. "I'm familiar with the intimate details of your personality, so I know you'd never renege on a promise. Except when you're really emotional. You can't help it. That's human nature."

He sounded disparaging, but Ariock wasn't going to feel ashamed of being human. "Then you make the offer to them," he said.

"You think they'd trust me?" Thomas gave a lopsided, bitter grin. "I'm the Betrayer of the Torth Empire. I'm less trustworthy than a slave."

The Torth were so proud of their power to read minds, yet it seemed to Ariock that they ignored the best possible uses of their power. They should be able to trust. They should be able to have rational conversations and accept reasonable truces.

"Just decide where we're going." Thomas gestured at the holographic globes. "The more time we waste, the less chance we'll have to sneak through temporal streams without being caught."

Ariock lay against a chair, wondering why he'd even considered that a bargain was possible with people who routinely tortured slaves. The Torth would continue to rule the galaxy. No one ever challenged them.

Except for him and Thomas.

He needed to stop thinking about that and focus on getting himself and his friends to safety.

# CHAPTER 2

# THE GALACTIC DISK

Ariock studied the holographic spheres. A world of doom, a world of ice and bugs, a world of vicious megafauna, a world of slow suffocation, and a world of unpredictable bioengineered monstrosities. Which planet did he want to consign the rest of his life to?

Vy tapped her chin in thought. "The supernova planet? Um, I guess that one sounded okay." She gave Ariock a searching look. "Is that the best choice?"

Everyone watched Ariock with respectful intensity. Weptolyso, Kessa, Cherise, the ummins, even Thomas…everyone. They apparently expected him to make this decision alone.

As if his judgment was flawless. Had they forgotten his mistakes already? His mother wouldn't have forgotten.

"This decision will lay the foundation for the rest of our lives," Ariock said. "All of us." He included Thomas, hoping for some expert-level advice. "We should all have a voice."

No one spoke.

The threat to Earth must be weighing on their minds, or maybe they still had lingering fears of being captured by Torth. Ariock understood that. He had to keep reminding himself that the battles were over.

"Which planet do you recommend, Thomas?" he asked.

"I couldn't care less." Thomas sprawled in his hoverchair, looking bored.

"Really?" Vy said. "It's your future, too."

"I might care if I had a future." Thomas spoke without emotion. "But I don't. Just make a decision already."

Ariock had glimpsed the inside of the NAI-12 case when Vy had administered a dose to Thomas. Most of the vials were empty. Their supergenius friend was going to die young unless they could get more of his unique medicine.

The medicine only existed in one place: Boston. On Earth. It was a prototype, not even in production yet.

Thomas's fatal genetics were just one more gross injustice piled upon a heap of them.

"Keep in mind that these planets are wildernesses, without spaceports," Thomas said. "That means we won't be able to launch this ship. Once we land, we won't be able to leave unless Ariock uses his powers to get us off the planet."

That figured.

"Does the tropical planet have plants we could eat?" Ariock asked. "And fish that we can catch with nets?"

"Yup," Thomas said.

It sounded like a world where Ariock could avoid using his powers. He imagined himself suntanning on an alien beach and—dare he hope?—kissing Vy under a blue sky.

"Maybe that one sounds all right," he said, tentative.

"Is that your final decision?" Thomas turned toward the piloting console.

"Wait. Hold on." Vy settled next to Ariock, so close that he felt her body heat. "Do you really want to live on the suffocation planet?" she asked in a low voice.

Ariock leaned back against the curved wall. "I don't want to use my powers," he admitted. "Not if there's any way to avoid it."

If Vy was disgusted by what must seem like weakness or cowardice to her, she didn't show it. "You had a lot thrown at you," she said. "I don't think you should beat yourself up about it."

Ariock met her blue gaze. She had such kind eyes.

He tried to explain what sort of monster he was. "When I lost control, I lost my human perspective. I wasn't Ariock Dovanack anymore. I don't think I was even human." He didn't want to see her dismay, so he looked away. "I can't keep taking risks like that."

Instead of flinching away, Vy gently touched his arm. "You protected us."

Barely.

Ariock tried, again, to make her understand. "Do you know what it feels like when I use my powers?"

She listened, as if expecting a recipe instead of a nightmarish description.

"People are tiny little sparks to me," Ariock said. "Everyone is an ember, easy to snuff out. And I can't tell the difference between an ummin, a human, or a Torth. You all feel exactly the same."

"You kept us safe," Vy said stubbornly. "You killed the Torth and protected us."

"Sort of," Ariock admitted. "But it was pure luck. Some vestigial part of me remembered that I was supposed to protect the life sparks behind me and kill the ones in front."

That shameful admission should drive away anyone with common sense. At least the ummins were sensible enough to avoid him.

"You're a good person, Ariock," Vy said.

"I can't believe you're not afraid of me," Ariock said.

"I saw what happened," Vy said. "You didn't kill your mother. She crawled out of safety and into a chaotic war zone."

As if that was an acceptable excuse. Ariock held back his retort.

"We can drive ourselves crazy with guilt." Vy looked away. "I think we all have something we're ashamed of. When I was a slave…"

She trailed off, apparently in shame. Ariock glanced at her, curious despite himself.

"There were times when I considered leaving your mother behind, to survive on her own," Vy admitted. "I desperately wanted to move faster so I could survive. I know it was terrible to think that way. I was just so exhausted and afraid all the time."

She hunched her shoulders in shame.

"I understand." Ariock had no right to judge her innocent desperation. He had murdered beasts with his bare hands. "The desperate times are over."

"As long as you make a decision soon," Thomas called from across the room.

"If you want to avoid using your powers," Vy said, turning to Ariock, "that's all right. I respect that."

He studied her in amazement. It seemed a lot to ask, to accept him with such a major flaw.

"We can defend ourselves using blaster gloves." Vy gestured toward the bin where they'd stored their high-tech weapons.

Those gloves were too small for Ariock to use. Maybe the refugees could use them for hunting, or for self-defense, but Ariock wasn't going to stand around, helpless, while predators ate the refugees he was supposed to protect.

"Those gloves never run out of ammunition," Vy said. "They're actually pretty cool. They just need a few seconds to recharge between rounds and then they're good to go again. So I'm okay with a planet that has predators. What do you think?"

Everyone else looked ambivalent. Ariock gave a tentative nod.

"Supernova planet?" Vy asked.

"Supernova," Ariock agreed.

"Excellent." Thomas waved his fingers over the control panel, and the holographic planets vanished, replaced by a glowing cobweb with strands that blended into a fog. "Its official name is Reject-81. Plotting a course."

Several ummins watched him work with fascination.

"Is that a map?" Vy walked toward the cobweb holograph.

"It's a representation of temporal streams," Thomas said. "This is how we leap ninety-five thousand light-years."

He waved his fingers, and a green beacon flared inside the fog.

One of the ummins was bold enough to ask a question. Thomas made an offhand reply in the slave tongue.

"Are those tiny strands all temporal streams?" Vy asked.

"Yup," Thomas said.

"The whole universe is mapped like that?" she asked.

"Only our galaxy," Thomas said. "The Torth Empire sent multigeneration colony starships to other galaxies, but one by one, they devolved into anarchy and lost contact. As far as the Torth know, they never got anywhere. And the Majority eventually voted to stop sending exploration crews beyond our galaxy."

Ariock remembered Thomas saying that the Torth did not allow the development of faster-than-light communications technology. The Torth Majority would never permit any individuals to gain enough power to escape or to compete with Torth military might.

"What happened to the civilization that invented the temporal streams?" Kessa asked.

Most of the technology used by the Torth Empire was hijacked or stolen. According to Thomas, the Torth had even stolen their power to traverse the stars.

"No one knows," Thomas said. "But there's historical evidence that the Torth obliterated a few ultrapowerful high-tech civilizations. They didn't enslave the ones that were truly threatening. They got rid of them entirely."

Such a casual sentence for such huge catastrophes.

"They obliterated entire civilizations?" Vy asked with quiet sorrow.

Thomas nodded.

Ariock wondered what would become of Earth while he was hiding on a reject planet. Would humankind put up enough of a fight for the Torth to consider them truly threatening?

How many weeks would the Torth need in order to conquer every remote outpost of humanity on Earth? With their power to read minds, they might only need a few hours.

"Where is Earth?" Vy gazed at the glowing map.

Thomas moved his fingers above the panel, and the cobweb contracted. More threads appeared at its edges, then more.

"There," Thomas said. "I zoomed out. Let me make it easier to see."

He fiddled with the controls—and the view outside their spaceship changed dramatically. All of a sudden, instead of drifting through empty space, they soared through a dense, breathtaking, cottony cobweb of stars.

"Oh my God." Vy stared up at the dome.

"It's a computer simulation," Thomas told her dryly. "The walls can display anything from the database of celestial star maps. Here." He waved, and a fiery blue beacon glowed in the distance. "That's Earth."

The last time Ariock had traveled in a spaceship, wrapped in chains, he hadn't imagined the wonders of these navigational illusions. Even though the view was just a harmless illusion, the change made him uneasy. Thomas had an awful lot of control over their environment.

It reminded Ariock that their streamship was actually a tiny habitat. This room was no larger than his sky room back home. It was an enclosure.

Like a cave. Or like a prison cell.

The refugees gawked with shock and awe. To them, it was all magic.

Kessa's large eyes reflected the dense starlight. "Where is Umdalkdul?"

Thomas did something to the controls. "There." An orange light flared in the mass of stars.

"And where is our destination planet?" Vy asked.

Thomas made another light glow, far in the distance. "If you'd like to see all the habitable worlds in this region," he said, "here we go."

The view became a violent mass of colors, blotting out everything else. Ariock had to squint.

"This is just a little sliver of the Torth Empire," Thomas said, possibly responding to someone's thoughts. He worked the controls, and the view zoomed out, faster and faster. The clusters of lights knitted so close together, they formed hard crystals.

Everyone shielded their eyes, but the colors condensed even more, flattening into a disk. Its edges ran into spiral trails.

"Here's the Torth Empire," Thomas said.

The galaxy hung below them in stunning detail, a cottony formation of colored lights.

"It is so much." Kessa gazed at the immense view.

"It's beautiful." Vy looked troubled, and no wonder. The Torth must own millions of planets. No one could possibly challenge all that.

"Can we see a close-up of the planet we're aiming for?" Ariock asked.

"Unfortunately, no," Thomas said in his uncaring voice. "Terrestrial maps have to be downloaded from an external source. The Blue Rank who owned this streamship only stored local maps of Umdalkdul and its moons."

He flicked his hand, and the stunning view washed away, replaced by the starry sky.

But a violent-looking halo swallowed much of that sky. Its center was utterly black, its iris a chaotic tangle.

"What is—?" Vy began.

"That's the supernova we're heading toward." Thomas poked icons on the control panel.

Ariock resisted a temptation to expand his awareness, to reach out and feel the supernova. It must be full of mysterious energies.

No. His Yeresunsa powers were dangerous. He needed to stay small. Or as small as he could be, anyway.

"Well, that was easy." Thomas leaned back. "We now have four days of boring, slow travel ahead of us. I suggest we ration the water and food." He floated away from the console and yawned ostentatiously. "It's been a really long day. I'm going to sleep."

"Wait," Vy said as he began to hover away. "Are we on autopilot?"

"Of course," Thomas said. "Don't mess with the settings. Wake me up if you see flashing lights."

Ariock watched Thomas float to an alcove at the edge of the room. There wasn't much privacy.

No one had washed the bloodstains off Thomas's clothes or hair. Was he going to sleep like that? In his hoverchair? Without a pillow or a blanket?

Maybe he was taking pains to not treat his companions like slaves.

"Good night," Thomas said pointedly.

Vy stood and walked toward him. "Thomas, I think you need some care." She looked at his medicine case, nestled next to him. "Aren't you overdue for an injection?"

"I'm making the medicine last." Thomas gave her a resentful look. "I don't need or want help. Just go away."

Vy hesitated for a second.

Then she grabbed a washcloth and a canteen.

"Don't waste water on me." Thomas sounded irritable. "I'm the most expendable member of our crew. Once we land? You won't need me."

Vy began to wash the bloodstains out of his hair. "You're not expendable. You saved our lives. As far as I'm concerned, you're a hero."

That was truth.

Ariock got to his feet. He scooped up one of the threadbare blankets and a water gourd. Both items were tiny in his hands. The holograph felt like cool air as he passed through part of it, padding toward Thomas.

"You don't need to help me," Thomas said, enduring the sponge bath. "We'll be safe in four days. After that, you'll have your own futures to worry about."

Ariock did have concerns about surviving on a wilderness planet with bare-minimum supplies. But he was even more concerned about Thomas's mind-set. Did he want to die? Or was he just resigned to it?

And his health. Anyone could see how sick Thomas was. His chest was concave, and his malformed limbs were withered from years of atrophy. He might need hospitalization within weeks.

"Maybe I'll figure out better ways to use my healing power." Ariock gently tucked the blanket around the boy. Healing was a lot nicer and safer than storm powers. It was worth experimenting with.

"You can't save me," Thomas said with acid in his tone. "There's nothing you can do."

Ariock folded the blanket so Thomas could rest on a makeshift pillow. Ariock had failed to protect his mother—but that didn't mean he accepted failure in general.

What were his promises worth if he shrugged them off?

He needed to be able to trust himself.

He needed to keep Thomas alive, no matter what it took. He refused to fail again.

"Would you like to sleep on a sofa instead of in your hoverchair?" Vy asked.

Thomas groaned. "I'm sick of overhearing everyone's thoughts. Just leave!"

Vy gave Ariock a look, and he took her cue. They both left, so Thomas could have whatever privacy and quiet time they could afford to give him.

# CHAPTER 3

# OPENED SECRETS

"Teacher?" an ummin queried.

It was Varktezo. Again.

Thomas forced his breathing to stay in a sleep rhythm. He kept his eyes closed and ignored the drool on his cheek. This streamship was designed for one Torth with two or three slaves, not a crowd of more than one hundred and fifty. Sleep—or the pretense of sleep—was his only escape from the noise.

Most of the passengers were respectful enough to leave Thomas alone. Their ummin voices blended in a background buzz reminiscent of college auditoriums. It soothed him enough to catch a few hours of real sleep, in between bouts of discomfort caused by his position in the hoverchair.

"Is he ever going to wake up?" Varktezo asked one of his adolescent companions.

"Why are you so impatient?" she asked.

"I'm not impatient!" Varktezo said. "How can you wait so long? He should teach us how to read Torth glyphs, and how this ship works, and how the Torth Empire works. Don't you want to learn?"

Thomas sensed Varktezo studying his face. The ummin was actually considering shaking the Teacher awake.

"Perhaps he is ill," the other adolescent suggested. "Just leave him alone."

"Ooh! I'll ask the Bringer of Hope to heal him. Good idea." Varktezo sped toward the far side of the room, where Ariock was resting and chatting with Vy.

Great. Thomas knew that his quasi escape was about to be interrupted.

But once they landed…he could hardly wait. His vacation would be eternal. He would finally allow himself to die.

Just two more days.

"Thomas," Ariock said, approaching along with Vy and Varktezo.

Thomas stretched and pretended to wake up.

"You've been sleeping a lot," Vy said. "Are you all right?"

Thomas tried to work some saliva into his mouth. "I'm just tired."

Ariock raised his hands in the healing posture, and glorious relief washed through Thomas. He shivered as his aches and pains subsided.

"Don't do that." Thomas glared. "I don't want your healing."

"Why not?" Vy looked mystified.

"Because it's wasteful," Thomas said. "Ariock isn't getting enough to eat. Powers are tied to health. It's idiotic for him to waste his limited energy on a problem he can't ever fix."

Ariock made himself comfortable on the cushioned floor across from Thomas. "This is why we need to have a conversation."

Vy held a canteen to Thomas's lips. "You sound like you need water."

Thomas sipped. The canteen was almost empty. He hoped they were being conservative with their supplies.

"Have you ever—" Ariock began.

"Yes." Thomas answered his unspoken question. "I've brainwashed people before, but I'm not going to do it to anyone here. Okay? I got peppered with inhibitor. It's still in my system, so you don't need to worry."

Ariock looked pained. "Sorry. Could we talk about—"

Thomas coughed weakly. "How about if we have this conversation another time?"

He sensed Ariock's inward search for countersuggestions.

"You'll just keep putting us off," Vy said to Thomas. "You've been avoiding talking to us."

She knew him too well.

"I don't know anything useful about Yeresunsa," Thomas admitted. "The Torth Empire lost a lot of knowledge from their earliest era. Since then, Yeresunsa powers were outlawed and research into Yeresunsa is forbidden."

"But you—" Ariock began.

"Frankly," Thomas said, "my personal history is none of your business. I don't need to tell you the sordid details of how I learned what I could do. My childhood trauma is completely irrelevant to our situation. We don't have the same powers."

Vy studied him, as if he was a patient she meant to cure. "Have you ever told anyone?" She glanced meaningfully across the room, to where Cherise sat among her ummin friends.

"Never." Thomas forced himself to calm down. "It happened when I was a little kid. All right?"

The nearest refugees were paying attention, wary yet curious. One of them tugged Kessa over. They wanted translations.

"All right," Vy said in an agreeable tone. "You have a past that we don't get to know about. Meanwhile, you know every secret we have. That's fair, right?"

Ouch. She had a point.

For a moment, Thomas considered telling them what he had done at that foster home in Maine.

But he knew it was a terrible idea. If the refugees and Cherise were avoiding him out of fear, then revealing his huge mistake would only exacerbate their fears. He didn't want to soak that up.

He especially didn't want Vy, Ariock, and Kessa to downgrade their respect for him. They actually thought of him as a hero. He didn't want that change.

Besides, the Torth had forced him to relive this trauma during his Adulthood Exam. Must he suffer through it again?

"How would you like me to reveal the worst moments of your life?" Thomas asked Vy. "How about that guy you went on a pity date with?" He turned to Ariock. "How about all your suicide attempts? I could tell everyone about the time you nearly jumped off a bridge—"

"Enough." Ariock cut him off in a tone that made all the ummins fall silent.

Vy looked frustrated. "We're not trying to humiliate you. That's not our intention."

"Then stop prying." Thomas wanted to escape, but he was as good as cornered. The ship was too small.

"You rescued us," Ariock said. "Yet you act like a Torth. My instincts say you'll never betray us. But Cherise won't go near you, and everyone is afraid of you. Including me. Should we be afraid?"

Thomas opened his mouth, but any definitive reply would be false.

He could not say for certain what sort of person he was. He didn't know, himself.

"I'm sure you know more about my powers than I do," Ariock said, searching his face. "All I want is some information. I need to know who you are."

Thomas slid lower in his hoverchair. Ariock and Vy had valid arguments. The other passengers saw Thomas as malevolent and mysterious, and he knew perfectly well that if he were to open up and demystify himself, that would go a long way toward equalizing their differences. It might even lay the groundwork for friendships.

He just didn't think friendships were worth the effort.

What was the point? He was going to die. He had failed in his friendship with Cherise. He would surely fail with everyone else.

He just didn't dare admit those truths out loud. It would confirm everyone's worst fears that he was secretly an emotionless Torth.

"All right." Thomas let out a breath that trembled. "Fine. You win. You'll get to hear my darkest secret."

Ariock had expected to walk away without answers or trust. His huge shoulders relaxed. "Thank you, Thomas," he said. "It means a lot to me that you're willing to share something painful."

"Whatever." Thomas glared at the onlookers. Not only were dozens of ummins listening, but Weptolyso had ambled over, and he understood enough English to follow along. And Kessa, of course.

Even Pung, his former slave.

They all wanted to hear the story that made the Teacher so uncomfortable.

The only English speaker who wasn't paying attention was Cherise. Thomas used to yearn to tell her this dark secret. She might have loved him for trusting her with such a weighty confession.

Or not.

In reality, Cherise probably would have backed off and begged for a transfer to another group home. That would have been wise.

"How about if we do this without an audience?" Thomas suggested.

He sensed consternation. Pung thought he was a hypocrite, eager to soak up everyone else's secrets while remaining aloof.

"Okay. Whatever." Thomas was outnumbered. He had the minority opinion, and the majority usually won.

He yearned for a tranquility mesh.

The intense curiosity of his listeners reminded him of press conferences. He used to endure microphones waved in his face along with rapid-fire questions. *Just how fast can you calculate?* *Is your memory as legendary as your coworkers say it is?* And sometimes, *Do you wish you could meet your birth parents?*

Those reporters used to watch for cracks in his polished demeanor. They'd wanted him to scream or to weep. Emotions would grab their audiences.

But emotions would rob Thomas of respect. Little kids wept or threw tantrums. Not him.

"My story won't set you at ease," Thomas warned his audience. "Are you sure you want another reason to fear me?"

Vy and others looked unsettled. Even Kessa looked slightly worried.

But Ariock did not budge, and neither did his thoughts. "Just tell us."

Thomas squeezed the armrests of his hoverchair and tried to gather his nerves. Maybe he should soften the story?

No. He wasn't going to stoop so low as to lie.

He was a traitor, a thief, and practically a mass murderer. If he took advantage of nontelepaths by lying to them, or by playing with their expectations, then he might as well quit his mission of bringing them to a place of safety.

He needed a shred of honor. That was the only way he would die in peace, and with some modicum of self-respect.

"How old were you?" Vy asked.

"Six."

They were silent, letting that age sink in.

"Where were you living?" Vy asked. "A foster home?"

He nodded, avoiding their gazes, not wanting to let them see his haunted look. "It was a group home in northern Maine, for disabled kids."

Vy snuggled against Ariock, making herself comfortable. Ariock tentatively reached around her, and Vy clasped his arm like it was a blanket.

"Will you describe this home?" Kessa asked.

Thomas remembered, with his flawless total recall, ratty rugs and plastic tarps over broken windows. He remembered every sad, broken child in that home, with no hope.

He had been one of them.

He hesitated.

But what the hell. If he could endure abusive foster parents, a billion ugly memories, bullies in foster homes, his debilitating disease, persecution by the Torth Empire, and his own impending suicide, then surely he could relive this trauma one more time. And he could do it without breaking down and weeping.

"It was summer." He began to speak in a steady voice.

# CHAPTER 4

# ONCE UPON A SUMMER

Thomas Hill, aged six, studied an obsolete college textbook about neuroendocrinology. The book weighed half as much as he did, and he couldn't have lifted it even with all his strength. His limbs were underdeveloped, short and atrophied. The best he could do was turn pages.

His older foster sister Donna, who was blind, had kindly bought the book for him, and she had placed it on his lap. Donna did a lot to help him out.

The text and diagrams on each page spread got branded into his memory. Thomas couldn't seem to forget things, no matter how hard he tried. He could recite the exact script of every infomercial on TV. He knew every crumb of dirt on the kitchen linoleum, the exact layout of the grassy patches in the weed-choked yard, and every wakeful millisecond of his own life, dating back to before he'd become self-aware.

He hated knowing so many things that didn't matter.

Sometimes he considered asking Donna to steal beer for him, just to see if intoxication would blur his memories. The fridge always had plenty of beer, if nothing else.

Or he could try the pain medications his foster mother swallowed every day. Her addiction made her tremble, and he didn't want to add to his own massive physical problems, but what if opioids affected his memory?

It would be worth it.

He really wanted to learn about neurochemistry, plus anything that might help him diagnose his many problems. This textbook was a rare treasure. The public library didn't offer in-depth books about neuroscience, and neither did the local bookstores. Thomas wasn't allowed to touch the computer. Even if he risked it, he would never be able to wrangle enough time to hack into college databases and read his fill of online textbooks.

So he had talked to Donna, the only one of them who had an outside family member who regularly gave her money. Even though she was blind and couldn't read textbooks, he had persuaded her to buy a few secondhand books. In return, he promised to tell her anything she wished to know, any time she asked.

They both thought it was a pretty good bargain.

A sense of danger interrupted Thomas's scan of the textbook. Crackling flames. A burning stench. He looked up from the book.

The drapes were on fire.

Jerry, one of the developmentally disabled boys, had apparently found the cigarette lighter, and now he gaped at the curtains. He thumbed the lighter on and off, backing away in stunned disbelief. Thomas sensed that Jerry wanted it to work like a TV remote control. He wanted to make the flames stop.

"Fire!" Thomas's voice was high-pitched and squeaky with fear, and so weak he wanted to cry. "Help! There's a fire!"

A lampshade began to burn. It flared rapidly, and flames danced across the carpet. Soon the fire would head toward the ratty couch where Thomas sat.

Jerry threw the lighter away and sped past Thomas, out of the room.

The doorway was so close, any able-bodied person could have run to it and escaped. But Thomas could not walk. He could not stand up without help. His basic-model wheelchair was folded up in the kitchen. The "parents" of this home provided their wards with minimal aid. They spent most of their meager income on beer and pain meds.

Thomas sucked in as much air as his weak lungs could hold, and he shrieked.

He was going to die horribly, trapped and helpless. No one would care. His birth parents, whoever they were, would probably laugh with relief when they heard about his death in the news.

He shrieked again and again. His throat burned, his chest ached, and he knew that he would die horribly.

"What is it?" his foster father roared. "What…?" He leaned into the room and peered at the fire with intoxicated, bloodshot eyes.

"Help!" Thomas sounded like a wheedling child. It was not the sort of voice that Mr. Gotte respected. As far as Gotte was concerned, most kids were greedy, self-absorbed pests, and Thomas was the worst. Gotte believed that Thomas exaggerated his weakness in order to manipulate everyone around him with pity.

Gotte gave Thomas a smug grin. His thoughts were unmistakable.

He was going to pretend that he had missed seeing this particular problem.

He would get insurance money for the burned-down house, and one less disabled kid to feed and clothe. Good riddance to Thomas, the creepy know-it-all.

"They'll know you could have saved me!" Thomas screamed, desperate. "People can hear!"

Gotte hesitated.

"Just pick me up!" Thomas cried. "Be a hero!"

Gotte seized Thomas in his burly arms. For one instant, Thomas felt sure that he was safe. His foster father was going to do a nice thing for once.

Gotte radiated a noble mood, but at this close range, Thomas sensed his private intentions. *I'll do the world a favor. Get rid of this demon forever.*

Gotte believed that he was evil. Possibly the Antichrist.

He prepared to chuck Thomas into the fire.

A healthy kid would have struggled. All Thomas had was a mouth and a brain that infuriated grown-ups.

He used his last second of life to burrow deep inside Gotte's mind, desperate to find a humiliation or a trauma—anything that might induce his murderous caretaker to stop. Thomas was so panicked, he accidentally overshot his goal, tearing through layers of vile secrets, arrowing straight into the primeval knot at the core.

All people and animals had a primeval knot buried at the core of their minds. This was the foundation, the instincts upon which everything else was built.

Thomas wrapped himself around that primal core, as if he could wrench it. His own terror seemed to give his mind a weight that it didn't normally have.

Gotte's primal core broke. Thomas sensed it twist and snap.

He withdrew his intense focus just in time to brace himself as he fell. Gotte seemed to have forgotten about tossing him. Instead, his foster father stood slack-jawed, ignoring the fire and everything else.

Thomas landed on the carpeted floor. He was small enough so that it didn't hurt too much.

The room was boiling. His skin prickled as his sweat evaporated.

Gotte seemed to be in a numbed state of shock.

"Please," Thomas whimpered, even though it must be useless. "Please carry me away from this fire."

Instead of kicking Thomas, or sneering at him, Gotte leaned down and seized him without any apparent forethought. He slung Thomas over one hairy shoulder and trotted into the kitchen.

Only one thought dominated the shattered remnants of Gotte's mind. All he wanted to do was carry Thomas away from this fire. Carry Thomas away from this fire. Carry Thomas away from this fire.

The girl with cerebral palsy gave them a frightened look.

"Mr. Gotte?" Thomas said. At least the air was easier to breathe in the kitchen. "Can you stop the fire?"

Gotte moaned in agitation, shifting from foot to foot. He heard motivational significance in every word, but it contradicted the priority that he should carry Thomas away from this fire. He could not process what was expected of him.

His ability to make decisions seemed entirely gone.

"Put me down," Thomas said. "On the kitchen counter."

Gotte began to fling him down.

"Be gentle!" Thomas yelled.

Gotte switched from rough to gentle in an instant. He set Thomas on the counter as if handling a fragile baby.

"Okay." Thomas wondered if he could fully control the drunken rage beast that used to be his foster father. Maybe he could get this broken-minded adult to do anything he wanted?

"Mr. Gotte?" he said. "Go and do everything you can to stop that fire."

Gotte raced into the fiery living room. No fear. No precautions. He was even more suggestible than a sleepwalker.

A series of heavy thuds ensued. Thomas leaned, but he couldn't peer around the doorway, and he was too far away to read Gotte's mind.

"Mr. Gotte?" he called, unable to see what was happening. "Are you okay?"

No answer.

The body-slamming thuds continued. It sounded like Gotte had gone berserk and was tearing the living room apart.

"Use the hose!" Thomas figured that high-pressure water must be a good way to stop a big fire. "It's in the yard," he shouted helpfully, just in case Gotte had forgotten.

A second later, he heard glass shatter. It sounded as if Gotte had smashed through a window in order to get to the hose in the yard.

Thomas cupped his hands around his mouth to amplify his squeaky voice. "Turn on the water first!" He should probably choose his commands with care. Gotte seemed to need accuracy. "Once the hose is working, spray water on the flames until they go out, okay?"

He heard the roar of high-pressure water.

The girl with cerebral palsy stared into the living room, transfixed with horror. She had a better vantage point than Thomas, and thankfully, she was close enough for him to peer through her eyes.

Now he could see, and what he saw was a blistery, bubbly mess of skin. His foster father looked like a wreck. All his hair gone. His clothes were charred remnants.

He must have rolled in the flames like a dog in grass.

Now he hosed down the remaining flames with robotic accuracy.

Two more foster children joined the girl, staring into the living room. One of them glanced at Thomas, and Thomas offered a smile. It must look dopey, since he was lying on the counter, too weak to sit up, but he wanted the kid to feel reassured that they were safe.

The kid ran away.

Thomas inwardly told himself that he wasn't evil. No one liked him, usually, but he might finally gain a friend or two once they realized that he was in control and that he was better than a grown-up. He was smarter.

"Mr. Gotte?" Thomas called. "You can stop now."

Gotte paused, then continued to water the furniture. The living room was a sopping mess.

"Stop," Thomas commanded.

Through the eyes of other kids, he saw Gotte go still. Gotte dropped the hose and seemed to await further commands. Blood oozed from cracks between his massive blisters.

Maybe he needed a doctor?

But if Gotte went to a hospital, the household would run out of food and the toilet would back up. Also, nurses and doctors would ask questions. Scary questions. They might figure out that Thomas was to blame for his foster father's condition.

Thomas would gain a juvenile record. He really didn't want that. He was only six.

Or worse. What if a bunch of grown-ups decided that Thomas was the Antichrist and needed to be murdered?

"What happened?" a shrill voice demanded.

His foster mother staggered into the kitchen on her high heels. She threw her purse on the cluttered counter and stared in outrage from Thomas to the kids in the doorway.

Then she peered around the corner and saw her husband. "Mitch? Oh my God. Mitch!"

Gotte did not react to his wife.

"Mr. Gotte, go turn off the water," Thomas said. "Then come back here."

Gotte strode through the broken window with single-minded purpose.

Mrs. Gotte turned her stunned stare to Thomas. Too late, Thomas realized how weird he must look on the counter, self-assured in spite of the wreckage. He usually pleaded for his foster parents to leave him alone.

"Demon!" Mrs. Gotte launched at him, her hands stretched into claws.

Thomas cringed. Of course, his weak little arms weren't going to shield him...but the instant she entered his telepathic range, he plunged into the depths of her mind.

He hurtled past her rage and her memories, all the way down to her core. He wrapped himself around that primal core and twisted it.

Mrs. Gotte tottered and pinwheeled her arms for balance. Her thoughts shattered and evaporated. Thomas sensed that a tiny section of her mind shrieked in horror, but that part of her was stifled, trapped below the level of her damaged consciousness.

She stood inert. Her blue eyes went glazed and empty beneath her mop of hair.

Good.

"No one likes you, Mrs. Bleating Goat," Thomas said, daring to use the nickname that kids called her behind her back.

It felt wonderful to speak such a plain truth. He had never spoken this honestly to anyone before.

"Go gather some bandages," Thomas told. "Bandage up your husband's burns."

The command dominated her mind. She stood and walked away with single-minded purpose. Nothing would stop her from gathering bandages and bandaging up her husband's burns.

Thomas imagined ways to keep other grown-ups from finding out what he had done. Mr. Gotte was a mechanic. His wife ran a nail salon. They both had friends who visited their home. There were visitors nearly every day.

"Um, the fire department?" Donna clutched the kitchen phone as if it was a lifeline. "I guess."

Thomas dived into her recent memories and realized that she was on the phone with 9-1-1, the emergency services hotline.

"Donna," Thomas said sharply. "Don't tell them anything. Hang up. Right now."

She burst into terrified tears.

Thomas realized that his tone had come across as a threat. "I won't hurt you," he said, appalled. "I'm disabled. Remember?"

She dropped the phone back into its cradle, then fled toward the bedrooms, sobbing.

She might alarm the other kids. They might panic and do something stupid.

Thomas figured he needed to persuade them that they were afraid of the wrong thing. They should be afraid of grown-ups, not of him.

Mrs. Gotte bandaged her unresponsive husband with workmanlike efficiency. She used toilet paper, since their bandage supply was depleted.

"Mr. and Mrs. Gotte?" Thomas called. "Come here."

They obeyed.

"There's nothing to worry about," Thomas called toward the bedrooms. He had soaked up enough random memories from strangers to know how parents were supposed to take care of kids. So he would command the Gottes to act nice. Soon enough, Donna and everyone else would be happy with him.

Maybe he'd even get Mr. and Mrs. Gotte to tell jokes, like parents on TV.

"Mr. Gotte?" he said. "Put me in my wheelchair."

Once he was seated to his satisfaction, he turned to Mrs. Gotte. "Open the note app on your phone."

She obeyed.

"Okay. Write this list." Thomas recited a list of groceries needed, pausing long enough for her to type. Their refrigerator contained nothing but peanut butter, expired milk, and several packs of beer. After today, each child would get a nutritious meal. Plus their favorite desserts.

"Good," Thomas told her. "Now put your phone into your purse."

She dropped the phone into her purse without her usual flourish.

"The next time I say 'groceries,'" Thomas said, "you will pick up your purse and go shopping for the items you just listed on the note app of your phone."

Mrs. Gotte listened with all-consuming intensity.

In the dim hallway, Thomas's foster siblings listened as well. Jerry made a sound of agitation. The others shushed him, and Thomas pretended not to see or hear his unsettled audience.

"While you're at the supermarket," he told his foster mother, "you will act normal. Act the way you should in front of people. You will act normal any-time you are away from this house."

He mentally reviewed his commands. Mrs. Gotte seemed to comprehend what "normal" meant. That should be enough to ward off suspicion.

"Groceries," he said.

Mrs. Gotte slung her purse over her shoulder. Thomas was pleased that she did this in a normal fashion.

She trotted out the front door, and it banged shut behind her.

Thomas exhaled. So far, so good. He could surely whip the Gottes into shape as parents. Soon everyone would adore him instead of whispering about him behind his back.


On the streamship, thirteen-year-old Thomas realized that he was hugging him-self, the way he used to. It was a good thing his listeners couldn't sense his mood.

"So," he said, "that's my story. I was just a kid. I thought I was helping people, and I was wrong."

Ariock nodded with sympathy, but his mind radiated suspicious curiosity. He guessed there was more that Thomas had neglected to tell.

Vy was all sympathy. "You acted in self-defense," she said. "And what you did was heroic."

Thomas looked at her, startled.

"I mean, it's a scary power," Vy admitted. "But your intentions were good. You have nothing to feel ashamed of."

Thomas supposed that, if viewed a certain way, without certain knowledge, then maybe he had done a good thing. He had been trying to save impoverished disabled children, after all. That wasn't evil.

"Did the emergency services arrive?" Kessa asked.

"Eventually."

"Did you twist their minds, too?" Kessa studied him with a piercing gaze.

Thomas forced himself to unclench his hands. The child he used to be was long gone. He was no longer that person. "No."

"Why not?" Kessa was relentless.

Thomas sank lower. Kessa was almost as curious as Varktezo. She was going to drag the worst part of his story out of him, even if no one else did.

Well, he hoped they weren't expecting proof that he was safe to be around.

He began to talk, emotionless and robotic. Let them hear what sort of monster he was. Maybe his friends would actively aid his suicide once they heard the whole story.

That was just fine.

# CHAPTER 5

# THE WALKING DEAD

A normal burn victim would have begged for help. Brainwashed, Mr. Gotte ignored the agony of his suppurating wounds. He merely existed. Anything he could do to lessen the pain would be a decision, and he no longer made decisions.

Six-year-old Thomas appreciated that.

He micromanaged Gotte through household chores. They did three loads of laundry, washed dirty dishes, collected empty beer cans into a trash bag, and made a pile of wreckage to throw out later. Gotte did let out an involuntary scream every once in a while, but Thomas told him to drink water every so often, and that seemed to keep him functional.

As the evening shadows lengthened outside, Gotte seemed less and less able to follow complexities. Thomas had to revise every single command into simplistic step-by-step instructions.

And where was Mrs. Gotte? Summer days lasted a long time, but she should have returned with the groceries at least an hour ago.

When he replayed his memories after the groceries command, he could not recall hearing any sound of an engine, or tires crunching over gravel. It seemed insane that Mrs. Gotte would have gone shopping without a vehicle. The nearest supermarket was seven miles away.

Thomas supposed he ought to find out for certain.

"Let's go outside," he said with reluctance. "Open the door."

Gotte turned the doorknob in vain. It was locked. He kept trying.

"Unlock the door." Thomas waited for Gotte to obey. "Now open the door. Now go behind my wheelchair and push me outside."

Gotte stank worse than roadkill combined with an outhouse. Belatedly, Thomas realized that he'd neglected to tell his zombified foster father to relieve his bladder. The zombie had wet himself.

"Stop," Thomas said, once they were on the front porch, amid cooling air and chirping crickets.

The beat-up old pickup truck was still in the driveway. That was the only functional vehicle the Gottes owned, amid rusted shells. Thomas wanted to punch himself for being such an idiot. He should have told his zombified foster mother to *drive* to the supermarket. He should have given her explicit instructions.

Instead, she must have walked the seven miles.

In high heels.

Thomas sucked breath through his teeth. Maybe controlling other people wasn't as easy as grown-ups made it look. "Go inside the house," he told Gotte, "and fetch the truck key from the kitchen counter. Then return."

After many painstaking instructions, Thomas sat buckled into the passenger seat of the pickup truck. He tried to ignore the stench of his foster father.

"Roll down the windows," he commanded.

Crickets chirped in a loud, ominous way.

"Turn on the headlights," Thomas said. "Back out of the driveway."

Gotte made bestial noises instead of obeying the last command. His eyes were glassy, and he didn't blink enough.

Thomas sensed the problem. Gotte was trying to back out of the driveway on foot while he remained buckled into the driver's seat. Conflicting commands swirled in his broken mind.

"Stop backing out of the driveway," Thomas said with a weary sigh. "Okay. Place your right foot on the brake pedal. Press the pedal with your foot. Shift the gearshift to the *R* symbol."

As a six-year-old, Thomas shouldn't know how to drive a pickup truck, but he helplessly absorbed skills from anyone he spent more than a few minutes around. He understood how to repair transmissions and radiators. He could theoretically give someone a perfect pedicure, thanks to memories he'd soaked up from his foster mother. He even knew American Sign Language and braille.

"Gently press the gas pedal," Thomas instructed. "Steer us backward onto the road."

He was too short to peer over the dashboard, so he had to assess the road through the zombie's damaged mind. Gotte stared straight ahead without a care in the world. He did not care about laws. They would smash into trees if Thomas didn't stay alert and tell him when to slow and when to avoid a pothole every few seconds.

The headlights barely penetrated the gloom.

As they drove, Thomas strained to see any sign of a lone woman trudging along the road with groceries. What if she'd wandered into the woods? What if a hapless driver had picked her up?

None of Thomas's breaths felt deep enough for the necessary oxygen. If she got lost, or was assaulted, or if she died, it would be his fault.

Even if she was safe, someone would probably bring her to a hospital, where grown-ups would ask pointed questions. Authorities would probably figure out what Thomas had done to her.

Then they'd lock him up.

He would never get a chance to sit near neuroscientists and absorb useful knowledge. He would die from his undiagnosed disease. He would never get a chance to grow up.

"Swerve around that pothole," Thomas said, letting his mouth run on autopilot. "Stay to the right of the double yellow line. Ease off the gas. Now accelerate a little more."

They drove one mile. One and a half. Two. Every tree looked like a distorted figure in the headlights.

Had Mrs. Gotte chosen to walk instead of drive?

Maybe a horrified piece of her broken mind was still self-aware enough to make a choice. When presented with a loose command that gave her some leeway, she could have interpreted it in the most suicidal way possible. Walk instead of drive.

She must hate Thomas.

Because she was right about him. He was evil.

Thomas resolved to fix his foster parents as soon as he could engineer an ideal situation, where he could be sure of looking innocent. Surely he could reverse the damage he'd done to their minds.

Or could he?

Neuroscience did not have answers for his most salient questions. In fact, the whole scientific industry seemed rather...skimpy...on the nature of consciousness. They never delved far enough. They dismissed telepathy as fiction, and fiction writers usually got the methodology wrong.

Thomas had never met another person who could overhear thoughts or twist minds. Self-proclaimed psychics always turned out to be disappointing frauds. He feared that he was a lone virtuoso.

Even if he could figure out how to fix the Gottes, he wasn't entirely sure he wanted to.

First, he would need to get himself transferred to another group home. Then he'd fix the Gottes and leave before they killed him.

The truck bounced over potholes, approaching the bridge into town. Through Gotte's dry, unblinking, uncaring eyes, Thomas saw a figure, laden with groceries, stumble and stagger toward the far riverbank.

"Pull over!" he told Gotte.

The truck nearly overturned as Gotte jerked the steering wheel, uncaring if he sent them over a cliff or crashed them into a tree.

"Hit the brake!" Thomas said.

They slammed to a stop.

While Thomas reeled off the minutiae of parking the truck, Mrs. Gotte staggered closer to the river. It had a strong current and white rapids.

She was taking the most direct route home, heedless of her own life.

She must have used the bridge on her way to supermarket, but somehow, she'd become more unhinged, or more suicidal. She'd gotten off course and now she was likely to drown with the groceries.

"Mrs. Gotte!" Thomas yelled through the open window. "Stop!"

Mrs. Gotte slipped on the steep embankment. She fell, picked up the groceries, and kept walking. The river's roar must have drowned out Thomas's squeaky voice.

Thomas analyzed scenarios in his head, searching for the best outcome. Mrs. Gotte was already in the water. He needed to save her within the next thirty seconds.

"Unbuckle your seat belt," he ordered Mr. Gotte. "Open your door. The next time I say 'go,' you will run to your wife, careful not to slip, and you will gently bring her up here, to the truck." He took a deep breath of humid air. "Go!"

The zombified Mr. Gotte sprinted down the slope, toilet paper bandages rippling behind him.

Thomas arranged himself to lean out the window, so he could see what was happening. The command was a good one. Mr. Gotte grabbed his wife and pulled her out of the river.

She fought like a wild animal.

"No." Thomas was horror-stricken. He hadn't intended for their orders to conflict. He hadn't meant to put either of them in life-threatening danger.

His voice wasn't loud enough to reach them. All he could do was scream, "Stop!" while the zombies tried to kill each other.

Some scrap of logic inside Mr. Gotte's broken mind must have reasoned that a corpse would be easier to handle than a maniac, especially if he was supposed to be gentle. He seized his wife's head and gave it a gentle twist.

It happened so fast. Mrs. Gotte collapsed, head lolling at an unnatural angle. Her hair hung like party confetti.

Hot tears spilled over Thomas's cheeks. "No!" His voice was a babyish whine.

Mr. and Mrs. Gotte had been right about him all along. He really was evil. A helpless, evil baby who never should have taken control of grown-ups. If he ended up in a juvenile detention center, or dead, well, he deserved it.

He needed someone else—a better person—to take control of Mr. Gotte.

But he was more alone than ever.


"I'm sorry," Ariock said.

Unshed tears stuck in Thomas's throat and made him hoarse. With his flawless memory, retelling this experience put him in two places at once. He was in the overcrowded streamship but also at the summertime river in Maine.

"You saw her get killed like that?" Vy sounded stunned.

Thomas nodded. "Her feet were a bloody mess from walking all day." He spoke in a dead tone. "I think part of her knew that she wasn't going to recover. When she saw an opportunity to die, she took it."

His audience was silent, absorbing that horror.

Weptolyso and Pung had both prudently moved back, putting themselves beyond his range of telepathy.

"What happened to the other zombie?" Kessa asked. "Your foster father?"

Thomas forced himself to continue in a measured tone, detached in a way that his younger self never would have been capable of. "Well, I tried to fix him."

That had been the worst disaster of all.


The last thing six-year-old Thomas had wanted to do was ride home next to a muddied corpse. He considered commanding Mr. Gotte to dump the corpse in the river.

But that was the sort of thing an Antichrist demon would do.

"Mr. Gotte?" he said.

Gotte's mind sharpened like a dog hearing his master's whistle.

"Place your wife on the seat next to me."

Her head sagged, her dead blue eyes flecked with dirt. Each of her manicured fingernails was painted with a tiny flower. She had wanted to use those fingernails to hurt Thomas.

He reminded himself that Mrs. Gotte hadn't deserved to pay for her mistakes with her life. A few people really seemed to love her, such as her mother and her sister. They'd be gratified if she got a Catholic funeral. He shouldn't rob them of that closure.

Soon he was directing Gotte to drive them home. The zombified man was worse than a drunk driver, spinning the wheel with more force than needed, jamming the accelerator or the brakes too hard. The corpse flopped with every bump in the road.

The stench of the zombies wormed its way into Thomas's mind. That, combined with the lurching vehicle, made sickness roll through him.

He leaned over and vomited. The oatmeal he'd eaten that morning spewed onto one of Mrs. Gotte's black-caked feet.

A flashing blue light penetrated his nauseous, tired perceptions. A police sedan and a fire truck were parked at the Gotte residence.

Thomas was almost relieved at the idea of turning himself in. Grown-ups could be wrong about a lot of things—he had learned that before he got his first wheelchair—but they did often excuse children for things that they would never excuse themselves for. Sometimes they said that children who chased each other or who stole from each other were just being cute.

Would they dismiss accidental manslaughter as a six-year-old just being cute?

It was best not to test that. He decided to try to fix Gotte's mind before anyone found out how badly broken it was.

"Brake," Thomas told Gotte, "and park."

His zombified foster father obeyed.

"Turn off the ignition."

The truck grumbled into silence. The headlights remained on, illuminating the front porch, with its door wide-open.

A police officer in uniform emerged from the house. "Sir!" he yelled. "Sir, are you all right?" He shielded his eyes from the headlights.

Thomas took a deep breath of clean air from the open window. "We're all right!" he called, letting the cop know that he was a child. To Gotte, he said, "Leave your wife here. You're going to step out of the truck, then walk around the front of it with your hands open and visible, then open my door and pick me up."

Soon Thomas was cradled in slimy, revolting arms. A second police officer, this one female, emerged from the house and stared in horror at Gotte. The first cop spoke into his radio, probably demanding backup.

"Put me in my wheelchair," Thomas whispered, hoping the cops wouldn't overhear him commanding the zombie. "Be gentle!"

The two cops sized up Gotte like nervous squirrels assessing a dangerous dog.

"Are you Mr. Gotte?" one asked uncertainly. "Sir, you look badly injured."

The instant Thomas was safely in his wheelchair, he forced himself inside the nasty dregs of Gotte's mind. Now was the time to fix the damage he'd caused.

Everything inside the broken mind was disjointed. Thomas bypassed nonsensical memory fragments. This was worse than exploring someone else's nightmare. Yet emotions did still exist in the mess, albeit confused and sickly. Fear. Unease. Hatred.

Here was a path Thomas could follow. He chased threads of emotions down to the primal core…which was silently shrieking.

Immense pain, rage, and terror screamed in endless alarm.

All of Gotte's pain was buried here, subconscious, disconnected from the rest of his ruined mind. A vital link must have been severed.

Thomas tried to reattach the subconscious to the conscious, but he couldn't guess how. It seemed impossible to untwist what was broken.

And the collateral damage had been massive. He might as well try to glue sand crystals together to form a house. This required more education and time commitment than Thomas was capable of.

Frustrated and helpless, Thomas withdrew from the ruined mess.

"What is going on?" the policewoman asked her partner.

"Hey, kiddo," the partner said. He walked over and crouched down to Thomas's level. "Do you know what happened to your foster dad?"

If Thomas spared attention for the cops, he knew he would lose what little control he had over the situation. They were able-bodied grown-ups. They wanted all the control. They had no idea that he could zombify them, like he had done to the Gottes. He could turn them into living zombies who needed commands to drink, to eat, to use a bathroom, even to blink enough.

Mr. Gotte might need commands for the rest of his life. Without Thomas to give those commands, he would die.

"Mr. Gotte?" he begged. "I want you to go back to being normal."

It was like watching a trapped rat gnaw its own leg in an attempt to escape. Gotte had a vague impression of what "normal" used to mean to him, but only in a dim way.

"You have the ability to make decisions for yourself." Thomas assessed the listening mind. "Do you understand?"

Gotte tried to make a decision, and failed. He kept trying, like a turtle knocked onto its shell, unable to obey yet still trying.

"This is weird," the male cop muttered to his partner.

"Where is their mom?" The policewoman shone her flashlight over the truck. "Is she in there? I'm going to check the vehicle."

"Got it," her partner said.

"Mr. Gotte?" Thomas said, desperate. "You can stop obeying me now. Obey other people from now on. Okay?"

His words dominated the zombie's mind.

The cops gaped as Gotte ran past them, into the house.

Thomas had a bad feeling about his last command to Gotte, but he was so frightened, he couldn't imagine exactly what might go wrong. All he could do was try to follow. Unfortunately, his wheelchair was the cheap, nonpowered type. He was too weak to roll it.

"I need to follow him," he told the male cop. "Push my chair?"

"She's here," the female cop told her partner. "Looks deceased. I'm going to try resuscitation."

The other cop hesitated, torn. Mr. Gotte had looked insane. He had sprinted inside a house full of disabled children with a single-minded look of purpose on his damaged face.

"I'll be back." The male cop drew his gun and chased after the zombie.

"Please bring me inside," Thomas begged the other one. "It's really important!"

She looked disturbed, having seen the condition of Mrs. Gotte. But when she turned to Thomas, it was with pity. She saw an innocent child.

He tasted her opinions about him. Not only did she see him as helpless, severely disabled, but she assumed that he must have behavioral issues. Why else would his foster siblings speak of him with hatred and fear?

She had met them. They had yelled things such as, "*You need to catch Thomas. He probably killed our foster parents!*"

"*He's the devil!*"

"*He knows secrets about everyone. Even people he's never met. He probably knows everything about you.*"

Thomas began to weep. He hadn't expected the other kids, especially Donna, to still hate him so much. Didn't they realize that he had saved their house and possibly their lives?

Well, no. They probably had no clue.

He normally pretended that their hatred didn't affect him. To show a reaction was to show weakness, which only made him more of a target. But now he wanted to look vulnerable and innocent. So he forced his tears to well up, to be visible.

"Please?" he begged. "I just want to go inside and make sure everyone is all right."

"All right." The female cop rolled his wheelchair to the front stairs. She carried him up the ramp and pushed his chair inside.

Moths fluttered around the kitchen light. The door had been left open too long.

"He just…!" The male cop was frantic. "Holy…!" he swore.

Gotte swayed as blood poured from one side of his head. He had apparently plunged a screwdriver into his ear. Now he wiggled it.

He pulled out the screwdriver with a wet squelching sound.

Blood ran down the ruin of his neck and torso. He appeared to not have a care in the world, but Thomas knew the truth. Gotte felt everything. He just couldn't express it.

"Obey my commands again!" Thomas yelled.

But it was too late. Gotte had already plunged the screwdriver in his other ear, as deep as it would go. Unable to hear, unable to read minds or read sign language, Gotte had rendered himself unable to obey commands.

Gotte's shrieking core must have sought a good excuse to mutilate his own brain. Thomas had given him one.

"I'm so sorry." Thomas could no longer pretend to be innocent. Everything people said about him was true. He was worse than evil. He was depraved.

He began to sob for real, unable to suppress it, aware of how much he'd caused the Gottes to suffer, and all too aware that he had destroyed his own chances for curing his disease and growing up. "It's all my fault," he confessed. "I'm so sorry."

The policewoman laid a hand on his frail shoulder.

Thomas tensed, expecting her to snap his neck, or shoot him in the back of the head. He deserved death.

Panicked, he tunneled into the depths of her mind. He needed to get to her primal core before she could murder him. He needed to wrench that core, and protect himself…

"This is not your fault," the policewoman said in a kind tone.

Shocked by her unexpected kindness, Thomas slowed his panicky drill into her primeval core. He allowed himself to sense her intentions instead.

Warmth glowed in her thoughts. She believed that Thomas was a victim who needed to be rescued from insane foster parents. As far as she could tell, the parents must have warped everyone in their home to hate this poor little boy.

She wanted to pick up little Thomas and hug him.

She wanted to assure him that he was wonderful, no matter what anyone else said.

And he had nearly destroyed her mind.

Thomas screamed. The policewoman leaped back, but he was done pretending to act like a grown-up. He had nearly zombified her. If he had, then he would have lashed out at her partner, too, and anyone else who threatened him. His destruction might have never ended.

Both of the cops radiated pity, but Thomas knew how guilty he was, even if the grown-ups didn't believe it.

He must never trust himself with this power. He must never twist another mind, never, no matter what. He would never use his power again.

*CHAPTER 6*
# EVIL

"That's it." Thomas let his limp hands dangle over his armrests, wrung out. Now they would judge him: guilty.

At least people would stop expecting his help. They'd write him off as a disaster.

"I'm so sorry, Thomas," Ariock said quietly. "No child should have to endure what you went through."

Sympathy was so unexpected, Thomas had no reply.

"Thank you for having the courage to tell us about it," Ariock said.

Thomas tentatively explored Ariock's mood, sure that he would find hatred or distrust buried beneath the sympathetic tone. But Ariock was genuine.

Kessa studied Thomas with a grave expression. *A mind reader*, she thought, *who feels guilt.* Although Thomas had imparted his history in a cold, clinical tone, Kessa had nonetheless inferred guilt from his word choices and the hunched position of his shoulders.

"I'm sorry," Vy said. At least she sounded shaken. "Did Mr. Gotte die in the kitchen, in front of you?"

"No." Thomas kept his tone clinical. "He went into a persistent vegetative state and died a week later, in hospice care."

Vy winced with sympathy. She used to work with vegetative patients. She had some idea of what his condition must have been like.

"I assume you got moved to a different home?" Ariock asked.

"I got bounced around for years." Thomas didn't mention that the other kids had refused to share a home with him ever again. Donna had even accused him of witchcraft.

Exasperated social workers had recommended that he get placed far away. They'd sent him to Rhode Island.

That hadn't lasted long. No one liked him in that group home, either, so the system bounced him to Vermont. The Hollander home in New Hampshire had been his tenth placement.

Thomas used to wonder if social workers and foster kids could intuit that he was evil, despite his harmless appearance. It never mattered how much he downplayed his telepathic power, or that he made feeble attempts to imitate normal kid behavior. Normal people always wanted to get away from him.

His loneliness and self-doubts had vanished only once he'd joined the Torth.

It had been such a relief to stop worrying that he was an evil freak of nature, to know that the vast majority of the galaxy embraced him. Only ignorant humankind—stuck on their backwater planet—had judged him as evil, as disabled and young and conceited. Everyone else in the known universe had really respected him.

Now he wasn't sure how to judge himself anymore.

Was he evil? Thomas wasn't sure he could explain what evil meant, even to himself.

"I understand now," Vy said, "why you were reluctant to brainwash those Torth officials. You were trying to avoid zombifying them."

Thomas fidgeted. "Yes," he admitted. "It seemed especially risky to do it to a Torth."

"Why?" Kessa looked intensely interested.

"Because anyone paying attention through the Megacosm would notice if a Red Rank suddenly suffered brain damage," Thomas explained. "I figured it would cause an alarm, and we'd be surrounded by an army before we could get to the spaceport."

"But that did not happen." Kessa clicked her beak, trying to puzzle out what had happened.

"It turns out the Megacosm requires free will," Thomas said. "When I twisted the mind of that Red Rank, he could no longer decide to share his perceptions with other people. So he dropped out of the Megacosm without a second thought."

"And his orbiters did not notice?" Kessa asked.

"They didn't care," Thomas corrected. "That Red Rank had literally no idea what hit him. He dropped out without any fuss. His only thought was about how ordinary we were."

Ariock rested his chin on one massive fist. "None of them were suspicious?"

"Maybe a few were," Thomas said. "But that Red Rank was just one of many thousands patrolling the entry points of various cities. His audience was small, and when he dropped out, I'm sure most of them swung into the minds of nearby Red Ranks, waiting for him to come back online. They probably assumed he was taking a privacy break."

"Hmm." Vy tried to imagine it. "We got lucky."

"I hadn't zombified anyone since I was six," Thomas said. "Yeah, I'm glad it worked out the way it did. We got a few minutes' head start before the Torth

Empire figured out that their Red Rank wasn't just taking a privacy break. Those minutes saved our lives."

Ariock looked burdened by the destruction he might have caused. He could imagine himself forced to fight at the checkpoint instead of inside the spaceport. If that had happened, he realized now, he might have devastated the whole city. He might have killed millions of slaves by accident, without ever getting close enough to a spaceship to leave the planet.

"Was it just as easy for you to zombify a Torth as zombifying a human?" Kessa asked.

"Yes," Thomas said. "But your role-playing was helpful. Those Red Ranks were so focused on trying to figure out what sort of weird slaves and Torth we were, they never registered the fact that a supergenius was digging through their thoughts, up close and personal, instead of in the Megacosm. Normally, that would have made them wary or suspicious."

It had been a near thing, though. Thomas figured the Torth Empire would be on guard for a long time. Individual Torth would probably not allow a supergenius to dig into their minds like that.

"I wanted to try brainwashing in a lighter way," Thomas admitted. "But there wasn't time for me to experiment. I had to do it before they got too suspicious."

Vy shuddered.

"These powers are dangerous," Ariock said.

"I agree," Thomas said.

They nodded to each other with mutual understanding.

Thomas gestured toward the bin full of blaster gloves. "Those gloves contain microdarts of the inhibitor serum. We'll run out of them eventually, but if you ever want extra assurance…?" He nodded toward his skinny arm. "Feel free to dose me up."

Pung looked guilty. It seemed he had been considering doing just that.

Ariock stood, towering over everyone. "I'll dose myself up right now."

"No!" Vy jumped up and grabbed Ariock by the arm. "Please don't."

He gave her a raised eyebrow look.

"What if we run into trouble?" Vy said. "I'll feel safer if you keep your powers."

Ariock hesitated. But Vy's pleading look seemed to work on him, and he reluctantly sat back down. "I guess. But once we're safely landed, I think I need to work on ways to suppress my powers."

Vy gave him a frustrated look. Thomas sensed unspoken arguments. Apparently, Vy had already expended some effort trying to convince Ariock that he wasn't a monster.

Poor Vy. Thomas suspected that she would never win an argument against Ariock. Right or wrong, the giant was stubborn.

"I have questions," Kessa said.

Thomas sighed. Kessa always had questions.

"Why does your power have a range limit?" Kessa asked. "If Ariock can affect things very far away, why must you be so close to use your power on a, uh, victim?"

Ariock looked interested, despite his resolve to never use his storm powers again.

"Maybe my sphere of influence is tiny." Thomas shrugged, wishing he understood it better himself. "Or maybe storm powers are long-range. Ariock has to be very close to a patient in order to heal them, so I guess that healing and mind control are different from storm powers."

Ariock looked thoughtful, mulling that over.

"It seems that the Torth Empire took a major risk," Kessa said, "letting you join them."

Thomas nodded in acknowledgment.

"Why did they let you in?" Kessa asked. "So far, none of your answers are satisfying."

The mystery plagued Thomas, too. Torth baby farms generated all kinds of undesirable babies, including Yeresunsa. Some tiny percentage of those would also have a supergenius mutation, like him. Yet the Torth terminated Yeresunsa babies the instant they tested positive for powers. Without exception.

Except for him.

"A lot of factors influenced the Majority's decision to grant me citizenship," Thomas said, aware that none of his guesses were good enough. "The most well-respected supergenius in the galaxy vouched for me. And the news feeds were mostly about Ariock and the possibility of enslaving Earth. I guess people were distracted? I guess my medicine was impressive, too." He patted his medicine case. "It could have been a perfect storm of factors."

None of which added up to a satisfying answer.

Thomas suspected that he was missing some vital fact—the real truth. Perhaps there was something the high ranks knew that nobody below them could guess or suspect.

"Did they give you as much freedom as a typical Yellow Rank?" Kessa asked.

"No," Thomas admitted. "They kept me dosed with the inhibitor, of course, and I always had a lot of orbiters. The high ranks were definitely keeping an eye on me."

He became aware of a relentless stare from outside his circle of listeners. Cherise stood there, with orb lights painting golden reflections in her glossy black hair. The distant supernova cast one half of her face into shadow.

Thomas couldn't tell how much she'd overheard, or how it had impacted her. It felt strange that he had to guess.

"He never told me about the people he killed." Cherise's tone was just as clinical as his had been.

"Cherise," Vy said. "This was really hard for him to talk about."

"Was it?" Cherise made that a statement of disbelief.

His listeners—Vy, Ariock, and Kessa—were doing mental gymnastics to justify the murders, but not Cherise. She knew better than to excuse Thomas because he was a child. He had always admired that about her.

Thomas stopped himself from making a fumbling attempt to confess how much he had wanted to confide in Cherise. She used to ask about his sleepless nights. She had begged to know about his past.

But if she had learned the truth—and if she had not run screaming—then her pity would have dragged on him like a burden. Thomas felt pity from Vy and Ariock right now. It was like absorbing nasty backwash. He didn't need extra reminders of his own flaws.

Besides, how could he explain his childish fears that he was the Antichrist? He used to lie awake, terrified that he was a witch, or a demon; an unholy thing from hell. He hadn't known any better.

Part of him still wondered, in an uneasy way, if he was evil.

Cherise would not have related to his growing pains, either. She had never understood his near-constant frustration with adults who seemed too slow, too stupid, too obtuse. Nor did she understand how it felt to suck up other people's memories as a glorious escape from his frustrations.

Sometimes he had barely restrained himself from twisting a mind.

Only his memories of the Gotte disaster held him in check. The freedom of self-determination seemed fundamental to being a human, or so it seemed to Thomas. Without free will, a person was no longer really a person.

So he had vowed to rely solely on his telepathic power, even if his life was threatened. He could not shut off his telepathy. Let that be his only advantage; he didn't need any extras. He certainly didn't need to rule the world or control adults.

Maybe he should have had the courage to tell Cherise all of that. Maybe.

But even if she had embraced him…what if she had mentally elevated him to an even higher hero status? Thomas could not help but view himself through the perspective of his closest friends. If Cherise had begun to worship him, where might that lead?

Nowhere good, he imagined.

"What I don't understand," Cherise said to Vy, "is how you keep forgiving him. He just confessed that he murdered two people in a horrible way. And you think he's a nice boy?"

Vy looked pained. "He was a child. He had to survive in a bad situation."

"Oh," Cherise said. "I guess he's entitled to do whatever he wants, then. I guess he gets endless forgiveness."

Cherise gave Thomas such a disparaging look, he lost all desire to read her mind. She must see him as pathetic. She would probably help him die faster.

"I was a child, too." Cherise strode away, back to the ummin friends who awaited her.

Vy looked flummoxed. "Cherise?" she called, standing.

It was useless. Thomas understood all the things that Cherise had made clear beneath her words. She wanted nothing to do with him. In her mind, Thomas was in the same toxic category as her abusive tyrant of a mother. She felt betrayed by someone she had loved more than anything. She was angry. And there was nothing he could ever do to make things right.

He hoped the aliens were better friends to her than he had ever been.

"For what it's worth," Ariock told Thomas, "I think you did what you had to."

Thomas gave a tolerant nod. He had broken his own vow to himself, to never brainwash another mind. Only Cherise found that troubling.

Most nontelepaths only saw the surface of people. Ariock saw Thomas as an innocent child, a victim.

Thomas was fairly certain he'd never been innocent.

He made his voice steel. "I want to reassess our autopilot settings. Are we done?"

Vy looked anguished. "I'm sure she didn't mean what she said. She's just…"

"Hurting," Thomas supplied. "I know."

His friendship with Cherise was broken, no matter what Vy wanted, no matter how much he wished it were otherwise.

He was toxic.

Cherise understood that.

# CHAPTER 7

# FOR THE BETRAYER

Ariock wished he had a way to jot down notes. "So if I say *olirda*, that means 'come'?"

"It means 'please come,'" Vy corrected.

Ariock had to remind himself to keep his gaze on Vy's eyes. Her lips and other parts were also nice to look at. She was extremely appealing, lying on her side with her head propped in one hand, her soft skirt knotted over one hip.

"*Irda*," Pung said in an exaggerated tone, "is demand," he said helpfully in English. He seemed fascinated by Ariock's struggle to learn the pidgin language that all slaves were fluent in.

"Okay," Ariock said. "So *Ol* means 'please'?"

Pung gave him a pained look.

"Sort of," Vy said. "It makes things polite. Did you ever study another language, back on Earth?"

Ariock shook his head, ashamed. His mother had never followed up on his homeschooling after sixth grade. Vy probably knew a lot more than he did about every academic subject.

"Okay. I want to make a comparison to Asian languages." Vy went on as if his lack of schooling didn't matter. "Some Asian languages use different forms, depending on the status of the person you're addressing. The slave tongue has something like that, equivalent to being unfriendly versus friendly."

"A Torth says *irda*," Pung put in. "You say *olirda*."

"Right," Vy said. "*Irda* is how people talk to strangers, or people they wish were strangers. But if you're talking to a friend, you'd say *olirda*."

Ariock had so much to learn. Sometimes he envied mind readers. "Got it."

"You're picking up the language really fast," Vy assured him.

"Thanks." Ariock supposed he had come a long way after a few practice sessions. Some of the conversations he overheard among the refugees were beginning to make a bit of sense.

Vy said a simple sentence in the slave tongue. Something about Earth, something about sky. "What did I say?" she asked.

"Earth has a pretty sky?" Ariock guessed.

She smiled. "I said Earth has a big sky."

Ariock tried to hide his embarrassment. He really ought to know the word people most often used to describe him.

But Vy looked so innocent, and so nice, he couldn't help but smile back.

She snuggled against Ariock whenever they slept. It seemed a miracle that she felt relaxed and safe near him. Ariock had worked up enough courage to hold her gently. She seemed to like that, when she was sleeping, but he didn't dare touch her otherwise. Nothing was worth the risk of offending her and losing her friendship. He'd watched enough TV to know that women had mysterious limits, and he needed to respect those limits.

Pung said a sentence, something about "delicious." He munched on a grassy wafer from their rations. Only ummins seemed to like those things.

Vy watched Ariock, expecting a translation.

"Um. The food is delicious?" Ariock guessed.

Pung grinned, chewing with his beak open. "Good!" he said.

Vy laughed. "Not to us. Ugh. I wish we had some eggs, or toast, or something."

"One more day till we get there." Ariock lay back and gazed at the stars. He missed the hot meals his mother used to cook. The only food he found edible aboard their streamship was sort of like birdseed granola bars, and those were far too salty and not nearly filling enough. He was so hungry.

Vy said another sentence in the slave tongue, enunciating each word. Something about Earth.

She used Earth in most of her examples. Maybe she didn't realize it. Ariock had quit trying to ask about her life, because the aching homesickness she felt was clear.

If only they could go to Earth.

Ariock glanced toward Thomas, who slept all the time and didn't seem to care about anything. With the right amount of persuasive pressure…maybe Thomas could be induced to change his mind? A visit to Earth might be worth a few life-threatening risks.

Red light suffused the room. The view outside the ship suddenly glowed red, like liquid magma instead of outer space. They seemed to be inside lava.

Ariock squinted in disbelief. Was he suffering from some kind of space-radiation sickness?

The molten glow faded. Soon the view was the same as before: a starry night sky, with ghostly splashes of distant ruination from the supernova.

"What the hell?" Vy glanced around, and so did Pung. They had noticed the magma.

It crept back, the whole sky shifting again to that molten red glow.

A shifting view might be some sort of alert message. Did red mean there was an emergency?

Thomas continued to sleep, oblivious, while the magma faded to starry blackness.

Seconds later, it flared again.

Passengers exchanged worried looks. Timid ummins approached Thomas while a much larger crowd moved toward Ariock, chatting in the slave tongue. He understood a few words. "Bringer of Hope" and "help."

Maybe he should expand his awareness, just to figure out if there was an obstacle out in space?

But how far would he have to expand until he encountered whatever the problem might be? A mile-wide radius? Ten thousand miles? Space meant huge distances. If Ariock let himself grow until his human core was just a speck, he might lose track of who he was and whom he was protecting.

No. He needed to remain normal and tethered to his human body. Any threats that lurked in space—a black hole? An asteroid?—could surely be avoided with good navigation.

"We'd better go wake the pilot." Ariock kept his tone light and reassuring.

The dome flared red again, throwing odd shadows.

Unpacked bags lay scattered across the floor. Ariock and Vy stepped with care, and adolescent ummins darted in front of them, snatching away the mess.

"Thank you," Ariock said in the slave tongue.

The adolescents gave him proud looks.

Refugees jostled aside to make room for Ariock, their owlish eyes hopeful. Thomas slept with his head on a folded cloth, mouth open. The crowd, and the red pulses, apparently weren't enough to wake him. Maybe he wasn't getting enough to eat. Maybe he wasn't getting enough of his NAI-12 medicine.

"Thomas?" Ariock touched his friend's bony shoulder.

Thomas murmured incoherently.

The dome turned red again, furious magma swirling against the glass. Everyone looked nervous.

"Thomas." Ariock gently shook the boy's shoulder.

Thomas made a cranky sound.

"Is that an emergency signal?" Ariock asked as the magma pulsed again.

"Ugh." Thomas stretched his scoliosis-bent back. His medicine case began to slide off the seat, and Ariock caught it before it could fall.

Thomas yawned. "Looks like it."

He seemed unconcerned. Ariock hoped that meant it was a false alarm, but with Thomas's uncaring attitude, he could not feel sure. "What does it mean?" He tucked the boy's medicine case back where it belonged, next to him on the seat.

Thomas floated toward the piloting console, his hair mussed up. "Let me check."

Refugees backed away and made room, allowing Thomas access, with Ariock and others following.

Thomas waved through strings of geometric symbols. They all watched. Ariock didn't want to loom, so he sat carefully on the floor, first checking to make sure there were no ummins in the way.

"The Torth build redundant fail-safes into their ships," Thomas explained as he worked. "This is probably just a sensor misfiring."

An adolescent began to pester Thomas with questions. Ariock thought he remembered the name of this one—Varktezo.

Thomas shot back lazy answers as he swiped through holographic displays.

The dome flared red again. Thomas blinked sleep out of his eyes and grew more alert. Symbols flitted by so fast, they blurred.

Thomas began to look concerned. Ummins shushed each other.

"What is it?" Ariock tried to assure himself that it was a fixable problem. Torth spacecraft had to be robust. If a Torth got stranded in space, they could call for help in the Megacosm, but help might still take a few days to arrive. Surely their luxury streamships were built to withstand problems?

Thomas poked through layers of floating menus, opening and closing them in rapid succession. The red glow flared, and faded, then flared again.

"Weird." Thomas slumped in his hoverchair, frowning at holographic schematics as if they were offensive.

Why couldn't he just explain what the problem was? Ariock considered how to ask without sounding threatening.

"What?" Vy asked.

"We have energy depletion." Thomas looked troubled. "This ship utilizes ambient dark matter, and it seems we're not moving. It's possible the ionic combinators wore out, and somehow, the problem never got logged. But then the ship would have been towed from its previous voyage, and it should have been in a repair bay. This seems like…" He frowned at the display. "Incredibly bad luck."

Ariock relaxed. If inertia was the problem, or steering, he could probably propel the ship with his powers. He just hoped he wouldn't need to expand his awareness too much.

"Is there anything we can do to help?" Vy asked. "Can we do something to repair the problem?"

"Maybe." Thomas leaned over the console. "Let me finish the diagnostic."

He scrolled through more geometric symbols while the rest of them watched.

"Hm." Thomas's tone became heavier. "That warning should have come on earlier." His fingers flicked symbols. "That doesn't make sense."

"What doesn't?" Vy asked.

Thomas ignored her, scrolling through multiple menus at once, alert and frustrated. Holographs blinked into existence and vanished faster than Ariock could track with his eyes.

One of the holographs generated another, spilling out a large blob of an image. Its blue glow counteracted the red flare. Thomas jerked his hand back, startled.

The blob gained three-dimensional detail, turning into...not a planet, but a person.

Ariock recognized the obese, life-size, ghostly recording. This was the Torth who had threatened planet Earth. She had stolen Thomas's medicine and mentored him.

The supergenius known as the Upward Governess floated in a hoverchair embossed with flowery vines.

Her holographic image glowed with fairy light. She gazed into space, unable to see her audience. A girl's voice rasped from hidden loudspeakers on the console.

"Now that you understand how completely I've won," said the raspy voice, "you will want to kill yourself, Betrayer. Too bad. I don't think your friends will let you."

Her lips curled into a cold smile.

Ariock realized that she spoke English, not the slave tongue. Her words were not meant for slaves or former slaves.

"Your death awaits you in the Isolatorium," she went on, her message apparently prerecorded. "You will suffer like your mother." She paused. "You could have chosen greatness. Instead? You've reaped payback. I win."

The holograph vanished.

Thomas stared at the empty air where her recording had been, eyes wide with dawning knowledge and terror.

"What was that?" Vy demanded. "What is she talking about? What trap are we in?"

Everyone asked questions, but Thomas looked like a terminal cancer patient. He shifted his haunted gaze to Ariock. "I'm sorry. I'm so sorry."

"Why?" Vy begged. "What is the problem? Just tell us!"

Ariock did not beg. Thomas was too stunned to talk, and Ariock might be able to find out what threat their ship faced without badgering the boy.

He had to know. He had to protect his friends.

So he reached out. He sent his awareness beyond the hull and into the vacuum of space. He kept expanding, farther and farther outward. Soon the whole ship was just a teensy capsule inside the immense void he contained.

He sensed emptiness, punctuated by the usual mystery arrays of particles. Nothing alive. Nothing big. Nothing to worry about.

Then his awareness rammed into something immense and tough.

A lot of things.

Fortresses, impossibly huge, and they sheltered life sparks. Not just a handful, but thousands.

Millions.

More than stars in a sky. More than grains of sand in a desert. The formless extension of Ariock ghosted through endless battleships and missile launchers and war machines. He couldn't keep track of that much complexity. The edges remained unknown to his awareness, the entirety too much for him to explore.

He could not hope to fend off so many missiles if they launched toward his core self.

This would be many magnitudes greater than the barrage he'd suffered in the spaceport, and it could go on for hours. Maybe days. He would need to throw all his focus into defense. If he got distracted, even for a split second, that would be the end of him. If he lost track of who he was, that could be the end of Vy and everyone else.

And there must be innocent slaves aboard the largest of the warships. Slaves didn't deserve to become collateral damage.

Their streamship seemed to be disabled, and the Torth Empire was aiming enough firepower at them to destroy a moon.

Ariock snapped back to his human body, reeling. He would have fallen if he'd been standing.

The view outside appeared to be empty deep space—but that view was fake, a Torth illusion. Someone must have programmed their ship to display a screen saver instead of what was really out there.

"There's an armada," Ariock said. "They have us surrounded."

# CHAPTER 8

# TO DIE WELL

A low hissing sound seized Ariock's attention. Air was escaping somewhere.

"Knockout gas," Thomas said.

His helpful hint sounded far away, because Ariock had already spiked out his awareness again, scouring their ship for any unusual airflow. Foggy puffs spewed from nozzles underneath seats. The puffs were low to the ground but quickly adding up. They would poison all the breathable air within minutes.

Ariock used his powers to crumple each straw-like hose, one by one, in quick succession. That stopped the gassy clouds.

They must have a source. He focused on one of the gas lines and traced it underneath the carpet, then below a floor panel. He raced his awareness down the pressurized line until he found the canister compartment where it was coming from.

Ariock widened his awareness enough to detect the surrounding area, full of incongruent machinery. A utility closet.

He couldn't guess how to eject the canister into space without wrecking their ship. Maybe he could defuse it somehow?

He probed the canister with his awareness, searching for valves. There were several. He poured himself into each valve, sealing the canister tight.

Then he snapped back into his body. "I shut down the toxic air," he reported. "We're safe." Then he remembered the armada outside. "Uh, our air is safe, anyway."

Vy and Kessa looked appreciative.

Thomas gave a nod of respect. "Thanks." He leaned over the holographic pedestal and worked furiously. "She might have planted more traps. I'll check."

"When did the Torth have time to put traps here?" Kessa asked.

Ariock had not even had time to wonder that.

"They must have installed the same sabotage code in every ship on Umdalkdul," Thomas explained, not pausing in his work. "Or every ship within a thousand miles of Duin, at least. They predicted that I'd steal one. My nemesis buried the hijack in substrate shells, knowing I'd be too smug or lazy to check every branching layer."

He sounded furious. Ariock hoped some of that fury was aimed at the Torth Empire rather than at himself.

"This is because I was stupidly avoiding the Megacosm," Thomas went on. "She got a large-scale project underway because she knew I wouldn't ascend and I'd be clueless. The whole operation must have taken at least a day. Maybe two!" He was growing angrier. "I gave her time. She had time to record that message and package it into the hijack macro, and she set a trigger so it would spill out when I finally figured..." His voice grew strangled with despair. "I'm sorry. I assumed we were safe."

"None of us—" Vy began, but Thomas cut her off.

"I know her. I should have guessed. I told you before, I thought our escape was too easy, but I failed to follow up on my suspicions. And now we're dead!"

Dead? Ariock stared at Thomas, wishing he would calm down. The refugees didn't need to see their pilot having an irrational panic attack.

Thomas met Ariock's gaze. "You're going to wish I was being irrational."

"We're not dead," Vy pointed out, gesturing around.

But they might be soon. Ariock had a sinking feeling. He didn't want to use his powers on a massive level again.

Yet if the Torth gave him absolutely no other choice...

Thomas swiped a holograph, and the domed window view changed dramatically. Spiky black warships surrounded them from every angle. Artillery barrels pointed their way, large enough to launch skyscrapers—or nuclear warheads the size of skyscrapers.

A nimbus backlit the armada. They must be near a star.

"That's the reality of what's outside." Thomas refreshed the cobweb holograph. "And this map shows our real location. Not the route I planned. Her hijack kicked in as soon as we slid into that first temporal stream."

Vy gazed at the armada, stunned.

Ariock studied the endless array of warships, looking for weakness. Any chance was better than none. "I should be able to push aside some of those ships," he said. "Enough for us to escape."

"They're here to wear you down." Thomas's voice had a fearful edge. "They can bombard you nonstop. Eventually, you'll have to take a break, or you'll have a lapse in focus."

"So they're not going to kill us?" Ariock said hopefully.

Thomas gave him an incredulous stare. "They don't need to. Our ship is dead in the water, so to speak. We don't have propulsion. She destroyed that."

Ariock took a moment to process the problem. "Well, I can—" He began to volunteer to propel their ship.

"We have nowhere to go." Thomas ruthlessly cut Ariock off. "Unless you count deep space, which is suicide. We don't have enough water to last for a long trek to some distant solar system."

"I thought we could jump through wormholes?" Vy asked.

Thomas gave her a withering look. "Temporal streams require exact calculations. If we get one little nuance wrong? We implode. I have a mind that can calculate those points, but there's no way I can communicate all that to Ariock. He'd have to be a mind reader to get it."

"All right," Vy said, frustrated. "But we could just—"

"There's no waiting them out," Thomas said. "They can rotate through endless forces. We don't have enough water and food to last through a siege."

Ariock considered that he might try to fix the damaged propulsion system. Maybe Thomas could walk him through it?

Thomas turned to him before he could speak his suggestion. "I've already thought of all your ideas, plus extras. Our ship needs a repair bay. We don't have the resources to make fuel or parts." He shifted his yellow gaze to Kessa. "That's a good idea, to take over one of the Torth battleships. A few problems with it. One, Ariock isn't willing to slay every life spark. He can't tell Torth apart from slaves unless he's visually able to see them. Two, we'd be vulnerable in any docking situation. Ariock can't split his focus that well. And three? You can bet the damned Upward Governess took precautions. I'm sure she has a kill switch installed in every ship out there."

Thomas fell silent. He seemed defeated, but no one else was ready to give up.

"Is there somewhere we can escape to?" Vy asked. "If we can hide out for a while, or swap our ship for—"

"There's one habitable planet nearby," Thomas said. "And it's the most dangerous planet in the universe for us—it's a training ground for Servants of All. It's home to two billion Red Ranks who want to prove how tough they are." He looked disgusted. "I'm sure the Torth want us to land in Stratower City, right near the Isolatorium. That's where they want to put me."

Everyone went silent, absorbing that.

"I do have a plan," Thomas said.

They looked at him with wild hope, but Ariock was wary. He heard dark despair in Thomas's tone.

"We have a tiny bit of propulsion capability left," Thomas said. "Instead of trying to dock somewhere, I could send us in an unexpected direction." He swiped menus, and a ghostly solar system appeared over the console. "We could rocket past the Torth Homeworld and toward their sun. Ariock can probably keep the armada off our backs for the hours it will take to get there. If not? Oh well. Maybe we'll die in an explosion."

Kessa and Vy exchanged looks of puzzlement. Ariock was glad he wasn't the only one who failed to follow Thomas's reasoning.

"It would take less than a second for us to burn to death at the speed I'm proposing," Thomas said. "We'd pretty much vaporize."

Ariock struggled to comprehend the suggestion. Surely Thomas wasn't talking about mass suicide?

"It would be painless," Thomas said. "Mostly. And it would end quickly."

Vy stared at him with disbelief. "What are you saying?"

Cherise had none of their confusion. "Coward."

Ariock was startled to see her, decked out in an outfit she must have sewn and knotted together. She looked like a pirate. The blaster glove on her hand only enhanced the impression that she was a fighter of some kind.

"Do we get a choice?" Cherise asked. "Or are you just deciding for everyone? Like a Torth?"

Thomas looked ashamed, unable to meet her gaze. "I don't want to die from torture," he said in a small voice. "If that makes me a coward, then I'm a coward."

Ariock thought about it. Spontaneous combustion was probably nicer than losing oneself in prison arena combats, reduced to a slavish, bloodthirsty animal. Maybe.

"He wants to die." Cherise's glare indicated Thomas. "He's wanted that for a while. The Torth got inside his mind and turned him into a coward."

"I never wanted you all to die with me." Thomas was pleading. "I should have… I'm sorry. I failed you."

As if their situation was solely his responsibility.

Ariock felt just as responsible. He should have guessed that their stolen ship would turn out to be a trap. Ever since they'd left Duin, he had felt a storm brewing. He had felt the same way just before the Torth abducted him from the Dovanack mansion. He couldn't foresee the future—who could? Anyone with that ability would be ridiculously overpowered—but he did have gut feelings. Hadn't he been ignoring his intuition that something was wrong?

Innocent people had lost their lives because of his unexamined fears. His mother. More than half the population of Duin.

He kept trying to hide. Yet the Torth kept targeting him.

They wanted to force him to slaughter thousands of people.

Maybe they didn't know what they were asking for.

Ariock pushed himself to his feet, towering over everyone. "If the Torth force me to fight," he said, "I will give them a war."

A few of the refugees looked worried, but Ariock felt certain. His peaceful retirement on a reject planet was an unobtainable fantasy. It always had been.

Even his peaceful life on Earth had felt unbearably stagnant and dull. Ariock was as unsuited to peace as Thomas was unsuited to spending all day in classes at school.

Ariock had come alive as a gladiator.

And when he had unleashed his Yeresunsa powers in the spaceport, that was the most alive—and the most powerful—he had ever felt. Ariock knew he had a lot of potential inside himself, still locked away. He actually wanted action.

"If I die fighting," he said, "then I will die well."

Weptolyso gave him a fervent look and snorted agreement. "I fight with you. If you die, I die." He snaked his head in a nussian salute.

Ariock returned the salute with a grateful nod. He turned toward Vy and the crowd of refugees. "What about you? Do you want a quick death? Or do you want a fighting chance?"

Pung translated.

Refugees showed their hands, encased in blaster gloves. They had tied the gloves for a better fit on their sharp little fingers. They clicked their beaks, and Ariock knew they were ready for a war of survival.

"We don't have a chance." Thomas's mouth trembled, like he was a hermit forced to confront unruly children. "It's best to have a fast death. At least we can rob the Torth of their triumph."

He reached for the navigation icon. With a minimal gesture, he would send them on a suicidal course toward the sun.

"I'm sorry," Thomas said.

Ariock pushed Thomas away from the piloting console before he could enact disaster. The hoverchair glided like a boat.

Thomas glared in outrage, and Ariock wondered if he was bullying a disabled kid. Thomas surely had a good grasp of the situation. He must know what was best for all of them.

But.

Ariock was just not ready to give up and meekly accept death. He had done enough of that in his life.

He would rather die fighting.

"The Torth will have to go through me first." Ariock assessed his own potential weaknesses. To maximize his strength, he should probably eat a few more of those tasteless seed-meal bars. And his flimsy rags were not enough protection. One microdart of the inhibitor serum would disable his powers.

During that spaceport battle, he had had to pour focus into shielding his bare skin. That was focus that he could use to better attack the Torth. Or to protect his mother. What a disaster.

He needed full body armor.

The ship's cushy upholstery might work. Better yet, the utility closet door was framed in metal. Ariock could bend metal.

He sent out his awareness, seeking the strength of metal. He worked himself all the way into the door frame, sensing where it was fastened to the rest of the wall. Hoping that it wasn't vital for life support, he forced the metal to bend and break, tearing the wall apart.

Wherever he found metal, he wrenched it away with a thunderous cracking sound. The ship's interior began to resemble a hollowed-out wreck.

Ariock flattened those metal extensions of himself, hammering them into rough-hewn steely plates.

He held out his arms and contoured the plates to fit his immense torso, arms, and legs. His metal self cinched around his flimsy clothes. He made sure that each sinuous plate overlapped. Crude hooks and fasteners held it all together.

He twisted and flexed, testing his motions, refining the makeshift suit of armor until it almost felt comfortable. It was ugly and imperfect, and small gaps appeared when he moved in certain ways, but it should protect him.

He added more coverage for the gaps. Thorny shoulder protections. A neck guard. He thickened crude knee guards and gauntlets, then smoothed out his armored plates, making them thin enough for dexterity. He forged protection for his feet, holding up each foot to sculpt metal insoles.

If only he had time to perfect the armor. Oh well. It would have to be good enough.

When he returned to himself, everyone was staring.

"That's amazing," Vy said in a tone of respect, as if Ariock had created a masterpiece.

Weptolyso rumbled with admiration. "Very good."

Along the ruined utility wall, torn wires hung like dendrites, emitting faint electrical buzzing noises. Half the chairs were ruined beyond recognition. The ship was a mess, and the makeshift armor seemed poor to Ariock, like something designed by a clumsy child.

But the refugees looked awestruck. They seemed to approve.

"Nice." Thomas sounded as if the admission pained him. "Uh, I guess if you're going for armor, you should forge a helmet as well."

Ariock collected the last scraps of metal in midair and began to sculpt a helmet around his head. He wished he had a mirror. It was going to be an ugly helmet, since he was working by Yeresunsa touch rather than his own eyesight.

"I can give you a mirror," Thomas said, "if you'll let me back at the controls. I won't crash us."

Ariock used his powers to gently push Thomas back to the console.

Thomas swiped a few icons, and one section of the wraparound window grew opaque and reflective. It became a mirror.

Ariock used to avoid glimpses of his own reflection. He'd had a tiny mirror in the sky room, for personal hygiene purposes, but otherwise, he had not looked at a full-body reflection of himself since he was a kid.

Now he assessed his armor.

Overlapping metal plates emphasized his big chest, the width of his shoulders, and his gigantic height. He looked like someone who could throw a tank.

Maybe that wasn't such a bad thing.

"Would the Torth have malware installed on every single ship on that planet?" Vy asked.

"Probably not," Thomas admitted. "They'll expect us to try to overtake and board one of the armada ships. They won't think we're crazy enough to land on the Torth Homeworld and try to steal someone's personal streamship from the most fortified planet in the galaxy."

"So if we do that—" Vy began to say.

"They'll scramble to install the malware," Thomas said. "And I'm sure they've already taken other precautions."

"But it's possible for us to steal a ship," Vy said, "before they have time to sabotage it, or stop us?"

Thomas looked sour. It seemed he didn't want to admit even a remote possibility of survival. "You're talking about very long odds," he said. "It's an almost nonexistent chance."

That was better than nothing.

Ariock fitted his new helmet to his head, ironing out the lumps. He used his powers to pinch a crest. As an afterthought, he crushed the crest into a serrated blade. He hoped the Torth could feel terror.

"They can't have traps set up for every square mile of that whole planet," Vy said. "Can't we land somewhere unpredictable?"

"We'll want to get the hell off the Torth Homeworld soon after we land," Thomas said. "So it has to be a spaceport. And there are a limited number of those. Only four." He looked forlorn at the controls. "Are we sure about this?" He begged Ariock. "We don't have enough propulsion to change course once we get going."

Ariock clenched his armored fists. He sent a fraction of his power shivering up his arms in staticky crackles.

His friends looked impressed. They should not have to fear or suffer.

The Torth Empire needed to learn some limits.

"I control the weather." Ariock's voice was huge and dark, like a thunderhead. "Let the Torth come at me. I'm ready."

# CHAPTER 9

# TOXIC PLANET

Warships began to move. They reconfigured in an ominous way, forming a wall. Vy figured that Thomas must be steering them toward the planet.

"Just remember," Thomas muttered, "I recommended a quick death."

Vy braced for an imminent crash into the nearest warship. But that warship moved aside. So did the next, and the next. A tunnel swept open for their little streamship.

One glance at Ariock told Vy that he was putting all his focus into tunneling through the armada. Encased in armor from head to foot, with his shoulders rigid, he looked unmovable.

It was hard to believe he'd forged that whole suit of armor in mere minutes. If Vy hadn't watched him reshape the torn-up metal, she would have guessed that all he could do was wreck things.

Maybe that was because Ariock himself seemed to think he was nothing but a talentless oaf. Everyone seemed to think that—including the Torth Empire. Including Thomas.

But Vy remembered the giant-size couches and tables in the Dovanack mansion. Ariock had built those without help, possibly without instructions. He was a craftsman. His newly forged armor was utilitarian and plain, but it was well-made. He really might throw the Torth Empire a new challenge.

"What can we expect on the Torth Homeworld?" Kessa asked.

"I expect the Torth to pummel Ariock for as long as possible," Thomas said, "to exhaust his powers, or his attention. Or both. They'll look for a way to distract him. If his attention wavers even for a half second, that could be enough to doom us."

"We won't give them that chance," Cherise said.

"The Torth will present Ariock with bad choices to make," Thomas went on. "Dilemmas that cause him to think, that will make him pause, that will lead to him making mistakes. A mistake can get him killed. Then we'll all be easy pickings."

Vy glanced at Ariock. He didn't seem to be mentally present, so maybe he couldn't hear the conversation, but even so, she wished Thomas would stop outlining everything that could go wrong. Ariock had enough to worry about.

"Maybe they'll send kamikaze slaves at him," Thomas said.

"What is kamikaze?" Kessa cocked her head, wanting a definition.

"Slaves who are forced to fight us." Vy adjusted her blaster glove. "We'll show them these," she said, waving her gloved hand. "Once they see ummins wearing blaster gloves, they'll abandon the Torth and join us." At least, she hoped so.

Weptolyso and Kessa exchanged a doubtful glance.

Ships slammed into each other, shedding parts and rippling with explosions. It was impossible to see far ahead with all the debris.

Ariock's grim look of focus intensified. Liquid fire splashed against an invisible shield around them.

The missile fire became so intense, Vy had to squint against the fireworks. It was eerily quiet, and their ship remained steady, so the explosions seemed like harmless illusions.

"I'll bet she set up a hack to shut down our life support at an inopportune moment," Thomas muttered. He scrolled through long blocks of geometric Torth symbols.

Vy watched from afar, feeling useless. "Thank you." If only she had guessed how dangerous the Upward Governess would be. She would have… Well, there was nothing she could have done. Challenging a Torth was like challenging a god.

"Is this world the place where Jonathan Stead freed a thousand slaves?" Kessa asked.

Hope surged through Vy. Ariock's great-grandfather had escaped from the Isolatorium, according to lore and legend. Old Garrett, otherwise known as Jonathan Stead, had survived on the Torth Homeworld. And from here? He had successfully escaped the Torth Empire!

"No one knows how he did it." Thomas sounded cross. "But he managed to surprise them. We cannot. Every Torth in the Megacosm sees us."

"Even so—" Vy began.

"Jonathan Stead wasn't bogged down with people he had to protect," Thomas cut in. "He was smart enough to stay solo. Nor did he attempt to wreck and kill his way toward safety. After he broke free from the Isolatorium, he wisely spent the rest of his life sneaking around and hiding. He never openly killed again. He sneaked into that spaceport. And he sneaked his way to Earth."

"Even so," Vy said.

"The Torth won't fall for the same tricks twice." Thomas gave her a flat stare. "They won't write us off as dead until they have our corpses in custody, and I'm sorry, but"—he nodded toward Ariock—"he isn't built for sneaking."

Vy ran out of arguments, but internally, she wasn't done. She felt hope.

"Look," Kessa said.

The interlocked layers of warships had finally thinned out. Through the gaps, Vy glimpsed a looming planet, stippled with cloudy froth and murky purple shadows. Refugees stared at it with curiosity.

"There it is," Thomas said. "The Torth Homeworld."

To Vy, the planet resembled a bloated blood clot. Its colors were unhealthy. The strangest thing was what looked like an enormous spike that emerged from somewhere over its horizon.

"Is that a space elevator?" Vy guessed.

"No," Thomas said. "That's the tallest skyscraper in the known universe. The Stratower. Yeresunsa built it before the founding of the Torth Empire."

Vy wished she could have a real conversation with her foster brother, the way they used to. She wanted to know all about ancient Yeresunsa and the Torth Homeworld. But these days, Thomas no longer volunteered information with friendly exuberance. He had become hard to talk to.

And depressed. Vy figured that must be a result of the way Cherise was treating him, plus the thousands of unhappy lifetimes he had absorbed.

She just didn't know how to reach him.

"Yeresunsa built that?" Kessa gazed at the improbable skyscraper. "Why?"

"No one remembers its original purpose," Thomas admitted. "But it's a seat of power now. Servants of All have secret meetings and train there. It's where new Servants are made." He poked at holographic menus. "There's a restricted-access spaceport near the top of the Stratower, but I expect they'll have set up a lot of traps. I suggest that we head toward a big public spaceport instead." He shuddered. "And let's not get anywhere near the Isolatorium."

Vy wondered how many awful thirdhand memories he had absorbed from tortured prisoners. No one should be subjected to that much pain and horror.

"You said there are only four spaceports on this planet?" Kessa sounded skeptical, and Vy inwardly agreed. The Torth Homeworld sounded like it was the center of galactic civilization. It must have a huge population.

"No one really wants to live on the Torth Homeworld," Thomas explained. "It is where the Torth originate from, but it's become something of a backwater. It's, uh, not like other planets." His look of dread worsened. "It has a lot of weirdnesses."

Vy wondered what he was holding back. "Like what?"

"It has toxic urban wastelands," Thomas said.

That sounded evasive, to Vy, but the chaos outside was intense. Warships spun away, battered aside by Ariock's power.

His face was unreadable under the crude helmet, but he stood perfectly balanced on the rolling floor, whereas everyone else had to brace themselves.

Tendrils of electricity rolled down his armor and winked out. Loose items floated as if eager to obey his silent commands. Bowls. Packets. A roll of twine.

"Ended that program," Thomas said with satisfaction, swiping a menu. "Yeah, she tried to sabotage us in a few different ways. At least that's taken care of."

Vy pushed down various levitating objects. Ariock seemed unaware of these signs of his imperfect control. He must be keeping track of a lot of things, pouring himself into this fight.

Torth ships kept pace with them as they drew closer to the planet's immense surface. The Torth Homeworld began to fill their field of view, dark and ominous. The armada appeared to be harrying them toward it.

The Stratower itself blotted out a swath of stars. The crazy skyscraper resembled an eroded narwhal horn, except it was also more ornate than a Gothic cathedral. It was definitely too artistic to be Torth architecture.

And it glittered. Those tiny points of light might actually be windows.

"Are those clouds?" Kessa frowned at the sickly striations that banded the whole planet. "Why are they so dark?"

"That's the storm layer," Thomas replied. "The Torth Homeworld has something like a nuclear winter effect going on—fallout from an ancient war."

That tidbit of information should have warranted more than a casual mention. Vy gave Thomas a despairing look.

"The climate is cold," Thomas said, "with toxic sludge falling from the sky in the form of sleet. It's eternal night. Nothing lives in the so-called dead city ruins, unless you count the mutant monstrosities."

In the back of her mind, Vy had assumed they could crash-land in a wilderness area, if worse came to worse, and survive off the land.

Apparently not.

"So we'll make this a quick stop," she said. "Grab a new ship and be on our way as fast we can manage."

"Sure." Thomas sounded bleak.

Their streamship lurched with a sickening drop. Lightning erupted across their view as they fell toward the planet.

"We're going to have a rough ride from here," Thomas said. "Hey Vy, would you mind anchoring my chair?" He nodded toward a double-handled device embedded in the floor. "Otherwise it's possible I'll slide around and lose control of the ship."

*You could have mentioned that earlier*, Vy thought as she snatched the handles and buckled them into the base of his hoverchair.

"Buckle me in." Thomas's voice changed, becoming very low, almost a whisper. "I'd rather not have anyone overhear this. But I am begging you. If

Ariock falls in battle, please, please, please use your blaster glove to blow my head off."

Vy paused in the middle of securing his hoverchair. Her heart ached for Thomas.

She used to be so fiercely proud of his gumption. On Earth, he had been unstoppable on his quest to survive to adulthood, conquering any obstacle in his way.

The Torth had stolen his ability to feel hope.

*You're loved,* she wanted to tell him. *You're wanted. This isn't the end.*

"I can't anticipate everything we're about to face," Thomas said, ignoring her thoughts. "It's possible the Torth have roped other supergeniuses into aiding them. I don't want to poke my head into the Megacosm. It's not worth giving them a chance to scan our situation. And to gloat."

Was that why he felt so hopeless? Did he think he was outmatched?

"We're definitely outmatched," Thomas snapped. "I'll do my best, but our odds are terrible."

All around them, refugees secured supplies and buckled themselves into the remaining seats. If they could hear a translation of what Thomas was saying, they would become demoralized.

Vy tested his hoverchair tether. She did not want to imagine a worst-case scenario, but she knew one thing for certain: anything was better than giving up. She would escape the Torth Empire, or she would die fighting.

"I'm not as brave as you," Thomas said, his voice cracking with despair. "If the worst happens? You have to kill me."

"No." Vy finished securing him in his seat. Only Thomas could navigate temporal streams. If they were going to have any chance at all, then they needed their pilot.

"I'm begging you," Thomas said.

Vy said nothing. She refused to imagine the scenario he was talking about, with Ariock dead and the rest of them doomed.

"Please?"

Vy knew that her brave, determined foster brother was still inside this hopeless Torth version. At least, she thought so.

She wanted to believe that.

"You're going to live," she told Thomas. "We all are. And don't you dare pester Cherise."

# CHAPTER 10

# DEAD CITY

The storm was a temptation.

Enormous towers of clouds loomed, forged into frightfully elongated shapes by racing winds. Lightning made him eager to spike out and see how fast and how strong his power could be. The very air was violent.

He wished to join it.

He could direct this storm. Make it his own. Winds flowed in ways that he could see and touch, and it would be the simplest matter to…

No.

He had a heart.

Ariock was a person, not a storm. The streamship was his heart, and the rest of him had to be arms, whipping around to form a protective shield.

He curved his awareness around the streamship, and he remembered to be gentle. Everyone he cared about was cradled within.

"I'm aiming for the busiest of the public spaceports," Thomas said. "That goes against my better judgment, but it's worth the gamble that the Torth haven't shut down all planetary commerce. They might be less prepared for us there."

Ariock glanced at Thomas. He was amazed that he could do that—glance at someone—while his awareness was stretched and busy. He was only vaguely aware of his human body. Half of his attention faced outward. Whenever he perceived a missile, he knocked it aside with a whip of wind. He was also the energetic wind surrounding the ship's hull.

He had not been able to handle this much at once back on the planet Umdalkdul. It was a lot to juggle, but he was getting more proficient.

The ship gained a plunging, roller-coaster sensation. Gigantic ghostly clouds appeared with flashes of lightning, but the lightning soon diminished to crackles.

Refugees gazed outside with frightened eyes. This no longer resembled the starry night of deep space. Their streamship descended into a sooty twilight beneath the roiling storm clouds.

Distant lights, brightly artificial, penetrated the distant gloom.

Ariock figured those must be transports. Thousands of them. A swarm. There was no way to be stealthy with so many watchful eyes out there.

"What are those splinters?" Kessa asked, peering downward.

Ariock squinted, trying to see through the darkness. Far below, a vast cloud blanketed the planet, like a dark, tranquil ocean riffled by wind. Shadows suggested needle-sharp points jutting up from it.

"Those are the skeletal ruins of ancient skyscrapers." Thomas floated at the piloting console, checking holographs that glowed against the gloom. "Most of this planet is covered in urban decay."

The Torth fleet stopped shooting. Ariock sensed many shuttles and transports out there, such a legion that they lent the sky a sullen glow, but they were flanking him, not trying to murder him.

For now.

Black streaks began to splotch their view. Each tarry spot melted almost as fast as it formed, but even so, their panoramic view became occluded by grime.

"That's the toxic sleet." Thomas did something to the controls, and the tar blotches faded away. "I never thought I'd end up in this hellscape," he muttered.

"Jonathan Stead freed a thousand slaves," Kessa said. "Where did they go?"

"They were never found," Thomas said.

"But—" Vy began.

"This planet has twenty thousand square miles of decayed, pitch-black ruins," Thomas said. "Full of toxic sludge. The Torth did search the area. They even bombed it for good measure. But they gave up after a few weeks. The escapees would have died of thirst, even if they survived sludge serpent attacks and bombings. There's no potable water down there."

Ariock decided to risk withdrawing his protection just a little bit, lending his human side enough bandwidth to ask questions. "But my great-grandfather survived," he said. "Right?"

"He must have found a hiding place," Thomas admitted. "And a way to survive in the ruins. The Torth never learned how."

Vy looked hopeful.

Ariock grinned. Maybe, if he was lucky, he would follow in his great-grandfather's footsteps. He craved details about the legendary hero who had later established the Dovanack family.

"Whatever methods he used," Thomas said, "whatever allies he had, his secrets died with him. *We* don't have a way to survive."

Vy began to argue.

"We cannot survive on this planet," Thomas said, ruthlessly interrupting her. "I'm telling you what I know."

Ariock gazed down at the mysterious cloud cover. The Torth had had trouble searching this area, despite all their slaves and all their vehicles. They could not see through ancient walls in pitch darkness.

But if he stretched his awareness? He might see things which the Torth Empire had missed.

It seemed worth a try.

Tentative, Ariock reached for Vy, brushing her arm with his armored fingers. If anyone could bring him back from losing himself, she could.

He held her hand, very gently. He was relieved when she clasped back.

Ariock closed his eyes and sharpened his focus. He protected their ship while simultaneously pushing his awareness downward. He twisted through foul air choked by grime.

The farther away that part of him went, the looser and less cohesive he felt. He was a cloud. He was a great expanse of tarry raindrops.

Those rainy parts of himself landed on broken towers that protruded from rubble.

Rail-thin bridges connected rusted remnants. Most of the bridges were broken, or they sagged, or else they arched in steepled lumps.

Many skyscrapers were fallen, supported by their ruined neighbors.

His awareness breezed through decayed walls, wafting over bare beams and through hollow places. Stalactites bearded every ledge. Inky sludge coated every exposed surface. There were life sparks here and there, but their lack of coordinated direction and lack of apparent gear hinted that they were animals.

Beneath tons of ruination and sludge, he sensed shapes like broken rib cages and skulls.

People had died in this city. Countless numbers of them.

Judging by the despair in the way they had fallen, they had died all at once, in some violent calamity.

This city did not feel gently abandoned. It felt abused.

He became aware of a subtle, low-key hum in addition to the life sparks of animals. It had the vibrance of a life spark, but instead of being concentrated, it was very diffuse, almost unnoticeable to him. Yet it seemed to be everywhere he went.

That lively hum alarmed him. It felt alien. He couldn't guess what it might be, and his ignorance here seemed very dangerous.

He gathered his vast self and snapped back to being just Ariock.

Such a quick return disoriented him. Ariock braced himself against the dome, reminded that his human form was very fragile and compact.

Thomas gave him a critical look. "Where'd you go? And what did you learn?"

Ariock realized that the boy was too far away to read his mind.

"The dead city feels cursed." Ariock hated to sound superstitious, but that was the best way to describe what he had experienced with his expanded awareness. "What happened down there?"

"There was a war."

Ariock did not need a supergenius to tell him that. The dead city was an enormous mass grave. But as inhumane as the Torth were, he figured they would rather enslave a population than destroy it.

"Who fought the war?" he asked.

"Yeresunsa," Thomas said. "It was a war between Yeresunsa versus the emergent beginnings of the Torth Empire. Billions of people died."

A knot tightened inside Ariock. He could imagine cataclysmic winds toppling skyscrapers and crushing people to death. Yeresunsa—his type of monster—had ravaged this world.

He might bring fresh devastation.

"Of course, we only know the Torth side of the story," Thomas said. "The losing side of that war was completely annihilated. We don't have any memories, or recordings, or written accounts from them."

Ariock wasn't going to answer the concerns in his friends' gazes. There would be time for conversations if they survived.

"This eternal night was caused by Yeresunsa?" Kessa said in disbelief.

"Yes," Thomas said. "They sparked huge storms that blocked the sun. It caused a runaway greenhouse effect."

Ariock had to believe that everything would go smoothly. They would steal a new streamship with minimum devastation and be on their way.

Colorful lights twinkled ahead. All of a sudden, the horizon was vibrant with neon colors, jarring against so much blackness.

"That's the living city," Thomas said grimly. "Where the spaceport is."

No one spoke. They barely moved, except to check their blaster gloves or to tighten the straps of their packs.

Their crippled vessel was a sanctuary, and every passenger was a warrior standing their last ground.

# CHAPTER 11

# STORMING

Polluted rainfall blurred the distant neon lights, turning them into something like an underwater carnival. The unreal horizon hurled defiance at the black ruins they were flying over. The Torth must find the colorful brightness to be inviting.

Ariock prepared for a fight.

He expanded his awareness, trying to assess how many enemy transports awaited them in the populated city. Too many to count. The air was clogged with traffic.

"Behind us!" Weptolyso said with alarm.

A missile slammed into Ariock's air shield. The enormous explosion ripped across the dome, so blinding that black cracks burned across the whiteness. One wedge of the dome flickered, wavering between a view of the outside and a gray blankness, evocative of a computer crash.

Everyone was on their hands and knees. Ariock pushed away from the curved wall, where he had fallen. At least he hadn't landed on top of anyone. In his armor, he might accidentally crush any one of his friends, except for Weptolyso.

"Our hull is damaged," Thomas said in a tight voice. He must be strapped into place, because he hadn't moved.

"Reinforce our hull, Ariock," Thomas said. "Otherwise we're dead."

Fireballs flared against their ship, causing it to careen off course. Ariock braced himself and sent his awareness crisscrossing around their hull. He absorbed shock wave after immense shock wave, trying to cement the fractured hull.

He struggled to do all that while hanging onto his identity. If he forgot who he was, he might just destroy his friends the way he'd accidentally killed his mother.

Vy touched his armored hand.

She did not ask if he was all right, but Ariock saw her concern. She helped him remember who and where he was.

Their ship soared over a pitch-black abyss. A wide ribbon of nothingness separated the dead city from the living one. There were no visible bridges or roads, no way to stroll from the dead city to the living one, or vice versa.

Ariock had no time to study the border that separated the cities. Bombs exploded from above. He poured himself into a frenzy of wind around the ship.

Then he was amid a dazzle of neon that might be akin to Times Square in New York City. Searchlights shone through the low clouds. Holographs glowed between otherwise dreary-looking fortresslike buildings. Bombs hit Ariock's extended awareness. He did not know, at a glance, what was solid and what was a mirage.

"They're trying to make us crash." Thomas worked the controls, and their ship banked one way, then another.

The Torth had waited, Ariock realized. They did not want to lose their targets in the dead city.

They didn't want a repeat of the Jonathan Stead incident.

Transports swarmed, shooting missiles, and Ariock solidified his air shield. Between fiery explosions, he saw blocky, geometric mounds. This was Torth-style architecture, seamless and overengineered, but it was different from the dusty sandstone buildings and glassy skyscrapers he'd seen on Umdalkdul. Here, everything was coated by layers of sludge and slime. Sharp angles were indistinct. There were no rooftop gardens or terraced plazas, no signs of luxury.

And all the people must be indoors.

Ariock extended his awareness briefly through a nearby building, and, sure enough, life sparks glowed here and there. A scattered flow of them must be a street full of pedestrians.

The local slaves probably never guessed what the outside really looked like. They would have windows and domes full of sunlight and other false things. Nothing was ever quite what it seemed in a Torth city.

"Oh my God," Vy said in a tone of awe.

She gazed ahead, and at first, Ariock couldn't process what his eyes saw there. It looked like a dark, baroque wall of ancient mechanisms, but it filled the whole horizon, and the sky as well. It extended into gloom and clouds. Distant transports flew in front of it, as tiny in comparison as fireflies trying to light up a field. Huge geometric buildings looked like tiny heaps collected at its base. Windows marched up its surface, millions of black points. Only a handful glowed like distant stars.

"That's the Stratower," Thomas said. "Ariock, pay attention."

Ariock forced his attention back to the onslaught. His human self could not hear the missiles fly through the air or explode, but his titan self sensed changes in air pressure and shrieking wind. He caught each missile before it could crater his hull.

Explosives began to shoot from below.

As Ariock added things to his self-awareness—humid air and sticky raindrops, structures made of alien materials, neon, illusions, bridges, chasms, transports, and explosives—he began to lose track of his human body in the complexity.

He kept one part of himself inside the ship, to remain present with the people he cared about, but there was too much to keep track of. All he could do was ensure that his body remained upright.

"Can't you dodge them?" someone familiar said. The pretty one.

"This is a streamship, not a transport." Another familiar voice; the boy. "It's not exactly maneuverable in an atmosphere. And we're on our last dregs of fuel, so to speak."

"Well, try!"

Another voice, the ummin elder. "Could you see where each Torth is, if you go into the Megacosm?"

The pretty one. "Oh, good idea!"

"If you want me to, I will." The distant reply sounded strained. "But it's a trade-off. If I get to see through their eyes, they get to see through mine. They'll know where I'm going and what condition we're in."

"It might be worth it."

Their ship flipped sideways and careened through the narrow passage between two skyscrapers, then flipped the other way to speed along a curved wall. They blasted through a neon-pink advertisement.

Missiles slammed into the tower behind them a split second later, sending chunks tumbling.

"I trust my brain," the boy was saying in a dark voice, while refugees slid across the floor. "But I can't work these controls as fast as an able-bodied person. My reflexes are crap."

His hands danced across the console, but they looked fragile. He trembled every time he had to reach far.

There was no time to train a second pilot, of course. Ariock made a mental note about prioritizing preparedness, if they managed to survive today. They should have used their relaxation time more wisely.

A large vessel roared up out of the depths to block their path. Thomas jerked their ship sideways to avoid it, and they ended up in a volley of missiles.

Ariock threw himself into that barrage. He became explosive shock waves. He was a giant of thunder, and when he crashed into transports, he knocked them down. Soon there was nothing alive inside them. Only the buzzing currents of machinery.

This stormy planet was electric with energy. Ariock wanted to chase each rope of lightning. He wanted to rush outward farther and faster, to encompass more.

More missiles flew at him. The cowardly Torth were hanging back, but their missiles were on target. And the more awareness he poured into self-defense, the less awareness he had of himself.

He realized, with dread, that he was losing control.

He could blow the latest swarm of transports away in one massive gale, but more would instantly replace them. He needed to try something more…final.

Ariock thought of the mighty storm that roiled the upper cloud layers of this planet. Chaotic energy. Chaos he might reshape and direct.

"Dodge them," he told Thomas.

It was all he could do to speak while fighting the barrage. There was no way to make his voice sound less detached. Thomas probably wanted to yell criticisms at him.

But Thomas really hadn't said anything insulting to Ariock since their escape from Umdalkdul.

No one had. Their wary glances made the why plain.

Ariock needed to address those fears. Later. Once they were safe, he would reassure everyone that he was civil.

Their streamship careened through missile fire, and Ariock pushed his awareness into vectors of wind. He became air currents high above the city, swirling around the Stratower, distantly aware of his chest and back pressing tight against his armor.

He drew the storm down in big, concentrated fistfuls.

A dark finger of cloud sagged in the middle of the swarm, sucking transports skyward. The cloud whirled into a furious pillar of doom, vacuuming up Torth vessels and hurling them in various directions.

Lightning stabbed down in huge, earth-shattering sheets. The lightning became a dancing wall of pure electricity that pounded the city hard enough to shake skyscrapers.

Ariock had intended a few stabs, not this strobe-light madness. Thunder exploded in a constant barrage. Anyone outside would have gone deaf. Lights flickered behind a heavy downpour.

His savage whirlwind expanded into a mile-wide tornado sweeping through the transports and destroying them. He dimly sensed life sparks winking out of existence.

He hoped that was enough to deter any more Torth pilots from attacking him.

"Ariock?" Thomas said desperately. "If you want to make it into the spaceport, I need a little help."

He flew their ship as if navigating through a pinball machine. They twisted around angular monoliths. They clipped an overhang with an inch to spare, knocking off sludge stalactites. Passengers clung to anything solid.

Two more tornadoes descended, nearly as thick as the first. The storms raged out of control.

"I've got this." Ariock sounded calm. He felt calm, in a strange way. There were a lot of things in the universe that he didn't understand, but he understood storms.

He connected to the nearest tornado and shrugged himself into it. Wind roared through him, as uncontrolled as his own pulse, just like the blood rushing through his veins.

When he'd familiarized himself with its vortex patterns, he scattered it, shaking off its energy. Five-hundred-mile-per-hour winds slowed to ordinary gusts. Rain spun outward, then gushed down. The twisted remains of missiles fell with the floodwaters.

The vortex fell apart like a demon called back to hell.

Ariock sent his awareness outward and dismantled a second tornado. Proud, he disengaged from wind and lightning and tightened his awareness around their streamship hull, close to his core self. That reduced him to almost fully human status.

But more cracks had appeared on their windshield dome. The cracks radiated outward from where his armored hands had braced against the wall, like etchings of lightning.

Ariock pulled his hands away and did not ask Vy or anyone else what he had looked like.

"The spaceport is sealed," Thomas said. "Ariock, you need to blast a way in for us."

Their ship popped above a tangled mass of wreckage and towers, gaining altitude. The Stratower dominated the sky like an impossibility. It must be large enough to hold a nation.

Their ship was the only flying thing in sight.

No more enemies. That seemed promising. Thomas looked sick with dread, but Ariock figured he must have an overactive imagination.

Their ship angled toward a beehive-like structure beyond one of the Stratower's low shoulders. Those tiers must be docks for transports. The sunken openings between each tonguelike wing of the building must be launch routes.

Their ship plummeted toward the beehive, falling into a shaft huge enough to encompass a skyscraper. Ariock wrenched a metallic blockage aside. It might be as strong as a vault door, but it was as flimsy as paper to him.

Steely walls flashed past during their roller-coaster plunge. Ariock kept his awareness extended ahead, ready to knock aside any other blockage that might appear.

He sensed life sparks.

Tens of thousands of life sparks. An army must be waiting for him.

It was too bad he couldn't just extinguish life sparks with a thought. But Ariock had learned that he could not connect with life sparks from afar. In order to heal someone, he needed to be in close proximity, almost touching, and he needed to pour all his focus and energy into that person. It was different than storm powers.

However, he could connect with everything else. The walls, the launchpads, anything inert. If he caused a ripple throughout the spaceport, he might shake up the army. Scare them away.

He imagined them, all wearing blaster gloves full of microdarts of the inhibitor. Some would carry missile launchers. They'd be on hoverbikes and weaponized transports.

Ariock was almost glad for the opportunity to see unprotected enemies up close.

Their ship emerged in a vast vertical space. Launchpads lined the walls, tier after tier. Those lily pad–like platforms should have cradled spacecrafts.

Instead, every single launchpad and catwalk was packed with nussians.

Their tough skin shone in natural shades of bronze, gold, and red. Their size, and their upright bodies with thorny spinal ridges, made them familiar to Ariock. These were the common guard species of prisons and slave zones.

And they all held what looked like cattle prods in their big hands.

Weptolyso snorted in dismay.

In the prison arena, Ariock had been forced to battle an enraged nussian, but Weptolyso was a friend. The former hall guard had forsaken his training and risked his life to help Vy and other slaves escape when he could have blocked their path to freedom.

"Suicide troops," Thomas observed in a tone of defeat.

Of course. The Torth would never entrust a "lesser species" with anything like blaster gloves. Those prods were probably designed to shoot one thing: microdarts of inhibitor serum.

No one cared if the spaceport nussians got killed in an attempt to take down the Giant.

"They've preemptively removed the ships," Thomas said. "They were ready for us." His yellow eyes looked large and haunted in his waxy-pale face. "This is it. We're out of fuel."

Their ship lost momentum.

They fell, on a collision course toward a launchpad laden with nussians.

# CHAPTER 12

# IN RUINS

Missiles exploded into Ariock's awareness. Automatic missile launchers were mounted everywhere in the interior of the spaceport. Even when they missed their target, they hit other things. Tons of nussians spilled to their deaths. Terrified alien guards shoved past each other, but the overcrowded balconies and piers lacked guardrails, and more fell.

Ariock connected to the air outside their ship and built a cushion so they wouldn't career into a wall. But Thomas seemed to have given up on piloting.

Maybe the boy was right to give up. He must have anticipated this disaster, along with all kinds of other disaster scenarios. Ariock was the one who was foolishly optimistic.

Hadn't enough innocent people already died for him?

He should have known the Torth would sacrifice tens of thousands of slaves to get what they wanted. Why had he insisted on fighting another day?

"Ariock." A thorny nussian hand gently scraped his armor. "We must survive," Weptolyso said in heavily accented English.

Ariock studied his nussian friend. Weptolyso gazed back with placid red eyes full of empathy. His alien face was difficult to read, but he understood the pressure of being a protector. He knew isolation due to his size, having been forced to guard much smaller govki and ummins.

The idea of slaying people like Weptolyso, or abandoning them to die in a condemned spaceport? Ariock couldn't do it.

"They are for the wrong side in this fight." Weptolyso eyed the hordes of nussians, and his huge nostrils flared in what looked like disappointment. "They will understand. They will wake up. Or not."

"We're crashing," Thomas announced.

Ariock shut his eyes and sent his awareness outward. He split himself in two, so that half of him embraced the ship's damaged hull. The voices of his friends faded to background noise as the other half of him expanded into the spaceport.

He became the launchpads, the walkways, the steel walls, the tunnels, the electric wiring, the pipes and vents. He crumpled missile launchers wherever he found them.

Amid it all, he tasted the multitudes of life sparks. He could dislodge most of those nussians with a flex, but he guessed that was why the Torth had filled this place with innocent slaves instead of with Red Ranks. The nussians had no idea whom they were fighting or what they were up against. They had no clue what a Yeresunsa was capable of.

Ariock wasn't going to murder them.

Bit by bit, he swallowed the entire spaceport inside his awareness. He inhabited every wall, every flow of energy or air. He was the frozen muck that hung off the exterior walls. He was the basement levels where slaves slept or died. He was the repair bay where vessels awaited...

He withdrew to his human self. "Go to the lowest tunnel on my right," he told Thomas. "There's a repair bay with ships."

Thomas gave him an amazed look. "They left shuttles in the repair bay?"

"Down and to my right." Ariock swatted away more explosive blasts.

They dropped in that direction, but a disturbing shock wave roared up from below. Ariock absorbed its deadly force, protecting their ship while launchpads disintegrated and hundreds of nussians died.

The force of the wave scalded his mind. He lost focus. He lost his ability to keep track of all the vaporized matter. He became just Ariock again.

It only lasted for a second. As soon as he could extend his awareness, he caught their ship's tumble. He also explored the repair bay...and discovered only burning wreckage. All the life sparks below were gone. The lower levels of this spaceport were ruined.

Ariock pressed his head against the wall. He couldn't see all the slaves who had just lost their lives, but he acknowledged their deaths.

The cruelty and wastefulness made chills run up his arms. How many innocent people had the Torth just murdered in order to prevent him from escaping?

"The repair bay is gone," he told Thomas.

He couldn't afford to mourn. There was no time. But he felt as if blood was leaking from every crevice inside his mind, reminding him that a battle against the Torth Empire was always far too costly.

He wanted to slam his armored fists repeatedly into Torth faces. Why were they so single-minded? So wasteful of lives?

"Ariock," Kessa said.

Her worried tone drew his attention.

"We are still here." She gazed at him with concerned gray eyes.

Ariock nodded an acknowledgment of her statement. He struggled to come up with a solid plan, but his overtired mind refused to take on any additional burdens. He was the ship's hull, he was the air currents around it, and he was also Ariock, and that really seemed like a lot.

"Get us out of here," he told Thomas.

"I can't. Our ship's too—"

"Just try!" Ariock didn't mean to let his anger out, but he was all too aware that his friends' lives depended entirely on him. He didn't need reminders.

Thomas worked the controls with a dubious look.

Ariock still wore the ship as an extension of himself, and he sensed which way the broken thrusters tried to aim. He propelled them upward, on a jet of air, in Thomas's intended direction.

They arrowed sideways and up through a brightly lit tunnel at a dangerous speed.

Ariock shot his awareness upward ahead of their ship, and it was a good thing he did. The launch route was blocked by a series of superdense gates. Ariock poured himself into the gates and wrenched them apart. Their ship careened past torn, sharp edges. If he had been a split second slower…

Disaster.

How much longer could he fend off Torth attacks? How much protection would his makeshift armor really give him?

Their streamship leaned heavily to one side. Something was fundamentally wrong with it. Ariock felt the mechanical problem the way one might feel a fatal wound in one's own body. This ship had traversed the void between stars for unfathomable years, and it had withstood countless meteorite impacts, but now it was dying. It would crash, and soon.

"It doesn't matter where we crash," Thomas said in a strangled tone of despair. "We're screwed! We have nowhere to hide."

Ariock thought of his legendary great-grandfather, who had supposedly hidden on this planet even while the Torth were trying to kill him. Jonathan Stead had survived. He had hidden amid the ruins and muck of the dead city.

Maybe that was the place to go.

"Nice try." A scratchy voice rasped from hidden loudspeakers. The glowing holograph of the Upward Governess flickered and solidified, blue and smug. "You are almost a worthy opponent."

Thomas frantically opened and closed control menus.

"Too bad you're weakened by your human heritage." Her voice twisted around the word *human*, as if tasting something foul. "You will never be in my league of brilliance—"

Thomas shut off her gloating live stream or recording or whatever it was. The holograph flickered out of existence.

Their ship shivered, gaining altitude only by Ariock's will. They emerged into the rain-drenched night. The living city blazed in all directions, low clouds reflecting its glow.

Torth transports swarmed like glowing hornets. But…were most of them flying away?

That was strange. Ariock wondered if they were trying to evacuate the city because of him.

"This can't be good," Thomas moaned.

"They're flying away from us," Vy said. "That's good. Right?"

"If they're evacuating the city," Thomas said, "they expect a major fight. Like, with nukes."

Clouds churned in a screaming, massive tornado, responding to the fury that pounded through Ariock's veins. All those fleeing Torth—those murderous thugs—were abandoning their slaves. They had tried to get Ariock to slaughter ten thousand nussians. Now they didn't care if this city got wrecked. They *wanted* him to kill the innocent.

He yearned to seize Torth throats and rip them apart. Teach them how it felt to be helpless.

"We're going to the dead city," Ariock said.

Thomas stared at him with unsettling yellow eyes. "Are you kidding? We're going down any second. The dead city is a dead end. At least the living city has slaves who might be friendly."

Ariock tapped the domed window, pointing the way. "Which way did Jonathan Stead go?"

"That was over a hundred years ago. It's not worth—"

"Show me the direction." Ariock tried to mitigate the undercurrent of threat in his deep voice. Why couldn't Thomas stop arguing and cooperate, for once?

Thomas tightened his mouth as if holding back a torrent of arguments. But he indicated a direction.

"Thanks." Ariock split his focus in a supreme feat of concentration. He thickened his shield around their hull, gluing damage together. At the same time, he was a jet of forceful air. He flung their ship toward the dead city at nearly supersonic speed.

"This is a terrible idea." The fear on Thomas's face belied his calm voice.

Ariock figured the farther they could get from populated regions, the better. He might defend a small bubble with his friends inside. But he was not going to attempt to defend an urban area, where life sparks might belong to either Torth or slaves.

"Do you have a better idea?" Vy demanded of Thomas.

He said nothing.

"Hey," Vy said. "Didn't you say there's another spaceport on top of the Stratower?"

"There's no way we can fight our way up through the thermosphere," Thomas said.

"How about if you check the Megacosm?" Vy suggested. "Maybe there's a weakness in their preparations."

If she wanted help from the collective knowledge of the Torth Empire, then she must be truly desperate.

"You don't understand how it works," Thomas said, his tone scathing. "If a Torth has knowledge that can help us win, then they'll purposely avoid the Megacosm until this battle is over. They know how fast I can soak up intelligence."

"You should try." Vy was pleading. "Any hint of help is better than none!"

"Their supergeniuses can soak up our situation," Thomas added. "They can peer through my eyes and feel how scared I am."

Missiles plummeted through the clouds, battering Ariock. He clenched his jaw and firmed up his protective sphere around their ungainly ship. The Torth were determined to see him crash in the living city.

Well, he was determined not to.

Ariock summoned his remaining concentration and spread his hands. Invisible wings unfurled from his fingers, sweeping out in shock waves that blew apart everything they touched. Ancient archways came apart and tumbled. His titan self sensed these things the way one might sense feathers brushing one's own skin.

Let the transports above deal with that.

In the midst of the chaos, Ariock sensed a falling bomb that felt different from missiles. Small. Ultradense. Deadly.

Thomas turned as if he wanted to shield his face.

The ultradense bomb exploded. At first, it was a fiery plasma that didn't quite touch Ariock. The detonation grew exponentially, violently bigger, as if the thing had a Yeresunsa awareness of its own.

It ripped through Ariock in a blinding, agonizing, impossible heat.

He managed to maintain his embrace around their fragile ship, but the outer layer of the hull disintegrated. All his thoughts—even his identity—died for a moment. All he could do was grit his teeth and wait for the radiant agony to fade.

The whole city lit up, a stark relief map. It must be blindingly bright out there, but the ship's adaptive skin seemed to filter out the harmful glare and radiation.

The shouts of passengers seemed far away, back where his armored body knelt.

"That was… Was that…?" Vy stared at the vast column of white fire behind them. It roared upward into the storm, its top spreading like a gigantic cap the size of the spaceport, the force of its updraft tugging Ariock and their ship along with him.

Passengers picked themselves up off the floor. None stood. They curled up or remained seated, afraid to get banged up.

Thick ropes of lightning danced around the mushroom cloud.

"Did they just drop a nuclear bomb?" Vy asked in horror. "On their own city?"

"Stratower City has weathered worse," Thomas said. "It can withstand a few nukes."

Ariock knew that the Torth would not care about minor structural damage. They had an endless supply of slaves they could work to death.

"They're spending so much effort on us," Vy said.

That was true. Ariock could almost understand why. He was dangerous. He commanded storms.

But he wouldn't have harmed anyone if the Torth had just left him alone to live his life on Earth. They were the aggressors. They had brought this upon themselves, hadn't they?

It was difficult to think while pouring so much of himself into absorbing shock-wave damage. He needed a plan. Once their ship crashed—which it must—he would need to cushion the impact. Then he would have to fend off Torth attacks, probably for hours. And hours. And hours.

The lights below vanished all at once.

Compared with their frantic entry into the living city, their exit was a low wobble. Ariock peered at the utter darkness ahead. All he saw were the vague outlines of ancient devastation.

Skeletal towers drooped like starvation victims. These remnants of skyscrapers looked rotten, missing vital parts such as walls and floors.

A nuclear glare lit the storm brighter than a supernova.

The inkiness of the dead city violently rejected that noonday brightness. It remained cataclysmic, dripping, and black. For the briefest of crazed moments, Ariock thought he saw shadowy apes climbing through a broken tower. That had to be his stressed-out imagination.

An unseen tsunami smashed into their ship.

Ariock was braced for the shock wave, but it was still more overpowering than he had anticipated. Screaming passengers tumbled against each other. Everyone and everything loose flew and crashed into one another.

Ariock struggled to regain his sense of self.

They sailed between the decayed ruins instead of above them. Ghoulish strands of lightning danced over the ruins. Ariock struggled to hold their ship aloft through sheer willpower.

He felt battered. He wasn't sure how long he could keep up this level of protection. Another nuclear bomb would wreck his ability to concentrate.

"I'll keep us going for as long as I can." Ariock's voice was as fathomless as the storm.

They glided for what seemed an improbably long time.

During that time, nobody spoke. The refugees held on for dear life, bracing themselves, prepared for a crash landing. Ariock kept almost hitting rotted towers, missing each one by a few feet.

Torth transports descended in the distance. Some were sucked into the churning storm, but most kept pace with Ariock.

Now he understood the Torth battle plan. They were chasing wounded prey. They meant to outlast Ariock. It was that simple.

The ship's belly grazed something solid that spun them in a violent arc.

It was all Ariock could do to expand his awareness, to shield them and cushion them as they smashed through a ruined tower top.

Bodies flew past him. People cried out in pain. Ariock braced himself against the tilting dome.

They crashed through ancient support beams. The floor was mostly gone. Ariock used all his focus to slow their momentum before they could plunge through the far side of the tower. They slid to a stop.

The ship rocked, then settled.

The domed window died. So did all the lights, plunging the room into pitch blackness.

# CHAPTER 13

# PRECARIOUS

Vy strained to see with her eyes wide-open, but it was utterly dark. She might as well be blind.

Disembodied voices worriedly called out names. "Are you hurt?" they asked each other in the slave tongue.

Vy could not triage injuries without light. She clambered to her feet, arm throbbing. She had smashed into something hard enough to leave a nasty bruise.

An electric blue-white light flickered into existence. It illuminated Ariock in his makeshift armor. He could apparently conjure electricity, and he held a jumpy orb between his armored hands.

"Who's hurt?" he asked in a tone as unwavering as he was. "Where's Thomas?" His shadowed eyes roved over the passengers.

Thomas sprawled halfway across the room with a dazed look. He had been thrown from his hoverchair.

"Are you all right?" Vy rushed to Thomas. Many of the refugees were stunned or had mild injuries, but Thomas was particularly fragile, with atrophied muscles that barely held together his underdeveloped bones.

An immense armored presence knelt beside her. Ariock held his hands over Thomas, and the electric sphere vanished as he poured his focus into healing. Sparks cast their own light. The air writhed, sparkling with friction. The force of healing lifted Thomas's fragile body partway off the ground.

When Thomas fell back, he looked more alert. He was probably as healthy as he was likely to get.

Ariock conjured his electric sphere again and peered around the ship's interior. "Who else is hurt?"

Their luxury capsule was transformed into a nightmare. Ariock knelt next to a refugee who seemed particularly injured.

"We can't stay here." Vy hated to bring up their dire situation, but she recalled the Torth transports they'd seen in the distance. "Ariock, can you move us again? Can you hide us?"

"The window display is broken." Ariock sounded detached, and Vy guessed he was focused on using his power to heal. "If I'm using my powers to quest ahead, while also levitating our ship, and while also shielding us, then I'm over-whelmed. I'm not as effective." He paused. "But I can try."

"Please," Thomas begged in the slave tongue. "Will someone shoot me in the head?"

Refugees stared at him with various degrees of incredulity or contemplation.

"Do not hurt him." Vy picked up Thomas and held him in her arms. "Where's your hoverchair?" She looked around and saw the ergonomic chair smashed against a wall along with other debris. It wasn't floating.

"It's broken," Thomas said as she set him in the crooked seat. "Hoverdisks are actually pretty fragile. They're not engineered to withstand getting smashed."

Nevertheless, Vy pressed buttons, trying to power the chair. She crouched down to peer underneath. Could she possibly figure out how the spinning disk could be made to spin again?

"The helimagnetic capacitor got shattered." Thomas spoke as if she was an idiot. "My chair is dead. And so are we."

"We can hide in the ruins." Cherise adjusted her blaster glove. "Unless we make a stand here?"

"Life-support systems are down," Thomas said. "We'll run out of air in an hour."

The stuffy air reminded Vy that spacecrafts were, necessarily, airtight.

"Even if Ariock cracks the hull so everyone can breathe," Thomas went on, "and even if he is still able to fend off nuclear bombs with the hull's integrity destroyed, the Torth will wear him down. His powers will get depleted. He has to sleep sometime. The Torth know that. They will be relentless."

"He's right." Ariock stood, and electricity rippled over his armor, casting enough light to illuminate all the scared faces around them. "The last bomb stripped layers off the hull. I don't think it will shield me much."

Kessa was gathering supplies. "Then we must hurry," she said. "We must hide in the darkness of the dead city."

There might be enough time to hide. The path of their downed vessel might not be obvious. All the ruined skyscrapers looked like decayed wreckage.

"Good luck," Thomas said bitterly. "There is zero chance of survival." He moaned. "I hope someone shoots me."

Vy really didn't want to hear that. She tried to feel hopeful, to give her foster brother enough reason to want to live.

"We'll survive." Ariock extended a hand toward the wall, and cracks appeared. "We'll hide." The wall twisted along the cracks, tearing apart. "If Jonathan Stead could do it, so can we."

Cold, damp air rushed through widening crevices. The air smelled as rank as sulfur. The dreary patter of rain became the loudest sound.

Refugees peered through the escape hole. Kessa spoke in the slave tongue, urging them to carry their supply packs and to hurry.

Pung bravely stepped out first. Others followed.

Ariock dimmed his electricity power. "Go," he urged everyone. "Escape."

Was he including himself? Vy stared at Ariock, silently urging him to lead the way instead of bringing up the rear. She didn't want him to try to hold back a Torth armada by himself, like a hero, while the rest of them fled.

The Torth would slaughter him. And then the rest of them would be alone in the dead city, wandering without his protection, while Torth prowled the ruins.

"You're coming, too?" Vy asked.

Ariock hesitated.

"Of course he is." Kessa spoke with certainty. "It is a solid plan, for him to hide with us, and then to use his powers to steal a transport from the Torth."

Ariock's face was partially obscured by his helmet, but Vy saw his look of comprehension. "Oh! Right." He gave a nod, accepting Kessa's plan.

Vy made a mental note to thank Kessa when Ariock wouldn't overhear. She should have thought to say what Kessa had said, to give Ariock a good reason to hide instead of acting like a hero. She was just so stressed-out and scared. Perhaps a lifetime of slavery gave Kessa nerves of steel to cope with life-or-death situations.

She adjusted Thomas on her hip. Carrying him through the rain-drenched ruins would be a challenge.

"Weptolyso," Ariock said. "Would you be willing to carry Thomas and protect him?"

Weptolyso set down an extra supply pack. Without hesitation, held out his huge arms to receive Thomas.

Vy didn't want to insult the guard, but his skin was so tough, he might hurt Thomas without meaning to. And she saw his nostrils flare with distaste. Until now, Weptolyso had avoided getting within range of the mind reader.

"Are you sure?" she asked him.

"I honor what the Son of Storms has asked of me," Weptolyso replied in the slave tongue.

"It's fine," Thomas said in a crabby tone. "It doesn't matter."

Vy gingerly let Thomas go. "Be careful," she told Weptolyso in the slave tongue. "He's very breakable."

She picked up a blanket-wrapped supply pack and tried to set aside her misgivings. At least she could move quicker.

"Are you hurt?" Ariock held his electric orb near Vy, assessing her.

She began to say that she was fine. But Ariock saw the bruise on her arm, and his orb vanished as he focused on healing.

Physical relief washed through Vy from her scalp down to her toenails. All her aches vanished. Even her weariness was gone. She felt fit enough to run a marathon while carrying an ummin under each arm. The suddenness left her gasping in surprise.

"Thank you," she whispered. "But we don't have time."

Refugees slid outside, into the night, bustling with supply packs.

One small ummin struggled with a heavy load. Cherise lifted the pack and hefted it over her own shoulder. The pained anger in her eyes was gone, replaced by determination.

"Cherise," Vy said.

Cherise gave her an impatient look, and Vy struggled to think of a way to articulate her worries. She felt as if she was losing everyone who mattered in her life. Her mother, on a faraway world. Her foster brother, who was suicidal and convinced that he was a Torth. And now Cherise was ignoring both of them, spending all her time with ummin refugees.

"I won't abandon you," Vy whispered. "We're sisters."

Cherise gave her a searching look. Then a solemn nod. They stood together for a moment.

"We'll look out for each other." Cherise ducked into the night before Vy could beg her to include Thomas as well.

Vy had a feeling that she was forgetting something vitally important. Her instincts told her that it had to do with Thomas, but he had already left, carried by Weptolyso.

Then Varktezo rushed past her with his arms wrapped around the NAI-12 medicine case. That case was instantly recognizable, plastered with stickers and Cherise's drawings of phoenix birds.

"Thank you, Varktezo!" Vy whispered.

Varktezo gave a nod. The case made him clumsy, but he clutched it as if it contained the secrets of the universe.

The ship's interior was nearly empty. Vy gave Ariock an urgent look. Then she ducked out through the makeshift exit.

She immediately missed her winter parka. Rags were hardly warm enough. And the cloying air made her want to gag. It was humid, but also frigid, so that she exhaled puffy clouds.

"The floor is dangerous," Pung said in the slave tongue, speaking to everyone. "Step with care. Go slow."

Vy took a few steps and soon understood what he meant. Glacial, oily water seeped through her foot wraps. Some of the puddles were ankle-deep. The remaining girders of the floor were sticky in some places, like old chewing gum, and dangerously slick in other places.

A moaning wind came from below. Its tone spoke of the sheer drop, although the pattering rain obscured it.

One misstep, and any of them might fall to their death.

"Do not run," Kessa told the youngest of the refugees. "No matter how much you want to go fast, we cannot run here."

Pung hopped along a rotted floor beam, splashing through muck. More fearless ummins ventured onto the beam after him.

Ariock ducked out from the shipwreck. He straightened to his full height, towering over everyone. The armor and supply packs he carried made him look even bulkier.

The wreckage seemed to exhale as he withdrew his Yeresunsa power from it. Something broken fell, and everyone flinched as the debris slammed into beams below in a series of echoing thuds.

"Sorry," Ariock whispered.

"Let me carry some of that." Vy held out her hands.

Ariock gave her a questioning look, but he let her have one of the extra supply packs.

Freed up a bit, Ariock seemed to imbue everything he saw with his power. Girders straightened and shed mucus. Gobs of muck drooled off the floor and into the darkness below.

Ariock conjured his orb of electricity. The jumpy blue-white light illuminated a vast, open-air stretch of crooked pillars and crisscrossed floor beams, seemingly held together by strings of black goo.

Runnels and broken pillars showed where their ship had skidded to its halt. Vy gasped when she saw how precarious the wreck was. Half of their ship hung over an abyss. Another foot, maybe another inch, and they would have plummeted off the tower and into oblivion.

Ariock must have stopped them just in time.

"Turn off the light, you idiot!" Thomas whispered.

Ariock let his electricity wink out.

"We need to be able to see," Vy said, her voice as quiet as the rain. "This floor has holes."

"I'll help with the lighting situation," Thomas said. "Once we're farther away from the wreck." A candle-like flame flickered in front of his face, illuminating him and Weptolyso with an orange glow. Then the meager flame vanished.

The inhibitor must have worn off, at least a little bit. Vy felt heartened. No matter how hopeless Thomas seemed, no matter how scared he sounded, he was on their side. In his own way, he was just as good as Ariock.

They had two Yeresunsa knights with them, not just one.

## CHAPTER 14
# STORM TITAN

Ariock took one careful step. The girder he stood on creaked alarmingly.

He stepped sideways, testing a relatively straight girder. When he put his weight on it, the beam squealed and began to sink. Weptolyso rumbled in alarm.

"It's all right," Ariock told everyone. "I'll make sure we survive."

He quested outward with his Yeresunsa sense. First, he wanted to locate a good hiding spot. Perhaps a lower floor…

Life sparks lurked in the depths. Dozens of them.

"I think there are Torth in this tower," Ariock warned in a low voice.

"Already?" Thomas sounded offended by the idea.

Ariock reexamined the beings that moved inside his expanded self. He did not sense any hint of gear. Were they naked? The life sparks were roughly the size of Torth, but they lacked the dead-weight bulk that he associated with armor. He didn't have time to closely examine whether the material he did sense was rags or fur or fabric.

And he did not detect any transports. Nothing hovered or flew nearby.

"Maybe they're animals," Ariock admitted. "I don't know."

"If they were people," Vy whispered, "we would see flashlights."

"Not necessarily," Thomas said. "Servants of All have ocular implants. They can see in infrared."

Vy sighed. Ariock dared not let himself feel outmatched. It was pointless to wish for better gear, or a helmet that covered his whole face without leaving any skin exposed.

"There's a shaft we might be able to climb down." Ariock pointed. "That way. We'll hide, and I'll try to steal a transport for us."

The refugees fanned out in that direction with confidence.

Ariock retracted most of his awareness. He wanted to explore every potential hiding place, but his attention was limited. He could not keep himself expanded across a hundred stories without losing some attention to detail.

Storms did not require as much attention. If he wanted to send a deadly wave of destruction through the air, he did not need to inhabit every raindrop, or touch every cubic centimeter of cloud vapor. But he had noticed that some materials accepted his awareness more readily than others. And some powers consumed more of his focus.

Healing, for instance. He could only heal someone if he poured all of himself into it.

Anyway, he could not afford to get careless while holding the floor together. Ariock put most of his undivided awareness into the treacherous floor. He edged out farther, sure-footed no matter how the beams creaked.

Artificial lights swept through broken ceiling beams above. Someone cried out in surprise.

"We're okay," Ariock said, hoping it was true. Maybe the Torth hadn't spotted him.

He took extra care with every step. He was the grime-caked floor beam beneath his feet. He was the humid air, and he was the broken girders overhead. Rain fell in spurts as transports crisscrossed the sky. He was the wind. He was the missiles rocketing toward—

Crap.

Ariock solidified the air overhead just in time, throwing his arms up to create an extensive shield. Fiery explosions lit the tower top with bone-jarring impacts. Pillars and beams glistened against stark shadows.

Ariock arrowed his focus into the air currents overhead. He knocked transports aside.

"Keep going," he urged his friends.

Every time he pushed transports out of the way, more descended from the clouds. They were as numerous as raindrops.

But Ariock knew how to end a rainstorm.

He condensed his energy. Lightning thrummed across his armor, snapping into whips that he hurled upward. Never mind shoves. He aimed to kill.

Transports fell. The pummeling lessened. Ariock took the opportunity to unfurl his awareness even farther, at least a mile outward.

He grasped rotted skyscrapers with a multitude of enormous arms.

He was ruination. He bristled with power. His sole purpose was so simple, so straightforward, he managed to remember it even while he existed as many ossified skyscrapers. He spoke that purpose with a mouth that controlled tons of ruins and muck.

"DIE, TORTH."

He shrugged many shoulders.

Corroded struts and girders came apart. Lightning grew in jagged sheets, blasting apart the remains of the tower tops, slamming transports into each other, causing them to crash in screams of steely wreckage and thunder. An avalanche of devastation rained upon the Torth fleet.

Ariock snapped wholly back to himself as the military fleet came apart. He anticipated the change in his stature, so it was no longer so disorienting.

He boomeranged his awareness outward again, firming his shield, protecting his friends. He probably looked berserk, but so what? This was just like the arena battles—except this time, he was unfettered.

He was a storm titan. And he was going to chase the Torth until they gave up. This might be his final battle. He must win or die.

# CHAPTER 15

# THE SCREAM

Outside the protection of a ship, Vy felt like an ant underfoot in a battle of titans. Goo exploded in black fountains. She threw herself down into muck, deafened and blinded by hammer blows of destruction.

Refugees shouted.

"We're on your side!" Pung yelled.

Vy risked a peek.

A troop of five nussians prowled toward the refugees. Where had this troop come from? A military transport must have dropped them off, sneaking past Ariock by coming in from below, or an unexpected direction.

"We are not your enemies!" Kessa yelled. "Join us! Disobey the Torth!"

But her volume was mostly drowned out by the storm.

The nussians fanned their spinal ridges in a sign of aggression. Like all members of the guard species, they were naked, without so much as a slave collar. Their pebbly gold-bronze skin gleamed like armor. They wielded spear-like prods, ready to fend off attacks.

Ariock was too busy storming the fleet to notice.

Vy unlocked her blaster glove, but she was not as fast as Pung or Irarjeg. They opened fire, and immediately, two nussians spun from devastating impacts.

One bellowed in pain, forearm blown off in a bloody gout.

Another nussian toppled off the edge of the floor and smashed into what-ever was far below.

The others reared in confused fear. They seemed shocked by the sight of um-mins wearing blaster gloves. As far as they knew, slaves never touched weapons.

"They're runaways!" a surviving nussian said in the slave tongue, with a harsh accent that must be local to this planet. "They stole those gloves. Rip off their arms!"

Tanklike nussians barreled toward the refugees like a deadly stampede of rhinos.

The battle became more savage as refugees defended themselves with blasts.

It was a lopsided battle. Vy almost felt sorry for the nussians. They might have been threatened with torture in the Isolatorium if they failed here, but they were massive targets.

Nussians roared in pain. They died quickly.

Vy scanned the storm-swept area, peering into shadows. A few sparse figures crept in the edges of gloom. They blended in with the monochromatic dead city. Eyeless helmets gave them an insectile alienness. Their forearms were bulked up with guns, their smooth white armor stippled in hues of gray.

Torth.

One sneaked toward Cherise. Vy nearly screamed a warning, but she silenced herself in time. She had a dark certainty that the Torth wanted screams. They wanted Ariock's attention. They wanted to trip him up.

He was busy hurling skyscraper wreckage at the sky fleet. Lightning raced off him in waves. So many explosions hit Ariock's invisible shield that he glowed, a giant encased in molten fire. Bullets or missiles must be melting in that furnace of destruction.

He probably didn't have time to blink, let alone listen to a rundown of individuals who needed protection.

If Vy screamed for Ariock's help, and if he actually heard her, he would lose track of his shielding. He might lose track of the floor and send them all tumbling to their deaths. Or he'd make some other devastating mistake.

No. Vy and her friends needed to defend themselves while Ariock destroyed the fleet.

Vy aimed her glove. She didn't want to kill anyone, not even a Torth, but she valued her freedom. She wasn't going to be a helpless victim ever again.

The Torth near Cherise tossed a dangerous-looking ball at her. Mechanical legs emerged and splayed outward.

The device clutched Cherise's supply pack and began to whip out chains.

Cherise struggled in a tightening cocoon. When she fell, the victorious Torth placed one booted foot on her helpless form, leaning his weight on her. He casually leaned down to yank off Cherise's blaster glove.

He clearly took his victory for granted. Torturing a human girl was nothing to him.

Vy aimed at the Torth's head.

She had the eerie feeling that she was in immediate danger herself. Torth always moved as if choreographed. Perhaps a faraway tactician was organizing them into strategic configurations, like someone setting up chess pieces for a checkmate?

Vy thumbed her trigger but whirled around at the same time.

She came face-to-face with the silent enemy who had sneaked up behind her. Her blast knocked the armored Torth backward and drilled a gory tunnel into his chest.

He staggered, still alive. Vy blasted him again.

The enemy toppled in a sludge puddle, his arm half-detached. His helmeted head vanished in a rainfall of blood as Vy, shaking, blasted the corpse again. She was all too aware of how close she had come to being a helpless victim.

Her blasts turned the enemy into a mangled mess. She had won.

Vy kicked the corpse off the edge of the floor and out of her sight. This wasn't like being a slave. This time, she was victorious.

"Vy!" Thomas yelled. "Free Cherise! Undo the chains!" His reedy voice was hard to hear over the thunder. "There's a toggle on the hub. You have to pump it!"

Vy skidded to her knees in the sludge next to Cherise and shot the nearby Torth in his stomach. As that Torth fell, Vy shot him again.

Refugees were struggling in nets of chains. Grabber balls careened toward them, and any ball that landed immediately spat out chain links.

One grabbed onto Dugwon. It knocked the adolescent backward and unspooled chains in a mechanical way, ratcheting tight around the terrified ummin.

Vy searched for the mystery toggle, terrified that she would get chained up if she failed to free her foster sister fast enough.

But there weren't many Torth in the vicinity. The few Torth in sight were sneaky and skittish. Perhaps they felt rattled by so many ummins with blaster gloves, despite their armor? Or maybe they had overwhelming mental audiences?

Wildfire lit the night.

Three Torth circled Weptolyso like sharks drawn to blood-churned waters. Thomas's eyes were intense as he tried to engulf his attackers in flames. But either he was too slow, or Torth armor was fireproof. Perhaps both.

As Weptolyso turned in circles, snorting like a warhorse, the Torth aimed their gloved hands. Whatever they shot, it was not blasts. It seemed to be something invisible.

The flames died as if someone had shut off a gas vent.

Microdarts of the inhibitor.

Unlike Ariock, Thomas did not wear armor. Weptolyso could not cover him entirely. Thomas had lost his powers, and his nussian protector did not even have a weapon. Blaster gloves could not fit on nussian hands.

Weptolyso hurled one of the grabber balls back at the Torth who had thrown it. He stomped on another device and crushed more of them, gingerly cradling Thomas in one arm while he dodged and fought. With his spikes fully extended, he looked a bit like a mutant hedgehog.

Vy toggled the chain release on her foster sister. The chains retracted, and Vy prepared to leap up, to help defend Thomas. The best way to kill Torth, she remembered, was to take them by surprise.

One Torth was strutting around without a helmet. Loose blonde curls spilled over the back of that one's dirt-splashed, feminine armor. When she turned, Vy recognized her pallid face.

The Swift Killer seemed to recognize Vy as well.

She stepped on a chained-up refugee, never looking down as she approached. "Just the one I was looking for." Her voice was disturbingly normal. She must have imitated humans before.

"Run, Vy!" Thomas shouted.

Vy aimed at the Swift Killer with her blaster glove set to maximum blast and thumbed the trigger.

But she was too slow. The Swift Killer suddenly leaped at her. Her speed seemed superhuman. Maybe she had muscular enhancements?

Excruciating pain exploded in Vy's skull and disintegrated all coherent thought.

She jerked and missed her shot. This sickening punishment was worse than any she'd ever suffered. It felt like death.

"Scream," the Swift Killer commanded.

Vy clamped her mouth shut. She could guess why the Swift Killer wanted her to add her voice to the deafening battle, and she wasn't going to obey.

The Swift Killer kicked her.

Vy slammed face-first into toxic slime. She tried to struggle, to turn around, but shackles constricted her arms. Chains slithered around her torso and cinched tight.

She had lost.

But Thomas needed her. Everyone needed her to live. Voices babbled in the background, amid explosions and thunder, but Vy could not focus on any of that. Battle noise drowned out most of what Thomas was saying. Was he ordering Weptolyso to attack? The nussian probably wouldn't obey a mind reader.

Someone kicked Vy onto her back.

It knocked the breath out of her, and it hurt. Vy refused to make any more noise than a gasp for air. Let the Torth kill her. Let them carry her away. She would not distract her friends from their battles.

Ariock was a magnificent, seemingly indestructible center amid lightning and explosions.

Let him win. Let him slay Torth by the thousands.

The Swift Killer aimed her blaster glove at Vy with a triumphant smirk. "Scream, you poor little runaway slave."

Her aim was so reckless, it looked like a mistake. An empty threat. A signal of bravado. She might just be flexing her arm muscles.

Vy remained disbelieving even as the Swift Killer thumbed the trigger.

Raw, explosive agony tore through Vy's legs. The explosion sent her into the air. She could not struggle, she could not think. This was annihilation. This devastation could not be minor. This was not a scrape or a broken bone.

This was forever.

Vy did not recall landing in the muck. When she remembered that she had a voice, it came out in helpless, piercing shrieks of agony.

Later, she would remember her broken vow to remain silent, to disobey and not scream.

By then, it was too late.

# CHAPTER 16

# THE EDGE OF HOPE

Kessa figured the only reason she wasn't captured or dead was because she was small. She must look like a muck-covered piece of debris, or a shadow cast by fiery explosions.

She wasn't particularly fast. That was surely why the nussian troop had ignored her as a nonthreat. That troop was dead now, but they had been replaced by worse enemies.

Decades of city survival had honed Kessa's abilities to avoid the notice of Torth. She stood motionless, blending with shadows whenever a Torth swiveled to look her way.

Battle distracted the Torth often enough for Kessa to move on. Despite their streamlined armor, the Torth here seemed preoccupied, even jumpy. She was able to scamper from one chained-up refugee to the next.

She'd seen enough Torth devices to figure out how to operate the release toggles. All she had to do was pump the release button three times. Then the chains snaked away. Refugees jumped up, freed.

Most of Kessa's friends were packaged into miserable bundles. She had to disregard a lot of pleas and cries, since the captives lay within sight of a wary Torth or two. They were beyond anyone's ability to help. But Kessa was not the only rescuer. She glimpsed Pung darting around, helping refugees as well.

Someone shrieked in agony.

They must be fatally injured, to scream like that. Kessa tried to tune out the horrific sounds, which blended in with thunder and explosions and the background storm.

Until the storm seemed to lose its momentum.

"Vy?" Ariock said, turning toward the screams of pain. His eyes lost their malevolent emptiness and softened with concern.

Vy was sobbing. There was something wrong with her legs. Ariock hurried toward her.

And he staggered.

Kessa knew when he lost his powers. Everyone probably knew, because the storm's roar ceased, the Torth fleet bobbed into a stable configuration, and everyone stopped what they were doing and seemed to hold their breath.

Torth straightened. The rainfall calmed down. The wind died.

Wrecked skyscrapers remained slumped or leaning against each other, but chunks stopped hurtling through the air.

The ground must be littered with destroyed transports. Still, dozens remained aloft, bobbing together.

Vy was silent now. Cherise frantically tied a threadbare blanket around Vy's lower legs, one after the other. Vy herself had slumped over.

Ariock sank to one knee, curling in on himself.

The battleground became hushed except for the eerie whisper of rainfall and the purr of transport engines. A charred smell underlaid the rotten stench. Beams of light crisscrossed the scene, causing every broken beam and pillar to cast a shadow.

One by one, the armored Torth removed their smooth helmets, exposing clean, smug faces. No pupils or irises. They lacked expressions, really, but Kessa was familiar with the human faces of her friends. She thought she detected suppressed smirks.

*So easy this was*, their confidence seemed to insinuate. *Slaves are so pathetic.*

The Servants of All glided toward Ariock, blaster gloves raised, ready to obliterate him.

Ariock lifted his head. Within the shadow of his helmet, his gaze burned with rage.

A few Torth hesitated. One even flinched.

So they could feel fear, or whatever dull feeling they substituted for real emotions. But the Servants of All seemed to share an unspoken ripple of reassurance. They crept onward.

Pung shot a blast at them.

And the battle sprang into full action again. Ariock lunged toward his enemies like a berserk nussian. One moment he was hunched in defeat, and the next moment he was in the air, leaping over a missing part of the floor, with his feet tucked up to avoid blaster shots.

He landed on an unbalanced rust sheet with so much force, its opposite end flew upward and sent a Torth flying.

Ariock threw himself into the midst of the Servants of All, and they seemed so surprised, they hardly remembered to shoot. A few of them scattered.

Pulses streaked past Ariock and exploded against structural girders. Explosions ripped apart mucus webs and lit up the night.

Ariock seized a Torth and smashed him into a broken pillar. He kicked another into the abyss, snapped the neck of a third, stomped on a fourth, and whirled to face two behind him, throwing them off the edge of the tower.

Kessa watched with her beak agape. Without his powers, and unarmed, Ariock could not possibly hope to kill dozens of armed Servants of All. They would surely kill him.

Ariock continued to seize the enemies. Turn by turn, he used them as living shields, breaking them in half or whacking them against others, discarding each corpse and seizing another.

It seemed the highest ranks were reluctant to shoot each other by accident. They kept missing Ariock, waiting for an easy shot as he ducked and dodged and killed them with uncanny speed.

Pung and other refugees joined the battle.

Ummins made small targets, especially when they hid behind the nussian corpses scattered across the floor. Blasts tore the corpses into chunks, spattering gore everywhere, but the Torth could not avoid return fire. They had to defend themselves from blasts as well as from Ariock.

Weptolyso plowed into a knot of Torth at full speed, his wordless roar echoing like thunder. He must have deposited Thomas in a sheltered place. He jabbed spikes into the face of a Servant of All, causing her to scream like a slave. He shoved another Torth off the edge of the floor.

The two giants, Ariock and Weptolyso, were giving everyone a chance to escape. A chance for freedom.

This was exactly what Kessa's mate, Cozu, had sacrificed his life for. He would have seized this opportunity if he were alive and here.

Kessa ran from refugee to refugee, toggling the devices and releasing the chains that held them captive. Grateful ummins jumped up. If they saw a discarded blaster glove, they seized it.

"Please shoot me?" Thomas begged from the floor. He lay on his side, helpless and forgotten, shielded by a nussian corpse.

At least he was out of harm's way. Kessa had no time to answer him. Too many people needed rescue. She spared him a sympathetic look as she rushed to free more refugees.

"We're not going to win," Thomas said. "I know you know that, Kessa."

All her life, Kessa had practiced reminding herself that freedom was a myth. She knew that the Torth always won.

Yet Ariock was still fighting in spite of his defeat.

He was fighting—and winning.

Ariock and Weptolyso yanked Torth arms out of their sockets, stomped on spines, and crushed helmeted heads. They were deadly titans at the center of the battle, one dark and shaped like a god, one red-gold and thorny. Blasts streaked past them, finding targets only in pillars. Meanwhile, they ripped Torth in half or kicked them off the building.

Several Torth sent rapid-fire blasts at a decayed girder. It collapsed, and Ariock jumped away from the corroded cross-section it had been supporting, just in time.

But Weptolyso wasn't quite fast enough.

He plummeted. Weptolyso was gone faster than Kessa could open her beak.

Ariock grabbed a Torth and used her like a club, whacking enemies out of his path, twisting away from fiery streaks.

Deep down, Kessa knew that Thomas was right. Slaves never won. It was impossible. The Torth had all the firepower in the universe, plus their ability to give pain seizures and their power to read minds. They owned everything. There were too many of them. Ariock was more skilled in physical combat than she would have believed, but he was only one person. And he had lost his storm magic.

So she wasn't surprised when a blast knocked him backward.

She did not see which one of the many Torth had dealt the offense, but Ariock slammed to the floor with a crash that seemed to shake the tower.

Such a blast would have torn apart a normal-size human or Torth. Ariock tried to get up. Even in the dim light, Kessa saw how massive and devastating the wound on his upper chest was. It looked like a gory tunnel, oozing blood.

Refugees shot defiant blasts. Some of the fire sizzled through grime-encrusted pillars. The remaining Servants of All switched their focus to dealing with rebel ummins. Grabber balls extruded chains and ratcheted tighter. Refugees cried in horror as they fell, recaptured.

Ariock shuddered in the muck. He was badly injured, but even so, a few Torth pumped their gloves at him, no doubt overdosing him with inhibitor. They threw grabber balls at him. Shaken, they watched the net tighten, ready with their blaster gloves, just in case.

Ariock struggled. But his struggles weakened. He was trapped in a metallic net.

The Torth began to relax.

The dread that seeped into Kessa's bones was nothing new. It was the resignation that all slaves felt. She did not think that Ariock would rise again.

Death and defeat were natural for her kind. This was the fate of anyone who challenged the Torth Empire. Dead ummins littered the floor between steaming piles of guts that used to be nussians. Mucus dripped from broken beams. Without fiery blasts and sheet lightning, the air was rapidly losing its warmth.

"Kill me?" Thomas begged in a desperate whisper.

Kessa still wore a blaster glove. She considered switching it to deadly mode and obliging Thomas. Without Ariock, what hope could the rest of them possibly have?

Maybe she deserved death. She was a runaway.

*Survive.* The ghost of Cozu whispered defiance inside her memory. *Never give up*, her mate would have urged.

Cozu had known the importance of freedom long before Kessa did. In the lifetime since Red Ranks had dragged Cozu away and tortured him to death, Kessa had blamed him for abandoning her and for bringing misfortune upon himself. But he had died proudly.

In his heart, Cozu had never been a slave.

Kessa had loved him for that.

Victorious Torth trotted around, collecting weapons. They kicked refugees for good measure. They ignored their own dead, not acknowledging their mistakes.

That was what Torth did. They did not learn.

Everything was fed to them, even knowledge. They were so accustomed to easy victories and easy answers, they had almost lost this battle against cornered opponents who lacked even a fraction of their resources.

Perhaps the Torth were not done making stupid mistakes?

Kessa scurried away, into shadows, as transports hovered lower and Torth leaped out. Maybe Weptolyso had landed on girders below. He might still be alive.

She sent reassuring thoughts to Thomas, just in case he was close enough to read her mind, but she would not reveal her position by shooting him. She did not want to die with a slave collar around her neck.

Newly arrived Torth unrolled a streamer of ornate cloth. They layered it over filthy puddles and oily muck, forming a clean pathway.

A gaunt Torth strode down the carpeted path. She had the eyes of a Servant of All, empty and blank, although Kessa knew that such eyes could peer into people's souls. A white shroud billowed behind this Torth, supported by horns that seemed to grow out of her shoulder mantle. Spirals glowed on her breasts and thighs, while the rest of her armor gleamed like bone.

This was more than a high rank, Kessa knew. This was the elected leader of the Torth: the Commander of All Living Things.

Her skeletal face remained expressionless as she glided toward the still form of Ariock.

Kessa silently crept past puddles and concealed herself behind debris. The Torth were gloating. But she saw their carelessness, and she remained alert, ready for any opportunity.

The Torth believed they were done with this battle. But Kessa was not convinced it was over.

# CHAPTER 17

# TELEPATHIC CANNIBALS

Thomas was beyond dignity. He had none left. He lay in filth, sniveling like a defeated child.

The Commander of All Living Things deliberately placed one boot atop the chained-up body of Ariock. She posed like a trophy hunter for her galactic audience. Teeth flashed in her skeletal face.

"That was quite a chase," she said.

In English.

Thomas cringed. Her use of the language of his homeworld was a subtle jab at him. It was a reminder, to all Torth, that she had been stationed on Earth three times during her eighty-year stint as a Servant of All. She was considered an expert on the primitive species known as humankind. Not only did she possess the elite clearance necessary for covert missions on wilderness planets, but she was signaling that she was fit and ready to lead a conquest of Earth.

Monsters.

Thomas curled in on himself. The Torth Majority would undoubtedly blame *(the Betrayer)* their renegade supergenius for every loss and setback they'd suffered during the chase. He would die mewling and helpless, never given a chance to recover.

*blood a feast of meat smell it this way*

Stray thoughts tickled the back of Thomas's mind.

This was the way Torth communicated—except instead of being clinical and rational, it was all emotion. There were no words, nothing with structure.

*so hungry mmm but wait*

This was too unexpected to ignore. Thomas strained to explore the bestial minds, unable to shut off his curiosity despite his own dire situation.

Telepathic animals prowled the darkness directly below him. They scraped through his range of telepathy, using their own mental sensitivities to navigate past rubble or pitfalls.

*too bright too warm it is dangerous just wait*

The Swift Killer approached Thomas, along with several other Servants of All. Their eyes served as windows for billions of viewers on a myriad of planets.

The unseen telepathic animals on the floor below scattered. They perceived too many intelligent minds within their range, and complexity unnerved them. Their own minds were purely emotional. Fun. Fear. Raw flesh. Copulation and the hunt. That was what those telepathic creatures cared about.

*Wild zoved*, one Servant of All thought to another, identifying the animals. *Below Us.*

*Ugh*, the other agreed. *Dead city vermin.*

Thomas had never researched the wildlife of this planet. He had only vaguely known that the Torth Homeworld had mutant telepathic animals, the result of long-forgotten bioengineering mishaps. He strained toward the Megacosm, thirsty for knowledge.

Why not?

All his reasons to resist temptation were gone. He could no longer protect anyone. If the Upward Governess wanted to gloat, well, he couldn't get any more miserable than he already was. The Megacosm would allow him to escape from his terrible situation for a few seconds, at least. He could bask in other minds for as long as other Torth were willing to tolerate his presence.

Thomas rose into the galactic symphony.

While his body lay helpless on a broken tower in the cesspool of the dead city, his mind sampled wonders. He joined distant Torth who lounged in holographic parlors or soaked in spas. They got massages. They sipped nectar drinks. They wore meshes that altered their brain waves so they could feel at peace.

Most of them shrank away from his *(toxic) (criminal)* gargantuan mind.

But not all. A few distant Torth orbited him, curious about his renegade *(illegal)* thoughts.

Thomas milked every millisecond. Within a second, he'd learned everything the Torth Empire knew about wild zoved. No one remembered where the vestigial name came from or what laboratory failure had released the telepathic apes. But they roamed the dead city in cannibalistic packs, preying on each other. Anyone who waded through the dead city needed to wear bright lights and blaster gloves in order to stay safe.

Thomas expanded his knowledge about the dead city. There was the infamous "dead city sickness." According to common knowledge, Torth who dared to wander alone in the dead city for more than a few hours would begin to hallucinate primitive sapiens hidden within pitch-black ruins. Sometimes Torth chased those phantoms. Many of those mysteriously dropped out of the Megacosm, never to be seen again.

Fascinating.

The Torth Homeworld was also infamous for a weird myth among slaves who dwelled in Stratower City. They believed that a spirit known as the Weeper visited slaves who were dying and alone. She looked like a Torth, but she wept. How odd.

*The Betrayer does not deserve to partake in Our collective knowledge.* The Commander of All Living Things stared at Thomas.

Her condemnation infiltrated every corner of the Megacosm. Thomas's inner audience began to abandon him in droves.

Thomas blundered this way and that, seeking minds to merge with, but he was like an unsightly leper in the midst of an upper-crust neighborhood. Torth whirled away.

What a bunch of cult members, so blindly obedient to their leader.

Torth were idiots. He knew it. Every supergenius knew it. They hadn't built their own wealth or power. They were thieving parasites. They ought to vomit in shame!

His inner audience evaporated. Torth did not want to share the experience of being a hate-filled emotional wreck. That wasn't what being a Torth was about. They were gone.

And just like that, he was puny and solo.

No one orbited his mind. He was as singular as he'd been when he had first encountered the Torth.

To add to the insult, Servants of All peppered him with a fresh volley of microdarts. More inhibitor. Thomas whimpered as chains ratcheted around him. They were packaging him with extra precautions, like he was a fearsome giant.

The Commander of All Living Things stepped off Ariock and walked toward Thomas with slow magnificence.

Soon she stood directly over him. She was so close that the toe of her boot nearly touched his nose.

*We (the great and magnificent Torth Empire) shall enslave humankind while the Betrayer rots in the Isolatorium,* she promised.

She stood within Thomas's range of telepathy. He sensed her orbiters. He sensed her approval rating skyrocket.

*We will enslave all humans!* her millions of sycophants chorused.

*Earth has sheltered (empowered) too many rogues and renegades.*

*It is time to curtail that freedom!*

*Launch the warships!*

*Send an invasion fleet!*

Thomas shivered in cold muck, feeling worse than he'd ever felt in his life. Had his own decisions condemned Earth?

If only he had risen in rank. Sure, if he had remained obedient to the Upward Governess, then his friends would be dying or dead. But he might have grown influential enough to sway the Torth Majority against conquering humankind.

*That's right.* The Commander of All Living Things stared down at him with billions of Torth peering through her eyes. She basked in glory.

Thomas held in a sob. The last thing he wanted was for the entire galaxy to know how he felt. His lost future taunted him.

*Back away*, the Commander of All silently commanded the nearest Torth. *I desire a private moment with Our little Betrayer.*

The nearby Servants of All obeyed their elected sovereign. They stepped out of range, some of them suppressing curiosity.

The highest authority in the known universe dropped out of the Megacosm. She gave Thomas her full, undivided attention, her shroud billowing like an aura.

Thomas dared to gaze up at her, wondering why she wanted to confront him alone. The Commander was strong enough to kick him in the face. He didn't even have enough strength to spit at her boot.

*You could have had everything*, the Commander of All thought with cold simplicity. *You could have become a governor. Maybe you could have risen to become a Servant of All.*

Thomas lay in the muck, chained up and shivering. Where had that last part come from? The Torth Empire kept their supergeniuses disabled and dying young.

*We would have made an exception for you*, she thought.

Why?

Why had they made so many exceptions for him? Why would they have continued to do so?

Thomas sought a way past her mental guards. There was a secret she was dancing around.

Her mind vanished from his senses as she backed away. She had exited his range of telepathy.

"You could have had anything you desired," she said out loud. "If only you had remained loyal. Instead, you chose a painful death."

Thomas stared at her, perplexed. Her gloating was weird. Physically disabled Torth never joined the ranks of the Servants of All. Would they really have made an exception just for him?

Maybe the Servants of All had wanted something unique from him.

"*They were using you.*" Ariock and Kessa had both said that.

Mind twists.

It almost made sense. Only the best Torth—the most ambitious, the most worthy—got promoted to the rank of Servant of All. They tended to be overachievers. Although they served the Majority, they might want more power. They might desire an extra tool in their arsenal; a friend who could influence the influencers.

Thomas could literally change minds.

Maybe he could have learned how to do it more softly. Maybe he could have twisted minds without causing massive brain damage. And then he would be a perfect tool for the Servants of All to wield in secret. He could keep secrets. He could change minds.

Armored Torth bustled around the battlefield. They seized blaster gloves from netted refugees.

*mmm still too bright too many too dangerous*

On the floor below, the pack of wild zoved milled about. Individual apes swung through Thomas's telepathic range, and he sensed how tantalized they were by the smell of carnage. They yearned to gorge on nussian carcasses.

*we wait big feast*

They were just animals, yet they were telepathic.

Thomas's powers were inhibited. But he might be capable of changing minds, even without twisting them.

*Come up to this floor*, he silently urged the wild zoved. *Why not feast on Torth? Bite their faces off.*

The telepathic apes paced, fearful. Thomas's invitation was too dry, too alien. It lacked the bloodlust they associated with feasts. Doubts bounced back and forth to each other.

*a trick*

   *just wait till lights go away*

     *then feast*

The Swift Killer circled toward Ariock. She wore a heavy-duty blaster. She probably meant to blast the Giant's head off.

Thomas turned his head, straining for a better connection with the ravenous apes. He gathered his courage—what little he had—and rephrased his suggestion. This time, he did not bother with abstract concepts. The apes were wordless.

He gnawed thin air and imagined it was raw flesh.

Mmm.

A few Torth stared at Thomas with disgusted fascination. They probably thought he was having a mental breakdown.

Thomas tuned out everything else. He chewed. Imaginary blood squirted past his imaginary muzzle and down his throat. All that existed was the delight of digging his imaginary snout into the gaps of armor, to savage warm, struggling meat. If all he really chewed on was air, it didn't matter. He used his supergenius ability to juggle perceptions and enhance his bloodthirstiness.

*FOOD HERE TOO GOOD TO RESIST*, he emphasized, drooling over the delicious taste of the too-proud armored invaders. *COME EAT!!!* He pretended to bite the faces off every Torth in sight.

He sensed the apish monsters change their minds.

Wild zoved swarmed out of shadows, climbing the eroded girders of the ancient building. They emerged in a ceaseless tide, hackles raised, knobby and skeletal, covered in filth, their enormous mouths grinning with rows of carnivorous teeth.

They bit everything their mouths could reach.

One tore through a supply pack like a wolf shaking its prey. Another chomped an ummin refugee, drawing screams. And the Torth...

The Torth froze. Thomas could all but hear their *(!!!)* surprise. They had never expected an attack from telepathic, cannibalistic apes.

Of course not. Among Torth, bloodlust was taboo, starvation unheard-of. Most Torth drugged themselves in order to fit in with polite society. It would never occur to a Torth to allow oneself to gnaw and drool and take savage bites. They had never attempted to mimic or befriend or relate to animals.

The night blew up with explosions as Torth abandoned the prisoners and hurried to defend themselves.

Skinny apes exploded in ropes of gore and blood, but it didn't slow the horde. Apes kept pouring out of shadows. They snapped up chunks of their dead kin until there was nothing left, while others leapfrogged over those, seeking more meat.

They savaged the carcasses of fallen nussians. They bit ummins, trying to gnaw past chains.

In the fiery strobe light of explosions, Thomas glimpsed how widely the apes could distend their jaws. Razor teeth lined their huge mouths. And there were far more wild zoved than he had guessed. The broken skyscraper must have sheltered multiple packs. Either that, or the local pack had called faraway packs to join them, or others had been attracted by the violence—or maybe they had simply come here to seek shelter from the storm.

Wild zoved scampered past Thomas. One paused, then another, close enough for him to sense their tormented hunger and inhale their foul stench.

He was easy meat.

Thomas dared not suppress his emotions, and he dared not trigger their carnivore instincts against himself. His only hope of survival was to be a wild zoved. So he renewed his saliva-inducing fantasy of savaging the Torth. He imagined himself to be a strong ape, panting and snarling with the rapture of killing. *MMM RUNNING OR STANDING MEAT IS BEST.*

A detached part of his mind observed this mental exercise as absolutely revolting.

Thomas stamped down on that logical part of his brain. He was no longer a Torth hybrid but a savage ape who lived only to hunt and to win and to feast.

Wild zoved launched themselves at fleeing Torth and swarmed over everything in their path. Even the Commander of All Living Things fled toward the safety of her luxury transport. Servants of All tried to protect her, but they were shooting nonstop, and sometimes their blaster gloves needed a moment to build up a charge.

They fell.

And they died.

Perhaps some of the Torth belatedly tried to command the wild zoved. If so, they failed. Cold, calculated commands would have no effect on ravening beasts in the grip of a blood frenzy. Such animals only understood emotions.

Thomas screamed with crazed triumph and amped up his savagery.

# CHAPTER 18

# MEEK

To Kessa, it was if the dead city had vomited up their battle. Explosions roared but failed to kill enough of the toothy beasts.

They were skinny, filthy, naked, and Torth-like, with enormous mouths. The sea of skeletal hunger rushed toward anything, living or dead. Ummins were fast, but these beasts were faster, lunging with merciless intensity. Whenever one of the horde fell, the survivors feasted on that corpse, too.

Kessa glued herself to a pillar and didn't move. She had to listen to screams for help and do nothing, because she was just an elderly ummin.

Even Servants of All were fleeing. Their armor wasn't enough protection. Beasts chomped their exposed faces. The apes piled onto them, knocking them off floor beams, causing them to stagger and plummet off the edge of the tower.

The Torth fled, abandoning their victims. They left Ariock unconscious and wrapped in chains. They even left Thomas, despite all the effort they had gone to in order to catch him. The Torth had to shoot blasts continuously in order to survive. Whenever they had to pause to let their gloves recharge, they got taken down or piled upon.

Kessa saw Cherise rummage through a pack. She pulled out one of the precious canisters of healing foam, a thing Pung had packed at Thomas's behest, back when they were in the city. Thomas had said that the foam would stabilize open wounds.

Cherise rushed to her foster sister and used healing foam on her damaged legs.

Vy remained unconscious. Kessa was not certain she would ever wake again.

The tone of the battle changed as Torth fell victim to beasts or leaped into hovering transports. The explosions lessened and happened farther away. The night darkened. The wet air grew colder.

Vicious shadows surrounded the fallen victims, slurping and gobbling. Kessa gawked as she realized that some of the beasts were violently copulating, mounting each other amid the carnage.

These things could not be related to Torth. Mind readers were vile, yet they valued cleanliness. Torth feasted with utensils in dainty silence. As far as anyone knew, Torth never did anything lustful. They did not mate.

The Torth were gone.

At least for now.

*This is the only chance we'll get*, Kessa knew.

The beasts gorged on heaps of fresh carcasses. That should keep them busy for a while.

Kessa crept out of hiding and tiptoed toward Naglitay, the apprentice herbalist who had been carrying the other canister of healing foam. She was alert for the smallest change in chewing sounds. She would much rather stay safely hidden, but she knew that right now, hiding meant shivering and waiting for death. This was not her world. She did not understand how to survive in pitch-black coldness where carnivores lurked and Torth ruled. If she and her friends were going to make an effort to survive, they would need Thomas. They would probably need Ariock as well.

Artificial light filtered through the broken ceiling beams, just enough for Kessa to see by. Torth vehicles hovered in the sky.

Were they waiting? Afraid?

Kessa could not picture Torth allowing fear to stop them. Even if they felt fear, they would strive to prove to their comrades that it was false. They must be preparing to attack again.

Kessa knew mind readers well enough to guess what they would do next. They were sending cargo transports to this battle, packed with nussians. They would probably force their enslaved nussian troops to slaughter the beasts for them. Maybe the nussians would only serve as fresh meat. Either way, the Torth would be able to return once the beasts were gorged and sated.

She released the chains on Naglitay. "Don't attract attention," Kessa whispered. "Use your healing foam on Ariock. Try to heal his wound."

The freed adolescent gave her a frightened nod. She grabbed the canister and sneaked away.

*We can survive*, Kessa assured herself.

Her dead mate, Cozu, had never let doubts stop him. This tower must have hidden pockets, dark zones where Torth would likely not dare to venture into without bright lights. It wasn't much of an advantage. But it was something.

"Find the shaft that leads downward," Kessa whispered to the next refugee she set free. "Free others—tell them to free others." Hopefully they would relay that message.

More and more refugees stood up, murmuring. A few were hurt. A few were dead, or lost and gone, like Weptolyso.

Mamlay. Etlaga. Bormaray. There were other names, but Kessa stored them all in her memory for later mourning. It hurt to hear the creatures feasting on what might be the remains of her friends, but such an end wasn't much different than sending a dead friend down a garbage chute. That was the burial most city slaves expected. No one really knew what happened to garbage, but there were rumors. Everyone knew the Torth stocked garbage pits with toothy monsters.

"How can we survive here?" someone complained.

Beasts looked his way, snuffling through the bloody gore that stained their jaws.

"Shh!" someone else said.

But it was too late. Some of the beasts abandoned their half-devoured meals and swarmed toward the refugees.

The rest followed. The beasts all seemed to share each other's thoughts, eerily cooperative. Like mind readers.

Kessa unlocked her blaster glove. She doubted that a bunch of scared ummins could hold them off.

"Kessa," someone called weakly from a distance. "Bring me closer."

She turned and saw Thomas. He lay chained up.

"I might be able to tell them to go away," Thomas said weakly. "They're telepathic."

"What?" Kessa surveyed the horde of drooling carnivores. If they could read minds, that explained how coordinated they were. One row moved one way, while another row moved in the opposite direction, and a further row closed off any possibility of escape.

"Wild zoved," Thomas said listlessly. "The creatures. They want to eat us."

"Wait." Kessa looked at Thomas with a stunned expression. "Can you control them? You had them attack the Torth?"

"Sort of." Thomas laughed weakly. "The Torth got me with inhibitor serum. All I can do is hear their minds. I can't control them."

Part of his ear looked chewed off. He was filthy. Yet he had somehow overridden the animal instincts of the predators and caused them to attack a troop of armored Torth.

"But..." Kessa backed closer to other refugees. "You saved us. You told the...wild zoved? To attack the Torth."

"I did." Thomas sounded ashamed to admit his act of heroism, and Kessa wondered why. Thomas had saved all their lives. He should be proud. It was something to brag about, not something to hide.

Kessa turned to the nearest strong ummin, one of the young salt miners. She took a moment to remember his name. "Hemjeg? Bring the Teacher here, please. Leave your pack."

Hemjeg scurried toward Thomas, but his fast movement triggered the wild zoved. They surged toward him in a hungry tide.

Cherise strode out of the darkness with a grabber ball in each hand. Kessa realized that those balls were actually a better weapon than blaster gloves in this situation. Blasts did not leave much meat. These beasts ate their own kind. A netted zoved would look like an easy meal to other wild zoved, which could potentially distract a lot of animals and pacify the horde.

Kessa saw undetonated grabber balls on the floor. She seized several and began to hurl them at the ravening beasts.

It worked. Ummins had excellent depth perception, so Kessa and other refugees were able to throw the balls with accuracy. Every time they netted a wild zoved, ten or twenty more beasts dived for the struggling victim. They snapped and drooled over the meals. The horde slowed, piling up like a barrier.

They crushed each other. They ate each other. Even so, more beasts poured over the top of the flesh barrier. Kessa no longer had any grabber balls to throw. How was Cherise still able to…

Oh.

She saw that Cherise was only pretending to throw grabber balls. Her gloved hands were empty.

Yet the beasts were fooled.

They reared back. A few wheeled around. Only a few at first, but once the biggest beasts slunk away, all the others followed. They turned around in droves.

Thomas must have had something to do with that. The wild zoved had decided, all at once, that fresh meat from bony refugees wasn't worth the risk of getting chained up and then devoured alive by their brethren.

The wild zoved loped back to the meals they'd abandoned. Soon they were gobbling corpses with disgusting relish.

Only refugees were left standing. The meek. The exhausted.

"We must carry those who are injured." Kessa's quiet voice seemed too loud. "Hemjeg…" She turned and saw that the stocky ummin had already unchained Thomas. He was struggling to carry the Teacher.

Refugees rushed to gather their scattered supplies. They called to each other about injuries.

"What about Ariock?" someone called.

The Bringer of Hope still wore his makeshift armor, dented and smeared with blood and muck. Refugees had removed his chains and his helmet.

He looked dead.

Kessa forced herself to sound calm and assured. "I will check on him." She hurried to do so. They needed Ariock at his full strength. If he was dead…or worse, if a bunch of worn-out ummin refugees had to carry the injured giant through pitch-black ruins…? Well. That would be an especially cruel challenge.

"Vy is badly hurt," Cherise reported. "I did everything I could. But she's lost a lot of blood."

Kessa did not show her worries. "Can you carry her?"

"I can try." Cherise sounded apologetic. She was a lot smaller than her older foster sister, but she was bigger and probably stronger than any of the ummins.

Kessa spread her hand in front of Ariock's nose. She felt a stir of breath. He was alive.

Kessa climbed onto his armored torso, certain that her lightweight size would not hamper his breathing. She needed to look at the wound. Maybe it was only superficial?

No.

The wound was wide enough to engulf a curled-up version of herself. Ariock's chest plate was partially disintegrated, along with most of one shoulder guard. A hardened, semitransparent foam stopped the huge wound from bleeding profusely.

Kessa did not dare touch the medical foam. It seemed to be the only thing holding Ariock together.

"I think he will die." A frightened voice spoke from behind Kessa, and she turned to see the apprentice herbalist from the slave farm of Duin. Naglitay had lost her head cover in the battle. Muck spattered her dome to keep it from reflecting lights. "Are we going to die, too?"

"Not if I can help it." Kessa resisted an urge to clamp her hand around Naglitay's beak. Survival depended on being proactive and purposeful. They did not need despair to be voiced aloud. "Do you have herbs that can speed up healing and relieve pain?"

"Oh." Naglitay looked down at her belt pouches, apparently surprised that she was still wearing them. "I guess I have russet leaf powder? But it's supposed to be in a broth," she added apologetically.

"If that powder might help Ariock and Vy and our other injured friends, then use it," Kessa said.

"Okay!" Naglitay looked grateful to have an errand.

"Kessa." Irarjeg sounded grave. "We cannot help him. And we cannot carry him."

Kessa straightened, but she had no solutions. The refugees could barely carry their own wounded friends.

Lusty chewing sounds warned everyone that they might only have a short time. They could not afford to argue.

"It's hopeless anyway," someone moaned.

"Most of our supplies are ruined," another adolescent said. "There's not much left."

Too many of the refugees had a despondent look in their eyes.

"We can survive." Kessa was trembling, and she was ashamed of that. These brave refugees deserved the Bringer of Hope. She was too old to be a hero.

But people seemed to be listening to her.

"We must leave this place." Kessa hopped down off Ariock. "And we must move fast."

An unexpected creaking sound drew everyone's attention. Something enormous emerged from the shaft in the floor.

Someone squeaked in fear.

But the hulking, inky-black figure looked like a nussian, to Kessa. Thorny spikes unfolded. And then Weptolyso spoke in his gravelly voice. "Is the Son of Storms all right?"

"Weptolyso!" Pung cried in relief.

Sure enough, the inky giant was their friend, coated in grime.

Kessa felt real triumph for the first time since the battle had begun. Not only had the Torth failed to capture Thomas and kill Ariock, but they had also failed to capture even a single runaway slave. They had not even managed to kill Weptolyso.

"Ariock is badly injured," Kessa admitted. "Weptolyso, would you be able to carry him?"

"Of course." Weptolyso lumbered across the unstable floor, testing every step, but he seemed honored. His small, reddish eyes filled with concern. "Did the Torth blast the Son of Storms? What happened?"

Kessa explained. She did not comment on how severe Ariock's wound was or what she thought about his chances for survival. "A clean blanket would help protect the injury," she suggested. "Can anyone find a blanket in their packs?"

"I have a blanket you can use!" A sturdy ummin offered up a rolled bundle.

"Thank you," Kessa said.

Weptolyso shook black mucus off his huge arms, then shook open the blanket. He snorted in worry when he got a look at Ariock's wound, but he said nothing about it. He seemed to realize that the survivors did not need extra reasons for despair.

The runaway hall guard hefted Ariock off the ground. With help from refugees, he wrapped the blanket around Ariock's chest, and he folded it in such a way as to create a makeshift sling for Ariock's arm, to take pressure off his more injured shoulder.

"This should hold." Weptolyso tied the ends behind Ariock's neck. He tugged the knot tight.

"Thank you, my friend." While Weptolyso had worked, Kessa had rushed to gather everything she could carry. She scanned the floor for lost canteens. Clean water must be precious on this filthy planet.

"Won't the Torth just follow us?" someone fretted.

"Torth are afraid of the dark," Kessa said. It might not be true, but the more she learned about Torth, the less invincible they seemed.

"What about the Teacher?" someone asked. "Who is brave enough to carry a mind reader?"

One of the salt miners had propped Thomas up against an eroded pillar.

Kessa began to respond, but a stocky adolescent cut her off. "Let's leave him behind. He is clearly the one the Torth want most, anyway. We don't need him."

"Thomas has kept us alive multiple times." Kessa glared at the stocky salt miner. Choonhulm, she thought his name was. "I believe he summoned those beasts to save us. He sent them away when they tried to attack us. We will not leave him behind."

Choonhulm looked ashamed. "Ah," he said in a small voice.

"I will carry the Teacher." Irarjeg stepped forward. "If someone else carries my pack?"

"I've got it!" Varktezo said, slinging the pack over his thin shoulder. "Also, I have the Teacher's medicine case."

Thomas spoke up, his voice raspy. "You can toss my medicine away. Maybe it will send the Torth looking in a wrong direction for a while."

"Do not," Kessa told Varktezo. "Hold on to the medicine."

Varktezo looked happy to oblige her command.

"Whatever," Thomas said carelessly. "But when we get caught, please throw it off the edge of something." His yellow eyes seemed to burn with an inner fire. "I don't want my nemesis to get it."

"We will not get caught." Kessa herded everyone toward the shaft.

"We don't have a chance," Thomas said in a conversational tone. "Ariock and Vy need hospital care. We don't have enough supplies for a trek. Even if—"

Kessa faced him with all her exasperation. "Shut up."

Thomas looked shocked.

But he stopped talking. That was good.

"Ignoring misery is how slaves survive," Kessa told him. "It does not always work. But when it does, we live."

Thomas looked troubled, but his concerns seemed directed inward rather than toward Kessa. He seemed to be reevaluating something within himself.

"I have survived for a long time," Kessa said, "and I don't plan to die just yet. We are alive. We have a chance."

Slurping sounds from the wild zoved undermined her point. Nevertheless, the refugees looked heartened, and they streamed toward the shaft. Weptolyso gently carried Ariock. Cherise struggled with Vy, aided by her adolescent friend Dugwon.

Even Thomas looked cautiously hopeful as Irarjeg picked him up. Maybe he understood. This was at least a partial, temporary victory. The Torth had retreated.

"Kessa, you're the best survivor I've ever known," Pung said. "Tell me what to do, and I will do it."

Kessa handed out supply packs to the few refugees who were not overburdened. The gnawing sounds continued, and the fleet of transports continued to hover above. One need presented itself as their top priority. Everything else was secondary.

"We must get away from this tower top." Kessa lowered herself onto the oil-slick first rung of an ancient, eroded ladder.

# PART TWO

*No hope. In the future, I see darkness. A thousand generations of darkness. And then there is one chance for light.*

*He will come to you in darkness…*

—Preserved scrap from the lost Prophecies of Ah Jun

# CHAPTER 1

# A SHIFTING PARADIGM

The Upward Governess faced her ivy-cloaked butterfly garden, squishing a gel toy in her hands. The squishing sensation felt good. Gel squirted around her pudgy fingers. She squished harder, wishing it was alive so she could kill it.

On one of the many levels of her psyche, she knew her rage was illegal. It was a crime worthy of execution.

But no one was watching. She lay in a hammock inside her private palace, at the top of her city, and none of her hundreds of slaves or bodyguards could see her face. She was below the Megacosm. She would have to avoid her inner audience until her anger ran its course.

*I handed the Betrayer and the Giant to the Empire*, she thought. Both had been chained and inhibited, ready to be carted off to the Isolatorium. *I had a foolproof plan.*

Except a fool was in charge of executing it.

The risk-loving Commander of All Living Things had cornered them with too few troops. She had let the enemies escape into the black labyrinth of a ruined tower.

Now the enemies might be anywhere inside it. If they were fast, they might even be beyond the tower. If they were smart—and they would be, with the Betrayer among them—they would spread out into hiding places and set up traps.

The Upward Governess was so sick of being stuck as an Indigo-Blue governing rank. She really ought to be the Commander of All Living Things herself, or at least a Servant of All. But of course no supergenius would ever be promoted above the color ranks. As humans put it, she was pressed against a glass ceiling.

In a sudden fit, she flung the gel away. It splatted into the grass.

There must be a way to flip this disaster to her advantage.

The Betrayer was trapped within the cold, swampy ruins of the dead city, where Servants of All practiced their wilderness survival techniques. Nuclear arsenals ringed the planet. The Upward Governess had chosen the Torth Homeworld as an ideal battleground on which to defeat the Giant, and that goal, at least, had been accomplished. The Giant was severely injured with his powers disabled. He would be unable to protect the Betrayer, at least for the next few days, and probably forever.

So the Giant was no longer an obstacle.

The Upward Governess watched butterflies alight upon flowers. Such delicate creatures. They had such short life spans.

As the gears of her mind turned, her fists loosened. All was not lost.

She snap-beckoned to a slave to demand a nectar smoothie. She kept her face smooth as the slave gently placed the drink between her hands.

This slave was a boring mute who was uninterested in gossip. It felt strange that she needed to be secretive around slaves, but she knew this one would not spread rumors about her emotive facial expressions.

Emotions were wrong. Volatile. She would keep her outburst hidden beneath mountains of trivial data and never think of it again. Embarrassing things must be buried.

Fully composed, the Upward Governess ascended into the Megacosm.

Lesser minds bowed to her massive one, although not as many as she was accustomed to. Puffs of discussion eddied in her wake.

She promised victory.

She ought to be demoted.

The Upward Governess kept her responses bottled up. But really, if the Torth Majority was reduced to throwing blame at a child—at a dying, loyal supergenius—well, then they couldn't be happy with the leadership, either.

Hm.

The Upward Governess almost felt as if she was eating her favorite dessert. A day ago, she never would have dared to challenge the most powerful being in the universe. But now? Now she might safely point out the bungling leadership of galactic civilization.

She did her best to keep her smile out of her mind.

*You.* The Commander of All Living Things soured with dissatisfaction when the Upward Governess entered her mental orbit. *Your plan failed, supergenius.*

Their respective audiences swelled. Attentive listeners wrapped the Upward Governess's mind like a mantle of power. Millions of Torth tuned in. They invited yet more listeners, until billions swirled around her mind like solar systems around a galactic nucleus.

Some members of her mental audience were supergeniuses with their own enormous orbital audiences. There were the Twins, a girl and boy who were each nearly as learned as herself. The eleven-year-old Death Architect became a listener, as well. The Rind Topographer. The Geodesic Flux. There were even a few toddler supergeniuses on baby farms, each unripe mind a tornado of facts and curiosity.

The Upward Governess would normally shrug off the youngest ones. She distrusted any mind that might grow into a mental giant and siphon away all the attention she had earned.

But now was a time to play to every one of her listeners.

*When a plan goes awry*, she thought, reclining in her butterfly hammock, *a smart leader will think fast and adapt to changing circumstances. You (a leader) should be able to think fast. If You are unable to adapt, then (perhaps) You are unfit to command.*

The Torth Majority seemed to hold its collective breath as they awaited the Commander's response. Baby farms paused their child-testing activities. Servants of All on the Torth Homeworld listened carefully, invested in the showdown.

Billions of Torth nudged their companions, bringing even more attention to the conflict between the Commander of All and the eldest, highest-ranked supergenius.

The masses thrummed with talk of the Commander's failure. Many were already campaigning for replacement candidates.

The Upward Governess indulged in a brief fantasy of being promoted to the role of Commander of All Living Things. If only the Majority would elect a dying child!

The Commander of All remained at ease, a perfect example of emotionless logic. *No one expected wild zoved (those normally timid apes) to attack Us. That was unexpected. Your scheme should have taken every possibility into account. Instead, when We were attacked, You (lazy self-serving coward) fled the Megacosm.*

Military ranks chorused in agreement. *Yes.*

She *(the fat supergenius)* dropped out at a critical moment.

*Why???*

The Commander of All was ready with a suggested explanation. *Could it be, perhaps, that the Upward Governess was bankrupt of genius solutions—and ashamed to admit it?*

Her massive audience surged with triumphant agreement.

The Upward Governess slurped her nectar drink in order to cool down her bristly feelings. True, she had made a forgivable misjudgment or two, but at least she could recognize when a plan spun out of control and needed to be revised.

*You should have invited more bombers to that location instead of bringing Your own luxury fleet on-site*, she accused. *Thanks to Your selfish ego, You let the enemies slip away. Now You are risking superior lives in a dangerous search.*

Teams of Red Ranks currently scoured that tower and its surroundings. They shone bright lights into black crevices.

But everyone knew about the dead city sickness. Lone Torth tended to suffer hallucinations and madness and sometimes vanished in the ruins. The Red Ranks were reluctant and jumpy.

*The Torth Homeworld was a bad choice of battleground*, their captain let everyone know. The Nerve Agent was in charge of the hunt in the dead city, having been quickly elected to replace the Pure Moment, who had gotten smashed and killed by the Giant.

*The plan was faulty from the start.* Symphonic agreements layered over each other.

*Couldn't We have lured the enemies to somewhere better?*

*Like maybe an abandoned space station?*

*Right. We should have lured the enemies to a more contained battleground, where We could control all variables.*

The Upward Governess did not bother to go over all the potential disasters she had calculated with a siege scenario. She had strenuously explained why it was dangerous to back the Giant into a corner when he was near his full strength. He had to be overwhelmed, depleted or injured or dead, before they could hope to catch the Betrayer. Her plan had proven the truth of that.

*The Giant is defeated (thanks to Me)*, she reminded her massive audience.

Minds churned, unwilling to count it as a total victory.

*The Giant suffered an injury that should have been fatal*, many thought. *But.*

*But his body is gone,*

*carried away by runaway slaves.*

*There is a remote chance that he might recover.*

The Upward Governess conceded that point. Somebody had healed slaves in Duin. It had to be a rogue Yeresunsa, although healing powers were considered to be long bred out of Torth genetics. She calculated a 0.0001 percent chance that somebody *(the Betrayer?)* would heal the Giant.

Once the inhibitor wore off.

Maybe.

*We ought to be sure that the Giant is dead.* The Upward Governess paused, reluctant to broach an unpopular opinion. She firmed up her resolve and forced herself to continue. *Here's how We win: drop a hundred-kiloton thermonuclear bomb on the region where they vanished.*

Her suggestion sent tidal waves of dismay and skepticism throughout the Megacosm.

*!!!!!*

*I know.* The Upward Governess, of all people, had solid reasons to want the Betrayer to suffer in the Isolatorium. She wanted justice. She truly wanted the remaining vials of his NAI-12 medicine. Even so…

She had mentally readjusted her expectations in light of this bungling.

*The Betrayer is an enemy supergenius*, the Upward Governess reminded everyone. *I am uncomfortable with letting him live when We don't know his location. I would rather give him a quick (and certain) death than allow him even the smallest shred of a chance for escape.*

Other supergeniuses in her orbit stirred. They hid their opinions, but the Upward Governess sensed them recalculating their own estimation of the danger posed by the Betrayer. Until now, no high ranks had suggested killing the Betrayer rather than sending him to the Isolatorium. Was he really that dangerous?

The Swift Killer oozed disdain. *It seems the Upward Governess believes that she is great enough to overrule the entire Torth Majority all by herself.*

Debates flared throughout the Megacosm. A growing minority of Torth sided with the Upward Governess. The Giant and the Betrayer had already cost too many superior lives.

Red Ranks on the Torth Homeworld were especially vociferous. They did not want to hunt the enemies through cold, swampy ruins, contending with an unknown population of wild zoved and sludge serpents and potential craziness. They all sided with the Upward Governess, voting to turn that region of the dead city into a radioactive crater.

But the Majority of the Torth Empire overrode them. *Let's not overreact,* they soothed their inner audiences.

*Nuclear devastation?*
  *For a nearly dead prisoner and a dying child?*
   *If We (the Torth Majority) (civilization) panic,*
    *and abandon Our principles out of fear,*
     *then how can We call Ourselves any better than slaves?*
    *We don't need to wage a war.*
     *The enemies are not an alien civilization with battleships.*
     *They are just a few pathetic rogues and runaways.*
     *The Betrayer deserves (torture) justice.*
     *Not the mercy of a quick death.*

The Upward Governess screened her own private introspection. Had irrational fear influenced her decision at all?

She thought not. Yet she secretly felt things only slaves were supposed to feel, and on one level of her subconscious mind, that troubled her.

She could not fully explain why the Betrayer seemed so dangerous. Objectively, he was no threat whatsoever. He was an outcast. His mental library was much smaller than hers.

So why did her subconscious mind keep sounding an alarm about him?

Why did the Betrayer seem worse than any threat the Torth Empire had ever faced in its long and venerable history? Why did she feel so much disquiet about his continued existence?

Maybe she really was being irrational.

*The Giant can withstand nuclear detonations*, a minority of fearful minds pointed out. *How is he so powerful?*

The Upward Governess took a deep breath, dampening her impatience. The Giant was a hybrid freak, but despite his monstrous strength, he was just a slave. Too many Torth were focused on him when they ought to worry about the true danger: the Betrayer.

She replayed a recent memory of the Giant, injured and unconscious. *He has the inhibitor in his system. He is weakened. Now is the best time to kill the enemies.*

Her audience swayed.

The Commander of All Living Things spread her hands, both literally and in the Megacosm. Her fingers branched into every branch of the debate. *We (the mighty Torth Empire) should not panic.* She pictured Torth running around like frightened slaves. *Remember, My predecessor (the previous Commander of All) struggled to appease a fearful and demanding Majority. He gave up on hunting and recapturing Jonathan Stead because he didn't want more Red Ranks to lose their lives. So he settled for merely "killing" Jonathan Stead, instead of sticking to his promise to deliver that rogue to the Isolatorium.*

She stopped, allowing listeners to recollect the grim ending of that event. Jonathan Stead had faked his death, fooled the Torth Empire, and lived to old age on Earth, remaking himself into a new person named Garrett Olmstead Dovanack.

*I am more pragmatic than My predecessor*, the Commander of All Living Things assured her audience. *That is why You elected Me. I will not bomb the Giant and assume that is good enough. I shall not be certain of his death until I (and forensics experts) examine his corpse. And I shall not allow the Betrayer any chance to escape.*

An overwhelming Majority of Torth approved. They clamored for her to get on with her job and be victorious; after all, they had elected her for good reasons. She had been widely admired as one of the most capable Servants of All.

The Upward Governess resisted an urge to insult the Torth Majority. That would be suicidal.

Instead, she withdrew enough to become an observer, just part of the audience in orbit around the Commander of All.

She caught a flash between Servants of All. Something like, *emergency meeting.*

It was just a pulse, the type of subtlety that most people would miss, but the Upward Governess was attuned to the nuances of many minds.

She had been suspicious for a long time. Now she was certain. The Servants of All were hiding a major secret.

A conspiracy.

They always backed up the Commander of All Living Things, or vice versa, no matter what. Their solidarity was greater than that of an average special interest group.

The Upward Governess kept her suspicions veiled by layers of mundane trivia. Perhaps she would be demoted. Perhaps she would lose any chance to live to adulthood. But knowledge was power, and secret knowledge was leverage.

She would require lots of leverage if she was ever going to gain another chance to obtain more NAI-12 medicine from Earth.

# CHAPTER 2

# A TROUBLED CHASM

Searchlights pierced the gloom every time a Torth transport whooshed past. Transports flew low between the toppled remnants of towers.

So Kessa dared not sneak in the open. Instead, she stayed beneath overhangs, and she sent volunteers to cautiously scout ahead and find paths through the muck. In that manner, she led everyone from one ruined building to the next, and the next.

She chose dark zones. Never mind the slithery creatures that lived in the sludge.

When a serpentine monster reared out of the darkness to strike, Cherise stabbed its snout. She wielded their sharpest weapon: the wavy-edged ionic knife. Everyone had tucked away their few remaining blaster gloves. They dared not call attention to themselves.

The serpent thrashed like mad.

Weptolyso carefully set down his burdens—Ariock and Vy. He hurried to pin the serpent down, and Cherise stabbed its eyeless head.

No one complained. The surviving refugees seemed determined to prove their bravery.

But they had slogged for a long distance with hardly any rest breaks. They had to give up on cleanliness. Kessa had tucked away her head cover, trying to preserve it as a semiclean piece of cloth.

"Keep moving," she urged. If only she had the strength of a Yeresunsa, so she could scoop everyone up and carry them.

They had no chance to steal a transport. Torth pilots were not foolish enough to abandon their vehicles, or even to land in this filthy mess.

But Kessa wasn't planning to quit until her own aching, arthritic limbs collapsed.

The longer the Torth failed, she suspected, the more they would question their own leadership. Torth could collectively make mistakes.

"Thomas." Kessa slogged closer to Hemjeg, whose turn it was to carry Thomas. The salt miner wore a makeshift harness as an aid, cradling Thomas against his chest. "Do you know of any routes through the dead city?"

Thomas laughed without humor.

"We must get to a place where we might steal a transport." Kessa pointed to the barest hint of a glow that limned the horizon. In the far distance, beyond crumbling cliffs and broken towers, the Stratower loomed. Its countless windows were like stars in the hazy night, almost too vague to see through the rainfall.

It looked impossibly far away.

"We don't have a chance," Thomas said.

"We will get there." Kessa made herself sound confident. People seemed to believe her.

"I can give you a bit of light," Thomas said.

Kessa looked at him.

"Take my wristwatch." Thomas pressed a button on the device he wore, and a meager glow lit his face. Hemjeg looked incredulous.

The light was colorless. Kessa doubted that the wristwatch would have illuminated much in the slave Tunnels, but here, her eyes were thirstier.

"Thank you," she said.

"It's not much," Thomas admitted. "There's a button. You hold it down."

Kessa gently took the wristwatch. She toggled the light on and off once, familiarizing herself with it by touch. She didn't want to overuse it. Torth and other vile creatures might see this feeble light.

A skittering sound echoed somewhere nearby. Refugees froze in fear.

"What was that?" someone whispered.

It might just be clumped sludge falling off ledges.

Kessa silently nudged the refugee ahead of her to keep moving. It was easy to mistake trickling slime for footsteps, or drooling, or chewing. Sometimes the wind sounded almost like a slave moaning around unseen corners.

Later, though, a series of splashes echoed from the darkness off to one side. That sounded like footsteps.

"Hide," Kessa whispered.

She crouched behind debris and strained to listen. Torth might have ocular implants or goggles that allowed them to see in the dark, but they could not wade in silence. They were too big.

A voice pierced the silence, sounding lost and frightened. "Help me!"

Kessa felt colder than she had ever felt in her life. Refugees had plunged out of sight during the battle, just like Weptolyso, but not all had returned. Three remained missing.

What if they were wandering, lost, through the ruins?

Thomas whispered nearby. "Shh. That's a Torth."

Another desperate voice called out from a different direction. "Please help. I'm lost!"

It sounded scared. It spoke the slave tongue. Yet Kessa realized that the harsh accent was not that of a farm slave from Duin, or from anyone she knew.

"Kessa?" someone whispered.

"Shh." Kessa crouched lower. Torth knew how to imitate emotions. They absorbed slave memories all the time, and many of them were capable of spoken speech.

Her friends passed the message along in low whispers. "Shh."

The despairing cries echoed off grimy walls.

"Help me."

"I'm lost."

The voices moved across a vast space at a quick pace, far too sure-footed to be lost ummins. The ruins were pockmarked with sludge pools and other pitfalls. Kessa's crew had to move with care, using makeshift poles—debris they had scavenged—to feel their way past tar pits.

Red light skittered along piles of rubble.

Kessa hardly dared to breathe. The laser squiggled right past her and her friends. Jagged ruins hid them, and the light moved on.

So did the squelching footsteps.

The false slave calls came again, more distant. "Help!"

Kessa waited until she was certain the Torth were gone. Her feet and hands were numb from the cold, and her wrinkled skin yearned for the dryness of a sunlit desert.

"Let's go," she whispered.

Refugees adjusted their packs and picked up their burdens. They slogged for what Kessa judged to be more than a work shift. But they were slowing.

Especially Weptolyso.

The runaway hall guard had to stop more and more frequently. He wasn't hurt, but he struggled to carry the armored and injured Bringer of Hope. He had also slung Vy over one huge shoulder. He kept needing to set down his burdens.

They came to the lip of a cliff. It seemed they had hiked to the edge of a plateau, and from here, there was a dark view.

The scope of flattened buildings looked like the result of an ancient cataclysm. The destruction extended into gloom, farther than Kessa could see. If there was a way down, she did not see it. The ceaseless rain fell into an inky abyss.

Somewhere beyond that horizon, though, slaves thrived in Stratower City.

"We'll go this way." Kessa hiked along the canyon of ancient wreckage, sticking to the shelter of rubble. No time for rest. No way to sleep.

A deep, exhausted voice spoke in the language of humans. "…Sorry."

Ariock.

Kessa sloshed toward him. Weptolyso had set the giant down, taking a rest break. Muck covered both of them.

"Naglitay?" Kessa called softly. "Where is she?"

The refugees located Naglitay and urged her forward. Kessa had to direct the herbalist to mix her russet leaves into a water jar.

"Drink this," Kessa told Ariock. "It should ease your pain."

Ariock ignored the offer. "I'm sorry." He sounded miserable. "For my failure."

Kessa looked at him in the darkness, not quite daring to press the wristwatch button so she could use light to read his face. Why would Ariock blame himself for what the Torth had wrought? He had fought valiantly. Did he expect to keep winning against an armada? Not even Jonathan Stead had done that. Not even the gods.

"You did not fail us," Kessa explained, using his native language so that no one else would feel alarmed. "We are not dead. We have a chance, and you gave us that."

Ariock fell silent, perhaps mulling over her words.

"Drink this medicine. Please." Kessa braced herself for an argument with the Bringer of Hope. They needed him to survive and recover his powers.

After all, he was the descendant of Jonathan Stead. Ariock could heal the injured and scan for anything alive. He could probably transform cold sewage into a sunlit habitat. He just needed his powers.

She did not need to say all that. Ariock accepted the jar, which was small in his huge hand. He drank.

"Stop," Kessa told him with reluctance. "You should save some for later." *And for other people*, she did not say.

"Right." Ariock handed it back to her. "Thank you." He thought a moment. "Did you give some to Vy?"

Kessa was unsure if Vy would ever wake again. She corked the jar, but she inwardly resolved to try and get Vy to swallow some. "I will."

"Son of Storms," Weptolyso said, "do you think you can walk?"

Ariock began to stand, using a wall as leverage. Refugees watched in awe.

But he did not rise fully. He winced in pain and remained hunched, holding the blanket in place over his wound.

"I will help you." Weptolyso rose slowly, clearly exhausted.

"No." Ariock braced himself against the wall, his voice tight with pain. "I got us into this mess. I'll walk."

Kessa suspected that he would ignore his injury and take stupid risks. His powers probably had him convinced that he was invincible. "Weptolyso," she urged. "Help him."

Ariock took one limping step. Then another. Everyone watched, heartened. If the Bringer of Hope could ignore his injury and walk, then perhaps they would all ignore their problems.

"Will you lead the way?" Ariock asked. He switched to the slave tongue. "I follow Kessa the Wise."

Kessa felt some awe herself.

She tightened her supply pack and led the way past sludge and ancient ruins. Perhaps that painkiller mixture had given Ariock enough strength to go on.

The farther they walked, the more distant the Torth seemed. Their searchlights lit a faraway area. But Kessa saw bestial shapes lurking in ancient buildings, or hiding behind blasted walls. She heard sounds in the rubble.

"Those ape monsters are stalking us," Cherise whispered. She gripped the ionic knife, ready to draw it from its sheath.

There seemed to be more wild zoved every time Kessa checked. If only the monsters of this world could be satiated.

"Ariock?" Kessa moved closer to him so she could whisper. "Can you use your powers?"

"I've been trying." Ariock slogged alongside refugees with a look of grim focus. His helmet was gone. His hair was matted by toxic rain, and his armor was likewise coated by grime.

His rest breaks were becoming more frequent. Clearly, he was no longer capable of shaking the ground or demolishing skyscrapers.

"I can carry you," Weptolyso offered.

He made that offer several times, but each time, Ariock refused. He did not want to take Vy's place on the nussian's shoulders.

Creatures swung from the girders of a nearby building. Kessa didn't like how cooperative they were. Their basic body shape, even their behavior, was vaguely Torth-like. It was as if the toxic rainfall had twisted ordinary Torth into uglier monsters.

It made her wonder what the dead city might be doing to her.

"Those things must get water from somewhere," Cherise said in a low voice. "I wonder if there's a river?"

Water.

Kessa was not thirsty, but the humans and hybrids drank a lot. Cherise, Vy, Thomas, and Ariock seemed much more reliant on water than ummins. There was nothing left to clean everyone's festering scratches and bite wounds. If they did not ration it better, they would run out of water long before they reached Stratower City.

"Could I have more of that painkiller?" Ariock asked in English.

"I'm sorry. It's all gone." Kessa had already given him the last of the russet leaf mixture. Vy seemed to be dozing a lot, but Kessa had also managed to get her to drink some.

"Could I get some water?" Ariock asked with pained hope.

Kessa fumbled in her supply pack and pulled out her jar. "It's almost empty," she warned him.

Ariock licked his lips. "Then I'll go without."

"If you need it…" Kessa said.

Ariock seemed too fatigued to respond.

More of the skinny, knobby creatures stalked alongside their group, not just from one direction, but from two directions. The beasts might be animals, but they were smart enough to hunt in packs.

"Thomas." Kessa fell back to join Irarjeg, who carried Thomas. "Are you able to send those wild zoved away?"

"What do you think I've been trying to do for the past twenty hours?" Thomas asked.

Kessa was surprised. She had assumed that the telepathic beasts needed to be close to Thomas, with their ranges overlapping, for him to communicate with them.

"They're sending scouts close to us," Thomas said. "They skirt within my range every so often."

"Oh." Irarjeg sounded unnerved.

"So I've been telling them." Thomas sounded like he was teaching simple mathematics. "I've been pretending that we're Torth, to feed their fear of us. But I can't force them to believe it. My powers are inhibited."

Kessa nodded, accepting that.

"They expect emotionlessness and bright lights from the Torth," Thomas said. "Instead, we're showing them fear. We smell and radiate fear like a gourmet feast." He swallowed. "And they're very hungry."

"Your efforts are becoming threadbare," Kessa realized. "The wild zoved no longer believe you."

Thomas nodded.

Kessa scanned the crowd of refugees. She could not see everyone in the gloom, but she would not ask them to pretend to be Torth. Their situation was too strained.

Wild zoved crept closer. A third pack had joined the first two. By now, everyone realized it, and the refugees crowded closer together.

A battle was inevitable.

"Don your gloves," Kessa said. She herself did not own a glove. Torth had stolen quite a few, and there were not enough to go around. Kessa had already preselected the largest ummins to help form a protective perimeter around everyone else.

Perhaps they had hiked far enough so that Torth would not see or hear blaster shots?

"Kessa?" One of the adolescents hurried to her, pointing toward the chasm. "There's a bridge! Do you see it?"

In the dim light from cloud glow, Kessa saw the dark silhouette of what might have been a scaffold, or a very ancient and broken bridge. It looked ready to collapse. Stalactites hung from its struts. Its far reaches vanished into gloom.

"There is no way that will hold Weptolyso," Irarjeg observed.

The chasm was a desperate gamble, Kessa knew. That ruined bridge might collapse, or it might dead-end in nothingness. A Torth transport might fly over the chasm at the wrong moment. More starving monsters and dangers might lurk in the gloom.

Yet what choice did they have?

The Stratower dominated the sky beyond the horizon. That city held water, medicine, transports, even space shuttles with launchpads. No doubt there were spaceships taking off for better worlds.

They just had to get there.

And find a way to steal what they needed.

One step at a time.

The horde of wild zoved circled tighter and closer, emerging from the ruins. They bared sharp teeth that jutted from their oversize jaws. Drool glistened on yellowed fangs and incisors. But none of them came from the direction of the chasm.

Maybe they were afraid of tumbling to their deaths.

Kessa backed toward the ancient ruins of a bridge, knowing that others would follow her.

"We'll risk the bridge," she said. "The lightest people will go first."

# CHAPTER 3

# DEVOID

Filthy, knobby apes moved closer, strings of drool hanging from their massive jaws. And refugees rushed onto the precarious remains of an ancient bridge.

Thomas studied the danger. If his carrier, Irarjeg, slipped while inching along that rain-slick, skeletal structure…

They would tumble for many seconds, in the dark. And then an impact. His own fragile body would break.

He would die alone, without any mourners.

Just like Delia had said he would. And maybe he had reaped a terrible death, like his own birth mother's death, just like the Upward Governess had said. Maybe it would be poetic justice. His errors were so colossal, everyone in the galaxy had a right to sneer at him.

He should have seen this trap coming.

He had known the Upward Governess well enough to anticipate anything she might do. Instead? Thomas had proven to himself, beyond any shred of doubt, that he was blinded by his own arrogance.

He had made this mistake. And his failure illuminated other mental errors he had previously hidden from himself.

For instance: a powerful group of Torth had tried to uplift Yellow Thomas and grant him power. There was a conspiracy. It involved the Commander of All Living Things and many Servants of All. Yellow Thomas should have investigated who, what, and why. They might have been trying to weaponize him, to use his power to brainwash people.

But he had been too blinded by greed, too pathetically needy for acceptance, to question their easy embrace of Yellow Thomas. He had failed to investigate the hints of conspiracy back when he'd had the opportunity to do so. He had not cared enough.

He should have been wiser. And braver.

He should have freed Cherise and Vy and Ariock sooner.

And he should have been brave enough to salvage whatever friendships he used to have. He had failed to even try.

His own cowardice overwhelmed him with shame. Even now, he was tempted to keep silent and let wiser people, like Kessa, take the lead.

"Kessa, what are you waiting for?" Pung complained. "Come on!" He stood on the bridge and beckoned her.

She hesitated, full of concern for the people who carried heavy burdens.

"You said that those of us who are lightweight must go first," Weptolyso pointed out. "That includes you."

Kessa clicked her beak in annoyance and doubt. But she ventured onto the bridge. "Do not leave anyone behind," she called over her shoulder.

The rickety bridge trembled and creaked as refugees made their way onward into darkness, and possibly downward. Any stairs would have long since rotted away. The ancient struts seemed held together by mucus. A few broke off as ummins touched them.

The wild zoved were clearly afraid to get too close to the chasm, but as the refugees left, the monsters grew bolder. The biggest ones circled closer.

"Set me down near the edge of the chasm, Irarjeg," Thomas said. "Where the bridge begins."

Irarjeg emanated bewilderment.

"It's necessary," Thomas said. "I'll give the rest of you time to escape. You need me to fend off the wild zoved."

"That is very brave," Irarjeg said, full of doubts. "But then how will you get across the bridge?"

"I'm sure Kessa will send someone back for me," Thomas said.

He was sure that Kessa would want to.

But it was apparent that Ariock was too weakened to keep his balance on the rickety ruin. He required aid from Weptolyso, and with both of those titans on the shaky remains of the bridge, it would almost certainly collapse.

There would be no rescue for Thomas after that.

And then Thomas would be able to choose his own lonely death. He could plunge down the chasm, or he could get eaten alive by carnivores.

Maybe Cherise would slit his throat with the ionic knife?

Cherise and her friend Dugwon hurried past, carrying Vy. They were going to attempt the bridge with an injured burden to carry. Vy was feverishly in and out of consciousness, with both of her lower legs swaddled in a grime-soaked blanket. Thomas had seen the blast blow off at least one of her feet. A tourniquet could only do so much. Her injuries would be fatal if left untreated for much longer.

"Good luck," Thomas said softly as his foster sisters passed by.

He would not beg for a mercy killing. Cherise had enough trauma to deal with. Let her survive for as long as she could, and without any guilt. He would not compound his mistakes with her.

"Go on," Thomas urged Irarjeg. "Cross that bridge. Protect your people."

Irarjeg gently eased Thomas down, propping him against a piece of slime-coated wreckage. He straightened, but he was full of concern. "I could wait. I'll cling to the bridge, close by, and when…"

The wild zoved lunged into their midst.

Weptolyso swung a piece of debris, wielding it like a club. As soon as an ape entered Thomas's range, he thought without words, *DELICIOUSNESS IS THAT WAY.* He mentally indicated a direction, tongue on his lips, as if the grime there was salty blood. He pretended to be in rapture with raw meat.

The ape rocked onto its hind legs. Several more behind it swiveled their elongated heads to peer through the rainfall, all looking in the same distant direction. They sniffed the polluted air.

Thomas redoubled his efforts. *THAT WAY. HUGE PREY. MMM.*

The lead apes loped in that direction. A few other apes followed.

Then the horde broke apart, scampering to catch up with their pack leaders. Some of the wild zoved cast hungry looks back toward Ariock and Weptolyso, but none broke away. They stuck together.

Irarjeg beamed with amazement. "You saved us."

"Don't get too relaxed." Thomas opened his eyes. "I sent the monsters on a wild hunt. That trick will last maybe five or ten minutes, at the most. It was the best I could do."

Weptolyso looked fascinated. "What will happen after that?"

"The wild zoved will come back," Thomas said. "Ravenous and pissed off. And they'll know where to find fresh meat."

"Then we have to use this time." Ariock shuffled wearily toward the bridge.

"I will help you, Son of Storms." Weptolyso hurried after him.

Irarjeg bent to lift Thomas.

"No." Thomas spoke in a strong voice. "That horde of wild zoved will return, and they'll be angry enough to swarm down the scaffolding and over the bridge. I'm the only person who has a shred of a chance to stop them. You need to leave me until the last moment."

Irarjeg gave Thomas a penetrating stare. He did not like the idea of leaving their pilot alone, without protection. "That sounds risky."

Ariock also looked unsettled. He stopped, hardly able to stand yet unwilling to leave. "We're not going to abandon you, Thomas. We need you."

Of course. Everyone thought they needed a supergenius. Everyone wanted to use him.

"I know," Thomas said. "I'm your pilot."

"Not just for that." Weptolyso snorted.

"You're our friend," Ariock said.

Thomas looked away, unsure about the kindness in their eyes. He was fairly certain that slaves could never befriend a Torth. They were saying things by rote, not truly examining their feelings for him. They were fooling themselves.

"Get going," Thomas urged. "Ariock, you'll need a while on that bridge. You need me here, holding off the horde."

Irarjeg readjusted his pack, yet he hesitated, too. "You must take care of yourself. Stay alive."

"Just go." Thomas put the right note of despair into his voice. "There isn't much time."

"Make it a promise," Ariock said.

Thomas said nothing. A sharp edge of metal poked out of the muck nearby. No one else noticed it, in the gloom, but Thomas detected every variation in his environment. Although he lacked the strength to walk, he might be able to writhe close enough, and position his neck in just the right way, so that a fall would kill him.

That would be better than getting devoured by cannibalistic apes. Better than falling off the cliff and plummeting for seconds before snapping his spine on some hard surface. Light-years better than the Isolatorium.

"You've got to go," Thomas whispered. "Look. They're coming."

Indeed, apish figures bobbed over the ruins in the rain-drenched distance. They moved with fluid ease, coordinated like a flock of birds or a school of fish.

Irarjeg hurried away. "Stay safe. We will send someone. You are a hero."

As if.

Thomas sensed more arguments brewing from Ariock, but the big guy barely remembered why he was arguing. He was beyond exhausted. His injury would be just as fatal as Vy's if he did not receive major medical care.

And perhaps Ariock realized how hopeless their situation was. Thomas could sense his attempts to stretch his awareness. Every attempt ended in dizzying failure. The big guy didn't want anyone to notice how weakened he was.

He eased his way onto the bridge, one step closer to Stratower City.

Struts groaned. The bridge trembled.

"Let me help you, Son of Storms." Weptolyso braced Ariock, ready to catch him if the structure collapsed.

"Don't call me that," Ariock murmured. "Can I just be Ariock?"

Weptolyso seemed perplexed, but he offered a rubbery grin. "Certainly." He tested the name. "Ariock Dovanack." He flared his nostrils in a nussian gesture of approval. "I will be happy when you have your powers back."

"Me too."

Ariock was probably deluded enough to believe that he would actually recover his powers. He had forgotten that Yeresunsa powers were tied to health.

Weptolyso cast one more look over his shoulder. "Stay safe, Thomas," he called.

They made their way across girders, stepping with care, struggling to keep their balance on slippery surfaces that creaked and swayed.

Thomas had a perverse urge to beg for a rescue. He suppressed it. No one truly wanted him around.

Besides, he had known that he was doomed from the moment the Upward Governess sent her holographic message.

Heck, he'd known it for most of his life. Everyone had told him to expect an early death.

Wild zoved scrambled over heaps of rubble. They sniffed the air. An ape in the near distance caught sight of Thomas, and it crooned to its hunting pack.

Thomas wrapped his thin arms around himself and shivered. He waited until everyone was gone, swallowed by the gloom over the chasm.

The dead city was extra dark to him now, without any other perceptions nearby. The wind seemed to carry whispers in a parody of languages. Maybe he was coming down with the dreaded dead city sickness?

His friends would probably not survive for much longer. They might never understand the luxuries and godhood he had rejected. That was a secret between Thomas and the Upward Governess.

His former mentor would likely not survive him for long, either.

For the first time since Thomas had joined the Torth, he stopped yearning for the Megacosm. That was over.

Those distant voices were strange, though. One sounded like Cherise. She was calling his name. Her voice echoed across the chasm.

Well, that had to be a hallucination. Cherise would never raise her voice like that, let alone sound so concerned for Thomas.

He was alone, and trapped with the most unpleasant company in the universe: himself.

He examined the jutting sharpness in the muck and calculated the best way to end his life.

# CHAPTER 4

# A RESCUE OWED

The bridge was a dead end.

Refugees found a way to climb down, hand over hand, into profound darkness. One of them had figured out a way to light up the display on her blaster glove. That knowledge was passed along, and so they had a bit of light.

A tiny, tiny bit of light in hell.

Cherise was more exhausted than she had ever been in her life. The bridge began to shake and clank before she and Dugwon had climbed all the way down. Weptolyso must be making his way across.

Cherise had Vy on her back with their arms tied together. The extra weight was painful as she climbed down, and she had to rest often. Dugwon climbed next to her, on the far side of the scaffold, ready to reach out a steadying hand or to offer Cherise a sip of water whenever she needed it.

"I think Thomas is really brave," Dugwon said.

Cherise made a noncommittal sound. News had passed down the chain of refugees, and they claimed that Thomas was staying behind in order to fend off the horde of wild zoved. That did sound heroic.

"I think he is different from other mind readers, because he is half human," Dugwon stated. "Like you. Humans are nice."

She must want Cherise to admit that maybe Thomas wasn't so bad after all. But Cherise wasn't going to do that. She had glimpsed Thomas's face as he sat there, on the edge of the chasm, and she did not see a hero. His reason for staying behind was dark and cold.

Thomas was going to kill himself.

Cherise understood. She had been there. Part of her empathized and wanted to hug him and to tell him that he had value.

But would he care about the opinion of a mere human?

The gruff kindness that Thomas used to have was gone, and Cherise was certain that it was never coming back. He was a Torth. Cherise was a member of a slave species. She meant nothing to him. None of them did. Thomas probably missed his Torth brethren, and if he wanted to die, it wasn't her place to ruin his plans.

Soft voices in the darkness below told Cherise that she was nearly there.

She trembled, lowering herself down the last few girders. She was so tired. So exhausted. So miserable.

She remained bent over, keeping Vy's damaged, blanket-wrapped feet off the oily ground. "Can someone untie Vy from my shoulders?"

There wasn't much to see at the base of the bridge. It was dark.

"Careful," someone said. "There is a sludge canal here. No way to know how deep it is."

"But there is a path with dry land," someone else said.

Refugees helped to lift Vy off Cherise's back. They laid her down, letting her rest. Vy moaned in pain. Cherise could commiserate.

She sat next to her foster sister. Her water jar was nearly empty.

"Do you want water, Vy?" Cherise asked.

"No." Vy's voice was weak. She radiated heat, yet she seemed unable to stop shaking.

"I think you need some," Cherise said.

"Pointless," Vy whispered. She turned her head away.

Cherise didn't know what to do.

"I'm dying," Vy said.

Cherise had no response for that, either. She wasn't a nurse. Vy was.

"I got us killed," Vy said. "I screamed."

"You aren't the reason we're here." Cherise was fairly certain of that. She supposed there was plenty of blame to go around, and if Vy was partially responsible, well, so was Ariock.

Grimy metal rails screeched, in danger of wrenching apart.

Refugees backed away. Cherise heard distant snorts of effort, and she knew that Weptolyso was climbing down. He probably had tamped down his spinal ridge and spikes so that he could carry Ariock over one shoulder.

A distant pillar began to buckle. Cherise heard it, even if she couldn't see it.

"Run!" someone cried.

Cherise seized Vy under her arms and called for help. Then Dugwon was there, and together, they scurried away from the bridge. The whole structure was coming undone, groaning as if in agony. Huge pieces splashed into what sounded like a sludge lake.

"Coming down!" Weptolyso bellowed. "Clear away!"

Seconds later, there was an enormous thud and splash. Weptolyso had landed.

The destruction went on. The ancient wreck of a bridge might have held on to its former glory for untold centuries or millennia, but it was broken now.

"At least those zoved things won't be able to come after us," someone muttered.

"I must rest." Weptolyso sounded as if he was on the verge of collapse. "The Son of…I mean, Ariock Dovanack…is with me."

"Is he all right?" Kessa's voice asked.

Ariock's reply was worn-out and curt. "No powers."

That seemed obvious.

"I meant, how are you feeling?" Kessa said gently.

Ariock made a noise of despair and frustration. Judging by the splashes, he was on his feet again.

"What about Thomas?" Kessa asked. "Who has him? Irarjeg?"

Silence.

"Maybe." Weptolyso sounded defeated. "He begged us to leave him up there."

"What?" Kessa sounded shocked.

"He is fending off the wild zoved!" someone else piped up.

"Yes!" another refugee said. "I heard it from Hemjeg, who heard it from Choonhulm, and he heard it from Irarjeg. The Teacher is saving us all!"

Cherise sat down on rubble, shivering from the cold drizzle. She had expected to feel relieved by the idea of slogging onward without Thomas. Instead, she felt something like despair.

"This is unacceptable." Kessa clicked her beak.

Cherise didn't think she had ever heard Kessa sound so angry.

"Where is Irarjeg?" Kessa demanded.

"Here," a faraway voice called.

Everyone listened as he sloshed closer.

"Did you leave Thomas behind?" Kessa asked, her tone full of threats.

"We have to run." Irarjeg sounded miserable. "The bridge collapsed. Last I saw, a horde of wild zoved was swarming toward the Teacher. He was beyond my reach. I could not save him. The bridge collapsed."

Refugees stirred, hearing his despair and panic. They gathered their meager belongings and prepared for another fearful slog.

"No." Kessa sounded coldly furious. "We do not leave Thomas behind."

"I am sorry, elder." Irarjeg sounded defeated. "I believe he is dead."

Cherise could not see faces in the darkness, but she could almost feel the devastation. It was palpable. She felt it herself.

"Did you see him die?" Kessa demanded.

Ariock swore. His tone sounded like he was standing at his full height, albeit weary. "Someone needs to go back."

Kessa translated that to the slave tongue.

"But there's no more bridge!" someone said.

"If there is even a remnant," Kessa said, "then the attempt must be made." A splash indicated that she had dropped her pack. "I will go, if none of you are brave enough."

"No!" several refugees cried.

A climb in this oily rain would be treacherous, if not impossible. Even if Kessa found a way up, even if she found Thomas alive, could she really strap him onto her back and climb all the way back down?

Cherise stepped forward. Someone had to intervene.

Pung got there first. "I'll go."

"It is my duty." Irarjeg sounded resigned. "My fault. If someone must go, let it be me."

"No need," Pung said. "I am a smuggler. I am used to dangerous situations."

Pung had not complained about his former owner since the night of their escape, but Cherise remembered well enough what slavery was like. Pung had suffered humiliations and at least one painful punishment from Thomas. He might be repressing a deep-seated grudge.

Cherise knew what that was like.

She stepped in front of Pung and placed her hand on the slimy surface of a remaining pillar. "I'll go."

She could feel shocked reactions. People must be staring at her in the darkness. No one had expected to hear her voice.

Cherise herself had not expected to volunteer.

Perhaps because this trek was wearing away her harsh feelings. The only thing that kept her going was the fact that people needed her. Vy. Dugwon. Kessa. And maybe even Thomas, if any remnant of his human self remained locked away in his Torth mind.

Sure, she didn't owe him anything. She didn't need to risk her life to save his. Except...

The origami lion he'd given her, long ago, nestled in her rags, crumpled and tattered. Cherise had kept that treasure all throughout her slavery. Even afterward, she had held on to the memento from home.

From Thomas.

*"There's a lion inside you,"* he had told her.

He had always known exactly what to say to give Cherise strength or to cheer her up. The lion was a talisman of the time when a more innocent Thomas had saved her life. Those two and a half years Cherise had spent in foster care with him...that was the only time she had felt happiness.

Everything else was betrayal, abuse, enslavement, and toxic pollution.

Her friendship with Thomas stood out. That time period glowed in her lifetime memories, stronger than the Stratower, more magnificent than a galaxy, endowing her with strength to survive worse times. It was the only reason she was alive.

And no matter how much she wanted to erase Thomas, she could not forget what he'd done for her.

She had told herself that she didn't care if Thomas went to rejoin his Torth kin, or if he died screaming; she'd simply wanted him out of her life forever. She had expected to feel relief when he was gone.

Instead, she felt devastated.

"You don't have to do this, Cherise." Vy's voice was weak. She must be worried that she would lose both of her foster siblings.

"Cherise?" Ariock sounded skeptical.

"It does not need to be you." Kessa must have the same concerns.

Cherise twisted a rag, readying it for use as a climbing rope. "I'm in better shape than any of you," she admitted. "And I think I owe him a rescue."

She remembered how once, during a trip to a local ski resort, she and Thomas had settled in a cozy corner by a roaring fireplace. Thomas had revealed funny secrets about every person who walked by. Cherise had begun to giggle at his dry commentary. She'd embellished each story, and she'd made Thomas laugh so hard, tears had leaked from his eyes.

That was when Thomas had confessed to her that he felt burdened by absorbing other people's secrets.

On that day, Cherise had understood why someone might sacrifice his or her life for another person. She'd understood love.

The pillar seemed to be leaning. It must have fallen against some more intact part of the bridge. Cherise inched her way upward. She hooked the rope over protrusions in order to hoist herself higher.

The arguments from below turned into wishes for good luck.

"Shout if you need help!" Pung called.

"Be careful!" Irarjeg said.

Wind moaned through the growing channel below Cherise. She didn't dare look down. Wind blew her hair back like a cape.

She used to accompany him beneath brilliant autumn leaves, or under summer trees. They used to discuss politics and ideology and epistemology, talking with each other like grown-ups instead of like the kids they were.

That version of Thomas had a way of making her feel valuable.

That version would never have tortured her.

That version—the one with the purple eyes—would have apologized to her if he'd gotten coerced into hurting her.

Everything about him had been a lie. Cherise hated her treacherous memories. The real Thomas wasn't human, and he never said, "I'm sorry."

She yanked herself upward, foot by foot, causing ropes of mossy sludge to sway and drip. The pole felt rotten and unstable. Wind swallowed the voices below her.

She hugged a trestle. She inched toward, bit by bit, too scared to stand up. The trestle swayed as if it was made of rope instead of ancient, eroded metal.

"Thomas!" she called, to let him know she was on her way.

The wind moaned. She heard nothing other than that, and rainfall and creaking metal.

She used to feel so inadequate around Thomas in her memories. She saw it clearly now. She had idolized him, like a child to an all-powerful parent. Thomas had saved her when she was ready to slit her wrists.

She had loved him.

With all her heart.

If Thomas was alive, he could not hear her thoughts at this distance, so it was safe to think that.

A tear spilled down Cherise's cheek. When she reviewed the sum total of her life, her only happy times were shared with the boy who had betrayed and tortured her.

So she would repay him for that. She owed him a rescue.

And if he died, however he died, she would mourn him, just a little bit.

# CHAPTER 5

# PRIMACY OF A SPECIES

Thomas scooted closer to the sharp edge of debris. He adjusted his seated position so that it would puncture his throat once he fell. It had to be a perfectly exact alignment. No second chances, since he was too weak to pick himself up and try it again.

He double-checked and ran extra analytics in the back of his mind. Meanwhile, wild zoved raced toward him from behind. He could hear them, splashing and slobbering.

"Thomas!"

He raised his head, disbelieving. That could not be Cherise.

Yet there she was, clinging to the remains of the scaffold. Her glasses picked up some reflective light from the clouds. Wind lifted her hair in fingers.

Now Thomas was certain the dead city had driven him insane. His own subconsciousness was foiling his suicide with a figment of his imagination.

"Come on," Cherise said, holding out an arm. "Can you slide toward that beam? If you can do that, I can meet you halfway."

Her voice was as liquid as Thomas remembered, but the note of independence was new. He was beginning to think that maybe she wasn't a hallucination.

He opened his mouth to speak. *I'm sorry*, he desperately wanted to say. *I should never have hurt you. I wish I could take it back.*

But wind roared through the chasm below, and wild zoved crooned behind him. All that emerged from his throat was a croak of terror as apes bounded toward their meal.

Thomas sensed their starvation as they entered his range. As each ape passed its perceptions to its comrades, Thomas caught images of Cherise as a tasty morsel.

She was really here.

And she was really clinging to the scaffold, with no way to flee the horde of carnivorous apes, no way to die gently or on her own terms. Because she'd tried to rescue him.

That seemed unfair.

Thomas squeezed his eyes shut. He didn't think he could fool the apes the same way he had been doing. They were getting wise to his methods. Never before had the wild zoved dealt with an outsider who pretended to be one of them, with their peculiar hungers and lusts and primordial fears. But they were beginning to accept that something new had entered their brutal world. Soon they would figure out that this new thing could be destroyed and devoured, no matter how alien he was, no matter how invulnerable his mind made him appear. He was an enemy. He was prey.

However, if there was one thing a supergenius could do well, it was think fast.

Thomas constructed groundwork for an elaborate scene in his visual cortex. This wasn't vague imagination. He boosted everything he saw. He added twenty-five Torth transports to the clouded sky, with searchlights slicing through rain. He layered in details, such as the hum of engines, near and far. The raindrops would refract just so. Searchlights and running lights would sweep the rain with conical penumbras. Transport speeds would vary, and Thomas built that variation into his scenario, along with other variables to add to the realism.

Then he played the scenario.

*DANGER DANGER DANGER!* Thomas trumpeted wordless alarm in his mind and lashed out with a pain seizure at the nearest wild zoved.

It screamed and fell off the cliff.

Panic rippled through the entire horde. Most of them had no clue why the forerunners were panicking, since they did not perceive any danger. Thomas's imagined scenario only impacted the apes within his limited range. Even so, one of their number had fallen off a cliff due to an attack by an unseen enemy, and that news spread through the rest, passed from mind to mind.

The horde cringed from shared perceptions of lights and danger. Their leaders whirled away from the cliff. Thomas sensed them deciding that this was a bad time to attack, with so much fear and uncertainty.

"You can still escape," Thomas urged Cherise. "Turn around. Tell Weptolyso to pull down the remainder of the bridge so the wild zoved won't venture out."

"I'm not abandoning you." She gave him an intense, defiant stare. "I didn't climb all the way up here just to give up."

All that connected the scaffold to the cliff was a swaying, slimy rail. Cherise would have to be insane to climb onto it. Yet she did. She wrapped her arms around the rail and made her way up, inch by inch.

"Go away," Thomas whimpered.

"Come toward me," Cherise invited. "I'll catch you."

Thomas shook his head, not daring to move more than that. Maybe he could crawl, if he exerted enormous effort, but he couldn't haul himself onto that diagonal rail over an abyss.

Cherise kept climbing. She would not be dissuaded. Death surrounded them, but Thomas couldn't quite bring himself to show her even more death and failure.

What if Cherise somehow had a future? Who was he to deprive her of a chance to escape this planet and live happily with her friends?

He had hurt her so much when she was a slave. Maybe he owed her some of his own humiliation and suffering.

He should meet her halfway.

Thomas stretched out one arm, then the other. His torn and filthy sleeves dragged in the muck. He pulled himself forward.

"You're doing well," Cherise said.

Thomas came to the edge of the abyss and stopped. His arms were too weak to clutch the slimy rail. He couldn't go any farther.

The angle was too steep for Cherise to work her way up. It might be safe for a squirrel, or a wild zoved, but a human would have a lot of trouble climbing.

A downward slide would be easier. An able-bodied person could do it, but not Thomas.

"I'm sorry," he said. He truly meant it.

Cherise yanked herself farther upward. A strong gust of wind made her cling tightly to the rail, swaying. Her hands were taut with the strain of her death grip.

"I can't," Thomas said.

"You saved me once," Cherise said in her wholesome voice that evoked Earth. "That's why I'm here."

Thomas edged slightly onto the rail. That put him just within telepathy range of Cherise—and the inner strength that radiated from her mind.

"Cherise," he whispered, wanting to reach for her. He didn't dare.

Despite the grueling trek, she emanated poise and defiance. It came from her core. Unlike most humans and slaves, Cherise seemed to float above atrocities like a fresh flower atop sewage. Her mind was beautiful in a way that Thomas simply could not ignore.

"You're frozen in fear," Cherise observed. "I know the feeling."

Thomas blinked back tears. He didn't want anyone to see him this way, especially not Cherise, but he was helpless to stop.

"Focus on my face," Cherise said. "Ignore what is below you, or behind you, and look only at me."

He obeyed her command. He owed her that much.

"Stay focused on me."

He did. Obedience actually felt good. It overrode his destructive thoughts about death and doom.

"Stay with me, Thomas." Cherise inched back. "Slide toward me."

He extended one hand along the rail. Then the other.

The chasm moaned, empty and black, like a monstrous mouth eager to swallow him. A stiff wind caused the rail to sway. Thomas clutched it as best he could, and all he could think about was staying on top. He trembled violently. His weak muscles would cause him to fail. The wild zoved might return at any second, and he couldn't spare enough focus to throw them another imaginary scenario…

"Thomas, look at me," Cherise said.

He didn't dare raise his head.

"Focus on my voice," Cherise said. "Remember how you used to help me practice speaking out loud?"

Thomas could barely concentrate on what she said, but as she went on, her words began to penetrate his fears.

"…on that beanbag chair. We always started with serious conversations, and we always ended up laughing."

Her voice was so warm, he yearned to get back within range, to reexperience those memories from her perspective.

He used to laugh.

That had been a warm feeling that spread through him. A pleasure. It was a distinct pleasure that Torth never experienced.

For the first time since becoming a Yellow Rank, Thomas considered his human heritage without disparagement. His unknown father was just a blur. He might have been a criminal or a nice guy, but he had probably known what it felt like to laugh.

Maybe Thomas had inherited something from him.

And maybe it wasn't a bad thing, to be human. Was Cherise really a different species from Thomas? Were they really so different?

"…I loved when you mimicked Mrs. Hollander," Cherise went on. "That was always the best."

And Thomas remembered something more pleasurable than laughter. That was making Cherise laugh.

"I remember," he whispered.

He yearned to bask in more of her memories. Cherise did not carry billions of Torth lives inside her. Most of her memories came from their home on Earth.

He trembled with the effort of staying with her. He made himself inch forward. Soon he hung over the chasm entirely.

Part of him was aware of her conscious manipulation. She was distracting him from his fears, yet he didn't care. He wanted more of her distraction. The last thing he wanted to think about was how devastatingly high up he was, and how long the fall would be.

The rail swayed sickeningly, and Thomas clutched it with a cry of despair.

"Thomas!"

He'd frozen again.

"Look at me." Cherise beckoned. "Focus on me. Unless you're too weak."

Thomas pulled himself forward on the shaky beam until he began to slide toward her. He kept his weight as centered as possible. If the rail moved unexpectedly, he would plummet to his death.

Cherise braced herself on a more solid part of the structure. That allowed her to hold out her arms.

Thomas slid fast at the steep angle and slammed into her waiting arms.

She was ready for the impact. He didn't weigh enough to cause damage, anyway. Cherise wasted no time; she was ready with a knotted carrying harness.

Without anyone to help her, Cherise had to secure Thomas against her chest. She tightened knots and tested each one in quick succession.

On Earth, this physical intimacy would have elated Thomas. It would have been a shockingly pleasant change in his daily routines.

But they were no longer on Earth. He was more than close enough to read Cherise's mind...and it shocked him in the wrong sort of ways. The rail was slippery and dangerous. As Cherise slid backward with painstaking care, she half expected Thomas to torture her with a pain seizure.

She thought he wanted to die that badly.

"I'm sorry," Thomas whispered, sickened by his own cruelty. He had incited so much distrust in her. When he had betrayed her with a pain seizure, he had damaged her almost as badly as if he had twisted her mind.

Wind whipped away his words.

"I didn't believe that you were a Torth, at first," Cherise said sadly. "When I was a slave, I kept saying, 'Thomas would never abandon us.'"

Yet he had.

Or so it had seemed to Cherise. And that mattered. He had abandoned her in that moment when he had tortured her—not in his heart, but he had hurt her as a performance for his Torth orbiters, and that was nearly as bad.

And he was continuing to abandon her.

Clearly, Thomas no longer cared about himself, and Cherise knew that she could not entrust her life to such a defeated person. She did not trust him to protect her or anyone she cared about.

She was right.

Thomas's mind reeled from that revelation. Cherise was right. He was wrong.

Cherise had been forced to reevaluate Thomas, forced to see the strengths of slaves and the weaknesses of their masters, and she saw what he himself had downplayed and ignored. She was mentally stronger than him. Ariock, Kessa, and Vy…they were all mentally stronger than Thomas. Every single one of the refugees was stronger than him.

Why?

As a Yellow Rank, Thomas had suspected that slave species must hold some undefined resilience, but he had not understood it until now. After all, he had rejected emotions. He had rejected humanity. He had told himself that they were an inferior species, whereas he was superior.

He'd been lying to himself.

Lying.

His mouth tasted sour. He had lied and lied and lied to himself. He'd woven a web of lies to justify his actions.

Yes, he had done it in order to survive as a Torth…but then he had held those lies close to his heart even after he'd severed himself and gone renegade. Even in the depths of his despair, he still thought of himself as superior. Better than ordinary. He never forgot that he was a supergenius.

Truth radiated from Cherise's core personality, and now that he'd learned her view of the difference between people like him and people like her, he could not forget it. Passions and hopes gave humans a strength that the Torth categorically rejected. Ultimately, slave species would outlast the Torth Empire. Their lives were infinitely richer than the lives of a trillion Torth. They had friends. They knew love. Those were the qualities that built civilizations.

The Torth could only steal what other species created.

"You…are superior," he realized.

Cherise did not understand what he was referring to, but she knew that it was a fact. She silently acknowledged it.

They balanced over the abyss, inch by inch, foot by foot, and yard by yard.

After an eternity, there was a babble of relieved voices from below.

"Is that Cherise?"

"She made it!"

"With the Teacher?"

Cherise slid down the last few feet, and there were cheers and relieved laughter in the darkness. Minuscule lights flickered on and off as people toggled their glove displays. Kessa wore Thomas's wristwatch.

"He kept us safe!"

"She is so brave!"

"It is a miracle!"

The overlapped voices were a disorderly mess, in contrast with the synchronized harmonies of mind readers. It would sound ugly to a Torth. Yet Thomas sensed an emotional undercurrent that was stronger, more organic, and more beautiful than a quorum of Torth.

Cherise unfastened the knots. "I need a rest."

"The Teacher is protecting us." Pung handed his supply pack to another stoic ummin. "I can take a turn carrying him."

Thomas wanted to spend more time with Cherise. He could hardly put his awe into words. Cherise had saved his life. She had done it as surely as a heroine out of a story…and she'd done it by talking.

Amazing.

For the first time since leaving Earth, Thomas permitted a smile on his face. It felt alien yet familiar. As Pung hoisted him into a harness, he faced Cherise. "Thank you," he managed to say to her.

Cherise had no return smile to offer; no warmth for the former friend who had betrayed her. "You know what I see when I look at you?" she said. "A boy who's lost everything. You have nothing to live for. I guess that's why you're so ready to abandon us."

She had always seen truths. She would not respect Thomas as long as he remained weak, untrustworthy, and uninvested in the people she cared about.

That was fair.

Thomas started to tell her that he was grateful, and that he understood, and that he was willing to try again. But Cherise walked away. A freezing barrier went up in her mind.

"We are even," she said.

# CHAPTER 6

# SPECTERS IN RUINS

Kessa was beginning to doubt that Jonathan Stead—and a thousand escaped slaves—had managed to survive in this frigid, dark swamp of endless ruins. Even with Yeresunsa powers to keep them alive, they would have needed to steal a lot of survival supplies.

From where?

And then Jonathan Stead had stolen a ship so he could fly home to the paradise known as Earth. He'd left the escapees stranded here. Alone. In the dark.

Those liberated slaves could not have grown old here, or had descendants, Kessa was sure. They must have fallen prey to wild zoved and sludge serpents.

Kessa and her people had tried to sleep, with everyone curled in a big heap. It was too uncomfortable, wet and cold, with everyone crushing one another. No one had slept much.

So they hiked.

They rested.

They hiked.

"Do you hear those voices?" Ariock sounded feverish.

Weptolyso snorted in a questioning tone.

Kessa listened. Maybe she heard carnivores gnawing on bones; maybe she heard the wind sawing past eroded struts.

"Never mind," Ariock said.

"What do you hear?" Kessa asked.

"I thought I heard whispers in the darkness. Like people whispering." He gestured. "There."

Kessa stared at the ruined skyscraper where he'd pointed. Sludge stalactites hung from the bare beams, hiding whatever might be within.

Not people, of course. That would be insane.

The hushed, whispery sounds might just be rainfall, but it did almost sound like conversations in an alien tongue. Kessa held her breath, trying to discern words.

"Does this place look familiar to you?" Ariock asked.

Kessa eyed him sideways. She suspected that Ariock had pushed himself well past any sane limit of endurance. He must be as feverish as Vy.

"I've been here before," Ariock mumbled.

Everyone sounded as if they were setting down their burdens. The load bearers must be nearing their limits of endurance, as well. Weptolyso looked as exhausted as Kessa felt, with drooping spikes and slumped shoulders. He had not uttered a single complaint, yet his short legs were not built for slogging through muck and across slippery boulders.

"Let's rest," Kessa said.

This trek was killing everyone. Kessa could imagine them all, including herself, becoming just a bunch of squishy corpses.

She sought Thomas in the gloom.

Irarjeg sat on debris, having removed the harness with Thomas. He had propped up the mind reader nearby.

"Thomas." Kessa sat next to him.

Thomas was close enough to read her mind, so she shouldn't need to explain what was needed or why their situation was dire. But his eyes were closed. He looked worse off than many of the injured refugees.

She kept her voice low and even. At least no one else nearby would understand her words in the human tongue. "Why don't either of you have your powers back yet?"

Thomas muttered something inaudible.

"We have been hiking for at least two wake cycles," Kessa said. "Maybe three." That was an estimate, but as a slave, Kessa thought she could judge work shifts.

They had run out of water maybe two or three work shifts ago, by Kessa's reckoning. The human types were always thirsty.

"You should have your powers by now," Kessa pointed out. "Can you try to spread your awareness?"

Thomas opened his eyes as if his eyelids were the heaviest things in existence. "Our powers," he said, "are connected to our health."

His eyes began to slide closed again.

Kessa shook him gently, until his iridescent-yellow gaze focused on her, brighter than anything in the darkness.

"So you can't use your powers?"

"No."

"When will Ariock recover?"

"He won't." Thomas spoke with his eyes closed, wheezing slightly. "I told you. He took a direct blaster hit in the chest. It's amazing he's alive at all."

Kessa prepared to ask if they were heading in the right direction. Down in this chasm, ruins and rain hid the Stratower from view much of the time. Whenever she did glimpse the monstrous building, it was the same unchanging size, an unfathomable distance away.

"Blaster gloves!" someone whispered fiercely.

Kessa heard refugees yank on their blaster gloves and crowd closer. They had learned, after several attacks from sludge serpents, that certain ummins were better lookouts than others. The lookouts rotated on the outskirts of their group. The most steadfast of those—the ones who kept their wits in the face of danger—were privileged with weapons.

Irarjeg got to his feet, yanking on his own blaster glove. "Light?"

Kessa flashed the wristwatch light. It was more powerful than any of the glove displays.

What she saw sent shock waves of icy fear through her system.

This was not a single pack of thirty to fifty wild zoved. The ruins writhed with the thin, shadowy figures. Predators moved everywhere the light touched. This was a massive horde of hunger, perhaps even larger than the swarm that had driven away the Torth.

Everyone brandished weapons or got ready to throw things. Cherise wielded the ionic knife.

As Kessa swept her feeble light over their doom, something unexpected caught her focus, and she stopped.

She moved the light back to that gaping wound in a tower, unable to believe what she'd seen.

Now there was only empty blackness.

She must have imagined those three upright Torth-like figures wrapped in black bandages from head to foot. Exhaustion and fear must be doing strange things to her exhausted mind. It was like the rainfall whispers.

A wild zoved lunged toward the refugees, jaws wide, lips peeled back in savagery.

That seemed to signal the rest of the horde. Wild zoved threw themselves at terrified ummins, jaws snapping, drool flying.

"They're going for Ariock!" Thomas cried out. "I can't stop them."

On the tower top, the wild zoved had devoured nussian corpses faster than anything else. It seemed they liked prey that was large and weakened. Like Ariock.

He sat on rubble, and Kessa knew that there was no more fight left in him. Ariock could not push himself any farther.

Refugees were splashing, fighting desperately, seizing rubble and hurling it. They tossed away supply packs so they could dodge or fight. A few had the presence of mind to swing empty canteens or other solid objects, but such weapons would not fend off the wild zoved for long.

Kessa lost sight of what was happening. She was too short. She clutched Thomas's medicine case for use as a shield, discarded everything else, and tried to weave her way toward Ariock.

Jaws snapped at her. She smashed a beast on its ugly snout and spun to fend off the next attack.

Teeth sank into the refugee next to her. That ummin screamed.

Muck splashed on her. No, too warm to be muck. It was blood.

A piercing wail dominated the battle. That sounded like Cherise, but she was anguished beyond reason. Vy must be under attack.

A refugee fell, helpless with his throat torn open, blood gushing out. Kessa whirled and slammed the case against a lunging, filthy, evil beast.

Time seemed to speed up. To Kessa, the battle turned in a strange way, and events happened in quick succession that she could neither understand nor explain.

A nearby carnivore fell in midlunge. Then another. Others trampled them, flattening them in muck puddles. They began to tear their fellows apart—but then they fell, too, with poles sticking up from their backs. The hafts quivered as if someone very strong had just impaled these wild zoved.

But no one in sight could have done such a thing.

Refugees twisted around in confusion. Between them, more and more wild zoved fell, pierced by sharp objects that arrowed out of the night, too fast to see.

Wind whistled. More creatures got impaled.

Kessa peered into the darkness, trying to see who was throwing with such impressive accuracy and bullet-fast speed. She half expected to see armored Torth. But there were no headlamps, no transports, no blaster gloves.

She nearly tripped over a corpse. Everything around her was a pile of death, mostly wild zoved.

The remainder of the horde finally whirled away and scampered into darkness. They had expected easy prey, not a real battle.

Kessa studied one of the quivering spears that pinned a dead creature to another corpse. She glanced down at her own torso, amazed that none of the ultrafast spears had hit her.

She did not see any wasted spears. Not one had missed a target. Every throw had apparently been aimed to kill a wild zoved, and all had succeeded.

There were many dozens of kills. More than one hundred.

And the slaughter had happened within a span of seconds.

Four figures approached out of the rainy darkness, so black they were as hard to see as sludge serpents. They moved like slender, diminutive Torth or humans.

"Are there mind readers among you?" one of the strangers called in a threatening tone.

She sounded human, but her version of the slave tongue was unusual, with a dainty accent.

Kessa did not lower the medicine case from the shield position. The Torth Homeworld was a planet of monstrosities. Bandages wrapped these strangers from head to foot, so they were indistinguishable from each other, as messy and obscure as the ruins.

The wild zoved feared them. Perhaps Kessa should fear them, as well.

# CHAPTER 7

# LUMINOUS PURPLE

Cherise knelt next to the mangled remains of Dugwon.

The battle had ended in an abrupt and unexpected victory. Yet no one was celebrating, and Cherise found it impossible to care who their rescuers were. The strange rescuers called out in the slave tongue, their accents full of flair. They sounded delicate and mushy.

"Do any of you belong to a mind reader?"

"Do you serve a Torth?"

"Point to the Torth among you."

The strangers looked humanoid, despite their dripping black bandages. If they were Torth, then they were unusual Torth, to ask questions out loud.

The traumatized refugees gave confused answers, unsure what the humanoids wanted to hear.

Not that any of that mattered to Cherise. She gripped the ionic knife by its hilt, too furious at herself to sheathe the blade. She had failed to protect Dugwon. She wasn't strong enough. She wasn't tough enough. With her human-length arms, she should have sliced more than a few wild zoved—but she'd been too afraid she might strike her friend by accident.

The quarters were so close. The creatures had attacked so suddenly. A nightmarish ape had sunk its teeth into Dugwon, and then a second wild zoved had ripped out her friend's throat.

Maybe Pung was right about the gods. He called them uncaring Torth, if they existed at all. They had allowed beasts to savage someone sweet and gentle, an ummin who had shown compassion to a human girl who must look like a monstrous slave owner.

If Cherise couldn't blame the gods, then she had to blame herself. She was a useless, pathetic nobody.

And she had failed to protect Thomas, as well. He had fallen over. There was a smudge on his forehead, possibly a bruise, and he looked asleep or unconscious. Had he gotten trampled during the heat of battle?

"Move away from that Torth," one of the strangers demanded, seeing Irarjeg gently pull Thomas into a seated position, cradling his head. Thomas's neck muscles weren't working. He had trouble moving his head even when he was awake.

He was definitely out of it.

"We will get rid of these Torth for you," another stranger said.

Surviving refugees jumped in front of Cherise and the other humans. They locked their arms to form a protective barrier around Cherise and Vy, as well as Ariock and Thomas.

Everyone was plastered with grime, but the smidges of skin that were exposed on Vy looked like the wrong color. Too chalky. She was asleep or unconscious.

Ariock was in bad shape as well. He slumped on the filthy ground, supporting himself with two hands, since his arm sling had slipped off. He looked like he was struggling with all his might not to keel all the way over.

Cherise was the only one of them standing.

"Expose your Torth," the most commanding of the strangers said. "This is our final warning."

She sounded hot-tempered, like a gang boss. The other three strangers trotted around, grabbing blaster gloves off refugees. Ummins yelped and surrendered far too easily.

"We have no Torth among us," Kessa said in a clear, firm voice.

The strangers whispered to each other in an alien language. If they found it necessary to communicate out loud, then they couldn't be mind readers.

"Our human friends resemble Torth," Kessa admitted. "But they are runaway slaves, just like we are."

Cherise squinted through the rain, trying to see if there were any other hidden attackers.

One of the shadowy strangers drew a wickedly curved blade. The three others shouted foreign words, but the lone attacker moved inhumanly fast toward Vy's head, sickle blade held at a murderous angle.

Weptolyso prepared to swing a dented chunk of debris, but he couldn't possibly match the speed of this attacker.

Cherise threw herself in front of Vy with a primal scream. She would not let another friend get torn up like Dugwon.

Her ionic blade flashed as she stabbed blindly. Not even dead city mucus could stick to its glossy surface. It shed whatever liquids it encountered.

The assailant stopped a few scant inches from Cherise.

"Stop!" Kessa yelled in a desperate tone.

The wavy-edged blade sliced through something solid, as easily as parting slime.

Something splashed into a muck puddle.

Cherise visually followed the line of her taut arm, blinking away raindrops, afraid of what she had done. The ionic blade could cut through flesh and bone without any effort.

Her gaze connected with shocked-looking purple eyes. Black wraps hid everything else about the humanoid stranger, but it had large eyes. Those eyes seemed to gather every shred of light from the dimly lit clouds.

Cherise's blade had sliced clean through a black scimitar.

All the stranger held now was a useless stub.

"What kind of weapon is that?" her assailant asked. He sounded like a young man, although he was barely a few inches taller than Cherise.

"It belonged to a Torth. Now it's mine." Cherise jammed the ionic blade into its ultradense sheath. She backed out of reach, unwilling to let the assailant disarm her.

The strange man sized her up with those pale, luminous eyes, and Cherise guessed he was trying to discern what she was. She wore eyeglasses and rain-drenched rags that leeched too much warmth from her thin body.

Most people mistook Cherise for a Brown Rank. But a Torth of any rank would have to be crazy to wander this far from the comforts of Stratower City, especially dressed as she was. Torth did not allow themselves to suffer.

These strangers ought to know that.

Any Torth with such grave injuries as Vy and Ariock would be airlifted to a biotech hospital, where they would receive the best medical care in the galaxy. And someone as fragile as Thomas would never venture into this hellhole.

Anyhow, who were these strangers, to be so judgmental? They could be Torth themselves. Although they seemed too at home in the dead city, like sludge serpents. Their eyes were a strange, luminous purple. Torth never used that color.

Then again, Thomas used to have plum-colored eyes before he'd become a Yellow Rank. Cherise used to associate his unusual eye color with his supernatural ability.

Ariock's eyes were also purple.

"Are you…" Cherise considered how efficient these people were at killing. "…Yeresunsa?" she dared to ask.

All four of the strangers looked shocked. Wraps hid their faces, but luminous purple eyes blinked in inky blackness.

"How do you know that word?" her assailant demanded.

"I don't think they are Torth," another stranger whispered.

"What is a human?" another asked.

The strangers huddled to exchange more whispers. They spoke at least two languages, the slave tongue and something else. Maybe they came from a hidden and unknown slave farm?

Cherise discarded that guess. Torth never permitted slaves to touch weapons. Whoever these strangers were, they were neither Torth nor slaves. They were anomalies in the Torth-ruled galaxy—like Cherise and her friends.

"We are running from the Torth," Kessa said in a ragged tone that begged to be believed. "They are hunting us."

Cherise was cold and miserable and very exhausted and thirsty. If these strangers were going to attack again, she doubted that she could keep fending them off.

"Please," she begged the stranger who had almost killed her. "Don't hurt us."

He looked pained, as if he regretted his attack. Maybe he was actually sympathetic.

The other strangers took on more relaxed, less guarded stances. When one barked a command in their foreign tongue, Cherise half expected a peace offering. Maybe an apology.

She was wrong.

Black cloth unraveled from each of the strange warriors. They remained swaddled in mummy wraps, but part of their wraps rippled away, flying through the rainy night like shadows that had gotten detached from their owners.

One cloth smacked against Thomas's unconscious form. It instantly snaked around his head, as creepy and autonomous as a grabber ball.

Another cloth wended its way around Ariock's huge head. "Hey!" Ariock clawed at the thing that was blindfolding him and cutting off his hearing.

The strangers each had one arm outstretched, fingers spread, as if controlling something invisible. The intensity in their luminous eyes was similar to how Ariock looked when he was conducting a storm.

Cherise knew, judging by the way the cloth ribbons reacted to their fingers, that they were using powers. They controlled the blindfolds.

They were Yeresunsa.

"Please stop!" Kessa said. "Those are our friends. They mean you no harm!"

One of the strangers gave a dismissive reply. "Quiet, ummin."

Another said, "We won't harm them. But they require evaluation."

Vy moaned as a black wrap began to twist around her head, cutting off her vision. It slid around her ears. She couldn't be fully cognizant of what was happening, since she was burning up with fever and pain.

Cherise drew breath to speak. She must convince these strangers that she could be trusted, no matter what she looked like.

Before she could say a word, a rain-drenched cloth slapped her in the face.

She tried to speak, but the cloth wound under her jaw, then over her hair. It tightened, crisscrossing her eyes and ears. Sounds grew muffled. The patter of rain faded away. Cloth wrapped under her nose, smelling like wet cotton with a musty odor.

Cherise resisted her instincts to fight and scream. She forced her hand to let go of the ionic blade's hilt. If she used that blade to slice away the blindfold, she would likely slice off her own nose along with the wrap.

Her captors were Yeresunsa.

She had tried to protect Vy. She had begged for mercy. She had destroyed the blade of her attacker. If none of that was enough...

Cherise listened to cottony silence, which was all she could hear. Her eyelids pressed against cloth. She couldn't see.

But that was okay. Kessa saw what was happening.

Cherise had suffered some major betrayals in her life, but never from an ummin. She inwardly calmed herself. The Code of Gwat entailed a constant reevaluation of everything one perceived, somewhat like the way an artist viewed things. Kessa had sharp eyes. If anyone could get them out of this situation, it was an ummin elder who had spent a lifetime analyzing reality and asking questions.

# CHAPTER 8

# WHEN WORLDS COLLIDE

Kessa shivered in the cold rain, blinking away weariness. She had believed—well, Thomas had believed, the whole Torth Empire had believed—that only two Yeresunsa existed in the universe.

So everyone was wrong.

There were other Yeresunsa, and they survived in secret in the worst place: in the rotten heart of the Torth Empire.

"Filthy cannibals," one of the black-swaddled Yeresunsa commented as he faced a pile of dead wild zoved. He used powers to pluck spears out of the corpses. The spears levitated in midair, one after the other, and the warrior grabbed them. He added them to others in the quiver on his back.

These four black-swaddled warriors—only four!—had very quickly slain more than twenty times their number of wild zoved. They might have killed even more if the horde had not fled. Their agile, fluid way of moving made her suspect that they had stalked her group for a while, undetected.

"Do any of you serve a Torth master?" This warrior had an unsympathetic voice, and she seemed to be their leader. "Answer truthfully."

"We have told you," Kessa said. "None of us serve Torth. We are fleeing them." She gestured toward her human friends. "Please let our friends see and hear. They are no threat to you."

One of the warriors made a derisive snort. "That one sounds like a slave."

Kessa clicked her beak in annoyance. If she were a slave, she would not dare speak out loud.

Anyone could see how ragged and injured the humans looked. Even if they were secretly mind readers, they were clearly in exile, unwelcome among Torth.

Pung joined in. "Have you seen the transports flying overhead? Those are Torth, hunting us!"

The warriors paused in their activities. They exchanged glances full of unspoken concerns and worries.

They had no problem showing off their powers, so why were they cautious? What were they afraid of?

"Who among you needs medical attention?" the lead warrior asked. "Point them out."

Tentative hands raised. Two of the warriors headed toward injured ummins, apparently willing to provide medical aid.

"Do you have healing powers?" Kessa stood. "Heal Ariock and Vy, please! And Thomas!"

Refugees pointed them out. The black-swaddled warriors shied away, clearly unwilling to get within range of someone who might possibly read their minds, no matter how injured or unconscious those victims were. They refused to tend to Ariock, Vy, or Thomas.

"We have some pure water for drinking and cleaning," the lead warrior said, her voice cold and unsympathetic. "Let us know if you need it."

Voices begged. The refugees wanted water and also blankets or anything that could ward off the chilly wetness of the dead city. They wanted food. They wanted shelter, if such a thing was possible. They begged for any aid these wonderful strangers might be willing to give.

The lead warrior's luminescent gaze swept over the refugees. "Which one of you is in charge?"

Refugees pointed toward Kessa before she could decide on an answer.

"That is Kessa the Wise."

"She is our chief."

Kessa tried not to act surprised by the grandiose titles her friends gave her. Even Weptolyso joined in, as if he'd forgotten that he used to be her hall guard.

The lead warrior approached Kessa, lithe and deadly-looking. Inkiness and dripping wraps hid her face and body, leaving only her luminous eyes visible.

"An ummin," she said, "in charge of Torth?" She sounded skeptical. "This is something I have never heard of. Tell me truthfully." She swept a gesture toward Ariock. "Does that gigantic…whatever he is…obey you?"

Kessa stood her ground. The strangers spoke like a gang of slaves, yet that might be deceptive behavior. The Torth Homeworld was full of monsters. These strange warriors might be incapable of smiling or frowning beneath their wraps.

"My *friends* respect me," Kessa said, emphasizing her word choice. "None of us are Torth."

The one in charge sized up the blindfolded victims, particularly Ariock. She plainly mistrusted them. "Where do you come from?" She blurted the question, as if it had been bothering her. "You are not Alashani, are you?"

Kessa tried to identify that word, but she had never heard it before. "No." She paused, unable to guess how grand, or how limited, the strangers were, in terms of knowledge. She decided to test a theory by offering a vague answer.

The warriors would figure out the rest…or not, depending on how much they understood about the universe.

"We come from another world," she said.

The lead warrior contemplated that reply with gravity. She seemed greatly troubled. "We have never seen a group like yours before."

"But you have met other runaways?" Kessa asked, curious in spite of everything. These warriors might have some idea of what had happened to the escaped prisoners freed by Jonathan Stead, so many generations ago.

"Yes." The lead warrior rested her arm on her sickle-shaped sword. "Our ancestors have encountered runaway slaves. It is very uncommon."

Kessa supposed that few runaways might survive in the dead city. Not for long. These warriors must have a shelter. Their layers of wraps clearly kept them warm, and probably dry as well. They might have quite a lot to offer.

Her hope surged when she noticed one of the warriors kneel next to a wounded ummin, and tiny sparks twinkled in the darkness. That was definitely healing magic. The air always writhed like that, crackling like static electricity, whenever Ariock healed someone.

The ummin sat up, amazed and much healthier.

"Please." Kessa resisted an urge to drop to her knees. She was exhausted, swaying from weariness, but she went on. "Please believe that our friends, the ones whom you've blindfolded, are harmless. They need healing."

"You sound like a slave." The lead warrior hardened her voice. "Are you a slave defending her master?"

Kessa met the warrior's gaze. She had been called crazy before, but somehow, this accusation—being called a slave—was far more insulting. The scar around her neck prickled.

"I will never be a slave again," Kessa stated. "My friends are Ariock, Thomas, Cherise, and Vy. They are my friends, not my masters. We have suffered together."

Pung brushed himself off. "Do you really think we're a bunch of slaves and Torth, out for a pleasure stroll?" he demanded. "Look. We are not wearing collars." He raised his beak, displaying the scar around his neck. "And what sort of Torth would allow their slaves to wear blaster gloves?"

Purple gazes flicked toward each other. The warriors looked a lot less certain.

"Torth are liars," one of the warriors suggested. "They will say anything to save themselves."

Refugees began to call out. "Cherise is not a Torth!"

"They're humans!"

"Worth saving!"

"Ariock almost died in his fight to protect us!"

"Thomas got us away from Duin!"

"Yeah! And he kept the wild zoved from killing us!"

Weptolyso fanned out his shoulder spikes. "If you want to kill the Son of Storms, you will have to kill me first. I am not his bodyguard. I am his friend."

The four warriors whispered and chattered in their foreign tongue. They sounded unsure of how to proceed.

When the lead warrior faced Kessa again, she sounded more friendly. "I am Jinishta, also known as the premier Yeresunsa of Hufti. These are Haz, Flen, and Nulshta." She gestured to her fellow warriors. "Your followers named you Kessa?" She paused, giving Kessa time to reject or accept the name.

Kessa considered offering her full, formal name: Kessatovtalun. She had shared it with Pung and Weptolyso, and also with Vy and Cherise, and Delia, when she was alive.

But such a secret was a gift.

"I am Kessa," she said.

Jinishta went on. "We are willing to help you and your people, Kessa. But we will not help *Torth*." Her tone twisted on that word, as if it was a curse. "And we do not help slaves. If you are loyal to Torth, we will turn our backs right now."

Kessa tried to suppress her wild hope. "We are enemies of the Torth."

Jinishta observed her warriors going around, healing ummins. "One of your so-called humans used the word *Yeresunsa*," she told Kessa. "Do you understand what that means?"

"You have powers," Kessa said.

"Yes." Jinishta opened her black-wrapped hand, and electricity flashed above her palm in crackling ropes. "How do you know about us, if you are not Alashani?"

The question caught Kessa off guard. She ran through potential answers and possible outcomes.

Pung began to answer. "We know about Yeresunsa because two of our friends—"

Kessa nearly clamped a hand over his beak. No doubt Pung was impatient to receive whatever hospitality these Yeresunsa could offer, but he had forgotten how dangerous they were.

She couldn't silence Pung in front of Jinishta. That would look suspicious. Instead, Kessa raised her voice, pretending to dominate the discussion. "One of us is a Yeresunsa." Kessa emphasized the singular word, determined to make Pung catch on.

He looked confused.

Kessa flicked her gaze toward Thomas's prone form.

Comprehension came over Pung as he remembered that these warriors labeled any mind reader as a deadly threat. Thomas behaved far more like a Torth than anyone else in their group. He never told lies. He would give away his ability the instant he woke up and said anything. At all.

So he needed stealth. He needed to seem as harmless and powerless as possible, for as long as possible.

Jinishta was so astonished by what Kessa had said, she reared back, completely missing the unspoken subtext between Pung and Kessa.

"One of you has powers?" She surveyed the refugees with fresh purpose and disbelief. "Which one? How is that possible?"

Ariock's powers could not remain a secret for long. Nearly one hundred and fifty refugees from Duin had survived the crash landing and the battles. Kessa had not had time to count the exact number of survivors. But they would talk. Grateful to be rescued, the refugees would undoubtedly tell their rescuers about Ariock and his storm powers. They'd reveal everything—unless Kessa got a chance to whisper in their ears about Thomas, and soon.

So she made no protest when some refugees pointed to the blindfolded giant. "Ariock," they said.

Ariock was yanking at the bandages with one huge, dripping hand. He exuded menace, even damaged as he was, due to his sheer size.

The warriors rested their hands on the hilts of their black scimitars, wary. Cherise's stalled attack must be fresh in their minds.

The one whose scimitar was destroyed reached for a throwing spear.

"Ariock is our friend!" Kessa pleaded. "He has saved our lives many times. Please let him live."

"That is a Yeresunsa?" Jinishta sounded disbelieving. "That thing cannot be Alashani."

"He is a human," Kessa said with frustration. "From Earth."

She mentioned the world of paradise only because it sounded like it could be a foreign slave farm. It made Ariock sound as if he came from somewhere, like he was a member of a slave species.

Jinishta stared at her with shocked, round eyes.

All the warriors froze in what seemed like surprise.

"That's right!" Pung leaped in, seeing how they'd reacted. "All the humans are from Earth."

"Earth?" Jinishta said with wonder.

Their knowledge of that distant world seemed unlikely, unless...

"Have you heard of Jonathan Stead?" Kessa asked.

All four of the warriors exchanged covert looks and a flurry of urgent whispers. Kessa discerned recognizable words in their mushy language. "Jonathan Stead," and "Earth," and "Yeresunsa." They seemed agitated, and they kept glancing at Ariock with incredulous eyes.

Maybe Kessa should risk telling them that Ariock was the direct descendant of Jonathan Stead?

Weptolyso tore the blindfold off Ariock's head. "This is Ariock, the Son of Storms," he proclaimed. "He is severely wounded because the Torth tried to kill him a lot of times. They shot him with a blaster glove." He pointed to the blanket that covered Ariock's chest and shoulder. "He is badly wounded, here."

The warriors looked awestruck.

To Kessa's astonishment, three of them began to chant in their foreign language. Their voices synced up, as if in song or prayer. They stared at Ariock as though he was a legend come to life.

Jinishta snapped at her colleagues, and they broke off their chant.

"Will you please heal him?" Kessa begged in the temporary silence.

Jinishta looked deeply troubled. Meanwhile, her colleagues spoke over each other, voices rising and falling in argument.

"This decision is too big for me," Jinishta said at last. She sounded angry about it. "I must present him to the council."

"What is the council?" Kessa asked.

Jinishta ignored her question. "I see that you are sick and miserable, Kessa. I want to help you. But I must ask again. None of your companions owns you, or claims you as property? You do not serve any of them? You are a free person, and not a slave?"

"Yes," Kessa said with pride. "I am free. I serve no master."

The pale gaze bored into Kessa. "And none of you can read minds?"

A few bedraggled refugees glanced toward Thomas. Pung spread his arms to block the warriors from shooting at him.

Kessa held her breath. If she claimed that Thomas was a nontelepathic human—if she said it loud enough—would every single refugee play along?

No. Too many knew about Thomas's abilities. Too many would talk. Thomas himself had a way of stating truths that angered people.

The truth, then. That was Kessa's only viable option.

She chose her words with care. "You survive by keeping secrets from mind readers?" she guessed.

When Jinishta did not argue the point, Kessa went on.

"Thomas is our friend. I trust him with my life. He has killed many Torth, and he has protected us on several occasions. Everyone here will tell you that is our friend. But..." Kessa braced herself for a reaction. "He can read minds."

The warriors gasped. One of them grabbed his blade only to realize it was a stub, thanks to Cherise's attack.

"Thomas is our friend," Weptolyso said in a dangerous tone.

"We will stand in your way if you try to harm him," Kessa said. "I am sorry, but his fate is bound to ours. He alone can guide us to other worlds. We absolutely need him."

Kessa stopped herself from saying more. Any attempt to detail her journey, while she was shivering and drenched by rain and blood and muck, would not help her credibility, or her dignity. She would come across like a desperately babbling slave, lacking in self-awareness. What she'd said would have to be enough.

Jinishta held up her hand and spoke in her unknown language. Her colleagues subsided, glaring toward the withered boy with hatred.

"There is only this one mind reader among you?" Jinishta asked. "Only that child?"

"Yes," Kessa said, through her shivers. "This I swear."

"And you trust him?"

Kessa chose to ignore Jinishta's condescending tone. "Very much. He risked his life to save my friends, and me."

Jinishta straightened and barked orders to her colleagues. The dripping wraps began to unwind from the heads of Cherise and Vy.

"The blindfold stays on the mind reader," Jinishta stated to Kessa. "None of you may communicate with him. You will stay out of his range of telepathy. That means none of you go near him. Tell your people. If anyone attempts to provide him with information, I will have no choice but to kill him."

Kessa considered how to gently ask for water for Thomas. Anyone could see how fragile he was.

"We will keep him alive, for now," Jinishta said, seeing Kessa's concern. "The council will decide his fate." She saw that Kessa still wanted to argue, and she added, "Understand that you have asked far more than you have any right to ask. The only reason I am allowing that Torth to live"—she gestured—"is because of the way you all pleaded for his life."

Kessa bowed her head. Although she did not have the strength of a warrior, she recognized mercy. "Thank you."

Jinishta hefted her scimitar, then let it fall back into its carrying hoop. "If any of you have lied," she said, "or if you are mistaken, my people will hold me responsible. But I will blame you. And I won't care about your reasons. First I will kill your owner, and then I will make you suffer. You will die in more pain than if you were torn apart by cannibals."

It was a promise. Kessa saw icy hardness in Jinishta's eyes.

Thomas would need to remain blinded and deafened for a while. He needed to feign unconsciousness, if he wasn't already doing so.

*One step at a time*, Kessa told herself. Her people needed help. Once they were safe, then, somehow, she would figure out how to persuade these powerful warriors that one mind reader could be trusted.

# CHAPTER 9

# CRY OF SALVATION

Refugees gathered their ragged belongings, eager to follow the Yeresunsa strangers to whatever shelter they might offer. The half-eaten dead would be left behind to rot. Again.

Cherise flinched when something draped over her shoulders. A blanket. Was someone pretending to care about her?

"This will keep you warm," Kessa said.

Kessa had removed the wrap from her own shoulders. She tucked it around Cherise, and Cherise remembered that not everyone was a faker. Her abusive mother was light-years away, in prison.

For the first time in what must be days, Cherise stopped shivering.

"I am sorry about Dugwon." Kessa wrapped thin arms around Cherise.

The fact that Kessa was here at all…that she cared… Cherise could not remember the last time she'd felt so well cared for. She melted against the ummin elder. Her sense of loss came out in helpless sobs.

Kessa rested her beak on top of Cherise's hair. She said nothing at first. She waited for the worst of Cherise's pain to come out.

After a while, Kessa said, "Here. Drink this water." She offered a thin flask that was wrapped in black cloth. "The Yeresunsa warriors gave it to us."

A sip of pure water revived Cherise more than she thought possible.

"We have to go." Kessa stood. "I am sorry, but this is not a place to mourn." She gestured at the heaped carcasses. "Scavengers will want to feast, and the Torth may notice and investigate. We cannot stay here."

Cherise understood how common death was among slaves. Kessa had never heard of funerals or burials. The deceased were garbage. Even so, Cherise hesitated. To leave the remains of Dugwon seemed like she was abandoning her friend in another way. She didn't want to reward this nasty planet by callously walking away.

The warrior with the broken scimitar beckoned for them to hurry. The whole group was in motion.

Cherise tried to recall what people said at funerals. Was there a prayer for losing a friend?

"Does the Code of Gwat give a guide for mourning?" Cherise asked.

Kessa clasped her hand. "Dugwon can no longer be with us. But we will remember her."

Cherise supposed the simplicity was practical.

"I am sorry, Cherise," Kessa said.

But there were living people to worry about. Cherise understood. Her foster sister was slung over one of Weptolyso's huge shoulders. Ariock wasn't in much better shape. He moved with painful slowness, and the nussian watched him, ready to catch him if he fell.

As for Thomas…

Cherise made a strangled noise of surprise. Thomas hovered in midair, horizontal, as if held aloft on an invisible platform. Muck dripped from his supine form. The enormous bundle of swaddling around his head made him look very much like a mutant.

Kessa's beak fell open.

A warrior focused on Thomas, apparently levitating him. Cherise recognized the Yeresunsa stare. She had seen the same glowing intensity in Ariock's eyes.

Cherise rushed toward Thomas. "Can he breathe in all that cloth? You've got to be careful with him. He's fragile!"

Another warrior casually blocked her path with one black-clad arm. It was the one with broken scimitar.

"You can't kill him!" Cherise begged.

"The *rekveh* can breathe through its mouth," the warrior said in a reassuring tone. "We left its jaw loose."

Indeed, Thomas's mouth hung slightly open beneath the mass of wraps.

Cherise turned to study the black-swaddled warrior. He spoke the slave tongue well enough, albeit with an accent. And with strange words. "What did you call him?" she asked.

"*Rekveh.*" The warrior made it sound offensive. "That is our word for evil. It means Torth. Or someone with the vile mental abilities of a Torth." He indicated her weapon. "May I examine it?"

Cherise placed a protective hand over the dagger's hilt. The warrior would probably steal her weapon, since he needed a replacement for his broken scimitar.

Then again, if these Yeresunsa wanted to steal from her, they could do so easily. They did not need to ask for permission.

"This weapon used to belong to Thomas." Cherise handed over the ionic blade. "He isn't evil. He's on our side."

Reflected light from clouds danced on the glassy blade, which then danced in the warrior's luminescent eyes. "It's beautiful." He eyed Cherise with the same caution he had used in handling the blade. "Is that why it's yours?"

"Uh…" Cherise was flustered. She didn't believe this polite warrior was actually complimenting her. She needed to figure out what he wanted.

"Your name is Cherise, I take it?" the warrior said. "That is what your companions call you. My name is Flen."

"Peace, Flen." Cherise automatically used the standard greeting in the slave tongue.

"Peace." He seemed pleased. "Well, I suppose this knife is still yours." He handed it back to her. "I would like to study it further, when time permits. Would that be okay?"

Cherise had no ready answer to that.

"Let's get going." Flen began to walk. "I have so many questions for you, Cherise of Earth."

"So do I," Cherise admitted.

She bowed her head to the remains of Dugwon one last time. Inwardly, she let go of the idea of a funeral. She would rather remember Dugwon as alive than dead, anyway.

She forced her aching legs to walk.

They trudged through muck puddles. The Yeresunsa warriors moved with swift purpose, although they paused to offer a helping hand to any refugee who slowed down too much.

Except for Ariock. The warriors avoided him.

"The Son of Storms needs to be healed," Weptolyso grumbled. "So does Vy. You should not ignore them."

Other refugees added their voices. After a few minutes of listening to complaints, one of the warriors snapped, "Fine." She darted close to Ariock and raised her black-wrapped hands. "I will heal him, but my power is drained. You will have to be satisfied with this. Any larger healing must be conducted by someone else."

The air writhed and sparked over Ariock.

Finished, the healer danced back, as if she feared the giant might step on her, or read her mind.

Ariock straightened his posture. He still looked terrible, but he managed to step away from Weptolyso. "Thank you," he said in the slave tongue.

The healer looked sick, herself. The one named Flen wrapped his arm around her. "Are you all right, Nulshta?"

Nulshta leaned on him as she walked. "I'll recover." She sounded woozy, like someone who had overdosed on medication.

Ariock studied the warriors with interest. "Did they heal Vy?" he whispered.

"No," the nussian replied.

Ariock raised his hand, and Cherise knew what he was trying to do. She watched carefully and hoped to see tiny sparks of writhing air.

Instead, Ariock hissed in a breath of pain.

"You're worn-out." Weptolyso shifted Vy to a better position on his shoulder. "Give it time."

The warriors held one of their whispered conversations. They kept sizing up Ariock, unsure what to make of him. Cherise thought they were unnerved, but there was a strange element of fascination in their attitude toward him. They seemed unwilling to let him out of their sight.

Flen glided next to Cherise. "Your friend from Earth," he said. "Ariock. He can heal injuries?"

"Yes," Cherise said. "But the Torth shot him with inhibitor. He needs time to recover."

"I see." Flen sounded confident, but his eyes were brooding, full of unspoken concerns. "What is…inhibitor? Is that a Torth magic?"

Cherise tried to keep her balance on a stepping-stone. It was too slimy, and she splashed into the puddle, arms out to brace for a fall.

Flen caught her with ultrafast reflexes. Before she even registered how she'd regained her balance, Flen steadied her.

"Thank you." She guessed these warriors must see her as pathetically clumsy.

"You come from another world," Flen said. "I suppose it is a world with fewer puddles and more light?"

Cherise laughed a little bit at the innocent description of Earth. "Yes," she said. "And fewer wild zoved."

"Wild what?" Flen said. "You mean the cannibals?"

"Is that what you call those monsters?"

Flen gave her a suspicious, marveling look. "You really aren't from this world," he said. "The monsters that eat each other?" He made gnawing sounds to demonstrate, and Cherise nodded. "Yes," Flen said. "Those are cannibals. They aren't very intelligent, but they are *rekveh*, like Torth. Only they are much easier to kill."

"Flen." The lead warrior, Jinishta, cast a warning look over her shoulder.

Flen fell silent, and Cherise guessed that the warriors weren't supposed to get too friendly with people who might be *rekvehs*, or puppets of *rekvehs*.

The other male warrior, Haz, wore a look of intense focus as he used his powers to carry Thomas. The boy floated through the rainfall like a wraith. Refugees steered clear, giving Thomas a lot of space, and Cherise heard the warriors give repeated warnings. No one was allowed to get within the *rekveh*'s telepathy range. Doing so would infuriate Jinishta to the point of murder.

"We are in no shape to argue with these Yeresunsa warriors," refugees whispered to each other.

"Kessa will convince them to be reasonable."

"Or Ariock will."

If Jinishta overheard the whispers, she didn't care. She led the party through a crumbled area that might have once been a dense urban zone but was now a maze of collapsed ruins. Tired refugees were forced to pick their way through sludge-filled alleys, under stalactites and over slippery boulders. As far as Cherise could tell, they were going nowhere fast.

"How much farther do we have to walk?" she asked Flen.

"We are close to an entrance," he replied.

Cherise glanced at his black-wrapped form in the darkness, wondering if his people used an underground system to get from one place to another. During their long trek through the dead city, Cherise had heard foreign whispers under the sound of rain, but she'd dismissed the sounds as her overactive imagination.

Had Flen and his colleagues secretly watched her?

Had they silently stalked her group when the bridge collapsed? What about when they ran out of water? What about every time they stumbled in the dark, desperate for help?

"How long have you been following us?" Cherise forced her tone to stay casual, not accusatory.

"We weren't sure what you were," Flen said. "You looked like Torth and slaves."

"But we were speaking out loud," Cherise pointed out.

Flen's eyes looked embarrassed. "Yes. That is why we followed you for so long. You might have been runaways." He touched his scimitar and seemed surprised that it was just a broken hilt. "Jinishta pushed us to keep watching. She figured there was a chance you might be runaways in need of help. And she was right."

Cherise clambered over a boulder, grabbing slime-coated ruins to pull herself upward. "So your people normally help runaway slaves?"

"It is part of our purpose." Flen offered a supportive arm, so Cherise could keep her balance while sliding through a freezing culvert of slush. Nothing seemed to upset his balance. "When a slave makes an effort toward freedom, we extend our help. Quite a few ummins, and other enslaved species, live in freedom among us. We have a large population of nussians."

Cherise looked for any hint of deception. But Flen's eyes had a sweet, guileless look, and it made her very curious to see the rest of his face.

"What made you finally decide to help us?" she asked.

"Your voice," Flen said.

Cherise had to watch her footing, but she cast a sharp glance his way, almost certain that the warrior was making fun of her. She was Silent Cherise. Everyone at school had known that.

"No Torth would cry out loud, like you did," Flen said. "It is not in their nature."

Cherise remembered her anguished scream when Dugwon was ripped apart. She had thought her scream was useless.

"That is when we grew certain you were something different," Flen said. "We have seen Torth wander through this dead city. We take their heads as trophies. Sometimes we find them underdressed, or weaponless. Sometimes they have slaves with them. They might even give spoken commands. It is not unheard-of. But we have not seen anything like you."

Cherise touched her neck, glad that her head was still attached. "I am not a Torth." She felt a need to emphasize that fact.

"I understand that, now," Flen said with reassurance. He gently touched her arm. When she flinched at the unexpected touch, he quickly withdrew his hand, respecting the boundary she had shown. "I believe you, Cherise of Earth. You're just very peculiar."

He kept sneaking glances her way, plainly curious.

Jinishta led them into pitch blackness. The patter of rainfall faded as the group waded deep into a ruin, and Jinishta called over her shoulder, "Flen, will you light the way for our guests?"

Electricity crackled overhead. Miniature lightning zigged and zagged, forming a jittery glow overhead. It illuminated swampy debris, dilapidated pillars, and stalactites of muck.

Flen was making it happen. Cherise saw his outstretched arm, sparking with excess power. Ariock had done something similar, although his orb of electricity had looked a tad more masterful.

"Don't worry," Flen said. "I'm good at this. We normally go in the dark, but that's because we have powers to sense what's around us. I suppose you don't?"

"Right," Cherise said.

Damp ruins threw back the echoes of whispers, so it sounded like they were a thousand people instead of fewer than two hundred. Some of the conversations were about people they'd lost. Dugwon was not the only person to have died in the recent savagery. The refugees had lost ten friends from slashing claws and teeth.

That body count was worse than the losses they'd suffered after their crash. Their group's weakened condition was a heavy toll.

"Here we are," Flen said.

Ahead of them, Jinishta halted at the edge of a black scum pond. She faced an enormous squared-off boulder that rested against a far wall. Jinishta's luminous eyes fixed on the boulder, and judging by the stiff way she held her arms, Cherise knew that she was using powers.

Substantial powers.

The boulder must weigh several tons. Even so, Jinishta's power rolled it forward, sinking it deeper into the pond. Displaced liquid bubbled as it sank with deliberate care.

These Yeresunsa could hurl spears like bullets, move faster than ninjas, heal injuries, and manipulate electricity. But this heavy lifting was something Cherise would expect from someone the size of Ariock, not from Jinishta, who was as small as herself.

As the boulder moved away, it revealed the deteriorated wall it had leaned against. A rough opening in that wall looked just as decayed as most ruins in the dead city…except for the glow.

There must be oil lamps, or torches, around the corner.

The inviting glow looked otherworldly after such a long time in darkness.

The boulder realigned itself so that its flat top was level enough to walk on. It had been a barrier in disguise, now transformed to a causeway that led to another realm.

Jinishta sounded exhausted. "Nulshta, why don't you report our return? Tell them that you need a recovery rest." She hesitated. "You're going to need to speak to Chaniyelem. Tell her everything."

Nulshta jogged across the short causeway and through the ragged opening.

"Go." Jinishta stepped aside and gestured for others to cross the scum pond. "I will seal the doorway once everyone is through."

Cherise glanced back to see how Ariock was reacting to this latest display of Yeresunsa power.

He looked both inspired and wary. He could probably do everything that these warriors were capable of, but he was powerless right now. And judging by the way he looked at Thomas, still levitating and unconscious, he wasn't too happy about that situation.

"Are you ready?" Flen asked gently. He offered his black-wrapped hand to Cherise.

She had no idea what to expect next. So she accepted Flen's guiding hand and walked with him into an atmosphere that felt warm and dry—and infinitely nicer than the dead city downpour.

# CHAPTER 10

# HEADS

Ariock hated feeling so useless. His own bad decisions—his failures—had gotten everyone trapped in the dead city. It should be his responsibility to get them out.

So he would take whatever generosity these Yeresunsa strangers offered to him. After that brief healing, Ariock was ready for more. He still felt weak, exhausted, starved, and in horrendous pain…but where one healer existed, there might be more. A few dozen rounds of healing might actually make him strong again.

Then he'd be able to heal Vy.

Then he could figure out a way to bring his friends home to Earth, and maybe defend Earth from the Torth Empire. And then, maybe, he would actually become the hero everyone wanted him to be.

The passageway forced everyone to walk single file. Ariock had to hunch. Every time he passed a flickering torch on the wall, he edged carefully past it, unwilling to jar the blanket around his chest. Every motion hurt that wound.

Yeresunsa might have carved this tunnel using their powers. It curved downward in broad steps that looked engineered.

Ariock sighed in relief when the tunnel emptied into a vaulted, lamplit chamber with a soaring ceiling. He took a deep breath, glad to straighten his back…and he caught his breath when he noticed all the very human-looking skulls.

Yellowed skulls hung in clusters, impaled on spikes, arranged around the chamber like trees. Empty eyes sockets stared. Jawbones hung from attached wires.

Some of the skulls had mummified flesh attached. Those jaws hung agape, as if yawning or screaming.

One still had a face. It was blackened by rot, the eyes gone, but even without any telltale eye color, Ariock guessed the head had belonged to a Torth. The precise haircut gave it away. That was the level of grooming that a slave could provide.

"They say these are Torth they have slain." Kessa gestured to the spiked skulls.

One of the warriors was speaking, and Ariock realized that Kessa had kindly translated for him. He looked down at her in gratitude. Kessa had plenty of people to watch over, but she'd chosen to give her time to him, instead of to other refugees.

"They want us to rest here." Kessa sounded worried. "My guess is that they are stalling, so that their people will be prepared to meet a mind reader." She hesitated. "This might be like our arrival at the slave farm of Duin."

One of the black-wrapped warriors pointed to the rotted head with its hair and face still somewhat intact. He spoke in a proud tone, perhaps bragging.

"Haz says that he enjoys hunting and killing mind readers," Kessa said. "He has killed two Torth, but Jinishta has slain five. They've used this Hall of Heads for many generations."

Ariock reminded himself not to judge the barbarism of these alien warriors. After all, they were on the right side of justice. They understood that Torth were as dangerous—and yes, as evil—as a sapient species could get. Ariock had killed quite a few Torth himself.

He just didn't think he'd go so far as to display the heads of his defeated enemies.

It was gruesome, especially since the Torth bore a strong, if superficial, resemblance to humans.

"They let cannibals devour the headless bodies of the Torth they kill," Kessa explained. "Then they slay the sated cannibals. In this way, the remains of Torth cannot be found, not even by other Torth."

Ariock tried to look politely interested instead of vaguely disgusted.

"…Ariock?" Thomas said in a small, frightened voice.

Ariock searched the chamber and saw Thomas curled up in a fetal position and tied up in black wraps, on the floor between racks of skulls. No one dared to enter his range. Thomas could not possibly see or hear through the wraps on his head, but his jaw moved. He was able to speak.

"Ariock? Kessa?"

With no one in range, Thomas must be clueless about who had captured him or why. All he knew was that someone had tied him up and deadened his sensory perceptions.

And if he'd awoken while being levitated…

*Thomas must think I'm doing this to him*, Ariock realized. He and Thomas were supposed to be the only Yeresunsa in existence, aside from countless babies on Torth baby farms who were destroyed before they could draw their first breaths.

"I am worried for him," Kessa said.

Somebody ought to comfort Thomas. A friend needed to stand up for him, at the very least.

"We have to be able to speak with Thomas," Ariock said.

Kessa angled her head up to meet his gaze. "I have begged them. They say it is against their laws."

Ariock clenched his fists. These warriors were grossly overreacting to a helpless child. A friend.

Kessa tapped the armor on his leg. "Ariock, please be cautious. I do not think we are in a condition to fight."

That was an unfortunate truth. Ariock struggled against his own anger. A brainless battle was the reason he was in such a mess. He shouldn't need a reminder to avoid brute force.

Maybe he should attempt diplomacy?

These people had apparently eked out a survivalist society beneath the dead city for more than one generation. They probably had families with children. Surely they could be reasonable?

The lead warrior caught up with the rest of their group, and everyone listened attentively as she spoke. Meanwhile, attendants emerged from shadowy side chambers. The attendants exhibited the same slender, humanoid appearance as the warriors, except their faces were exposed.

They were albinos.

Hair and skin alike were ivory white. Only their pale-lavender eyes stood out, demurely downcast. Their hair was stiff, cropped, and tightly curled. They wore clean white tunics belted over swishy pants.

"They look like humans to me," Kessa whispered. "What do you think?"

The attendants poured water from earthenware jugs into a stone basin, perched on an altar. Their round, chinless heads and gracile necks were unlike any ethnicity that Ariock could identify.

Cherise stood nearby. "They're not Torth," she whispered. "But I'm pretty sure they're not from Earth."

The albino attendants examined the blaster gloves that had been stolen from ummin refugees. They placed each weapon inside a treasure chest, handling them with gingerness, as if they might explode.

"Cherise?" Thomas sounded distraught, close to tears. He paused. Then, "Vy?" Everyone ignored him.

The three warriors—the fourth had run ahead to alert their people—peeled off their bandage-like wraps. They dunked their heads into the water basin and allowed the attendants to rinse and wash their hair. Filth came off.

The warriors exhibited the same albinism as their attendants.

Flen and Haz had close-cropped white hair. Jinishta—the smallest and most delicate-looking of the three—had a cloud puff of cottony hair, restrained by metallic clasps.

"Who are you?" Thomas demanded. His voice aimed blindly at anyone who might listen, but only empty skulls faced his way. "Irarjeg? Weptolyso?" He cycled through more names. "Who took me captive?"

Ariock decided he'd had enough of wrongheaded rules. Let Kessa be diplomatic. She was good at it. "I'm going to him."

Kessa hissed a warning.

Thomas repeated his queries in the slave tongue. Then another language. He began testing a variety of alien tongues, pausing between each attempt in a methodical way.

Ariock strode toward Thomas.

"Stop, Ariock." Kessa sounded scared.

Weapons crisscrossed in front of him, blocking his way. The small albino men who wielded the halberds seemed unintimidated, despite the massive size difference between themselves and Ariock.

Halberds. Those seemed anachronistic on a world where blaster gloves were commonplace.

"Thomas needs us." But Ariock hesitated. Each halberd was crowned by cruel-looking spikes. The albinos saw the filthy blanket that barely covered Ariock's gaping wound. One swing would knock him down. It would be agony.

And Ariock was pretty sure his powers were still inhibited. The last time he'd tried to spread his awareness, he had suffered a throbbing pain in his head.

If he failed yet again—if he got himself killed—then he'd never be able to help Thomas.

And if he broke that promise, he might as well be dead.

His mother had known that he was unfit for the heroic role. His father, too. Everyone knew it by now. Ariock only brought death and suffering to the people who mattered most. He needed to stop doing that. Either he was the Bringer of Hope, or he was a hopeless burden.

"What about Thomas's medicine?" Ariock asked, looking at Kessa. "How can we take care of him if they won't let us into his range?"

Kessa carried the NAI-12 case, and she looked at it in surprise. "Oh. That is a good question." She called to the lead warrior and switched to the slave tongue. Ariock guessed she was explaining that Thomas needed regular injections in order to survive.

Jinishta planted her fists on her hips and harangued them in a lecturing tone.

"Jinishta says they need a lot of assurances." Kessa paused, listening. "Jinishta says she doubts that you are 'the one'?" Kessa's brow ridges furrowed in confusion. "I don't know what she means. Perhaps..." She trailed off, interrupted.

A commotion entered the Hall of Heads.

Despite his worries and pain, Ariock couldn't help but stare at these new arrivals. They were the same species, small and albino, but this group wore expensive-looking woolens and velvet vests. Gemstones and gold plates decorated their outfits and hair.

They were very clean. They were also out of breath, as if they'd run fast and hard.

The elderly woman in front spoke heatedly to Jinishta, like a mother chastising her daughter. Gold plates swung from her ears. A diadem crowned her white hair.

Jinishta listened with stoic pride, at first. But as the lecture went on, she began to look ashamed. She flinched at angry words.

The diadem woman pointed past Ariock, at Thomas. She said something that sounded like a command. It had to do with the "*rekveh.*" Ariock wished he could understand the slave tongue.

Haz and Flen each drew a black spear.

"No!" Kessa leaped to block Thomas. She spread her arms in a feeble attempt to protect him.

Ariock anticipated the attack, and he threw himself toward Thomas, heedless of the spiked halberds. He had promised to protect those who'd risked their lives to save him. He had failed to protect his mother. He wasn't going to fail the boy who needed him. If Thomas wasn't safe in this underground haven, then none of them were safe here.

There were shouts. A powerful force yanked Ariock away and hurled him several yards through the air.

He slammed heavily against a wall.

Waves of nauseating blackness rolled through him, along with agony, and he fought to stay conscious. He had to fight. Never mind that he was pinned by an unseen power.

Jinishta focused on him, her slender arm outstretched.

She had actually lifted Ariock and thrown him partway across the room. Not even a nussian could do that. She was a lot stronger than she looked.

Ariock forced words through his mass of pain. "Tell them," he said to anyone who might listen. "If they kill Thomas, then they need to kill me."

Kessa stared at him with concern.

Too often, Ariock found himself needing quick communication but stymied. "Tell them." If he lived through this, then he would learn the slave tongue as fast as possible. He searched for the correct alien words. "He dies? I die."

Weptolyso exhaled a threatening snort that sounded like the prelude to a roar. "I fight with Ariock." His spikes popped out. "I die with Ariock."

Ariock tried to expand his awareness. Pain crashed over him.

But for a split second, he became the stone floor.

Then he slammed back into his body, full of pain, unable to maintain his spread-out state.

Arguments broke out. The albino people gesticulated and yelled over each other, apparently debating something of vital importance. They were screaming. Kessa attempted to interrupt, but one of the flashy ones snapped at her in the slave tongue. Ariock could piece those words together. "Stay out of this, runaway."

The force holding Ariock set him down. Jinishta was letting him go.

She resembled a porcelain doll, with her minimal jaw, petite lips, and large eyes. That fragile prettiness only accentuated the ferocity of her stare. She watched him with deep mistrust.

Haz and Flen tucked their spears back into their quivers, and Ariock took that as a good sign. He tried to look meek.

But if it came to a battle? He was ready.

The finely dressed elders trotted toward Ariock, done with their vociferous argument. Everything about their outfits looked rich, the way Ariock imagined nobles had dressed in ancient India or Greece. Every golden plate was embossed with stylized figures.

Judging by the demanding tone of the elder with the diadem, she wanted Kessa to translate.

"This is Chaniyelem," Kessa said.

Ariock prepared himself for battle. Maybe the albinos were going to try to imprison him with their powers.

Instead, Chaniyelem studied him with watery violet eyes, as if searching for something. She asked a question in a polite tone of voice.

Kessa translated. "Several melt measures past—I think she means days—she felt the ground quake. Buildings fell. Many Torth converged in a frenzied battle. Chaniyelem wants to know…" Kessa paused, giving the question emphasis. "Was that you?"

Ariock had no doubt she was talking about his crash landing and subsequent battle. He nodded.

"Yes," Kessa translated.

The reply sent the albino people into a tizzy. They whispered and argued, sneaking glances his way. They reassessed him, their foreheads creased with unspoken worries.

Good. Maybe they would take his concern for Thomas seriously.

Chaniyelem seemed fascinated by the grimy blanket around Ariock's wound. She touched it with caution.

"May I see your wound?" Kessa translated.

Ariock held the filthy blanket-bandage in place, unwilling to reveal how injured and weak he was.

Then he reconsidered. Chaniyelem was polite, at least. That was better than pinning him to a wall and using power to get what she wanted.

Unsure what to expect, he twitched the filthy bandage aside.

The horror on their faces told him how dire it looked. Even Weptolyso winced in sympathy. Ariock didn't want to look, but he flicked his gaze down and caught a whiff of rot and a glimpse of necrosis. It was a wonder that his arm was still attached.

"That is no bite wound." Kessa translated for Chaniyelem, who spoke in a quavering voice. "She wants to know what created it. I will tell her."

The elders whispered in awe at whatever Kessa said. One of them, a round woman, began to chant in a melodic rhythm. "*Tem delin ramash haka...*"

She went on. Meanwhile, another elder spoke what sounded like a translation into the slave tongue. That allowed Kessa, in turn, to translate.

The words lost their rhythm in English. "He will come to you in darkness." Kessa had to pause and wait for each line. "He will come to you in need, but he will leave with an army at his heels. You will know him by his great height and the wound on his shoulder. Mind readers shall grovel—"

"Wait," Ariock cut in.

Kessa looked inquisitive.

"This isn't a prophecy, is it?" Ariock asked warily.

"I don't know that word." Kessa hurried to catch up with the translation. "Mind readers shall grovel for his mercy, save the one who has earned it."

Ariock had a sinking, twisted-up feeling. The specifics of the prayer, or prophecy, might seem to apply to him, but it must be just a gross coincidence.

He only wanted help for Thomas and Vy. Nothing more.

He didn't need yet another group of people praising him for things he hadn't done, expecting miracles he was incapable of delivering.

"He will be your salvation," Kessa translated mercilessly. "Only he can lead you into light and restore you to your former glory. Follow him or perish."

The albino people fell silent, gaping and staring up at Ariock like he was a legend made flesh.

# CHAPTER 11

# SAVIOR

Ariock felt set up to fail. Was he supposed to pretend to be the savior of these albino people, to claim their charity, to get help for his friends?

Well, he was done with pretense. When he met the watery gaze of Chaniyelem, he couldn't fake heroism. Thomas and Kessa were the main reasons why so many refugees from Duin had survived this far. Ariock had gotten their village condemned and a lot of them killed. He wasn't a hero. And he wasn't going to steal the heroic status that his friends had earned.

"No," he said.

Kessa gazed at him, her gray eyes profound and unreadable.

"Tell them I'm not going to do any of those things," Ariock said. "That chant they have is a fairy tale. It's a bunch of lies."

Kessa cocked her head. "How do you know?"

Ariock suppressed his frustration. There was no such thing as a savior, and a former slave like Kessa ought to know it. If these people believed the prophecy, or whatever it was, then they were idiots.

Jinishta, at least, continued to watch Ariock with suspicion. She had a healthy skepticism. Ariock found himself respecting her, even though she might be an obstacle.

"Certainty," Kessa said, "is not the same as truth." She swept a gesture toward Thomas. "A mind reader has your mercy. I believe that is the salient point. I will make sure they notice."

She chatted with Chaniyelem, and Ariock had to wait, letting Kessa hold a conversation on his behalf. He hid his concerns. If Kessa was using words like *salient*, then she'd picked up quite a lot from her conversations with Thomas, Vy, and Cherise. That much perceptiveness would be useful in dealing with aliens.

At last, Chaniyelem spoke to him in a gracious tone.

"Messiah," Kessa translated. "You are welcome to stay in our grand city, among our humble people, the Alashani. You shall have healing, and feasts to honor you, and a suite that fits your status as a great warrior. I will provide anything you desire. But..." Kessa's tone grew dismayed as she realized that Chaniyelem was serious. "No *rekveh* may enter our city."

Other jewel-bedecked elders spoke, and Kessa translated.

"It is forbidden."

Ariock absorbed that cold information. These people seemed to think that merely showing up with a mind reader fulfilled that part of the prophecy.

"Thomas needs healing and a safe place to stay," Ariock stated.

When Kessa translated, the Alashani people looked disbelieving. They whispered, but Chaniyelem spoke with concession. She was offering something.

"They are willing to let the *rekveh* live," Kessa translated. "They will return him to the place where they found him and leave him there for his kin to find."

"That's a death sentence for him," Ariock pointed out.

Kessa translated, her overly patient tone implying that she'd already made these arguments.

Sure enough, Chaniyelem and the other richly dressed people began to bicker. They stared at Ariock in frustration.

"They are very afraid of *rekvehs*," Kessa told Ariock, helpless. "They refuse to believe what we tell them about Thomas. Chaniyelem says you may ask any favor, but she will not condemn her people to death. She believes Thomas will bring death."

Kessa was distraught, clearly unable to think of a way to save Thomas. And if she couldn't think of a way...

Then words were simply not enough.

Chaniyelem and her people would argue until Ariock and Kessa collapsed from exhaustion, while their friends suffered and died. Vy desperately needed a healer. There was no time for this.

"All right." Ariock inwardly braced himself for the hardest decision he'd ever had to make. "If Thomas can't stay here, then I'll leave with him."

Kessa gaped at him in disbelief. Whatever she'd expected, this was not it.

Ariock picked up a discarded blanket and an empty gourd-canteen, both coated with grime. The refugees wouldn't need these supplies anymore. They were probably welcome among the albinos, at least.

Chaniyelem asked a question. Kessa replied. Chaniyelem made a curt response.

"She says you cannot leave," Kessa translated. "You are in grave condition, and you need healing."

Ariock searched for extra wraps with which to keep Thomas warm. "I'll be grateful for any healing they feel like offering to me and Thomas," he said with dignity that hid his pain. "But I won't stay where my friend isn't welcome."

Kessa looked devastated. "Are you sure?"

Ariock nearly apologized for abandoning her.

But he could not abandon Thomas, and he would never ask anyone to follow him and Thomas into cesspools full of cannibals. Not even Vy…although
leaving Vy behind would feel like tearing off one of his own limbs.

His friends needed healing and safety. He could not give them that.

"Yes," Ariock said. "I'm sure."

He approached Thomas, heedless of shouted threats from the albino warriors. He didn't dare try to use his powers yet, but he braced himself, determined to stay conscious through any agonizing headache and battle. Failure
was not an option. Thomas had no choice.

"I will go with you, Ariock," Weptolyso rumbled.

Ariock stared at the nussian, stunned. The trek would be awful and dangerous. In his condition, they would almost certainly die.

Then again, maybe having a fake guard along would help them sneak into
the Stratower?

"I will go, too," Kessa said.

The albino people—the Alashani—gawked with incredulity as Kessa and
a few other refugees began to gather their beat-up, depleted supplies with grim
determination. In short order, half the refugees were hugging their friends,
saying farewell in the slave tongue.

Behind them, an argument spun up.

Chaniyelem and the other richly dressed people sounded dumbfounded.
Perhaps no one from their underground civilization ever volunteered to go into
the cold, rainy darkness. They kept calling for Ariock to "Stop!" Jinishta spoke in
a menacing tone. He recognized a few words—*rekveh* and "death."

"We must be prepared, Ariock," Kessa said in a low voice. "I think Jinishta
may try to have us killed."

He looked at her, surprised.

"She says that we have not sworn the Warrior's Pact," Kessa explained. "I
don't know what that it, but she says that if we get caught by Torth—"

"Stop!" Chaniyelem cried in the slave tongue.

That sounded dramatic. Ariock turned to see all the Alashani staring at
him. Even the skulls seemed to stare.

The warriors clutched spears, grim, ready to fight or commit murder.

Ariock noticed, in the corner of his vision, that Weptolyso had popped his
spikes out, ready to fight. Good.

Chaniyelem spoke rapidly, hands outstretched as if to calm everyone. She
said something about the *rekveh*.

"They beg us to stay." Kessa looked interested. "Chaniyelem says that they
will allow Thomas to live! They are willing to protect him and keep him alive."

Ariock gave Chaniyelem his full attention. She had a unique way of speaking, pausing for effect like a preacher.

Kessa translated. "Chaniyelem says that aboveground is certain death. The ruins are toxic. The Torth city is protected by a border than kills anyone who tries to cross. She wants us to stay here instead. She begs us. But…we must agree to their safety rules." Kessa's translation lost enthusiasm as she went on. "The wrap must stay on Thomas's head. No one goes into his range of telepathy. No one feeds him information."

Ariock shifted his weight, every bruise and wound throbbing with pain. He felt so weak.

"They say they will give Thomas the medicine he requires," Kessa went on. "They will cleanse his wounds. They promise to take good care of him, but only if you agree to those conditions."

Her tone was a prod. Kessa wanted—needed—Ariock to agree. Not for herself, but for her exhausted people.

For Vy.

If Ariock turned his back, it would mean a battle, and it would be their deaths.

Thomas lay shivering on the floor.

"He's scared," Ariock said. "I need to able to say something to him. Even just a few words."

Kessa took a deep, reluctant breath, and translated.

Jinishta made a grimace of disbelief, and the other Alashani exchanged looks. They seemed unused to such obstinate refusal.

They let Chaniyelem speak for them. "We will care for your mind reader," Kessa translated. "If he proves to be as harmless as you say he is, and if you are truly the messiah, we will revisit this matter. That is all I can promise."

Ariock shifted from one foot to the other, aware that lives hung on this decision.

Thomas was smart and resourceful; surely he could endure a day or two in darkness and silence without ascending into the Megacosm? He had spoken aloud without suffering extra punishment. Maybe he would conclude that he wasn't in Torth custody and would therefore bide his time and wait for a rescue.

Meanwhile, Ariock and the people who depended on him sorely needed healing.

Once they were all healthier…once Ariock had his full strength and his powers…he could do whatever was necessary to rescue Thomas.

"All right." Ariock nodded slowly. "If you promise to keep Thomas alive, then I agree."

Kessa translated, and the Alashani conferred briefly.

Chaniyelem spoke and waited for Kessa to translate. "They will clean him and give him water and food and medicine, as needed. But if he dies from his innate weaknesses, they say that they are not to blame."

That sounded innocent, but the wording was careful. Maybe Chaniyelem was their equivalent of a lawyer.

"If you mistreat him," Ariock said, "I will have revenge. If you don't like that, then put him in my care."

Kessa seemed reluctant to translate. She did, but Ariock suspected she'd left his threat out of it.

The Alashani seemed to reach a consensus. "You and your friends shall receive our best care." Kessa smiled in relief as she translated. "They say they have awaited the messiah for generations beyond count. Chaniyelem and the council members welcome all of us to the Alashani city of Hufti."

# CHAPTER 12

# HIS GREAT HEIGHT

Ariock held still while the albino Yeresunsa used their powers to scrub him clean. It seemed ludicrous that they put higher priority on his hygiene than on anything else, even health and well-being. But whatever. When Ariock had complained about their priorities, they'd slowed down and held a debate. It seemed more efficient to stay quiet and let them work.

Plate by plate, his filthy, dented armor clattered into a pile. Grime rolled off his clothes.

"Their best healer is on her way," Kessa said, leaning around a pillar. "Her name is Orla, and she will be here soon. They say she will make you feel a lot healthier."

"Great." Ariock tolerated a wet cloth that sponged his face, levitated by a warrior. "Tell her to heal Vy first."

"I told them," Kessa said with patience. "Although I think they are a lot more likely to listen to you than to me."

Kessa was gone before Ariock could respond. She must regret having learned enough English to be the official translator for the messiah. He figured she must be concerned for her people, but she couldn't check on everyone while the Alashani kept hounding her, demanding answers and translations.

Dirt came out from under his fingernails and got gently scraped from every crevice. These people had an unnerving level of precision with their powers. Ariock usually spread his awareness into too many things at once, or too large an area, to act with such focus.

A tiny yet dangerous-looking blade suddenly hovered near his face.

One of the warriors, Haz, laughed, and mimed a haircut. Ariock tried to relax as Haz used powers to tug his beard, bit by bit, cropping it close.

Only the three warriors—Jinishta, Haz, and Flen, still clad in black wraps— had accompanied Ariock into this vaulted side chamber, to clean him up. It seemed like a job for attendants. Maybe only a few of Alashani had powers?

Someone giggled, and Jinishta, Haz, and Flen all stepped back to make room for what looked like a pink-cheeked teenaged girl. She stared up at Ariock with luminous eyes, as if starstruck.

Like the elders, this girl was dressed in diamonds and layers of gauze. Two thick clips held back her mass of white hair. A purple mantle draped her shoulders, like a short cape, pinned by a delicate brooch of silver.

The grinning girl approached Ariock with her delicate hands outstretched. That was the healing pose, but she looked too young to be their best healer. Surely that role should belong to someone with a lot more life experience? Someone professional?

Jinishta said something that sounded like an introduction. "Orla," she said.

The teenage girl, Orla, said something curt and motioned for Ariock to sit down. Her silly expression melted away.

Ariock realized that he was towering over her.

Bending was excruciating, but without the armor plates, he was more flexible. He managed to lower himself to the stone floor.

With a somber expression, Orla held out her hands.

Energy washed through Ariock in a tide of wellness. This was nothing like the minor healing he'd received earlier from Nulshta. Ariock had never tried major drugs or painkillers, but this must be better than any of them. His agony vanished. It wasn't being masked; it was entirely gone.

Orla swayed, as if light-headed.

Ariock pulled aside his bandage to study his wound. Instead of black rot and ghastly pus, fresh scar tissue stretched over raw, exposed muscle and the cavity beneath. The shrapnel was gone, too, replaced by clean, new-looking skin.

The hole had become a dent.

Ariock looked at Orla with amazement. "Thank you!"

She giggled tiredly and blushed.

Ariock spread his awareness, eager to use his powers. He'd start with something light, at first. Just a little stir of air.

His connection to the air snapped. Dizziness washed through him, and spots blinked throughout his vision. Pain knifed through his skull.

Orla gently slapped his chest with the back of her hand. She chided him in a tone of outraged concern.

"Orla says you're not supposed to use your powers yet." Kessa was out of breath, having hurried from somewhere else. "Why would you do that? She says it's crazy to use powers after such a major injury." Kessa had to speak quickly, every time Orla paused for breath. "If you work with a warning headache—sorry, I don't know what she means by that—then probably no one can revive you. You need to rest a lot. Eat a lot. Regain your physical strength first. Also, Orla says the healing is not yet complete. You need more. She will revisit you for a second session after she recovers. This healing took a lot out of her. You had better take care of yourself."

Orla finished her rant with a small "humph" sound. She folded her arms as if daring him to argue.

"All right," Ariock said, cautious.

That seemed to satisfy Orla. She gave him a smile with dimples.

"What about Vy?" Ariock said. "Please go heal Vy, if you haven't already." He began to stand up, to lead the way.

Dizziness made him hesitate. His pain was gone, but he felt weak and ravenously hungry.

Kessa translated, and Orla hurried away, offering a concerned reply as she left.

"She will heal Vy right away. But Ariock?" Kessa hesitated and moved closer, lowering her voice. "She said she does not think she can salvage Vy's foot."

Ariock pushed himself to his feet. He wasn't going to let light-headedness prevent him from making sure that Vy received substantial healing. After the way the Alashani had treated Thomas, he didn't like letting any of the humans out of his sight.

"Cherise is with Vy," Kessa said. "She'll make sure Orla does all she can."

"Good," Ariock said. "What about Thomas? Is anyone keeping an eye on him?"

"Pung and a few others," Kessa said. "They're reporting to me. Don't worry. We won't let the Alashani break their promise."

Jinishta said something and gestured for Kessa to translate.

"Jinishta says that our injured friends will be carried to a..." Kessa stumbled on an unfamiliar word. "I suppose that means a place where people recover."

"An infirmary?" Ariock guessed. "A hospital?"

"I don't know those words." No doubt Kessa wished she had time to learn. "Jinishta is assuring me that our friends need rest and care from healers, and they will be healthy in a few...um, days? I think that's what she means." Kessa twisted her beak in exasperation. "They all use strange words. They speak the slave tongue, but differently."

"That's all right." Ariock began to walk past Kessa, to seek Vy.

Jinishta spoke a word he knew. "Wait."

Ariock hesitated in midstep. If it had been anybody else, he might have kept walking. But Jinishta made him wary. She'd shown that she had enough power to toss him across a room.

Jinishta raised a hand, and all his dented, discarded plates of armor levitated. They'd been polished to a shine.

"You must look presentable," Kessa translated.

Ariock rolled his eyes but planted himself so that Jinishta could send polished armor plates to his body. "Tell her to hurry."

Kessa did not translate that.

Each armor piece jostled to assemble itself on Ariock, molding over the cleansed remnants of his clothes. Jinishta seemed unsure about how the armor overlapped, because some of the small pieces were in the wrong places. She left out a few parts entirely.

Yet she made it work. If a plate refused to stay in place, Jinishta sent black ribbons of clean mummy-wrap material to wind around Ariock and hold the armor in place. Soon he was clothed in metal and blackness. A metal plate hid his chest wound. Jinishta even wrapped his feet in the black material, which felt soft and luxurious.

The three warriors stood back to admire their handiwork. They made comments and adjusted a plate here, a sash there.

Kessa nodded with approval. "Impressive."

"Can we go now?" Ariock said. He felt ridiculous, dressed for a battle and yet unable to fight effectively.

Jinishta made a shooing gesture, and Ariock took that as permission. He ducked out of the vaulted chamber and back into the Hall of Heads.

Everyone was on the move. Richly dressed people glided down wide, tiered steps and through a massively ornate gateway. Attendants followed them, aiding limping ummin refugees.

The ummins looked dazzled and excited, and it was no wonder. They ran to examine the intricate stonework beyond the gateway. Gold glimmered on stone friezes, which depicted figures and lightning bolts in a style reminiscent of ancient Greek or Babylonian art. Everything glowed with golden lamplight.

But Ariock was more interested in how Vy looked. She lay on a litter carried by albino attendants, amid satin pillows and velveteen blankets. Her face was scrubbed clean. Her hair shone like copper.

"Ariock." She smiled up from her comfy bed, looking exhausted. "This must be the safe haven that Jonathan Stead found. It's paradise."

"Do you need healing?" Ariock gently touched the blanket over her legs.

Vy looked uncomfortable, and he withdrew his hand. He had dragged her through enough pain to last a lifetime. His very existence was why she had gotten abducted by Torth in the first place. After he'd killed his mother by accident, Vy might be ecstatic for a chance to get away from him.

"Orla healed me," Vy said sleepily. "She said she needs to rest before she can try again. I guess it takes a lot out of her."

Ariock wondered if Orla's power worked differently than his. He had never needed rest after he healed people.

Cherise walked over to them, scrubbed clean. "They have a hospital," she said. "It sounds like they have a lot of healers, like, maybe dozens. That's where we're going."

Ariock liked her unimpressed, matter-of-fact tone. Unlike the Alashani, Cherise looked at him and did not see the Bringer of Hope. She probably saw what he truly was: a guy who had failed.

Ariock wished more people could see him with that much honesty.

"I'm so sorry, Ariock." Vy looked away in shame. A tear glistened in her eye. "I screamed when you were fighting to protect everyone. We almost died. Because of me."

Did she actually blame herself?

For Ariock's failure?

"That wasn't your fault," Cherise said fiercely.

"Sorry," Vy repeated in a soft voice.

"You're apologizing for being human," Ariock said. "I'm the one who took you into a war zone."

"You had no choice."

"I made mistakes," Ariock said, aware that it was a vast understatement. "I might be making one right now, by not healing you. Maybe I can do better than what Orla did. But she told me not to use my powers yet, and I think I still have the inhibitor in my system, so I'm just—"

"That's fine," Vy told him firmly.

"But—"

"You kept the Torth off our backs," Vy interrupted. "And Weptolyso carried me all this way. That's enough. I don't know how Yeresunsa powers work, but you shouldn't strain yourself after a major injury. Any nurse can tell you that."

The litter bearers carried Vy down the tiered steps, through the gateway.

Ariock kept pace. "I don't know what to expect from these people," he admitted. "But if you need anything—anything at all—you just have to ask. Okay? Let me know."

Vy looked tired, but she gave him a smile that loosened knots inside his mind. "You got it." Her gaze roved over him. "By the way, I like the way they dressed you up."

Ariock had to laugh. He nearly said something about looking more human, now that he wasn't dripping with grime, but then he remembered that he wasn't human. Not entirely.

So he kept quiet. He didn't want to watch Vy struggle to pretend that he was a normal person.

"Agh," Cherise said. "I'm going to go see if Kessa needs help." She hurried away.

Jinishta shadowed them, listening without understanding their words. Despite her delicate appearance, her face had a hardness that most of the albino people lacked. Ariock wanted to keep her in sight, just in case she decided to throw spears.

Her fellow warriors, Haz and Flen, had joined a dozen albino guards around Thomas. Albino attendants had erected black curtains around the boy, shielding him from sight. They didn't want anyone to see the "evil *rekveh*," Ariock guessed, and never mind that Thomas was a fragile, disabled, swaddled child who couldn't hear or see anything.

Ariock made a low growl, not caring that Jinishta overheard.

They walked past ornate friezes. These Alashani people were not mere survivalists. It seemed they'd had time to carve a lot of art.

Grand colonnades loomed ahead, veined marble that reflected the golden glow of lanterns. A stream burbled through a shallow channel cut into the marble floor.

Ariock stared at the decorative canal. He hadn't imagined that this filthy planet had any pure water, let alone an excess of it.

Water trickled from open-mouthed stonework faces, adding to the stream. Most of the gargoyles looked like the albino Alashani people, but there were also aliens. Ummins. Nussians. Govki. Other species Ariock was unfamiliar with.

A distant cacophony made him think of fund-raisers at museums or hotels, the kinds of events that his mother used to take him to when he was a child. A lot of people were gathered somewhere.

Pedestrians began to appear, crossing their path. The people of this underground world all looked well-dressed, with beads or elaborate embroidery decorating their tunics. The albino women flattened their puffy hair with kerchiefs. The men carried satchels, or they dragged rickshaws with squeaking wheels, loaded with crates or barrels. Some had children or other passengers riding on top of the cargo.

Without exception, the strange pedestrians halted to gape at Ariock.

He almost wished for curtains to hide behind, like Thomas had. It was hard to ignore the shocked reactions.

However, when alien species began to show up amid the increasing crowds of pedestrians, Ariock stared back. There was a tubby-looking fur creature. And there was a mer nerctan, with a sickle-shaped head atop a neck with multiple joints.

But these aliens did not act like slaves.

Instead of rags, they wore woolens cut to flatter their alien figures. Their necks showed no hint of chafe from slave collars.

Ariock paused to look at a small group of ummins who were obviously not among the refugees from Duin. Two adults stared in dismay, as if offended by the sight of so many smelly, starving countrymen. The two child ummins paused in the act of licking popsicles. Instead of scrappy hats, this family wore pleated skirts around their heads, pinned into place by diadems with silver swirls.

The refugees stared with round eyes at these nonslave ummins. So did Kessa.

Chaniyelem led them onward, through crowded intersections that became increasingly impressive, hemmed in by imposing stone buildings of granite, onyx, or quartz. People stood on balconies with wrought iron railings. Lamps dangled from iron brackets over square-cut doorways.

There was artistry everywhere. Ariock had to duck beneath elaborate quartz-stone arches that seemed to serve no purpose other than decoration. The stonework flowed with impressions of nude albinos entwined with each other and more than a few salacious details.

It was finally sinking in: the Torth Empire did not know this place existed.

Not a single mind reader knew.

The rest of the universe believed that the Torth Homeworld was a world of decay and death, where freedom was impossible and misery was everywhere. If anyone ever happened to learn otherwise…if just one Torth learned of it… then this underground haven was doomed.

These people had to take great care to never get caught, or seen, by a mind reader, or even by a slave who might come into contact with mind readers. Most of them probably never ventured aboveground.

One tiny mistake, and everyone here would be enslaved forever.

That must be why Jinishta and the other black-wrapped warriors were so watchful. They guarded the black curtains around Thomas. They knew what was at stake. Their worry was palpable.

Ariock shoved aside his realizations for later consideration. He had too many new things to look at.

Vendors stood behind wagons, selling knickknacks or steaming food with smells that made his mouth water. Ariock nearly got in line at a food stall, but Jinishta tugged his hand and spoke in a commanding tone.

He remembered that he didn't have any money on this world. Anything these people gave him would be charity. So he walked on.

He passed a pedestal topped by a weeping woman with arms outstretched. Her flowing hair hinted at human heritage, perhaps. It was long and wavy and detailed, as carefully carved as her translucent stone tears.

They encountered a cheerful nussian who freely handed plates of unidentifiable stir-fried food to the refugees.

Ariock got in line, eager to sample the food and meet the jolly nussian. All the nussians he had met in the prison were too terrified to laugh.

Jinishta tugged his arm. "Come," she urged in the slave tongue.

An enormous gateway loomed ahead, opening to tiered steps lit by golden lanterns. Beyond that, the murmur of the underground city sounded like a vast audience.

Chaniyelem glided up the steps, but Ariock slowed. The Torth had forced him to murder alien beasts in a crowded arena. What if the Alashani wanted him to do something similar? At the very least, he hated being stared at.

Something prodded him in the back. "Follow Chaniyelem." Jinishta was insistent.

So Ariock took another unwilling step, and another.

He left Vy behind on her litter, and Thomas behind his curtains, and Kessa, and Cherise, and everyone else. Most of them were enjoying plates of warm food.

The steps were too narrow for his huge feet. He picked his way upward and finally joined Chaniyelem on the lip of a sheer cliff. Only a low balustrade enclosed the drop. Beyond that...

The cave stretched as far as Ariock could see.

Lamps dotted an underground city, twinkling over square-cut doorways and rooftop corners, until they blurred in the dark, hazy distance. Palaces glittered atop each other, sparkling with mica chips or other gems. Deep channels scored the valleys between palatial neighborhoods, crossing in a labyrinthian tangle. Even the channels were lamplit; alleys were knitted together by stairways.

Verdigris railings enclosed rooftops. Fountains burbled in intersections. Canvas signs denoted shops. Stairs were everywhere, ascending or descending, and people clogged every stairway, rooftop, street, and bridge. They leaned out from windows. They perched on grotto walls.

Tens of thousands of albinos and aliens all stared directly at Ariock.

He took a step back.

A horn blast sounded across the city-size cavern in a mournful note that lasted much longer than a human exhalation. It ended in a sharp jag upward. Ariock caught sight of the horn blower, a heavyset nussian bedecked with decorative chains and jewels.

The citywide audience went dead silent.

Chaniyelem walked to the edge of the marble lip and gazed down at the masses. "*Aonswa,*" she said, presenting him. "Ariock."

These people had never seen a Torth before, Ariock felt certain. Otherwise they would have mass-panicked at his close resemblance to Torth, with his dark hair, so unlike theirs, and his bolder features. And his size.

*You will know him by his great height.*

Chaniyelem began to chant. "*Tem delin ramash haka…*"

Many thousands of voices joined hers, a ritual prayer spoken by a congregation so large that it boomed like an avalanche. The immense audience gazed at Ariock with shining hope. Every chorused syllable reverberated in his bones.

Ariock wanted to back away. Instead, he stood his ground. Even if he fled, he would not easily escape their thunderous expectations.

# PART THREE

*The Bringer of Hope is of three bloods: the new, the old, and the ancient.*

—Preserved scrap from the lost Prophecies of Ah Jun

# CHAPTER 1
# BANQUET OF DECEPTION

Kessa picked at the heaping plate of food in front of her. When Chaniyelem insisted on inviting the messiah to a feast in his honor, and Ariock said yes, Kessa was given no choice. She was ushered through a lamplit grotto with fountains into a chamber where awestruck albino people offered to sponge-bathe her, and then they thrust a clean, fresh outfit at her and told her to wear it.

In the brightly lit banquet hall, they gave her a seat next to Ariock, within the penumbra of everyone's attention.

Vy was tucked into a bed to await more healing. Cherise was too quiet, and Weptolyso hardly knew the human tongue. That left Kessa as the only person who could satisfy everyone with her translation skills.

Ariock seemed unaware of how exalted he was. Like Weptolyso, he was devouring a fourth or fifth helping of delicious foods, possibly as a way to avoid all the curiosity and awe aimed his way.

Ariock and Weptolyso were a lot more interested in the banquet food than Kessa was. She'd eaten her fill, but she had already forgotten the savory tastes and aromas. Everything about this palace was alien and peculiar. She couldn't stop staring.

Especially at the ummin dinner guest seated across the table from her.

High Councilor Deschuba was unlike any ummin Kessa had ever seen. Gold plates weighted his hat, cascading down over the shoulders of his richly embroidered tunic. He was portly, unlike any slave, and Kessa estimated that he was old. Maybe even as old as herself. His skin had the same creased, worn quality as her own.

Those facts alone would have absorbed her attention. But the most peculiar thing was how the albino people treated him—with deference. A servile young woman replaced his goblet with a fresh one, and she seemed honored to do so.

Other high councilors sat at the table, all richly dressed albino people, and they conferred with Deschuba as if he was their equal. He spoke with them, and vice versa, as if there was no gulf whatsoever between their species.

"High Councilor Deschuba?" Kessa had to interrupt his conversation with a couple of nearby dinner guests, but interruption seemed the only way to get his attention. He'd been honored with a seat near Ariock, yet he seemed reluctant to speak with Kessa or any of the refugees. Perhaps he found their scrappy hats offensive.

"May I ask, Councilor Deschuba," Kessa cut in, "how did you escape slavery?"

Deschuba gave her a pitying stare. His gaze lingered on the scar around her scrawny neck. "I was never a slave. I have resided in Hufti all my life."

Kessa was stunned. Born free? It seemed impossible.

Pung leaned over from his seat at the adjacent table, half-chewed food visible in his beak as he gawked. "Is that common?" he asked. "Are slaves born free, in this city?"

Deschuba fiddled with his goblet, looking pained. "I told you. We aren't slaves," he said, as if speaking to a child. "I am sorry that you were a slave, but my people are not. I'm Alashani."

The albino people continued to eat or chat, not contradicting him. None of them stated the obvious fact that he was unlike them.

"But…" Kessa took a deep breath and decided to risk it. "Aren't you an ummin?"

"Of course." Deschuba gave her a look of pitying amusement. "Your eyes do not deceive you. I'm an ummin Alashani."

Kessa began to redefine that word in her mind.

"I thought the chalky-white people are Alashani?" Pung said.

"Yes," Deschuba said. "We are all Alashani. I am ummin Alashani, and they are shani Alashani." He gestured to nearby albino councilors.

"Ah," Pung said with exaggerated comprehension.

"But your ancestors…" Kessa hesitated, unsure if she might offend him.

"My ancestors were Alashani," Councilor Deschuba stated in a matter-of-fact tone.

Kessa drank the last sip from her goblet, trying to hide her disappointment. Deschuba must be gullible if he believed such an obvious lie. His ancestors had probably broken free from the Isolatorium, aided by Jonathan Stead. If he wanted to erase their heroism, then he was insulting his own heritage.

Pung seemed to agree. "All ummins are descended from slaves," he pointed out.

"That is simply false." Councilor Deschuba saw their skepticism and set aside his silver eating utensils. "I can trace my lineage back more than a dozen generations. My ancestors were Alashani as far back as the first recorded births and deaths, after the Age of Starvation."

Kessa stared in disbelief.

Pung gawked.

Another councilor leaned over and said, "Councilor Deschuba's family and mine go way back, for generations."

"Thank you, Karyum." Deschuba adjusted his gold-plated bracelet.

Kessa and Pung looked at each other, struggling to imagine so many generations of ummins who knew nothing whatsoever of slavery.

"There *are* slave descendants in this city," Councilor Deschuba went on, huffy. "And in other cities, such as Ellonch and Harashar. And yes. I did have one ancestor who used to be a slave." Deschuba looked ashamed to admit it. "He was one of the survivors with Jonathan Stead. He fathered my grandsire, Yupida. But that is the *only* former slave in my family." He reached for juicy tidbits in a communal dish. "Runaway slave," he corrected. "So, not really a slave at all."

Kessa supposed that by those standards, she wasn't a slave, either.

But she never could have escaped slavery without help. It would have been a guaranteed death sentence. Did Councilor Deschuba imagine that ordinary slaves had a choice? Did he understand that runaways and slaves were the same type of people?

Judging by the way he ignored the deferential albino woman who cleared away the plates he had eaten from, he must believe that slaves were an inferior type of person.

Councilor Deschuba gave Kessa a hard stare. "Were you among the runaways who threw a fit in order to bring a *rekveh* into our city?"

She returned his stare, unwilling to apologize for her role in saving Thomas's life.

"If so," Deschuba told her sternly, "you made a very poor choice. Our way of life depends on remaining apart from mind readers. All these riches you see?" He gestured at the candelabra, the chandeliers, the hammered gold wall plates, and the albino musicians who plucked stringed instruments to produce an otherworldly melody. "These riches are impossible without freedom," Deschuba said. "We have these things only because the Torth do not know we exist."

He must think Kessa was dull-witted. "I understand that," she said.

"I don't think you do," Deschuba said. "That...thing...you brought with you, into our city? That *rekveh*? It has the power to doom us all. With a mere thought. You may believe it is your ally—and maybe it has shown you kindness, or done you a favor, I don't know—but its mind is connected to all Torth." Deschuba tapped his gold-plated hat. "One slip of a thought, and all of this goes *pfft*." He made a zipping sound. "It will vanish."

Kessa hid her troubled thoughts with a faked sip from her goblet. She wished she could counter the fear Deschuba had presented her with, but there was truth to it. Thomas, for all his feebleness, had a doorway inside his mind. No one could hammer that doorway closed, or take it away. Thomas could destroy this beautiful, lamplit city with a stray thought in the Megacosm. He could almost do it by accident. He just had to glean some hint that the Alashani existed, and then ascend.

Even if Thomas remained cloistered away, even if he endeavored to keep the Alashani underground a secret, the Torth Empire hunted him with desperation. They wanted to take him alive. And there were Torth who could weasel a secret out of anyone. Another supergenius—such as the Upward Governess— could pry out any secret he tried to hide.

Kessa decided to refrain from enlightening the councilors about the scope of Thomas's mental capabilities. They had enough to fear from him. They didn't need to learn that he contained more knowledge than their wisest elders, or that he had a power to light fires and forcibly alter minds.

The more helpless he seemed, the safer he would be.

"Do Yeresunsa protect your city from the Torth?" Kessa asked, to steer conversation away from the dangerous topic of Thomas.

"Of course." Councilor Deschuba had a tone of strained politeness. "A free society cannot function without Yeresunsa. They do a lot more than protect us."

The woman seated next to him overheard. "Yes!" Chaniyelem said eagerly, decorative ovals swinging from her ears. "Yeresunsa pump water throughout our city and also throughout the livestock pens and the mushroom farms. Without them, there would be no water. Civilization would end."

Kessa noted that Chaniyelem did not include herself as a Yeresunsa, although she seemed to be the highest of high councilors. She wielded authority over everyone they had met.

"Are you a Yeresunsa?" Kessa asked.

"Oh my, no." Chaniyelem tittered. "I don't wear the purple. See?" She caressed her lacework dress, which was dotted with beads.

High Councilor Deschuba looked amused. "Very few shani are blessed with Yeresunsa powers," he said. "It is a rare gift."

"The messiah will need a purple mantle," Chaniyelem said. "We will make an extra-large one for him."

Kessa peered around at the many dinner guests and observed that some of them—including Jinishta, Haz, Flen, and Nulshta—wore a short purple cape over their shoulders. The mantles varied in style, and each used a different sort of brooch to pin it closed across their chest.

Except for those mantles, the warriors were now dressed like everyone else. They sparkled with gems over colorful woolens or gauze.

Yet something about their solemn expressions evoked the black mummy wraps they'd worn aboveground. Jinishta, in particular, never laughed or smiled. When she glanced at Ariock, her gaze was troubled, unlike the grinning councilors. Her food remained untouched. She seemed to have a lot weighing on her mind.

"So, Kessa." Jinishta leaned over. "Will you tell us about your journey from slavery to where you are now? I am very interested."

"Yes." Chaniyelem laced her fingers together and rested her delicate chin atop her hands. "Please tell us your story. I must hear it."

Deschuba became attentive, as well. All the councilors within earshot turned their focus to Kessa, and she dared not disappoint them.

So she talked. She started with her dreary existence as a city slave, and how the humans had enlivened her bunk room.

Beyond that, however… Kessa hesitated. The Alashani would not show compassion for someone who had betrayed their messiah and sentenced him to death by crucifixion. They would not understand what the Megacosm was, or why Thomas felt so compelled to ascend. Kessa barely understood that herself.

Instead, she said, "Thomas remembered his human heritage. He shed his Torth fakery and came to our rescue when we needed him, thereby proving himself to be far more human than Torth."

Pung, Cherise, and Weptolyso gave her dubious looks. Kessa silently willed them to play along, to say nothing of the way Thomas had tortured Cherise and Pung with pain seizures. That could not be part of this story. And Thomas could not have a supergenius mutation. That would make him seem extremely alien and threatening.

"Thomas is very human," Pung said agreeably. He took a swig from his goblet, probably hiding his amusement.

Cherise looked pained. But she kept quiet.

"So Thomas rescued us." Kessa continued the story, ignoring skeptical looks from Jinishta and a few of the councilors. "And he brought us to a slave farm called Duin."

Her lies became more elaborate as she spoke about their escape from the planet Umdalkdul. The Alashani did not understand what a pilot was, or what a spaceship was. They seemed unsure what Kessa meant by "other planets." They had no words for stars, or for daytime and nighttime. They had never seen sunlight or the sky.

Comprehension only showed in their eyes when Kessa spoke of Ariock's power to heal injured people. That caused a few happy glances. So Kessa embellished his powers, saying, "He defeated the army of Torth that was chasing us, and he used his mighty powers to fly us from Umdalkdul to this world."

"The messiah is great." Chaniyelem bowed her head.

"Wait." Jinishta leaned over her dinnerware, so she could fix Kessa with her luminous eyes. "He killed how many Torth?"

"Many hundreds," Kessa said. "Perhaps as many as a thousand."

Jinishta shifted her gaze to Ariock, studying him as if considering the best way to get rid of him.

"This must all be exaggeration," one Yeresunsa dinner guest said to another.

"No one can kill hundreds of Torth." That was Flen, another of the Yeresunsa.

Kessa suppressed her urge to correct them as they went on debating. Without any solid concept of the sky, they did not comprehend flying long distances, which meant they could not imagine what a Torth fleet looked like, or a spaceport. They did not quite grasp what a storm was.

"But," an elderly Yeresunsa said, "the Torth did defeat him. They shot him, and they nearly killed him. I daresay, shouldn't the messiah be invincible?"

"Right," Jinishta agreed with relief. "If he is so powerful, then why did we find him so wounded and desperate?"

"'He will come to you in need,'" Chaniyelem cut in. "So it was foretold."

"It was foretold," another councilor murmured.

All the councilors bowed their heads toward Ariock, including Deschuba.

Ariock glanced from one white-haired head to the next. Although he was cleaned up and looking satisfied from the meal, his expression soured. His large hand engulfed a stone goblet that was sized for the albino people. He drained the contents.

"He is the Son of Storms," Weptolyso put in.

The Alashani looked inquiring. They clearly had no idea what storms were. They shrugged with incomprehension as Weptolyso and Pung described nuclear bomb detonations.

But their eyes lit up when they heard that Ariock could use his powers to throw large objects.

"He picked up buildings and threw them at the Torth fleet," Weptolyso rumbled, eager to be a storyteller. "It is true. I was there. I saw him do it."

Ariock seemed apprehensive, unable to follow along in the slave tongue. "Kessa, will you tell him to stop? Please, tell them about Thomas and everything he did for us."

"That is a bad idea." Kessa placed her hand on his huge arm. "These people only tolerate Thomas because they believe he is powerless. They must not learn the things he can do. We must not ever hint that he has a power to access the Megacosm, or anything else. Or they will kill him."

Ariock considered that. After a moment, he slumped. "I guess you're right."

"I will warn everyone as soon as I can," Kessa added.

"Thanks," Ariock said. "That's good thinking."

Kessa dipped her head.

"But we need to communicate with Thomas," Ariock said.

"One step at a time," Kessa assured him. "We will think of a way."

Servile people entered and exited, refilling goblets and tending to candelabra and lamps. By the time Weptolyso had finished boasting about Ariock's power and strength, all the food was cleared off the tables, and the councilors sat in sleepy relaxation.

"Kessa," Chaniyelem said. "Tell the messiah that I shall provide whatever he wishes."

"Yes," another eager councilor said. "He need not work as long as he resides in Hufti."

"We will hold banquets and theatrical productions in his honor," Chaniyelem said.

"He will lead us to reclaim our lost cities!" another councilor said in rapture.

Jinishta stood and slammed down her stone goblet.

All conversations ceased. Dinner guests looked startled and scared. Even Ariock flinched after he'd begun to relax.

"The prophet Migyatel never said anything definitive about him." Jinishta flung a pointing finger toward Ariock. "Didn't our ancestors make a mistake like this?"

Her accusation fell like a stone in a pond, causing ripples.

"Have you all forgotten the fake chosen one? The liar?" Jinishta was so incensed, sparks rippled up and down her arms.

Everyone in the banquet hall grew tense.

"Jonathan Stead." Jinishta spat the name.

Ariock only understood the name, nothing else, and he folded his arms. "I guess my great-grandfather did show up here," he said with cynical amusement.

Kessa felt no amusement. Ariock could feel confident, but he was relatively powerless here. She counted eight purple mantles in the banquet hall. Other people in the city wore them, too. Dozens. Perhaps hundreds.

It was easy to imagine what would happen if the Alashani decided that Ariock was their enemy instead of their messiah.

## CHAPTER 2
# BLASPHEMY

Kessa had many questions as the dinner guests continued to argue, but she kept her beak shut. She gave Ariock a look that promised translation later. For now, she figured the best way to help him was to learn by listening.

"Jonathan Stead came to us in darkness, and in need." Sparks crackled along Jinishta's tense body. Her hair bristled. "Was it not said that he had great height? People saw his wounds, and did they not say, 'Here is the messiah, come to deliver us to our lost glory'?"

"Well, that was in Bebeshar," an elderly woman said.

"They are a bit foolish there," someone else agreed.

"And it was ages ago."

"Sit, sit," Chaniyelem urged Jinishta. "Can you deny that he has great height?" She indicated Ariock. "I think there is no mistake."

Jinishta folded her lace-covered arms. "The prophet Migyatel sent word asking for all premiers to search for runaways in the dead city. That is all she said. If he is truly the messiah…" She sized up Ariock with skepticism. "Surely the greatest prophet in ten generations would have mentioned that?"

Uncertain murmurs rippled throughout the banquet hall. Guests eyed Ariock with newfound skepticism.

"What's wrong?" Ariock asked Kessa in a low voice. "What are they saying?"

Kessa placed a hand on his arm. "They had a problem with Jonathan Stead. I will find out more, but I must listen."

A few dinner guests, particularly the ones who wore purple mantles, stood in solidarity with Jinishta.

"Our premier is right."

"Migyatel would know."

"She would have come to Hufti in person, to meet him."

Chaniyelem stood, confident against the rising tide. "I have, in fact, received word from Migyatel, just before this banquet."

Everyone else quieted. Kessa barely understood what a prophet was, but the dinner guests seemed to revere this prophet Migyatel.

"She is on her way," Chaniyelem announced.

That caused a stir. Dinner guests looked at each other, awestruck and excited. They murmured that they must prepare the city for such a grand visitor.

"Is she traveling from Bebeshar?"

"But that is fifteen pendulum orbits from here."

"Such a long way!"

"How far is she?"

"It is an arduous journey, even for someone in good health. She is as old as stalactites."

"I see your doubts, Jinishta," Chaniyelem said with a nod toward the premier. "But surely you will accept Ariock as the messiah once Migyatel announces that he is the one?"

Jinishta looked somewhat mollified. "I suppose."

"You suppose?" Chaniyelem arched an eyebrow.

"I would need to be there in person." Jinishta sounded grudging. "To see Migyatel speak. If the prophet publicly announces that Ariock is the one and only savior who will lead us to light and glory, then yes, I will have no choice but to believe."

"Of course." Chaniyelem seemed satisfied.

Jinishta's voice became firmer and more confident as she went on, staring at Ariock. "Until then? Ariock is an unknown Yeresunsa visiting us from another land. He is just a stranger."

Chaniyelem winced.

"I don't care if you find my lack of faith offensive, High Councilor." Jinishta took another step closer. "We both serve this city, and we both care about the people here. You can concern yourself with parties and banquets, but I have visited the darkness beyond our realm. I have beheld *rekveh*. Our world is far more fragile than you can imagine. If you want to continue enjoying your parties, then you will let me do my job."

Chaniyelem looked like she wanted to argue, but she reconsidered.

"The supposed 'messiah' will be under my command." Jinishta stated it flatly.

Kessa hoped that Ariock would not try to rebel. Jinishta seemed to wield a lot of authority in this room full of top authorities. She was equal or greater than the much older high councilor Chaniyelem.

Sure enough, Chaniyelem gave a stiff nod. "That is fair, Premier Jinishta. The messiah will serve us as a visiting Yeresunsa. For now. When Migyatel arrives, she will foretell his future for everyone to hear, and all shall know who he is."

"Very well," Jinishta said.

Ariock listened to the whole exchange without comprehension. Kessa felt almost as bewildered as he looked.

She leaned closer to Deschuba, the ummin dinner guest. "Who is the prophet Migyatel?" she whispered. "What is a prophet?"

High Councilor Deschuba gave her one of his pitying looks. "A prophet," he said, "is a rare Yeresunsa who has a power to see the future." He hesitated, then added, "Migyatel is never wrong. And she has lived for more than four generations. She was a child when Jonathan Stead arrived in Bebeshar."

"I heard that she predicted a great battle," another dinner guest said knowingly. Other chimed in.

"I heard that she is predicting a flood."

"Oh, that is just nonsense."

Kessa wanted to ask more questions, but she wasn't going to keep excluding Ariock. So she set about translating, assuring Ariock that he was probably safe for a while, at least until the mysterious prophet arrived.

She was in the middle of trying to estimate how long the prophet would take to arrive when Weptolyso caused a commotion.

"Do not call Jonathan Stead a liar!" Weptolyso stood, responding to some disparaging remark from one of the councilors. "He freed a thousand slaves and he had great valor." The nussian puffed up. "Also, beware, for you are in the titanic presence of his son!" He swept a gesture toward Ariock.

If the earlier discussion had caused ripples, this caused a wave. Silverware dropped. Dinner guests gaped at Ariock with renewed fascination.

"That's right," Weptolyso said, as if vindicated. "Ariock Dovanack is the heir of Jonathan Stead, the storm god. Ariock Dovanack is the Son of Storms!"

Ariock sighed. He knew most of those words, and he gazed into his empty goblet as if searching for reasons to leave.

Everyone spoke over each other with renewed vigor, amazed by the unexpected familial link. High Councilor Deschuba gazed at Ariock as if meeting a god.

Even Jinishta looked stunned. "So…" She sat and stared from Weptolyso to Ariock and back again. "Jonathan Stead went back to his home? He actually made it?"

"Yes," Weptolyso told a rapt audience. "He fooled the entire Torth Empire by faking his own death. He stole one of their transports and flew to the paradise from whence he came."

Soon the refugees in the banquet hall were inundated with questions. Haz and Flen interrogated Cherise about paradise. They seemed fascinated by her descriptions of Earth, and they kept interrupting each other, making Cherise laugh shyly.

"On Earth," Pung said, embellishing the slave legend, "in a great palace, Jonathan Stead raised his only child and heir, Ariock Dovanack."

No one mentioned other Dovanack family members. They were dead, and there was no need to complicate the tale.

The Alashani fascination with Jonathan Stead made it clear to Kessa that he had been a real person and not just a myth. For the first time, she had proof—besides the word of Thomas and the conjecture of her friends—that the legend had truly happened. Jonathan Stead was part of Alashani history. Some of their elders might even remember his visit.

But why did they call him a liar?

Kessa cleared her throat for attention. The Alashani were so wrapped up in talk about the messiah and his famous progenitor, no one heard her.

So she stood on her cushioned seat and raised her voice. "Excuse me? Councilors?"

A few councilors glanced her way, but they seemed disinclined to listen to a runaway slave.

Kessa went on, regardless. "I would like to know why you called Jonathan Stead a liar. What did he lie about?"

The hall quieted down.

"Well." Chaniyelem chuckled uneasily. "That is of no importance. It was a long time ago, before any of us were born."

"And it was probably a misunderstanding," another councilor suggested.

Jinishta huffed. "Jonathan Stead broke sacred laws," she said, humorless. "There was no misunderstanding. He claimed to be the messiah so he could demand food and ale and servitude. He took hospitality from the people of Bebeshar. He promised to lead us—all the Alashani—to light and glory. Every swing of the pendulum, he made tantalizing promises."

Kessa began to have an uneasy feeling.

"And then," Jinishta went on, lace-covered arms folded, "he abandoned the Alashani and threatened us all. He was a very powerful Yeresunsa, but instead of using his blessings to serve others, as any Yeresunsa ought to do, he served only himself."

"He ran away," a councilor put in.

"He endangered our world," Jinishta said with disgust. "He put every city, every Alashani, at risk by running to the Torth realm with our secrets. Instead of proving himself to be the messiah, he proved to be a coward. And a traitor."

"All right, Jinishta," Chaniyelem urged. "That's enough. You've made your point."

"He wasn't that bad," another councilor said tentatively. "He deceived people, yes, but he also saved the lives of many hundreds of runaways. He did good deeds."

Electric sparks fizzed across Jinishta's lace outfit and her hair. "Warlords used to do good deeds, in between their gluttonous orgies of destruction."

The councilor who had spoken wilted under her glare.

"We cannot allow Yeresunsa to run amok," Jinishta said. "You all know why."

"It's true," another councilor said meekly. "He was reckless."

"He should have been executed," Jinishta said. "Our ancestors should have tried harder to hunt him down. You have no concept of the Armageddon that would befall us if a Torth ever catches someone like him—someone who knows we exist. We would all be wearing slave collars right now. It is only luck that we remain free."

This missing part of the legend of Jonathan Stead made him sound less than heroic. He had deceived the Alashani. And later, when he'd hidden on Earth, he had assumed a false identity. He had invented the name Garrett Olmstead Dovanack and pretended to be someone he was not.

Layers of deception.

Kessa wondered what sort of person Jonathan Stead had really been.

"Translate for me, runaway slave." Jinishta shifted her disgust toward Ariock. "Tell your overgrown friend that laws matter. I don't care how powerful he is. We are not going to tolerate another Jonathan Stead."

Kessa turned to Ariock. "They are sensitive about the subject of Jonathan Stead."

As she went on, catching Ariock up on the conversation, his mood became introspective. "So my great-grandfather sneaked away from these people?" he said in a dry tone. "I can't imagine why."

Ariock seemed to think that his great-grandfather had gotten fed up with undeserved worship. Maybe that was so, but Kessa suspected that something much darker had spurred the hero to leave this underground haven.

After all, Jonathan Stead had sneaked away from safety. From friends. He had left in a hurry, without good grace or goodbyes, and without any guarantee of getting home to Earth. He had eschewed a comfortable life as a messiah, swapping it for loneliness and deadly risks.

Why?

What would a powerful Yeresunsa have to fear, in this place?

What could be worse than the risk of being recaptured by the Torth Empire and tortured in the Isolatorium for a second time?

Kessa recalled the gruesome Hall of Heads.

"Deschuba," she said, focused on the nearest councilor. "When Jonathan Stead was among your people, did he tell anyone that he could read minds?"

The immense hall was suddenly quieter than a Torth forum. Every conversation stopped. Dinner guests gaped at Kessa, and even servants paused in their duties.

"Right," Pung said, apparently oblivious to the dangerous tension. "If you don't allow mind readers into your cities, then why did you allow Jonathan Stead to live freely among you?"

"Blasphemy!" A warrior stood so fast, a platter fell to the ground.

"Blasphemy!" Another stood. Electric sparks crackled over his leather tunic.

Kessa shrank back.

Ariock thrust his arm in front of her, blocking the warriors from sight. "What's their problem?" His lighthearted mood had vanished. He eyed the warriors with apprehension. "What did you tell them?"

"Jonathan Stead," a councilor said, his voice shaking with fury, "was not a *rekveh*. Recant what you said!"

Chaniyelem was already on her feet and talking, trying to calm everyone. "Of course Jonathan Stead was not a *rekveh*," she said in a soothing tone. "He was an ordinary Yeresunsa. Right, Kessa?"

The truth was less important here than survival. "Right," Kessa said from behind the thick arm blocking her view.

Ariock cautiously pulled his arm away, but he remained alert. Weptolyso looked alert, too. And Pung. Those two exchanged dubious glances, no doubt wanting to argue the facts about Jonathan Stead.

"Kessa did not intend any offense," Weptolyso said with caution. "But every slave legend about Jonathan Stead says that he was a mind reader."

"Your legends are wrong," a warrior stated.

"Thomas confirmed it for us, though," Pung said.

Kessa signaled Pung to keep quiet, but he failed to see her and went on. "He told us that Jonathan Stead could read minds."

All eight of the warrior dinner guests stood. They looked ready to use tables and plates as weapons, and even the councilors seemed outraged. They might not worship Jonathan Stead as a hero, but their ancestors had, after all, mistaken him for their messiah. They had welcomed him into their underground paradise.

"The thing you call Thomas is a *rekveh*," Chaniyelem said calmly. "Of course it tells lies."

This time, even Pung sensed the danger of contradicting the dinner hosts. So did the refugees from Duin. They kept their beaks closed and tried to look agreeable.

Kessa recalled the first words she'd heard from an Alashani. *"Are there mind readers among you?"*

Jonathan Stead must have encountered this attitude, and as a mind reader, he would have known the danger of a truthful answer. He must have lied in order to avoid decapitation.

No one moved a hair. The room seemed to hold its breath.

"Chaniyelem? Jinishta?" Kessa considered her words with great care. "If you say that Jonathan Stead was not a mind reader, then you must be correct."

Councilors and warriors returned to their seats with nervous laughs and relieved smiles. Weptolyso and Pung were wise enough not to contradict the lie this time. They looked sour, but they kept silent.

"Runaway slaves tend to be ignorant," High Councilor Deschuba assured his friend Karyum. He turned to Kessa and said, "You will learn our ways. It takes time."

"You seem like a lovely person," Chaniyelem added.

Another councilor leaned over. "Please accept my apologies for overreacting to what you said."

"Of course." Kessa forced a forgiving smile onto her beak.

To Ariock, she said, "I think I understand why Jonathan Stead needed to leave this place. He was afraid they would learn the truth about him."

"What truth?" Ariock remained alert, eyeing the warriors.

"That he was a *rekveh*." Kessa marveled at how masterful Jonathan Stead must have been with his deceit. He must have faked every reaction he had, even his facial expressions. His moods. His words.

Given the same situation, Thomas would no doubt confess his ability to read minds. He would tell the truth even if it meant decapitation.

Now Thomas was isolated inside a prison somewhere, guarded by Yeresunsa who bragged about killing *rekvehs*.

This was a world where Yeresunsa hunted mind readers, apparently for fun.

Kessa hoped Ariock would get a lot of rest and recover his powers quickly. Thomas needed him.

# CHAPTER 3

# WORSHIPPED

Ariock awoke under a velvet blanket that covered his whole body, atop a soft mattress that was unbelievably huge. He could spread his arms and legs without reaching the edges.

For a fleeting second, he wondered if he'd reverted to childhood. Books and toys would fit comfortably in his hands, the way they should. Was his dad alive? Maybe he was in his familiar blue-and-silver bedroom, rather than a cave.

He opened his eyes to see a ceiling of hammered gold, which reflected the flicker of many candles.

Then he remembered that Chaniyelem had insisted that he sleep as a guest in her palace. She had personally led him to this ornate, immense bedchamber. His parents were dead—because of him—and Vy might be on the brink of losing her foot for the same reason.

If Ariock abandoned Vy, then she would surely never sleep nestled in the crook of his arm again, the way she had on the streamship.

He would lose the one and only person who could reminisce about Earth with him, the only person who really understood where he came from. Vy had visited his lonely mansion and met his mother. And she had forgiven him for whatever shortcomings that background left him with.

Ariock sat up. Water cascaded down one of the black marble walls in a soothing stream. Flames danced in soapstone sconces, illuminating baskets on marble shelves. Golden filigree accented stone surfaces.

"*Aonswa?*" An ivory-white woman knelt, bending her graceful neck in a pose of supplication. She offered up an earthenware plate with pale sashimi and a steaming bowl of porridge. Her laced robe was so transparent, Ariock needed to look away.

Another albino woman stood nearby. Her laced-up outfit did not hide much, either.

On Earth, their frilly chains and ruby diadems would have implied wealth. But such adornments seemed run-of-the-mill among the Alashani, and these women had the downcast eyes of maidservants or slaves.

"Thanks." Ariock accepted the breakfast platter, which included ivory utensils inlaid with black designs.

He was famished. His body had already forgotten the feast. Ariock had seen the people he'd healed eat ridiculous amounts afterward, and he guessed it had something to do with energy replenishment.

As he sampled the delicate slices of fresh fish, he wondered if his powers had recovered.

*Bad idea*, he thought, remembering Orla's scolding.

Yet he needed to know. Without powers, he was just a grotesque freak, helpless and burdensome. Vy wouldn't want him around. No one would. He needed Yeresunsa powers if he was going to do anything at all worthwhile.

Very cautious, very tentative, Ariock let go of his sense of bodily limitation. He let his awareness seep into the air that enveloped him.

No pain.

Encouraged, he began to spread himself farther, into solids such as the bed and the stone floor. Air was nebulous and slippery for him. Solids offered enough resistance to help him go slow.

"Ahem."

A feminine throat clearing startled Ariock, and he snapped fully back into his body.

The tall, arabesque double doors were open, and Jinishta stood there, with an ummin in an immaculate outfit by her side. Jinishta said something brusque in the slave tongue.

"Good morning, Ariock," the well-dressed ummin said.

"Kessa?" Ariock stared, disbelieving. Kessa wore a lacework tunic and an embroidered head cover. Tiny, jeweled fringes framed her face and hems. Such a superficial change shouldn't transform a person so much. Kessa still had her wrinkles, and the scar around her neck…yet somehow, she looked like a new ummin.

"Oh, these clothes are gifts." Kessa tugged her tunic and laughed in a self-conscious way. "Councilor Deschuba—well, Yenna, his life mate—wanted to dress me up. They will not let the messiah's translator wear old rags."

Jinishta said something that sounded more businesslike than "good morning." With her swishy outfit and purple mantle, she looked ready for a busy day. Frilly ivory spears poked up from the gold-fletched quiver on her back.

"Jinishta says it is lawful for a visiting Yeresunsa to obey the local premier, or leader," Kessa translated. "That is her. She will assess your capabilities today."

"Okay," Ariock said, uncertain what that entailed. "But can I visit Vy?"

"We will," Kessa assured him.

"And we have to be able to see Thomas. We can't keep putting that off."

"I know."

As they spoke, Jinishta used her powers to send a bundle of purple cloth toward Ariock, which unfurled as it flew.

"All Yeresunsa are required to wear a mantle," Kessa told Ariock. "It is illegal to hide your powers. Everyone must be able to see what you are."

Ariock doubted that anyone would mistake him for a normal person unless they were blind. Even then, his deep voice was unlike that of an Alashani. But he allowed the mantle to tug itself over his shoulders. It wasn't quite large enough to hang, like a cape, and the cloth stretched tight across his chest.

Pinning the mantle in place with her powers, Jinishta opened her small hand and sent a clasp flying toward him. She used her powers to deftly fasten the mantle.

Ariock tried not to show how impressed he was by her ability to multitask. She must have practiced for years, to master her powers with such casual ease.

Well, he could probably match her feats, if he really tried. Maybe he just needed a bit of practice.

Jinishta glided away, as if bored with him. She spoke over her shoulder in the slave tongue.

Kessa translated. "Jinishta says you may take a moment to finish eating your breakfast and washing. Get dressed. Make yourself look impressive. We will wait outside. Then you will come with us to visit Vy at the infirmary."

Those were the right words to get Ariock to hurry up.

He finished the meal in a few bites, all but inhaling the porridge, which had an earthy mushroom flavor. He splashed water on his face to wash and used gestures to persuade the serving girls to give him a privacy break. They obeyed, but only with pouty looks. Before they deigned to leave, they unfolded a massive woolen tunic, its frills weighted with bejeweled tassels. They made suggestive gestures that he should wear it.

Ariock pitied the knitting team that must have been commissioned to create this monstrous tunic.

He was eye-catching enough without any weird adornments. Instead of wearing the ridiculous thing, he washed up, then affixed a minimal number of armored plates over his undergarments.

Fit to be seen, he entered a lamplit corridor. Kessa and Jinishta lounged against a wall of polished granite, carved with friezes. A few dozen albino people seemed to be waiting with them.

"*Aonswa.*" A woman bowed as soon as she saw Ariock.

Awestruck people parted before him, squeezing against walls. Men and women bowed their heads, murmuring "*aonswa*" as Ariock passed by.

He didn't need a translator to know what that word meant.

Messiah.

Jinishta looked disgruntled as she led Ariock out of the palace, into a cobblestone alleyway that seemed scooped out of the stone buildings that cradled it. Curious people peered out from windows and square-cut doorways. Parents hoisted children onto their shoulders for a better view.

None were undernourished or glazed-eyed, like the slaves of Torth-ruled lands. They wore soft woolens bedecked with jeweled chains and gemstones.

Yet they begged for salvation.

A few people—richly dressed aliens—even prostrated themselves when they saw Ariock. Somehow, their solemn worship seemed more genuine than that of the albinos.

*"Aonswa."*

It was just a word. Just a harmless belief. Ariock relaxed his shoulders, not wanting to seem aloof. He wasn't going to act like a Torth, gliding past slaves, pretending not to see their needs. That would be rude.

He dared to offer a hesitant smile to the worshippers.

That transformed them. Their eyes sparkled as if he had showered them with gifts and praise. *"Aonswa!"* People laughed to each other and clapped each other's arms.

Not everyone greeted Ariock that way. He glimpsed a few suspicious frowns. The unbelievers peered around lintels or down through rooftop balustrades, but mostly they hid behind happier onlookers.

The most zealous worshippers wanted to touch Ariock, but Jinishta's stare made them flinch back. It even worked on a hefty nussian. Jinishta might be a delicate Alashani maiden, but her Yeresunsa cape endowed her with authority. She didn't need to make threats.

The Alashani knelt before the person they believed to be their messiah.

Apparently, they really wanted a savior. Yet they dwelled in a wonderland untouched by Torth or bombs or storms. Stone outcrops crowded each other, riddled with narrow stairwells, burbling grottoes, and tunnels aglow with lamplit gemstones. This underground city was carved with magic. It was magical.

As Ariock smiled and waved, he inwardly figured that the Alashani historians must have forgotten the reason for their ancient prophecy. They wanted light and glory. They wanted their lost cities. Yet eons must have passed—hundreds of generations—since their ancestors walked aboveground.

The Alashani had adapted to darkness. They were all albinos.

They would burn in daylight.

# CHAPTER 4

# VITALITY

White-shrouded people breezed in and out of openings that looked dwarfish to Ariock. Jinishta glided into one of the stone-carved doorways.

Kessa sized up the ancient, worn-looking staircase where Jinishta had gone, and she sized up Ariock. Then she shrugged, gave him a pitying look, and followed Jinishta.

Ariock sucked in his breath, twisted sideways, and ducked under the lintel. His shoulders pressed against the sloped ceiling.

Jinishta glanced back and made a dry remark.

"She says they should have used the nussian infirmary, as a courtesy to you," Kessa translated. "This is the main infirmary."

Ariock couldn't tell whether that was an insult or an awkward apology. He had to edge his way up the stairs, bent double.

They entered a rough-hewn corridor, also sized for people much smaller than Ariock. A billowing layer of gauze formed a wall, broken at intervals by stout pillars.

Ariock had to walk bent over. Every time someone squeezed past him, they leaned into the curtains while he moved aside, but he still felt as if he was blocking their path and towering over them.

Passersby gave him tight-lipped, curious, or businesslike stares. Not everybody in the city worshipped the messiah, it seemed.

"*Aonswa!*" Orla popped out from the gauzy curtains, seeming delighted to see him.

Jinishta urged Ariock and Kessa to follow the teenaged healer. Ariock pushed through curtains, into a lamplit chamber that was as long as the corridor. More gauzy curtains probably concealed bedridden patients.

He'd hardly taken two steps before Orla held out her hands in the healing pose and made a demand.

"Please sit down," Kessa translated. "Orla wants to heal you."

Ariock touched the soreness where his wound itched and throbbed. Surely other patients needed healing more than he did. "I feel fine," he said.

Kessa translated, but Orla made an impatient sound and snapped back.

"Sit," Kessa said. "Orla says otherwise you will fall over."

Ariock thought that was ridiculous, but Orla folded her arms across her Yeresunsa mantle, and Jinishta had a threatening look. One or both of them could force him to sit.

So he settled onto the stone floor, cross-legged. As soon as he was down, Orla stood on her tiptoes to spread her hands over his wound.

A titanic wave of health crashed throughout his body. His heartbeat strengthened. His pores felt clean. He felt vigorous enough to lift a truck.

And his wound?

Ariock tugged aside his Yeresunsa mantle and opened the garment beneath. What he saw, instead of exposed muscle, was wholly smooth skin, marred only by a knot of scar tissue.

Orla swayed dizzily. Jinishta steadied her.

There was more conversation, but Ariock was too busy trying to figure out how to express his gratitude. The Alashani really ought to focus their healing efforts on more deserving people, like Vy and Thomas.

One of the gauzy curtains swung aside, pushed by a white-shrouded woman. It revealed a cushy bed—and Vy on the bed, looking like she'd barely survived a grueling ordeal. Yet she looked serene as she studied Ariock.

"Orla says she was partially depleted when she healed you the first time," Kessa told him, translating. "She was able to do her best work this time."

Jinishta interjected a few words as Orla went on.

"They say you need more time to recover," Kessa translated. "You should avoid getting shot by Torth." That must be a joke, since Orla had said it in an airy tone, and she laughed. "You will have some raw power at your disposal now. Don't overuse your power. You must rest a lot, and be gentle with yourself for a few pendulum orbits. I mean, days. Behave as if you are recuperating from a serious injury. Which you are. The damage is healed, but your inner… sphere?…is depleted, and will take time to replenish."

"Thank you." Ariock walked to Vy's bed, keeping his head ducked to avoid the ceiling.

Jinishta and Kessa caught up to him. Jinishta's tone was pedantic.

"Jinishta says you can try healing a less injured patient," Kessa said. "She wants you to prove what you can do, but go easy. She wants you to resist healing Vy. 'We have plenty of healers taking care of her,' she says."

A white blanket covered Vy, flat over her lower body.

Too flat.

"Don't look," Vy said, seeing his attention where her foot should be. But her voice was frail. She couldn't stop Ariock from pulling away the blanket to reveal the extent of her injuries.

His heart lurched at the sight of only one leg.

"They couldn't save that part of me," Vy said in a faint voice.

Her missing leg still had part of a thigh, and a knee, but it ended just below that. Blood seeped through a cap of thick bandages.

Vy's other leg—her only leg—was disfigured, crisscrossed by a mess of bandages.

"They had to amputate," Vy said. Her voice was rough, hiding what must be enormous horror or pain. "There was almost nothing left. Just rot and broken bones. It was really a lot of damage."

Orla, the nurse, and Jinishta were all talking, demanding Kessa's translation services, no doubt instructing Ariock on what he should or shouldn't do.

They didn't matter. They weren't the ones in agony and anguish because of his stupid failure.

Ariock held his hands over Vy's lower body. Without further thought, he connected to her life spark and poured his newly restored energy into her. He kept at it even as Vy flushed, even as the air between them writhed and sparkled.

"Stop!" Orla and Jinishta both shouted in the slave tongue.

Ariock stopped only because he saw that nothing he did would regrow Vy's missing limb.

Her existing leg looked healthier. She sat up, refreshed and lively. She unwound bandages with amazement.

"I wish I'd done that for you sooner," Ariock said, full of regrets. "I should have done it right away."

Vy explored smooth, pink skin with her hand. Her stump of a knee looked healthy, with a knot of scar tissue at the bottom.

Her other leg was now whole. It looked withered, but Ariock supposed it would get stronger.

Ariock inwardly resolved to never make another mistake with his powers. He absolutely needed to master self-control. Normal people could afford mistakes. He had to be a lot more careful, or else people lost their limbs—or their lives.

Maybe the Alashani Yeresunsa could teach him how to attack and defend with precision, even in the middle of a chaotic battle?

Orla and the nurse made exclamations over Vy.

"That was reckless," Kessa translated for Jinishta, who spoke in a forbidding tone. "Very impressive—I am impressed—but you are recovering from a serious injury, and that must have depleted your powers."

When Ariock checked to see if he could spread his awareness, he did so with ease. He sensed every life spark in the vast hospital room.

Some of those life sparks were guttering. Dozens of injured people needed care.

Jinishta kept jabbering at him, and Kessa translated. "If you ignore a warning headache, I cannot guarantee that my power will be sufficient to revive you. So you must take care of yourself. You must— Where are you going?"

Ariock walked toward the next patient in the next bed, ignoring the scolding voices of Jinishta and Orla, and even Kessa.

He recognized the refugee who lay in the bed. She was one of the familiar ummins from Duin.

Ariock healed her.

Yells and protests followed him to the next bed, where he healed another ummin. And then another.

By the time he'd healed an eighth patient, both Orla and Jinishta fell silent. They followed him from bedside to bedside as he healed every patient in the room, including lots of albinos and other people he didn't recognize.

The healed patients got out of their beds. Ummins or alien people, they bowed to him and thanked him profusely. Some followed him to see what else he would do.

The inhibitor serum must be gone, or nearly gone, from his system. Ariock could not guess why Orla and Jinishta stared at him as if spooked. They should be glad that he wasn't enfeebled and bedridden, shouldn't they?

This was a hospital. People came for Yeresunsa healing, and he was able to provide that.

He felt fine.

# CHAPTER 5

# RAW POWER

"I want to see Thomas," Ariock said, his voice echoing off marble columns. "Where is he?"

Jinishta said something dismissive in reply to Kessa's translation.

After the hospital, Jinishta had led Ariock and Kessa through a food district, where she'd paid for meals they could eat while walking. Ariock wished he could have shared that experience with Vy, but Vy had declined to join them.

"I don't want to be dragged around in a handcart," Vy had said with shame. "Besides, Chaniyelem offered to get me fitted for a prosthetic leg. I want to meet the artisan as soon as possible."

If she was trying to avoid Ariock—if she detested him—then she was doing a good job of hiding it. So Ariock had wished her luck and promised to check on her later. Then he'd followed the impatient Jinishta.

But she hadn't brought him to see Thomas.

Instead, she had led Ariock to some kind of temple for Yeresunsa. Slender albino people emerged from vaulted side chambers, every one of them adorned with a short purple cape. Kessa was the only person in sight who wasn't a Yeresunsa. She seemed aware of it, clicking her fingers in a timid way.

Even Ariock felt small amid the fluted columns that spread up to a multichambered, vaulted ceiling, so distant it was lost in shadows. Friezes embossed every wall, depicting stylized albino warriors who shot lightning at ghoulish apes. Torches glowed behind translucent, frilly soapstone shields. The subdued glow illuminated trickling waterfalls that poured continuously into shallow channels of slick marble.

This chamber was meant to be impressive. But Ariock only felt annoyed and impatient. Was Thomas being mistreated somewhere?

Jinishta began to speak to the congregation. She paused frequently, giving Kessa enough time to translate.

"Ariock," Jinishta said, "has proved to have a generous power to heal severe injuries. He has raw power and talent as great as his father, Jonathan Stead."

The gathered Yeresunsa gawked in awe.

Ariock folded his arms. If this was an official introduction, he hoped they would hurry up and get it over with. How many times did he need to ask about Thomas?

Jinishta turned to Ariock and made an inquiry.

"What else can you do?" Kessa translated.

"I can cause earthquakes. And storms." Ariock wondered if they expected him to list every single feat he had ever done. "Lightning. Tornadoes. I can make things levitate. And shield myself. I can bend metal. And I guess I can kill a lot of Torth." He shrugged. "Um, I don't really know what else. I've only been using Yeresunsa powers for a couple of weeks."

Kessa gave a ragged sigh and translated.

The gathered Yeresunsa murmured with unease. Their surprise skyrocketed at the last part, but if Jinishta was impressed, she gave no sign of it. She calmly asked another question.

"Can you show us your production of electric light?" Kessa translated.

In response, Ariock held up his hands, connected to the air, and sent energy zipping from one immense palm to the other. Lightning crackled and twitched between his hands.

Jinishta nodded and asked another question. Ariock quit the lightning display.

"Can you channel water?" Kessa translated.

Ariock felt a little bit ashamed to admit his ignorance. "Uh, what does that mean? I don't think I've ever tried."

In response, Jinishta lifted a slender arm toward one of the soothing waterfalls. When she lifted her fingers, the water parted from the stone and twined upward, like a snake climbing around an invisible string.

She let the water splash down and gave Ariock an expectant look.

He gawked at where the water had been.

"Jinishta wants you to try doing it," Kessa prodded him.

"Um…" Ariock sent his awareness into the waterfall. "Okay."

When he tried to inhabit the water, it slipped away. It wasn't like air or solid materials. Instead of receiving his expanded awareness like a comfortable item of clothing, it rolled away.

Ariock poured more focus into it. He stopped paying attention to voices, and to the perceptions of his core body. He felt as if he could inhabit the water—he'd had it for a split second—but it kept rolling away. He must be making a stupid error somewhere.

"Ariock." Kessa poked his leg.

Ariock snapped back to his human body.

"Jinishta says you have potential with water," Kessa said. "But water is a difficult skill to master, and we will discuss it later. For now, show us your other powers. Can you infuse yourself with extra speed?"

"What?" Ariock said.

Kessa gave him a helpless look.

"Can't we do this later?" Ariock spoke directly to Jinishta, pausing to give Kessa time to translate. "I don't mean to be rude, but I'm worried about my friend, the one you promised to protect. How much longer do I need to wait to see Thomas?"

Surely a time estimate wasn't too much to ask.

But Jinishta suddenly yanked one of the frilly spears out of her quiver, and, in a blur of hyperspeed, she launched herself at Ariock.

He shielded himself with condensed air.

If Jinishta had hurled the spear instead of her whole body, then maybe she would have managed to stab Ariock. Instead, she bounced off his air shield. It didn't knock her down. She apparently sensed its invisible appearance, and although her momentum was too great for her to slow down in time, she ran up the shield and did a graceful backflip.

She landed lightly on her feet and tucked the spear away, all in one casual motion.

Ariock found himself gawking again, and he closed his mouth. Jinishta had just proved that she could have attacked him even faster than he could register her motions. She could have stabbed him.

But she'd intended no harm; this was just a display.

It had never occurred to Ariock to use his expanded awareness as masterfully as she had done. And he couldn't imagine how Jinishta moved with such inhuman speed.

Could he do that?

"Your shielding is impressive," Kessa said, interpreting as Jinishta spoke to him. "I have never seen anyone cloak themselves in air. But I suspect you may have a few unexamined weaknesses. Perhaps I do, as well." Jinishta asked a question, and Kessa said, "She wants to know if you will spar with her?"

Ariock opened and closed his mouth, unsure how to respond to such a request. No one had ever politely offered to fight him. He could deal with enraged or murderous enemies…but a well-dressed little woman who was supposed to be the equivalent of his boss?

It was unthinkable. He might accidentally kill her.

Jinishta gave him an exasperated look of pity and used her powers to telekinetically fetch a velvet bag. She pulled out something that looked like two round bars of soap, or two hockey pucks. She spoke to Ariock in a reassuring tone.

"Jinishta says, 'We aim to touch each other with charcoal, not to hurt each other,'" Kessa translated. "The winner is whoever marks the skin of the other person first with this charcoal."

Ariock found himself considering a sparring match, despite his worries for Thomas. He yearned to measure his unpracticed skill against that of the premier Yeresunsa. Had years of practice made Jinishta a better warrior than him? If he had any problematic weaknesses, then surely he needed to learn about those. He ought to correct his deficits before he made another devastating mistake.

"Jinishta says she knows you are weakened from your ordeals in the dead city," Kessa went on, translating. "And also from all the people you healed. That must have tired you out. She promises to be gentle with you."

Ariock raised an eyebrow to let Jinishta know that she was underestimating him. He felt as strong as ever.

Jinishta said something else, beckoning.

"She wants to take you to a sparring room," Kessa translated.

Ariock exhaled in frustration. "I have to check on Thomas," he said. "That's more important than—"

A disk zoomed in front of his face and hovered there, like a curious hornet, urging him to either swat it away or grab it. Only the center was charcoal. The rest was some kind of leather, for clean gripping.

Ariock grabbed the disk, but he wasn't sold yet. He glowered at Jinishta. "I'm not sparring with you," he said. "Unless—"

Jinishta sped away, faster than humanly possible.

The remaining Yeresunsa gestured for Ariock to follow her. They were growing rowdy, like sports fans getting psyched for the biggest match of the year. Someone used powers to shove Ariock in the back, urging him to follow Jinishta.

The shove nearly knocked him over. If he'd been on defense, with his awareness expanded, he would not have stumbled in such an embarrassing way. When he was in battle mode, he was immovable.

"Fine." Ariock gripped the sparring disk. "But this is it. Tell Jinishta that we have to visit Thomas after I win." He exaggerated that with a confident smile.

Kessa hurried to keep pace with his long strides. "Ariock." She sounded stressed-out. "Isn't it possible…" She seemed to inwardly correct herself, and tried again. "I mean, is it possible that you may not win?"

Ariock glanced down at the ummin elder, saddened by her wariness. She had missed his exaggeration. "I'm aware that I can lose," Ariock assured her. "Kessa, you can say whatever you want to me. I need a friend who can be honest. Tell me the truth."

Kessa's eyes crinkled. "I will be your Thomas. That is well."

Ariock felt tension ease off his shoulders. She had a quick wit.

"Perhaps," Kessa told him, "while you are learning techniques from the warriors, I will learn how well the Alashani guard their prison."

Ariock gave Kessa a look of gratitude before he ducked into the sparring chamber. Maybe he wouldn't need to do everything alone.

Kessa had loyal, unpretentious friends among the refugees from Duin. More than a hundred ummins might be able to befriend prison workers and learn secrets that the Alashani were unwilling to share with a powerful stranger.

# A BLESSING OF STRENGTH

The sparring chamber looked like an emulation of the dead city, with precipitous ledges, rubble, and dim lighting. The space was more vertical than horizontal. No rain, but it did have oil slicks and treacherous puddles.

Ariock explored crevices with his extended awareness. His opponent would be able to squeeze through most of the hidden passageways, whereas he could not.

It probably wouldn't matter.

He gripped his sparring disk and stood in the base of the chamber, facing the much smaller Jinishta. Blue agate clips held back her puff of white hair. She'd removed her decorative quiver and spears, but otherwise she remained confident in her elegant clothes.

Onlookers peered through cutaways at the very top of the chamber. Torchlight illuminated their faces. Kessa sat in one of those cutaways, probably boosted there by someone. The Yeresunsa were treating her like an honored guest.

"You may use anything within the sparring chamber." Kessa's voice echoed down to Ariock. "But do not use anything outside the chamber." Someone must have given her a rundown of the rules. "No killing. No maiming. Your goal is to mark the skin of your opponent with charcoal."

Jinishta had a ready stance.

Ariock thought of his mother, dead in his arms. He thought of Vy, with a leg gone. This combat match was designed to avoid results like that.

These Yeresunsa warriors learned to master their powers. They must hold the key to self-control, or else they would not have a functioning underground civilization. It would all be wreckage.

"If you are ready," Kessa said, "I will count down. The fight starts when I say 'one.'"

Jinishta's confidence bespoke skill. She was going to give him a taste of what self-control looked like for a Yeresunsa in battle mode.

Ariock gave a nod. If his opponent resorted to brute force instead of exhibiting skill, then he would quit and walk away. He wasn't here to learn brutality.

"Three," Kessa said. "Two."

Ariock wrapped himself in a shield of air for self-defense.

"One."

Jinishta's disk boomeranged at Ariock's face and smacked his air shield, leaving a puff of charcoal dust that never touched his skin. The disk returned to her waiting hand within a second. She looked slightly ashamed of the failed attempt, but she hopped upward.

About thirty feet upward.

Ariock gawked as Jinishta somersaulted high above him, flipping backward in midair to land on a narrow ledge. He had never dreamed of trying reckless acrobatic stunts. Usually, he wanted to minimize the space he took up. Every move he made was cautious, so he wouldn't accidentally hurt his friends.

Before he could throw his disk at Jinishta, she slipped behind debris, vanishing faster than a cat.

Ariock spread his awareness. He located her life spark speeding through a passageway, and he knew he could expose her by tearing down some debris. But that might endanger her. These albino people looked more fragile than ummins.

Something slammed against his air shield from behind.

He'd been so focused on the target of Jinishta, he'd forgotten that she could attack him from any direction, using her powers. Ariock firmed up his shield. He would not be shoved or beaten.

Maybe he should attack instead of react?

It would be a challenge while fending off Jinishta's rock projectiles, and to manage it without hurting the small warrior—

Ariock's own sparring disk jerked out of his hand.

He was so surprised, he lost his train of thought. That was when Jinishta picked him up.

She probably meant to slam him against a wall.

The sensation of being lifted off the ground by an invisible force was so unnerving for Ariock, he countered it immediately, rooting himself. He slammed back to the ground.

The pressure shifted and increased. Jinishta was still trying to throw him.

Ariock increased his own efforts as well. He connected himself to the ground like he was a tree, or a mountain. No one was going to knock him off his feet.

Abruptly, Jinishta changed tactics. The instant she stopped trying to throw him, Ariock remade his shield of pressurized air—just in time. Her rocks shattered against it.

Ariock sensed the life spark of Jinishta scurrying through unseen passageways. But she had stopped. Why?

One of her slender white hands appeared as if ready to catch something.

Ariock's sparring disk sailed toward her extended hand like a tiny frisbee. She was going to leave him weaponless.

He seized the disk with an extension of his awareness.

Jinishta tugged. Ariock tugged harder. She tugged more, but he was stronger. The disk whipped back into his waiting hand.

Jinishta could probably make the disk smack him for an easy win. Ariock trapped it inside his huge fist, careful not to let charcoal mar the skin of his hand. He wasn't going to let a technical mistake make him the loser.

His opponent remained hidden. Ariock could not see her body language or access her skin. He wanted to rip her disk away, but he couldn't see it. This chamber was riddled with places for someone Jinishta-sized to sneak around and conceal herself.

Maybe he should level the playing field?

Ariock hated himself for the thought. This sparring chamber was carefully crafted. He was here to learn, not here to wreck things.

But he needed to get to her if he was going to win.

Carefully, Ariock extended his free hand toward the rocky debris that shielded Jinishta. Very carefully, he dismantled a few rocks. The goal was to expose Jinishta. He would not hurt her or cause any excessive—

She telekinetically seized Ariock and threw him backward.

Ariock had to react fast, spiking out his awareness as he slammed against a wall hard enough to cause a mini avalanche. Rocks rained down.

But he had shielded himself in time, and he was unharmed.

Jinishta made no sound when Ariock used his powers to forcefully pin her against a wall, high up. She didn't plead for mercy. Instead, she crackled with the energy of a storm, not nearly as delicate as she looked. Shock waves rolled off her. Unseen tentacles of force tried to disrupt his invisible grip. Jinishta had the strength of a gorgon or a jinn, condensed into a tiny package.

But ultimately, she was no stronger than a Torth jumper shuttle. And Ariock had destroyed plenty of those.

He casually broke free from her grip.

Jinishta's eyes widened with surprised outrage as Ariock ignored her attempts to throw him, to pin him, or to whip him with shock waves. She was mighty, but he was the rocky ground. He was the air between them. He was the energy of the room.

He approached her, absorbing every attack, no matter how unexpectedly strong.

Ariock lifted his hand and levitated his sparring disk, ready to sail it through her crackling field of electricity.

A speedy sensation entered his extended awareness. Stalactites zoomed toward him. Debris walls ripped themselves apart and flew at him. Rock shards aimed to impale him.

The entire room was wrenched apart in an effort to kill him.

Ariock had to defend himself. As he firmed up his shielding, he felt Jinishta blast free from his force-grip.

She bounced, then flipped a somersault in midair, so hyperfast that he couldn't pin her right away. On her way down, she used her momentum to swipe her hand and send a charcoal disk spinning toward his face. At the same time, she forked lightning at him.

Falling boulders, stalactites, and lightning were too deadly for him to ignore, so he spread his defenses. He knocked away her tiny little charcoal disk as well. But while he focused on all that…his own disk jerked out of his grasp, wheeled up, and tapped him lightly on the cheek.

It fell away. Its mission was accomplished.

Jinishta slammed to the ground. Her lightning died, and the last falling rocks tumbled to stillness.

Ariock touched his grizzled cheek, unsure if the charcoal had really marked him. His fingers came away smudged.

"Jinishta is the winner." Kessa sounded relieved, and so did the rest of the audience. They laughed politely while staring, horrified, at the wreckage that used to be the sparring chamber. Dust motes swirled in the golden glow cast by the few remaining torches.

Ariock chuckled. At least no one had gotten hurt.

Jinishta remained kneeling, still panting from her efforts. Her clothes and face were smudged with dirt. Her mantle was askew, and her hair was in disarray.

Ariock supposed he ought to feel ashamed at his defeat, but instead, he felt hopeful that he might win next time. There were so many ways he could improve! So many new techniques to learn!

He offered his hand to help Jinishta stand. He had to kneel to reach her. "That was fun," he said. "I hope we can do it again?"

She looked chagrined, not victorious, as she gripped his fingers and hauled herself up. She gave a pained look at the remnants of the chamber and spoke in a rueful tone.

"Jinishta says that was not an ideal win for her," Kessa translated. "She broke your focus. Any trained warrior would have withstood such a simple trick."

Ariock nodded, ashamed that he had fallen for a simple trick.

He'd probably made sparring mistakes that he wasn't even aware of. He reviewed the match in his mind, determined to figure out how Jinishta had exploited his focus.

And how had she infused herself with extra speed? Extra strength, too. She could leap thirty feet straight up.

If Ariock could enhance his own strength like that…well. The next time he fought an army, he might actually win.

He needed to be able to protect all his friends, instead of leaving friends dead whenever he had a confrontation with enemies. He needed to learn.

Jinishta said something else in her dainty accent, mentioning "Jonathan Stead."

"Jinishta says she should have known you have freakish strength," Kessa said. "Like Jonathan Stead. Especially after you healed all those people."

Freakish. Of course. Everyone used that term to describe him. Ariock tried not to show his shame.

"Your strength can be a great blessing to the city of Hufti," Kessa said, translating.

Jinishta clasped his forearm in what must be her alien version of a handshake, and went on.

"That was the best sparring match she's ever had," Kessa said. "You have heroic potential, if you are willing to learn and to practice. She would be honored to teach you. Will you accept a schedule of lessons with her?"

Honored? Ariock nodded with a grin, happy to show his eagerness to learn. "Yes, please," he said in the slave tongue. He knew a few simple phrases, at least.

Jinishta gave him a very small smile, the only nongrim expression he'd seen from her.

"You should meet her at the monastery pendulum at the beginning of each orbit," Kessa translated. "I guess she means at the start of each wake cycle? Jinishta will teach you centeredness first. That should help you gain a better understanding of the limits and scope of your power."

# CHAPTER 7

# A SINGULAR MIND

Thomas craved the Megacosm with a psychotic level of need.

Sometimes he was able to claw his way into some distant Torth's mental audience for a second or two. It only worked until they realized how their own orbiters were reacting to his uncouth misery and his gigantic mind. Then they cast him out.

Thomas was a bedraggled orphan with festering wounds, starved and dying. He was unwelcome among the gods. No Torth wanted to experience the incessant, lonely, torturous curiosity that had become his existence.

Although the Upward Governess herself actually granted him a microsecond of her enveloping attention.

Just a crumb.

Just once.

His former mentor hadn't seemed to be gloating. She had, in fact, seemed entirely shocked *(!!!)* to experience his mind. It seemed the Torth military had carpet-bombed a portion of the dead city. The Megacosm was full of swapped visions of fiery explosions.

Which told him quite a lot.

The Torth Majority believed that their Betrayer was either missing or dead. He was not in the Isolatorium.

So his jailers were probably not Torth.

But who were they? The slimy stones that Thomas was propped against gave him too little information. The chilly, damp air told him almost nothing. A thick wrap muffled sounds and blocked his vision. Thomas could neither see nor hear.

His nose and mouth were exposed, so he knew that his environment was odoriferous. Some of the smell was his own urine.

His last cleanup and meal had ended eleven hours, twelve minutes, and forty seconds ago.

The mysterious wellness sessions came every twelve hours or so. But the jailers never entered his range. As far as Thomas could tell from exploring his environment, he lay at the bottom of a narrow well or shaft, and there was no pulley system, no ladder.

Yet somehow, washcloths operated on their own to clean his waste. His medicine seemed to inject itself. Bland gruel forced itself into his mouth once per day.

Since Thomas contained the collective experiences of millions of different cuisines, he was fairly certain that the gruel was mushroom-based. That made it anomalous for a Torth prison. It implied an underground society.

His jailers might be some secret breakaway group of rogue Torth who were operating illegal machinery, such as independent drone robots.

Or they might be using illegal Yeresunsa powers.

Or maybe this was actually the Isolatorium, and they had fooled him, misleading him with fake news in the Megacosm and inexplicable injections of his medicine. They had not even bothered to inhibit his powers.

Or maybe Thomas had contracted the dead city sickness, and he was hallucinating all of this. Ghosts were said to haunt the ruins and kill any Torth who saw them.

Whatever.

Thomas knew one thing for certain: his jailers, whoever they were, had a solid understanding of how to torment a telepathic supergenius with deprivation.

He yearned for new information. He shook with longing. Every second, every millisecond was an eternity of too little input. Since he couldn't have enough of the Megacosm, he would have settled for the internet of Earth. Or a crowd. Even a swarm of bugs. He wasn't picky.

Hell, he would have settled for a pack of wild zoved. Let them devour his flesh, if only he could feast on their minds, just to experience something even remotely new and different.

Eleven hours, twelve minutes, and forty-two seconds.

Thomas thumped his head against the wall. Wrapped and padded as his head was, he couldn't hurt himself.

He might be able to summon enough of his wildfire power to burn holes in his blindfold.

But what if the lack of inhibitor was a true oversight and not just a sick mind game? His jailers might be monitoring him through cameras or other means. It was best to hang onto any potential secret advantage he had, at least until he had collected more information.

If that ever happened.

Desperate for input, Thomas riffled through his own immense memory banks. A movie rehash? A book to reread? Maybe he'd relive an adventure from a Torth extrasolar exploration team?

But it was all stale data. Replaying knowledge he'd already assimilated felt repulsive to him, like eating vomit. If he did it too much, it became the mental equivalent of autosarcophagy—the act of consuming one's own flesh.

A creative endeavor? Thomas had mentally started several novels, as well as a film project.

Blah. It all seemed pointless. No one would care or know what he created solely inside his mind.

A simulation?

Thomas recreated a vivid scenario in his imagination. It was summertime. He sat in the recreational park a few blocks away from the Hollander home. To enhance the realism, he layered on details. A hue for every blade of grass. Randomized fluttering for three butterflies. Ambient sounds, including kids playing softball in the distance.

It felt real.

This was nice.

He and Cherise used to get ice cream in this park, so he savored a cup of lemon sorbet. Cherise sat on the bench next to him, licking a cone of mint chocolate chip.

*Do you ever wish you were one of them?* Cherise asked him in her mind, mentally indicating the softball-playing kids. *Normal?*

The simulation wavered as Thomas wondered how to define normalcy. That word no longer held any meaning for him. He had not really allowed himself to be human—was that normal?—for a long time.

He studied the simulation of Cherise, viewing her the way he used to when they had shared a home. Warm. Strong. Insightful. She would blossom out of her awful childhood and grow up to be someone formidable as well as lovable. Sometimes Thomas even felt a little bit inferior next to her.

He opened his mouth, to attempt an answer...

But the real Cherise disdained him.

Beneath the imaginary soft cardigan he wore, Thomas felt scratchy in his filthy robes. Instead of a summer breeze, he felt clammy. The fake taste of sorbet was a cruel joke.

This level of pretense was just another way to delude himself, the way he had done as a Torth. It was lies.

Thomas let the illusion fall apart. No more self-deception. Nothing was worth going down that path ever again.

He might as well go back to scientific challenges.

Not that he could accomplish anything useful. Not without lab equipment plus assistants plus a future. But he wanted to stave off insanity. He had to think. He had to learn. He craved knowledge more than any shipwrecked sailor had ever craved water and food.

He picked up where he'd left off on his superluminal communications theorem. He experimented with adding quartic interactions. Maybe his imagined scalar field was what the ancient aliens had used when they'd created temporal streams. Allotropism could induce tachyon condensation. If the field was conformally invariant…

Something tugged on the wrap around Thomas's head.

He lost his train of thought, because this was new. This had never happened before.

The wrap was unwinding. Coming off!

Thomas lifted his head away from the wall, trying to be helpful. This might be a prelude to more torment, or it might be a rescue. After several days of input deprivation, he still lacked certainty about his situation. So many unknowns seemed obscene.

His mind generated lots of hypotheticals, though.

For instance, what if the Torth Majority had voted to reward the Upward Governess with an endless supply of NAI-12? He hated that possibility, but it might explain why his tormentors were wasting the precious medicine on a condemned prisoner. They might want him to cling to a futile hope. That would also explain why his powers were not inhibited. He was so sickly and weak, he doubted he could light a candle, yet access to his powers did give him a sliver of hope.

The pressure on his ears lessened. Sound began to return. Thomas greedily analyzed the echoey silence.

Too much echo to be outdoors.

Was that a hint of dripping in the far distance?

Stalactites? A cave. That implied interesting possibilities when combined with the mushroom gruel. Thomas cataloged every fact, reshuffling the puzzle pieces. Sooner or later, he would glean something—a morsel, a tidbit—something useful.

"Thomas?"

The deep voice of Ariock echoed down from somewhere far above.

The last time Thomas had seen Ariock and Vy, they were dying from their wounds. Now Ariock sounded all right.

Thomas licked his lips and forced saliva into his throat. "Ariock?" It came out as a whisper. He remained blindfolded. When he blinked, his eyelashes brushed against cloth. "Is Vy okay? What about Cherise?"

"They're safe." Ariock sounded certain. He probably wasn't under duress.

Thomas leaned his head back, yearning to see Ariock, or to feast on Ariock's thoughts. He needed more.

"Are they feeding you enough?" Ariock asked. "And do they give you your medicine?"

This did not sound like a rescue.

Thomas forced himself to remain patient. His friends might just need time to work out an escape plan. "Are you all right? What about Kessa?"

Kessa's voice echoed down to him. "I am fine, Thomas."

She spoke in the slave tongue, although Thomas and Ariock had been using English. That was a clue. Someone else must be listening. His jailers. Kessa seemed to be demonstrating that the conversation was innocent, using a language the jailers understood.

Thomas reshuffled his scant deck of information.

His jailers did not know all languages. And they were treating Ariock and Kessa well. That implied that this was not the Isolatorium.

His jailers were not Torth.

Would a secret society of runaway slaves have the resources to hospitalize Ariock and Vy and nurse them back to health? What about the drones they must be using to keep Thomas alive?

Unless they were not using technology at all.

Thomas nearly asked if his jailers were Yeresunsa. The possibility was both ludicrous and tantalizing. But he dared not speak a guess that his captors might comprehend and feel threatened by. Thomas could not see them or hear them, but he suspected they were listening. They would shut down this friendly visit the instant they felt threatened.

"I need to get out of here." Thomas had meant to sound calm, but the plea slipped out of his mouth. "Please get me out of here. Please. I'll do anything. I'll make any promise. Just help me."

Silence.

Thomas clamped his mouth shut and analyzed every nuance of every distant drip of water, squeezing data out of the environment. He was terrified that he might lose contact with his friends. Kessa and Ariock sounded so far away.

"We want to help you, Thomas." Kessa's reply was careful, and in the slave language. "But we cannot help right away."

Thomas chose English for his next question. "Do my captors have powers like Ariock?"

A pause.

"We can't tell you." Ariock sounded frustrated.

"I am sorry." Kessa's response was carefully diplomatic. "Thomas, we need to learn if you are being cared for."

Thomas wanted to laugh and scream at the same time. After days of input deprivation, they expected him to give rather than receive?

His friends seemed focused on his physical welfare. Maybe his jailers were trying to show off the fact that he was in decent health?

"No." Thomas snarled the word in English, not caring if that angered his jailers. "No, I'm not okay." The damned jailers washed his wounds and fed him regularly, but that was not health. That was mere survival. "I need to get out of here. Get me out!"

"Thomas." Kessa's voice was low and urgent, echoing down to him. "This is important." She switched to English. "Do not use your powers. Do not show off your knowledge. It is vital that you seem harmless and unthreatening. We are working on a rescue, but we need time. You must wait. Do not use your powers, or I fear we will not be able to help you."

New possibilities zinged through Thomas.

If Kessa and Ariock were really up there, then they must be under the aegis of a secret society of runaway slaves or Yeresunsa.

His friends were safe.

That was what mattered.

And that meant that Thomas must never ascend again, not even for a nanosecond. He had promised to keep his friends safe or to die trying. The Torth Empire must never learn what he had puzzled out.

He needed to fully abstain from the Megacosm.

That realization stung like a physical ache. Thomas nearly wept. It was hard to believe that most sapients endured their entire lives with this much ignorance. Somehow, he would have to endure.

But couldn't he be allowed to see and hear again, at least?

The wrap began to wind around his head again.

"Kessa?" he pleaded. "Ariock? How long must I wait?"

Sounds became muffled. Terror and loneliness welled up inside Thomas, seeking a tearful outlet.

No. He would not grovel. He had done enough of that for the Torth Empire. He would never grovel to his supposed friends.

Thomas forced his chest to harden. "I'm suffering," he stated, even as the damnable wrap swaddled his ears and eyes. His jaw remained free enough for speech. "I will wait as long as I can, but I am losing my mind."

He didn't even know if Ariock and Kessa were still listening or not.

"Seven days," Thomas said. "I'll hang on that long. After that? I can't promise I'll be sane."

Silence. Darkness. Nothingness.

Thomas replayed the short interaction with his visitors in his mind, analyzing it, squeezing it for every drop of data.

He could only hope that Ariock and Kessa understood his urgency. If his mind took a final plunge into the chasm of insanity, well, he might end up getting creative with his depleted powers.

# CHAPTER 8
# A WORTHY WARRIOR

Ariock considered how miserable Thomas had looked at the bottom of that filthy well shaft.

The loneliest, lowest level of the dungeon labyrinth was full of pits and treacherous shafts. Thomas was all alone inside a cavern large enough to encompass a palace. Higher levels of the dungeon held lesser prisoners: thieves, thugs, and brawlers who yelled insults at each other. The chambers in between were mostly empty.

Every part of the labyrinth was cordoned off by gigantic vault doors only Yeresunsa could heave open or closed.

There were traps. Ariock had stretched his awareness to encompass the whole dungeon, so he knew. He had sensed deadly pits with saw-toothed spikes, gears that controlled gigantic gates, crushing boulders poised to fall, and several hidden lava pits. Yeresunsa warriors were stationed at critical junctures.

Within all that complexity, Thomas's life spark was interchangeable with that of guards and other prisoners. If Thomas was relocated elsewhere, Ariock would have a lot of trouble finding him again.

But finding Thomas and breaking him free wasn't the biggest obstacle.

Ariock could theoretically wreck the dungeon. He could wage a bloody war and slaughter prison guards and Yeresunsa warriors and demand that they let his dying friend go free.

The biggest problem was: And then what?

Slaves hated Thomas on sight. The Alashani wanted his head on a spike. Torth wanted him to suffer in the Isolatorium. If Ariock dared to poke his head aboveground with Thomas cradled in his arms, they were both likely to get obliterated by nuclear bombs before they could sneak their way to the spaceport at the top of the Stratower.

Was anywhere in the universe safe for a renegade mind reader?

Ariock might try it anyway. He could leave his other friends behind in this underground civilization and sneak toward a spaceport with Thomas in his arms.

But if even one Torth read their minds—only one Torth—then the flourishing Alashani underground civilization was doomed. And so were Vy and Kessa and everyone else he cared about.

"Do not despair, Ariock," Kessa said, seeing his mood. "I have been learning about the prophet Migyatel. The Alashani put great faith in her public announcements. If she declares that you are the true messiah? Then I believe you will be able to persuade Jinishta and other Alashani to do anything you want."

Ariock supposed that was meant to be reassuring.

He wasn't convinced that Migyatel would say what everyone expected her to say. She might just declare Ariock to be a fraud. That was the truth, after all. If she was an authentic prophet, then she would know that he was a loser, not the one and only messiah.

Even if she did give Ariock her blessing…would another reputation boost really help him to help Thomas?

Ariock doubted it. The public wanted to murder mind readers even more ardently than they wanted to follow a savior.

A massive gate loomed ahead, five stories of cast iron, thick enough to stop an armored transport. Jinishta led the way. She raised a slender arm and used her powers to rotate huge gears, which turned the winch system that lifted the gate.

Protesters swamped the street outside.

Many of them held canvas signs with crude illustrations of a head on a spike. Their depictions of Thomas's head included demonic yellow eyes and blood gushing from his severed neck.

Jinishta plowed through the mob, ignoring their shouts, somber in her black woolens and Yeresunsa mantle. The spears in her quiver did not look decorative. They were black and deadly, unlike the frilly golden spears she otherwise carried.

Ariock followed her. The protesters yelled and waved their gruesome signs. One of the protesters was an albino child who looked younger than Thomas.

Jinishta spoke over her shoulder to Ariock. Her tone was reassuring.

"Jinishta says not to worry," Kessa translated. "These are just ignorant low-class people. They are not permitted inside the dungeon. She has rotating shifts of warriors assigned to protect your *rekveh* friend. She promises that no harm will come to him."

"Thanks," Ariock mumbled.

He was ashamed. He had promised to protect Thomas, yet he knew that he could not be any more effective than Jinishta and her warriors. Ariock was only one person. He had to sleep sometimes. He simply could not offer Thomas protection around the clock.

Meanwhile, Jinishta commanded more than seventy warriors. The dungeon had traps, portcullis gates, nussians armed with halberds, and all kinds of barriers.

Thomas was safe there. Safer than he would be if he was hidden in a cabinet or anywhere else inside this lamplit city.

And he was miserable.

*"Seven days,"* Thomas had said in a tone full of threats. He would be patient and suffer for seven days.

And then what would he do?

Ariock could imagine mayhem. Thomas might burn off his blindfold. Maybe he would set his jailers on fire? Or try to brainwash them?

The Alashani had no clue that Thomas had Yeresunsa powers. They would be unprepared for an attack from their seemingly helpless prisoner.

In fact, they had no safeguards whatsoever against wildfire or mind control. Kessa had surreptitiously asked questions, and she had informed Ariock that fire was alchemy to the Alashani, not magic. Nobody in this underground could ignite fires with their mind or brainwash people. Such powers were unheard-of.

Ariock himself could not do it. He had tried. The closest thing he could manage was electrical sparks.

"Maybe we should microdart Thomas," Ariock suggested glumly. "To keep him from using his powers?"

Ariock really didn't want to prolong Thomas's suffering. Nor did he feel comfortable about disabling a fellow Yeresunsa. And yet…if the Alashani felt threatened by Thomas, that would be the end of any kindness or truce. The warriors would gain a perfect justification to execute the much-hated *rekveh*.

They might even manage to do it before Ariock could stop them.

"That is a good idea," Kessa admitted. "But our blaster gloves are under guard. They are in some hidden treasury room inside the monastery where Yeresunsa train. I could work on obtaining one, and then I can try to visit Thomas before the seven days are up."

Ariock nodded. He didn't trust himself to say anything. He was grateful to Kessa, yet full of self-loathing at the same time. What kind of a friend was he? Thomas did not deserve prolonged suffering.

*Neither did I.*

Thomas had never visited Ariock when he was alone in that Torth prison arena. Not once. And he probably could have.

Ariock lifted one of his huge arms, examining the heavy iron spike that poked out of his forearm like a mutant growth. The Torth had decided he looked better with iron spikes. They had used those spikes to chain him up and to guide him to and from fights. They'd hammered the iron into Ariock's bones without any warning and without anesthetic.

Alone and in pain, Ariock had been forced to fight alien monsters over a period of three months. During that time, he had been kept in ignorance. He'd had zero communication with anyone. The prison guards had never said a word to him. He hadn't known whether his mother or his friends were alive or dead.

He had been terribly alone.

And scared.

He would have said the exact same things Thomas had said, down in that well shaft.

But no one had assured him of rescue. Ariock had suffered for what seemed like an eternity before Thomas had figured out a way to help him.

And yes, Thomas was a true hero. Thomas had saved his life.

But if it took a hero like Thomas that long, maybe Ariock could forgive himself for struggling against a similar roadblock?

"I think you should try to befriend Jinishta," Kessa said.

Ariock glanced down at her. "Why?"

"You are under her command," Kessa explained. "But you act aloof. You do not trust her much, and she does not trust you. I think she expects you to become a problem. She is more likely to treat Thomas well if she feels friendly toward you instead of threatened by you."

Ariock supposed that made sense.

"Also," Kessa said, "I believe you may be underestimating Jinishta and her warriors. They are not as strong as you are, individually, but the Alashani have dealt with Yeresunsa warlords in the past. They used to imprison warlords in those pits where they are keeping Thomas."

Ariock nearly asked how that was possible.

Then he remembered his trek through the dead city, and he pieced it together. Injuries. Thirst. Starvation. If a Yeresunsa was kept in deplorable condition, they would lack the strength to break free.

"In these modern times," Kessa said, "that dungeon is no longer in use, except for Thomas. The Alashani no longer imprison Yeresunsa at all. If the council deems a Yeresunsa to be dangerous or unfit for society...?" She hesitated, gauging Ariock's face. "They hunt him and immediately execute him."

"Oh," Ariock said.

"There are no second chances," Kessa said. "They will not listen to reasons or excuses. If they decide that you are a threat, or an enemy, they will just execute you."

The implications began to dawn on Ariock. Kessa was telling him that he was in danger. If he risked a rescue and failed...or even if he succeeded but got caught...

There would be no imprisonment for him.

Just an immediate execution, or an attempt at execution. And if Ariock evaded it? Jinishta would pursue him with all seventy-plus of her warriors.

"Got it," Ariock said darkly.

He felt oppressed. The soot-blackened ceiling was too heavy and too low. It was no substitute for a sky. There were walls everywhere. His heart wrenched with the knowledge that Thomas was alone in an even worse, more enclosed space.

"They will not allow you to leave the underground, either," Kessa said, "until they trust you as someone who considers himself to be fully Alashani. Only Jinishta decides who is permitted to exit the caves and visit the surface. They go up there only for one reason: to hunt the heads of mind readers."

Ariock was beginning to get a clearer picture of why he needed to win Jinishta's trust.

"How do I become fully Alashani?" he asked.

"I don't know," Kessa replied. "Ask Jinishta."

Ariock lengthened his stride. It wasn't hard to catch up with the small albino woman. Jinishta walked fast, but he had much longer legs.

"Jinishta?" Ariock asked. "What must I do in order to become an Alashani?"

Kessa translated, slightly out of breath.

Jinishta gave Ariock an assessing look out of the corner of a purple eye. She looked as if she did not quite believe him. But she answered.

"Jinishta says that she hopes you will someday swear the Warrior's Pact," Kessa said. "When you have proven yourself worthy, you will be ready to help safeguard civilization."

Ariock straightened his back. Maybe, if he proved himself worthy to Jinishta, she would treat him like a person instead of a potential problem.

Maybe he would not need to face a bloody battle and death aboveground versus death underground.

"What must I do?" Ariock managed to say it in the slave tongue, although his accent was probably atrocious.

Jinishta's eyes seemed to glow as she reassessed him.

Ariock tried to look worthy. It was difficult to admit, but he actually liked the sour premier Yeresunsa. Jinishta treated him like a student. Not someone to be feared or worshipped, not a giant or a hero, but merely a student. She refused to be influenced by popular opinions.

Maybe she was a potential friend.

Kessa continued to act as translator. "You must excel at your lessons," Jinishta was saying. "But in truth, that is only one part of being an Alashani warrior. There is more to it."

Ariock showed Jinishta his look of interest.

"You must be hardworking," Jinishta said, with Kessa's translation help. "And willing to help. Yeresunsa are the pillars of civilization. I will show you this as part of your lessons."

Ariock thought of Orla, the teenaged healer who always looked exhausted. He had heard that a Yeresunsa artisan was crafting a prosthetic leg for Vy. Yeresunsa did seem to do a lot of varied tasks. He nodded.

Jinishta led the way into a nicer neighborhood, passing through an ornate archway with polished agate accents. Ariock had to duck underneath it.

"Also," Jinishta went on, pausing to allow Kessa time to translate, "Yeresunsa are part of society. We are not above it or outside of it. You must be part of Alashani society."

Ariock nodded.

Jinishta seemed to assess Ariock yet again. She asked a question.

"Do you have family?"

The unexpected question caught Ariock off guard. He couldn't guess what Jinishta wanted to hear from a prospective warrior.

"I know your parents are deceased." Jinishta paused on a cobblestone slope, studying his face in the light of a nearby lamp. Kessa translated. "What about siblings? Or aunts or uncles? Do you have any relatives whom you care deeply for?"

Ariock studied the premier Yeresunsa. If only he could say that yes, he had a wonderful family.

"No," he said truthfully. "I don't have any family."

"Do you have any living relatives at all?" Jinishta stopped walking so that she could stare at him. "Cousins?"

"No," Ariock admitted. "None who are alive."

Why did he feel so inadequate? Surely having cousins was irrelevant to being a warrior? Fictional warriors and soldiers never needed families. They were stoic. Fierce. Love and romance supposedly made soldiers weak.

"What about friends who consider you to be family?" Jinishta searched his face, as if looking for something crucial.

Ariock had a sinking feeling. He couldn't think of a single person who would count him as family. Maybe Vy? Maybe Kessa? Maybe Thomas?

Nah. Thomas would probably never trust him again, after this.

The others relied on Ariock as a protector, but that didn't mean they liked him. Vy's leg was gone because of his screwup. Deep down, they probably feared him.

"This is vital," Jinishta said through Kessa's translation. "Relationships are what make us better than Torth. Have you ever had a relationship?"

Ariock gazed at the distant lamplit vista, all too aware, now, that he was unworthy. He could not meet Jinishta's eyes. He had accidentally killed or failed everyone who had ever cared about him.

Jinishta would surely reject him. She would be right to.

"Ariock?" Kessa told him in a warm voice, "I consider you to be family."

Ariock swallowed. He did not deserve her kindhearted charity.

He felt like such a fraud.

"I will tell her." Kessa spoke to Jinishta, and Ariock knew that she was assuring the premier Yeresunsa that Ariock did have at least one or two friends.

Whatever Kessa said, it appeased Jinishta. She began to stroll up the street again, chatting contentedly.

Kessa translated, speaking of how a warrior needed to be a person first and foremost. That was essential. Yeresunsa had to fit in with people and not rule over them. That was more important than any amount of battle skill or power training.

Ariock gave her his full attention and tried to feel worthy.

But he couldn't help but remember Vy's amputated leg.

He needed to earn back her trust. He needed to somehow earn back Thomas's trust, as well. Whatever happened, Ariock knew that he must avoid maiming and killing innocent people. He needed to earn everyone's trust, and to win Jinishta's approval—whatever it took.

# CHAPTER 9

# STARS AND HEARTS

Vy sat motionless while an albino man slowly brushed her thick red hair. He hummed with each stroke, as if playing a musical instrument. He seemed entranced by her otherworldly tresses.

Had Vy not spent time as a personal slave, she might have felt amused to have menservants. They were all men who referred to her as "angel." It was a good thing they only wanted to pick out her clothes and fetch things for her, because they could be overbearing. They acted offended whenever Vy asked them to go away. They always returned within an hour.

All the servitude made Vy feel like a Torth.

She never, ever wanted to be mistaken for that sort of creature. If not for her leg situation, she would have categorically rejected the servile attendants.

But Nulshta had assured Vy that these men were valued employees who served in her family's palace. The Alashani underground did not have slaves. There were poor people. There were slums. But anyone could rise to the top of society if they happened to find themselves related—through blood or through marriage—to a merchant, a councilor, or a Yeresunsa.

One lucky cousin could boost his or her entire extended family.

Likewise, one disgraced cousin had ripple effects on the rest of their family, causing incomes to shrivel.

"Thank you, Chad," Vy told the manservant. She had trouble pronouncing his full name, which sounded something like Chadrorl. "Will you please get the ointment for my leg?"

Chad bobbed something like a curtsy and hurried to oblige her.

Vy knew that she was considered to be something like a cousin-by-proxy to the messiah, as far as the Alashani were concerned. None of them knew that she was the foster sister of the dreaded *rekveh* in the lowest reaches of the dungeon. Instead, Vy and Cherise were angels from paradise. The two of them were almost as exalted as Ariock.

But lacework dresses and a palatial suite did not make Vy feel exalted. Or angelic. Or full of grace.

"Hey, Vy." Cherise knocked on the door frame. "How are you doing?"

Vy could not summon a lighthearted reply.

"Flen and Haz invited us to a shopping bazaar," Cherise said. "We're leaving in a few minutes. Want to come?"

As if shopping would cure any of Vy's worries. Or soothe the newfound anger that seethed just below her surface.

"No, thanks," Vy said.

Cherise hung in the doorway. Diamonds shone in her black hair, connected by fine chains, as striking as stars in a clear night. She was resplendent in an embroidered cream-colored top and swishy pants. Alashani garb really flattered her.

"We could take a rickshaw," Cherise suggested. "You wouldn't have to walk far."

Vy blinked back tears. Couldn't her foster sister see that she wasn't going to leap up and go back to being carefree?

The manservant began to rub smelly ointment on Vy's stump, where her leg ended below the knee. The ointment was supposed to prevent chafing. It didn't. Not enough, anyway.

The farthest Vy had managed to walk, so far, was the palace district pendulum. There she could sit by a burbling fountain while an ornate pendulum swung in front of her, inexorable and reliable. Its swings knocked over toothy little stones, marking every half hour and hour. It made a full orbit by some mysterious means.

Every neighborhood had a pendulum. People used them as meeting places, and Vy did meet interesting people there sometimes. Talk helped her keep her mind off everything that was missing in her life. Like Thomas. Daylight. Earth. And the leg she needed in order to run, swim, and walk the way she used to.

Her new peg leg was beautiful. A skillful artisan must have spent hours carving the ivory prosthetic. The artisan had hollowed it out and embedded ribbons of molten gold for extra shine. It was a gorgeous piece of work.

But it was not a leg.

It had no foot. It was just a stick that could not bend.

"Just go," Vy told her foster sister. "Have fun."

Cherise shrank back at her uncaring tone.

"I'm sorry. I guess I'm not in the right state of mind." Vy wished she could be the big sister she used to be, on Earth. Cherise had turned seventeen while they were slaves. She ought to experience something like normalcy.

Vy fumbled for something kind to say. "Hey. Isn't Flen the guy who took you on a date yesterday?"

Cherise's cheeks went red. "Um, I guess. Maybe? He took me to an opera."

"An opera?" Vy raised an eyebrow.

"It was really beautiful." Cherise sounded embarrassed. "They had Kemkorcan feather dancers. Those are those serpentine aliens with bioluminescent patches on their skin?"

The manservant made an appreciative sound. "They will have an encore performance next orbit," he said helpfully.

Vy studied Cherise. "How do you feel about Flen?" She could not be the only person who was worried about Thomas. Cherise used to giggle behind the closed door of Thomas's bedroom in the Hollander home. Vy had passed that door often enough to hear them chatting in there together, even if those chats were one-sided. They used to spend so much time together.

Cherise shrugged.

"Do you miss Thomas?" Vy regretted the rude question, but she had to know how serious the rift was.

"I never wanted him to suffer." Cherise's gaze was downcast. "This was never what I wanted."

"I know." But Vy had overheard gossip, and she had seen protest signs. The Alashani believed that Thomas was a demon. "What does Flen think about him?" Vy dared ask.

"Uh…" Cherise's cheeks were redder than ever. "We don't really talk about the prisoner or anything like that."

Of course not. Vy tried to hide her disappointment.

"Flen and Haz do take shifts in the dungeon," Cherise said. "If you come with us, you could ask them yourself."

Vy shook her head. She could imagine what the two warriors were interested in talking about, and it wasn't their *rekveh* prisoner. They wanted ladies from paradise.

Her manservant was making suggestive eye movements. He wanted Vy to go on a date. In Alashani society, Yeresunsa warriors were ultradesirable, like star athletes. Everyone wanted to date a Yeresunsa.

But Vy wasn't in the mood.

Nor did she find the albino men to be particularly attractive. They all seemed wispy, too thin and weak. A lot of them had nasal, whiny voices. They were all shorter than she was by several inches or more.

Vy wanted someone substantial, someone who could wrap her up in one arm. Someone who seemed like a protector.

She wanted to feel Ariock's arm around her.

Vy gave a sad sigh. Ariock wasn't going to go for her these days, she felt sure. Not with her new disability. She would never be able to keep up with him.

Besides, the messiah could have his pick of swooning albino maidens who would do anything to show off their powers. He was like the star athlete on a heroic level. Everyone in the city wanted to please him.

"Thanks for the ointment," Vy told her manservant, and he got the hint and stopped rubbing her stump.

"I want you to know," Cherise said, "Thomas and I were never dating. It was just a friendship."

"Oh. I know," Vy lied.

"Anyway." Cherise began to plait a lock of hair into a braid. "I just really wish you'd come with me to the bazaar, or on some other double-date situation. Just to make sure..." She stopped herself, looking uncertain.

"To make sure of what?" Vy prompted.

"To make sure I'm not crazy," Cherise said. "Flen and Haz are both, um..." She trailed off, clearly embarrassed.

"Rude?" Vy guessed. "Overbearing?"

"No."

"Overeager?"

"Sort of. But that's not it. They're just really..." Cherise seemed stuck on a concept, afraid to speak it out loud.

"...alien?" Vy guessed in English. The attendant was listening, after all. "Like, not attractive?"

As an artist, Cherise must be aware that the albino Alashani resembled porcelain dolls. They had tiny chins and comparatively huge eyes. Their tunics were frilly.

"What? No." Cherise gave Vy an exasperated look. "I love the way they look. I'm fine with them being nonhuman. I'm not going to judge them for that. They're just...I mean..."

Vy waited. Maybe if she held still and kept silent, Cherise would explain how she really felt about the petite warriors.

"Why are they interested in someone like me?" Cherise's words tumbled out with passion. "Why not you? You're the one who actually likes to talk! You're tall and graceful, even with your leg. And I get that men are afraid to hit on someone the messiah likes, but it doesn't make sense for every man in the city to avoid you, and pay all this attention to...well, to the weird girl who hardly ever talks."

Vy blinked at her, stunned.

"I wanted you to come with me." Cherise folded her arms, protective. "Because I think I'm misinterpreting something. There has to be a reason why men are acting like they actually want to date me. You have to admit it's weird. I thought maybe if you were there, you'd have some insights."

Vy appraised Cherise. "I can think of a few reasons why Alashani men would choose you," she said dryly.

Cherise looked skeptical.

"You come from paradise," Vy said, ticking off each point on her fingers. "You're friends with the messiah. You're polite instead of acting like an oaf who talks too much. You're beautiful. And you're talented." She let her hand fall. "Gee, I wonder why men are falling for you?"

Cherise looked shocked.

Vy hid a wistful smile. "I'm sure Thomas would list all that and more, if he was here."

Thomas used to look at Cherise with a look of adoration. Maybe Cherise had friend-zoned him, but if so, he had been hopeful anyway. Vy was pretty sure about that.

"I saw Flen pick you up for that opera," Vy said. "He gave you jewelry for your hair. That's an expensive gift. I talked to a few people around here, to make sure there's no mistake about what it means, and yeah. That's a courtship gift. He's wooing you."

Cherise was speechless.

"When you go to that bazaar," Vy said, turning to the scrolls on her desk, "maybe try to choose between Flen and Haz. Or just let them both know you're not interested. Don't be afraid to tell them no. You're worth more than any warrior. You're an angel from paradise."

Vy suspected that there was even more to Cherise's appeal than what she had listed. Exaggerated shyness was a popular pretense among Alashani women. Cherise had the alluring mannerisms of an upper-class maiden, without even being aware of it. She also had a gracile body type, whereas Vy was ungainly in comparison.

On top of that, the most important deity in the Alashani pantheon—the so-called Lady of Sorrow, arbiter of birth, death, and water—had long, flowing hair. Both Vy and Cherise resembled the goddess.

Beyond all that, Cherise's reverential drawings of things like trees and butterflies captivated a lot of Alashani. Merchants were negotiating with Cherise for the rights to use her designs on their wares. Vy had overheard conversations about it. There was a strong likelihood that Cherise would gain status in this underground world without even trying.

Of course men wanted her.

"I'm going to work on learning the Alashani writing system," Vy said, resigning herself to another lonely day.

She half wondered if she was wasting her time by learning the loops and pretzels that symbolized mushy syllables. Among the Alashani, it seemed that only bookkeepers bothered to learn how to read. Most people were illiterate.

Cherise picked up her jewel-encrusted satchel, but she paused in the doorway. "You know," she said, "Kessa could use a break from acting as Ariock's translator."

Vy wished she dared to volunteer. She just didn't want Ariock to see her rocking on her peg leg, barely able to hobble across a street, while Jinishta taught him how to do backflips. Vy couldn't imagine being in that sad role. She didn't want to think about it.

"Mm," Vy said.

"Kessa might be able to learn something about the prison, and maybe help Thomas," Cherise said, "if you're around to help Ariock learn the slave tongue."

"Or you could teach him," Vy said pointedly.

Cherise looked pained.

"Ariock won't want a crippled person slowing him down." Vy slumped, hating to make that admission. She felt useless.

"Crippled?" Cherise dropped her satchel, turning her full attention back on Vy. She glared. "I never heard you refer to Thomas that way. Or me. Or anyone else."

Vy gawked at her own unintentional insult. It had never crossed her mind to compare her disability to those of others.

"Is that how you thought of us?" Cherise asked. "With that defeated tone of voice?"

Vy wanted to reel back her comment.

Instead, she admitted to herself, in her own mind, that she did feel reduced. She used to jog and ski and swim. Now she could barely walk. It affected everything she did.

"Ariock and everyone else have been respecting your wishes," Cherise said. "You don't want to go anywhere? That's fine. If that's how it is, then we'll wait, however long it takes. But never assume we're ashamed of you! That's ridiculous."

Vy studied Cherise for signs of deception or exaggeration.

There were none.

"Anyway," Cherise went on, "it doesn't matter whether or not Ariock wants your help. He doesn't get to be a diva. He'll take whatever translator we give him, or else he'll start to believe he really is the messiah."

Vy laughed, in spite of her worries.

Cherise picked up her satchel. "He keeps asking to see you."

That seemed unlikely. "He does?" Vy asked.

"Yeah." Cherise gave a sublime smile. "The same way Flen keeps asking to see me." She adjusted the satchel on her shoulder. "Sometimes, I guess, you've got to show the boy you're interested."

She slipped away.

Vy picked up the fountain pen and selected a blank parchment. But instead of experimenting with the loopy Alashani script, she found herself doodling little hearts and stars.

If Cherise could find an untapped well of courage, then maybe she could, too.

# CHAPTER 10
# STEAM PRESSURE

Steam whistled through pipes, clouding the iron girders that ribbed the rocky ceiling and obscuring distant laborers. Waterwheels churned two of four aqueducts into froth.

Ariock tried to look appreciative and interested. The aqueducts were the Alashani hubs of industry. Most of their textiles and foods came through this area. Jinishta kept emphasizing that. She explained the importance of every steam-powered process and every industrious-looking laborer, waiting impatiently for Vy to translate.

Ariock was more interested in Vy's sideline commentary. She kept making wry comparisons to jobs on Earth. She noted that this worker ought to get a raise, or that one was obviously trying to impress his boss. Some of her comments made Ariock laugh.

"This is the gristmill," Vy translated for Jinishta. "Workers unload mushrooms here, and this is where they get sliced up. And, I guess, sifted? Yeah. Sifted. Then they get packaged into those sacks."

Dozens of laborers, many of them nussians, piled heavy sacks onto industrial rickshaws, which were also drawn by nussians.

"That explains why everything tastes like mushrooms," Vy said.

Ariock nodded. He dared not comment, because whenever Jinishta heard his voice, she assumed that he must be speaking to her and not to his friend from Earth.

Jinishta walked rapidly onward. She paused, impatient. She did this deliberately every so often, pouting at Vy's slow pace. She had remarked, several times, that Kessa was a better and more professional translator.

Ariock supposed he agreed about Kessa's professionalism. But it didn't matter. He preferred Vy.

Vy had trouble walking because a peg leg had certain deficiencies. It wasn't her fault that the Alashani lacked the technology to make a comfortable leg prosthetic for her.

And it wasn't Vy's fault that the Alashani had locked up the one and only supergenius on this planet. Thomas could likely design a good prosthetic. If only the Alashani would stop being idiots and let him have regular visitors.

Seven days had come and gone.

The only good thing that had happened during that time was that Ariock was learning the slave tongue. Vy was now his full-time teacher and translator. That was nice.

But where was the prophet Migyatel?

How much longer would Thomas wait?

How safe were any of them here, really?

"Ariock?" Vy sounded concerned.

Ariock realized that small tools and debris were floating around him. His awareness had spiked out, carried by his frustration.

He set the items down using his power and withdrew his awareness. Jinishta's stern look was enough to make him ashamed. Yeresunsa were not supposed to lose control like he had just done. It was a major faux pas.

In Alashani society, Yeresunsa were the epitome of politeness. They did not get inebriated or get into brawls. People looked up to them, with their purple mantles and their magic powers.

The cost for transgression was high. Jinishta might let one or two mistakes slip, but she would not tolerate a Yeresunsa who repeatedly made people afraid. She was keeping a wary eye on Ariock.

He tried to look harmless and eager to learn.

Jinishta gestured toward an albino man who wore a purple Yeresunsa mantle. "This is Shevrael."

Ariock had learned enough of the slave tongue to understand simple phrases, so he did not need a translation for that. He nodded a greeting.

Shevrael paid no attention whatsoever. He sat cross-legged on a cushion with a look of intense focus aimed toward the aqueduct.

"Every city in the Alashani underground is nourished by the mighty River of Tears," Vy translated for Jinishta. "We—I think she means Yeresunsa—guide the water to where it is needed. Just as shepherds herd cave sheep, and farmers nourish mushrooms, Yeresunsa orchestrate water. This is the lifeblood of our world."

Ariock was tall enough to see over the heads of the factory workers. As he looked in each direction, he noticed people like Shevrael seated at intervals along the gigantic factory floor. They wore purple mantles as well as pristine clothing. An attendant in drab woolens knelt to serve a carafe to one of them.

"They work here all the time?" Ariock asked. "At all hours?"

Jinishta heard the translation and made an affirmative sound. She seemed pleased that Ariock had gotten interested enough to ask a question.

"They take shifts," Vy translated. "But all Yeresunsa must serve. You will do this noble and crucial job once I judge that you are ready."

"It looks mind-numbingly boring," Ariock remarked. "Don't translate that."

Vy laughed. Her reactions were definitely more fun than Kessa's politeness.

Jinishta never laughed. She gave Ariock a pained look, as if he was an over-grown child. She turned to Shevrael and asked him a question.

"She's asking Shevrael if he would like to take a break," Vy translated. "She's offering to have you take over his job for a little while."

Steam or sweat beaded on Shevrael's albino forehead. Veins stood out. It seemed Shevrael was putting forth a lot of effort, and he dared not shift his attention away from his job. But he mouthed a word of assent.

"Okay," Ariock agreed, curious.

Jinishta sat cross-legged on the damp ground. She patted the floor, indicating that Ariock should sit.

He settled himself down. Vy looked grateful to take a seat, as well.

"This job is especially suitable for young warriors who don't know their own limits," Vy said, translating as Jinishta spoke. "Jinishta says that she worked the aqueduct after she was newly sworn. She says the regular practice tested her limits and her endurance. It also helped her learn how to cooperate with other warriors."

Ariock sharpened his attention. Every Yeresunsa warrior he'd spoken with made a big deal about knowing their personal limits. It sounded vital for combat situations, but Ariock had yet to understand why. He didn't even know how one measured such a thing.

"Teach me," he said.

Jinishta understood that phrase. She gave him a smile.

Vy visibly steeled herself. Yeresunsa lessons were always a challenge to translate.

"All right," Vy said, doing her best as Jinishta spoke. "First, the aqueduct has many hidden channels and pumps. Can you explore them?"

"No problem." Ariock folded his legs in a comfortable way, stretched his arms, then let his hands rest. Jinishta had taught him why the meditative posture was important. The more in tune with his body he got, the more intuitive his awareness became.

He sent his awareness into the aqueduct.

There were many clever parts. Gears turned. Pumps sucked and pulled. Water surged. Ariock figured that some of that activity must be controlled by Shevrael, forcing water continuously through hidden channels, in and out of the main aqueduct.

Ariock spread his awareness farther out. He sensed more gears and pumps and channels. Each area had its own Yeresunsa.

And, Ariock realized, if any of them failed, a blockage or an overflow would damage the whole system. They could not afford to get distracted.

"Jinishta wants you to keep your awareness on Shevrael's section," Vy was saying. "Now, can you inhabit…uh, one-tenth?…of the inbound water flowing into the main channel?"

"I can inhabit all of it," Ariock said.

He didn't wait for Vy to translate. He needed more practice with water, and he wanted it.

It was a strange feeling, like exercising a muscle he rarely used, or thinking in a way he rarely did. The rest of the world faded as he poured himself into liquid. Ariock dominated the inbound water. Soon he controlled the outbound flow as well, because he was sure Jinishta would ask him to do so next.

His awareness kept wanting to jump outward and onward. He had to restrain himself from following the flow.

Shevrael sat back with a sigh of relief.

Jinishta watched Ariock with a careful gaze. She said something cautious.

"Ariock, you must speak up if you get worn-out," Vy translated. "Yeresunsa have died by showing off. It's never worth it."

All too often, Jinishta made Ariock sound like a frail, childish braggart. It was especially galling in front of Vy.

"Tell her I'm fine," Ariock said. "I've never gotten worn-out in my life."

Vy looked curious. Instead of translating, she gazed up at him. "Is that true?"

"Well," Ariock said, "except when I have a major injury and I'm dosed with the inhibitor serum. But otherwise? This is easy for me."

To demonstrate, he took over more of the aqueduct. He reached across water, to the next workstation, and inhabited the water flow there, pumping and shoving until whoever was controlling it let go and let him have control.

Then he reached in the opposite direction. The Yeresunsa seated there gave a whoop of surprise as Ariock took over her duties.

Jinishta and Shevrael jumped to their feet. They looked stunned.

"I could take over the whole factory," Ariock said.

He was gratified to see Vy beam with admiration. She grinned at Ariock even while Jinishta chastised him.

"Jinishta says that's enough," Vy said. "You can stop now."

"What's she worried about?" Ariock hoped they were all noting how he was able to carry on a conversation even while he simultaneously pumped water through multiple crucial junctures. Maybe they would hesitate to treat Thomas cruelly.

Maybe they would think twice before they dared to piss him off.

Ariock sought massive energy flows throughout the factory. He slipped his awareness into whatever machinery could use a boost in strength.

Stone aqueducts groaned as their load increased. Water roared everywhere it was supposed to go at full capacity. The Yeresunsa workers blinked in surprise at the unexpected interruption of their workflow. They gawked at each other, then at Ariock.

Laborers stepped back as Ariock took over gristmills, primitive steam engines, turbines, and pumps. They laughed in amazed awe.

Ariock had to quickly take over sacks and crates, also, to catch the results of sped-up productivity.

Vy laughed along with the workers. She actually clapped, twisting around to admire all the moving parts.

Jinishta seemed momentarily speechless. She opened and closed her mouth.

Ariock no longer had the bandwidth to talk, and he wasn't sure how long he could keep up this much multitasking. It was like juggling a hundred balls. But it was worth it for the reactions. He loved how delighted Vy was.

Ten Yeresunsa stared at Ariock with wide-eyed shock. Jinishta and Shevrael had a snappy argument with each other.

"Shevrael says you're definitely the messiah," Vy said, laughing as she translated. "You'll break the power crystal for sure." She added, as an aside, "I don't know what he means by that. Anyway, he's urging Jinishta to let you into the monastery. He says you should be allowed to visit the power crystal right away, even though you haven't sworn the Warrior's Pact."

Jinishta clearly disagreed.

Ariock was too busy controlling the factory to have any response. He was a thousand valves and pumps. He was grinding iron. He was fueling furnaces. He flowed with tons of water.

Getting out of this predicament might be more difficult than getting into it.

Ariock realized, with dismay, that he couldn't simply withdraw from everything all at once without destroying the factory.

He withdrew from one furnace. Then another. He just had to be methodical and gentle. He'd have to analyze the risks of every reduction in his stature.

Jinishta planted her fists on her hips and scolded him.

"Jinishta says if it's that easy for you, then maybe you can keep it up for the rest of this work shift," Vy said.

Ariock groaned. He realized that Jinishta actually wanted him to settle in as a happy workhorse.

After all, he was living off charity. He had yet to earn any of the clothes or food or lessons he'd been given. Unlike Chaniyelem and Shevrael and lots of other people, Jinishta saw Ariock as a freeloader. She didn't believe that he was the messiah.

She expected him to be grateful to have a job.

She expected him to just slowly forget about Thomas and any hope of escaping this world. He was supposed to work for Jinishta for the rest of his life. In dark, enclosed spaces. Underground. Forever.

"Sorry." Vy touched Ariock's arm in sympathy.

She probably thought he'd groaned because of the workload. Even so, her kindness reminded Ariock that he couldn't afford to be weak. Vy was counting on him to rescue her foster brother.

And to continuously protect Thomas from angry mobs. And the galactic empire.

And what about Earth? Vy had not said that she wanted Ariock to save humankind from enslavement, but wistful despair entered her voice whenever she spoke of home.

Deep down, Ariock did want to be that kind of hero.

He yearned to gain enough skill to show the Torth Empire that there were places in this universe they could not have. He wanted to prove his worth to Alashani society as well, and make them listen when he insisted that Thomas was not their enemy.

"I'll do this work shift." Ariock straightened. Speech was still an effort, but he had relinquished enough of the machinery to manage. The exercise in control would probably do him good. "But tell Jinishta to give me straight answers about the prophet. When will she arrive?"

Vy translated.

Jinishta seemed unnerved that Ariock was able to carry on a conversation while doing everything he was doing. She gathered her thoughts and responded.

"The prophet Migyatel is said to have departed her home city," Vy translated. "She is on her way. That is all anyone knows."

"Shouldn't a prophet be able to predict her own arrival?" Ariock asked.

Jinishta folded her arms, but her annoyed look seemed to hide shame. It was Shevrael who responded.

"Shevrael guesses that she got delayed on the road," Vy told Ariock. "People say she's old and frail."

Ariock didn't point out the obvious explanation for the prophet's leisurely pace: Migyatel might be just as surprised by his existence as anyone. The much-revered prophet might just be a standard charlatan.

After all, if her predictive power was reliable, then Ariock figured she would trumpet alarms about his demented, malformed plan to wreck the dungeon and barrel toward the surface of this nasty planet with Thomas in his arms and an army of Yeresunsa chasing them.

Ariock wasn't quite ready to take that leap and put Vy and Kessa and everyone else in danger. But he did keep toying with the idea.

"How does prophetic power work?" Ariock asked. "Does the prophet need to be near me? Is that why she's traveling to this city?"

"Yes," Vy said. "Prophecy is supposed to be a proximity power, like healing. And like telepathy. Migyatel needs to touch a person in order to see their future."

Ariock wasn't sure he ever wanted to be touched by a prophet. It sounded socially dangerous, whether she was a fraud or not.

If he was going to leave the Alashani peacefully—in order to have a chance—then he had to prove them wrong. Wrong about Thomas. Wrong about their messiah prophecy.

And Jinishta was wrong about the limits of strength she kept ascribing to Ariock. She kept assuming that he would get tired out or depleted. He never did.

"Tell Jinishta that Thomas needs to be treated better." Ariock met Jinishta's steely gaze. She must notice that he was literally doing the work of ten Yeresunsa. He was in control of the entire factory.

He could destroy their civilization, probably.

Maybe Jinishta could round up an army and stop him. Or maybe not. Did she really want to turn her beloved factory, or her city, into a battleground?

"Tell her," Ariock said to Vy, "that Thomas needs regular visitors. You should be able to check on him. You're his nurse. If you say that he needs medicine, or more water or food, or whatever entertainment? They need to defer to you. Tell Jinishta that."

Vy hesitated. She was clearly afraid, but she did turn to Jinishta. She spoke seriously in the slave tongue.

Jinishta took a firm look around at what Ariock was doing. She observed steam pipes whistling and stone half-pipes groaning with the extra load of water. Ten warriors stood back, grinning and enjoying refreshments during the unexpected break.

Everyone in the factory was happy, impressed with the messiah. People nudged each other and pointed to Ariock with pride.

His unspoken threats hung in the steamy air.

"All right," Jinishta said with a judgmental glare. "It will be as you say, Ariock."

She did not call him the messiah. She never did.

Ariock was stunned. Had his pressure actually worked?

Vy turned to him with admiration, more joyful than he'd seen her in a long time. "That was brilliant. You're amazing!"

Her joy gave Ariock extra energy. He conducted machines like his own blood and flesh. Everything fell into a symphonic rhythm, almost as easily as breathing. He had done something to help Thomas! It was a step in the right direction.

And he had done it without causing bloodshed or harming anyone.

"Thank you," Ariock told his mentor, and he meant it.

He would find ways to reassure Jinishta and her people that he was a good guy. All their overwrought fears would evaporate like steam.

# BIGGER MUSHROOMS

Cherise backed away from Flen's passionate, overeager kiss.

She didn't understand why he was obsessed with touching her. She must be desirable in some unknown way, like a blossom beckoning a hummingbird. But like a flower bud, her default state was curled up tight and hidden. She couldn't fake being a flashy Alashani maiden, even with the jewelry and makeup she wore. She felt too damaged.

Flen looked befuddled. "Have I hurt you?"

Cherise reminded herself that Flen was not a mind reader. He had no way to guess what sort of person she was.

"I'm not ready for kissing like that." Cherise took his hand, to prove that she meant no offense.

Anyone on Earth would have given up trying to date her, she felt sure.

But Flen treated her like a celebrity. "Then we shall simply explore," he said, as if enchanted by everything she said or did, no matter what. "Any path you want to take."

They strolled through a forest of gigantic mushrooms. The ribbon-like waterfalls were for irrigation, but to Cherise, it was an alien fairyland. Toadstools towered over her, fat and serene, their trunks mottled with zany pastel colors. Golden lamplight filtered down between colorful umbrella caps.

Although the Alashani underworld lacked sunlight, Cherise loved to explore the beauty it did offer. Albino cave fish in crystal-clear streams. Fuzzy little jerboa creatures. And so many gemstones, glittering in random grotto walls or forgotten statues.

"I love your world," she told Flen.

He gave a proud smile. As a high-status member of a powerful family, Flen could bring her to privately owned parts of the city. His cousin's father-in-law owned a fur farm. Some other cousin owned a gem shop and seemed excited to make customized jewelry for Cherise. And Flen's aunt owned this mushroom forest.

"So," Flen said. "The mushrooms on Earth are piddly little things?"

"Yes." Cherise approximated the size with her hands. "We have other plants that are…"

She stopped herself, not wanting to imply that trees were superior to mushrooms in any way. It was best not to go on and on about butterflies and birds. Or the animals of woodlands and grasslands. Mountains. Oceans. Sunset skies.

"Farms on Earth have less color than your farms," Cherise decided to say. It was mostly true.

Anyway, she really ought to distance herself from the homeworld she would probably never see again. It was time to change the subject. She hated to make Flen feel awkward, but she felt obligated to ask, "How is Thomas doing?"

Flen scowled. "The *rekveh* is healthy."

That wasn't exactly what Vy had said. According to Vy, Thomas's basic needs were being met, and torture was not involved. Yet he was withdrawn. He had not touched the puzzles or parchments that were given to him so he could entertain himself.

And he was refusing to talk.

That news had hit Cherise in a way nothing else would have done. On Earth, Silent Cherise was the one who never used to speak out loud. Thomas used to be the only person she felt comfortable conversing with.

"He's not a bad person," Cherise said. "He isn't a Torth." She hoped that was true. "I promise."

Flen studied her with pained skepticism. "You lived with that *rekveh*," he said, hesitant. "Like it was a member of your family?"

Cherise regretted having mentioned that on an earlier date. Flen had assumed she was lying. He had reacted with such strong disgust, she had decided to never bring up the topic again.

"Yes," Cherise admitted. She ambled beneath huge mushrooms and felt like an alien.

Among the Alashani, Cherise knew, people bragged about their best family members. They tried to hide anything bad, such as abusive birth mothers. Or foster siblings who joined the Torth Empire. Cherise never should have mentioned her relationship to Thomas.

"Did you live in a palace?" Flen asked. "On Earth?"

"Not really," Cherise admitted. "It was smaller than your home."

Flen seemed more skeptical than ever. "The *rekveh* was content to live in a small place?" he asked. "Did it order you around and treat you like a slave?"

"No." Cherise laughed a little bit, unable to imagine the human version of Thomas ordering anyone around. He had relied on caretakers.

He still did, she supposed.

"What is funny?" Flen asked.

Cherise couldn't think of a graceful way to answer.

"Did it read your mind?" Flen asked with concern-tinged fascination.

"He…" Cherise hesitated. She wanted to explain that Thomas had helped her to solve problems. And sure, he used to read her mind. She had actually liked it.

She had loved it.

But that would sound exceedingly weird to an Alashani warrior. It might even sound kinky in a sinister way.

"He was nice to me." Cherise knew that sounded foolish. It made her sound like the naive victim of a Torth mastermind.

But if she were to explain how Thomas had helped her to regain self-respect after her ma had thoroughly destroyed it…

No. Flen would lose all respect for her. He would realize that she didn't come from a good family. At best, he would pity her. He would see Cherise as a poor, unloved orphan who had been so needy, she had stupidly enslaved herself to a crafty demon who could read her darkest secrets and manipulate her endlessly.

Maybe there was even some truth to Flen's version of the facts.

"I think I am beginning to understand you, Cherise." Flen stopped walking and faced her. He gently brushed a lock of Cherise's hair away from her cheek and behind her shoulder.

Cherise gazed into his lavender eyes.

"This is why you don't like to be touched," Flen said. "Isn't it?"

She tried to understand what he meant.

"Did that *rekveh*…did he hurt you, Cherise?"

Had Thomas hurt her? Cherise remembered him on that huge round bed, his eyebrows and hair powdered with gold, his eyes an iridescent-yellow color. And he had hurt her. He had tortured her.

Her throat clogged with the truth she dared not speak.

But Flen was searching her face, looking for an excuse to hurt the prisoner in his care.

She had to say something in Thomas's defense.

"No," Cherise lied.

She had hesitated for too long. A stormy look entered Flen's gaze. Cherise half expected lightning to crackle along his slender arms. The very air seemed heavier.

"Thomas can't hurt anyone," she hastily assured Flen. "Have you seen him? He's like a baby. He's always been weak."

She pressed her hands on Flen's tense arms, but Flen still looked suspicious.

"Please don't hurt him," Cherise begged. "When I was enslaved, a lot of Torth hurt me, but I was never afraid of Thomas. He isn't a threat."

Her pleas finally seemed to reach Flen. Cherise's skin prickled as tension left the air.

She sighed with relief. Flen's polished mannerisms hid what he was capable of.

"I'm sorry." Flen looked ashamed. "I should not have frightened you. I am not like your hulking friend Ariock; I have total mastery over my powers. That is a requirement for warriors who swear the Pact."

"Oh." Cherise wasn't sure if any Yeresunsa was totally safe to be around.

"I will respect your wishes," Flen said. "I have affection for you, Cherise. If you don't feel the same way? It will cause much sorrow in my heart. But…" He looked too miserable to finish the sentence.

He started down the mushroom-forested path, heading toward the exit.

Cherise grasped his arm.

Alashani hugged or kissed each other at the slightest provocation. Cherise had seen respectable city leaders make out with their own chambermaids, in public, uncaring who saw. It was surely okay for her to grab his arm like this.

"I'm interested," she assured him.

Flen tentatively wrapped her in an embrace.

When Cherise didn't resist, he very carefully, very gently, brushed his lips with hers.

A tingling sensation ran through Cherise's face and body. It wasn't quite like an electric charge. It was nicer, kinder, warmer, gentler. She wasn't sure if Flen had used his powers to make her feel this way. Somehow, the sensation seemed entirely her own.

She pressed against Flen.

He pressed against her, and she felt the lithe shape of his body. They fit together.

"If I ever meet the monsters that hurt you," Flen said, "I will make them pay. No one who hurt you should live."

Cherise thought of Thomas and promptly tried to forget him. If Flen ever dared to attack Thomas…well, what if Thomas attacked back?

That was unthinkable.

"I'm sorry." Flen nuzzled her forehead. "You are too gentle for such cruel talk. Come. Will you join me in my palace?"

That was certainly an invitation. Cherise hesitated, unsure. Flen lived in a sprawling palace near the top of the city, rumored to have a hot spa.

"We can touch, or not," Flen said kindly. "But will you allow me to massage you with oils? I will have chambermaids arrange crushed velvet for us to relax upon."

Cherise nearly refused. Flen seemed convinced that she was high-class and worth pursuing, but he was mistaken. She came from the worst sort of family. She was a worthless...

She stopped herself.

Thomas had seen value in her. Now Flen saw value in her. Even Kessa and Vy seemed to believe that she was worth knowing.

Maybe her friends were right.

"Is that okay?" Flen asked.

"Yes," Cherise decided.

She let Flen take her hand and lead her uphill, back toward the palace district. It was amazing to feel so cherished. She had never felt this valued before.

Not even with Thomas.

Unlike Thomas, Flen didn't know her yet. He didn't understand her. Flen was exploring. He wanted to get to know everything that made her Cherise Chavez, and it might take years.

Possibly even the rest of their lives.

As Cherise strode next to the compact albino warrior with powers, she smiled. She felt as if she was embarking on a new adventure.

# CHAPTER 12

# OF THREE BLOODS

"What is troubling you?" Jinishta asked. She lounged against a rocky bench wall, where Vy sat. "Stop. Take a break, and let's talk."

Defiant, Ariock took another superpowered leap toward the faraway ceiling.

This cavern—the main city cavern—was the only cave big enough to accommodate Ariock's midair backflips. He could infuse his body with so much extra strength, he was able to fly. It was as if emotions and thoughts and physicality were woven together in a synergy that felt as natural as breathing. When Ariock added an extra twist to the airflow, he somersaulted just beneath the ceiling. He landed with easy grace, albeit with enough force to jolt loose a few rocks.

"You don't need to show off," Jinishta said.

The slave tongue was still foreign to Ariock, but these days, he was almost fluent. He asked for Vy's company solely because her presence irked Jinishta.

And because he secretly liked Vy.

She backed him up whenever he needed a friend. The best thing about Vy—other than her stunning beauty—was her unapologetic humanness. They had attended the same elementary school! They kept surprising each other with unexpected commonalities. How was it possible that Vy had such good taste in television, music, games, and books?

"Can we talk?" Jinishta asked.

"When are you going to let me go aboveground?" Ariock demanded.

He had a lot of unmet demands. When would the prophet Migyatel arrive? How many weeks of travel did she need? Would the Alashani ever let Thomas out of that dungeon pit? But most of all, Ariock wanted to know when he would get to swear the Warrior's Pact.

He needed to be allowed to leave the caves.

Until then, he could not hope to sneak away with Thomas hidden in his arms. Leaving had to be a simple, uncomplicated matter. As long as chambermaids spied on the palace room where he slept, as long as Jinishta trained him all day, every day, he could not sneak anywhere.

"Sit." The premier patted the bench seat where Vy sat.

Ariock didn't bother with the seat, which was too narrow for him. He plopped onto the floor and glared at Jinishta. How much more training did she believe he needed? Hadn't he proven his skills already? He was clearly more powerful than any warrior in the Alashani underground, including Jinishta herself. If she would deign to set up another sparring match, he would prove it.

"Tell me," Jinishta said, in lecture mode. "What is the Warrior's Pact?"

"It's proof that I am trusted by society," Ariock said promptly. "Only those who swear the Pact are allowed aboveground." Or into the dungeon, Ariock knew.

"But what is the Pact?" Jinishta asked. "What is it that warriors swear to do?"

Ariock hesitated.

He realized, with shame, that he ought to have learned the answer on his own. Jinishta probably expected him to hang out with other warriors and have friendly chats.

Instead, Ariock spent a lot of time chatting with Vy.

Sometimes he visited Kessa or Weptolyso. But other Yeresunsa? He didn't feel as if he had much in common with the elegant albinos.

They didn't exactly invite him to their artsy cocktail parties, either.

Most of the warriors seemed intimidated by Ariock. They lived in delicate palaces with crystal sculptures and gemstone grottoes. They didn't want him around. And Ariock preferred to spend his time in the nussian wrestling pits, down in the lower part of the city. Nussians had a good sense of fun.

"I guess warriors swear to protect society?" Ariock said.

Jinishta gave him a pained look.

"Please teach me." Ariock bowed his head.

"Whenever I go aboveground," Jinishta said, her tone heavy, "I carry poison with me."

Ariock felt as if he had missed her meaning.

"All warriors who swear the Pact carry poison," Jinishta said. "Because we must be willing to die quickly if we are caught by Torth."

She pulled a necklace out of her tunic. An amulet hung on the chain around her neck. Jinishta unscrewed the amulet and shook out a tiny nugget. She showed it to Ariock.

"This," she said, "is a suicide pellet."

Vy sucked in her breath. She seemed to understand.

"We must never, ever give Torth a chance to read our minds." Jinishta was emphatic.

She tucked the nugget back into the amulet and sealed it away.

Judging by her somber expression, she wasn't joking. Not that Jinishta ever joked.

Ariock was at a loss for what to say.

"If we are accidentally captured by Torth," Jinishta explained, "we do not attempt escape. We do not attempt a rescue. Death is the only option. We eat poison and we die fast."

Ariock wanted to reject that requirement. At the same time, he understood the necessity. Mind readers could absorb knowledge quickly. They could probe minds.

If just one Alashani encountered the wrong sort of Torth—someone like Thomas—their hidden world would end.

"Why do you go aboveground at all?" Ariock demanded. He tried to soften his tone, to make it less accusing. "Why hunt Torth? You should stay away from them."

Jinishta's reply was fierce. "Torth prowl near our homes. If we allow them to explore as they please, more Torth will always come." She glared in defiance. "They must fear us. Otherwise they will invade us."

Ariock recalled the holographic map of the galaxy, conjured by Thomas, displaying countless inhabited planets. All planets were colonized by the Torth Empire, except for a handful of rejects.

Jinishta had a point. If the Torth Empire ever lost its superstitious fear of the dead city, they would pave it over and build luxury high-rises—and unearth the Alashani underground.

"That is why we collect their heads," Jinishta said.

Over centuries, perhaps millennia, Alashani warriors had killed thousands of Torth, perpetuating Torth myths about the dead city sickness and random vanishings.

In the process, no doubt, a few black-clad Alashani warriors might have perished. Either they got killed by Torth, or else they ate poison. They invariably died before any Torth could read their minds.

"But a few Torth must have glimpsed you," Vy said. "Or your bodies? Surely it's happened before?"

"Almost never." Jinishta straightened. "This is why we go aboveground in groups. Four is the minimum. Usually, we go with five to seven. If any of us are captured by Torth…? The rest of us make sure the captive is not taken."

Ariock leaned back on his hands and studied his small mentor. No wonder Jinishta was so humorless. Had she ever used her powers to kill a fellow warrior in order to prevent a Torth from probing their mind?

How many times had she dreamed about swallowing poison?

"We swear the Pact," Jinishta said, "so that we can trust each other."

"I see." Ariock tried to sound willing. He imagined himself swallowing a suicide pill in order to avoid a confrontation with Torth.

His mind rejected that imagery.

It was far too much to ask. He never wanted to be in that position.

"I am sure you have heard warriors brag about killing Torth." Jinishta faced him with a frank expression. "We brag because we are still alive. We display Torth heads in order to please the Lady of Sorrow."

That was the Alashani goddess of life and death. Supposedly, the Lady of Sorrow shed a tear for every slave. Her eternal grief was the source of the River of Tears. But the goddess was also an arbiter of justice. According to Alashani lore, she appeared to people who hovered on the brink of life and death. She could choose a hero to return from the land of the dead in order to help the living.

Vy looked at Ariock, and he saw his own worries reflected in her eyes. "Maybe," she said in English, "you can swear the Pact without actually meaning it?"

That was one way to handle it.

Ariock didn't want to outright lie to the Alashani. He thought of his great-grandfather, who had sneaked away without swearing the Pact. Would Ariock be able to follow in his footsteps? Again?

Ariock could only follow Jonathan Stead up to a point. His forebear had faked his own death and hidden on Earth. Ariock didn't think he could do either of those things.

And Jinishta would be alert.

"Has anyone ever broken the Pact?" Ariock asked. "Aside from Jonathan Stead, I mean? How often does it happen?"

There had to be other rogues in Alashani history. Ariock wanted to know how observant Jinishta would be. If he dared to escape with Thomas, how far would Jinishta pursue him? Would she attempt to murder him from a distance?

"Right," Vy said, catching on. "It's hard to believe that in all of Alashani history, no one ever made a mistake."

Jinishta slumped on the bench seat. She looked ashamed. "Well," she muttered, "everyone knows the story of Eidelwen."

"I don't," Ariock said.

Jinishta laced her fingers tightly against each other. Why did she look so ashamed?

"Who was Eidelwen?" Vy prompted.

Jinishta jumped up, as if she couldn't stand to sit any longer. "Really?" She gave Vy a searching look, and then Ariock. "No one has ever told you?"

Ariock and Vy exchanged mystified looks. They shook their heads.

"Will you tell us, please?" Vy asked with politeness.

Jinishta hesitated for such a long time, Ariock felt sure that she would refuse. She looked ready to storm away. Maybe she would end their lesson session early for today.

Then she seemed to brace herself. "Eidelwen," she said, "was a premier Yeresunsa of Hufti."

Perhaps she was embarrassed to share a title with a deplorable outlaw?

Jinishta paced the other way. "She was also the sister of my great-great-grandmother."

Oh. That explained her shame. One bad ancestor could cripple the status of an entire Alashani family for generations.

Ariock recalled Kessa saying that she had overheard some gossip that Jinishta's parents and siblings lived modestly. They had probably grown up in a slum because of this Eidelwen person.

"Like me," Jinishta said, "Eidelwen was blessed with immense power. But so much power made her overconfident."

The story must be vital for Ariock's education, because Jinishta went on even as her pale face flushed bright red. She must be full of shame.

"During a hunt to kill Torth, Eidelwen accidentally became separated from her partners. Alone, she found herself confronted by a gigantic Torth dressed in armor."

Ariock could imagine the confrontation, in the rainy gloom of the dead city.

"She should have fled," Jinishta said. "But Eidelwen made a stupid mistake. She tried to decapitate the Torth by herself. She failed. And in her defeat, she also failed to swallow her poison."

A Torth who could evade the superfast skills of a Yeresunsa warrior must be an exceptional fighter. Probably a Servant of All.

Yet the Torth Empire had never learned about the Alashani.

Why not?

"The huge Torth savaged Eidelwen." Jinishta gave Ariock a strange look, as if he was supposed to recognize something about the story. "Then he threw her off a building and left her to die in muck."

"He didn't read her mind?" Vy asked.

"I cannot know." Jinishta paced. "But when Eidelwen failed to swallow her poison—when she let that Torth capture her alive—she nearly condemned all Alashani to slavery and death."

Ariock wondered if Eidelwen had distracted the lone Torth attacker, somehow. She must have prevented him from delving into her Alashani secrets.

"Eidelwen survived," Jinishta said.

Ariock focused on her, wondering what more there could be to such a story.

"Her partners found her, healed her, and brought her home. But it soon became apparent that..." Jinishta seemed to gather her courage. There was something dreadful about this story—something she was forcing herself to discuss.

"Eidelwen was pregnant," Jinishta said.

Vy blinked and sat up straighter, attentive.

"She had no lover," Jinishta said. "She was pregnant because of that Torth."

Ariock exchanged a look with Vy and saw that the implications had caught her off guard, as well.

The Torth Majority made lust and love illegal. But every once in a while, it seemed, a lustful Torth slipped out of the Megacosm long enough to defy the rules. Like Thomas's nameless mother.

And hadn't Jonathan Stead descended from a Torth father and…well, a something else?

If Torth hybrids such as Thomas Hill and Jonathan Stead could survive beyond infancy, there must be other liaisons. How many rare hybrid babies were conceived in secret? How many got aborted before they became known?

How many Torth never acted upon their secret lusts? How many Torth were suppressing emotional instincts?

"Everyone believed the baby would be a monstrosity." Jinishta grimaced with shame. "Monstrosities are not unheard-of, among us. Sometimes, even without a Torth involved, an Alashani will birth a baby who cannot see or cannot hear. Or one that is very disfigured."

Vy gave Jinishta a pained look. "Do you believe all babies like that are monstrosities?"

"No." Jinishta offered a weak smile. "I would not advise killing a baby with poor eyesight. One of our warriors, Lei, is blind. But a *rekveh*?" She made a face. "We cannot allow such evil to live among us. If a baby shows signs of reading minds, it must be killed. That is an unassailable law."

A fleeting thought crossed Ariock's mind. *Like the Torth.*

The Alashani were unlike Torth in most ways. Yet the Torth destroyed their Yeresunsa fetuses. Wasn't this the same thing? They told themselves they were getting rid of monstrosities.

"Go on." Ariock kept his tone flat. He remembered that giants on Earth used to be labeled monstrosities or freaks. Jinishta had no idea how wrong she was to label Thomas, or anyone else, that way.

"Eidelwen promised that she would have her baby suffocated as soon as it was born," Jinishta said. "It would not be allowed to live."

Vy winced.

"But in secret," Jinishta went on, "Eidelwen visited her sister, who was a seer. Her sister whispered that her baby would become a famous warrior with legendary strength. So Eidelwen became determined to give her baby a chance to live."

Ariock braced himself for a tragic ending. Eidelwen and her unborn hybrid baby had probably been torn apart by a mob of angry Alashani.

"Close to giving birth," Jinishta said, "Eidelwen sneaked away. She vanished into the dead city alone, even with her belly big with the pregnancy."

Ariock waited for more.

"No one ever saw her again." Jinishta regarded him as if she had conveyed a lesson.

Was the lesson supposed to be about overconfidence? In truth, Ariock admired Eidelwen for taking control of her own fate, and that of her unborn child, instead of allowing a mob to murder the baby.

"Is that it?" Ariock asked uncertainly.

Vy came to another conclusion. "That baby." She gasped. "He did grow up to be a famous warrior! Jonathan Stead?"

"Yes," Jinishta confirmed.

Ariock had a few reactions. He was a direct descendant of that strange encounter—that rape?—in the dead city.

He opened his mouth, then closed it, recalling that it was blasphemy to suggest that Jonathan Stead had been capable of reading minds.

But stubborn Jinishta knew! She knew that Jonathan Stead had been half Torth!

Yet she'd stridently denied that he was a mind reader. Apparently, she wanted no familial association with someone who could…

Family.

Ariock gawked at Jinishta. Her great-great-grandmother was a sibling to his. They were blood relatives!

Jinishta looked shy. "Jonathan Stead was not searching for his family," she said. "But if he had come here, to Hufti, instead of to Bebeshar, he would have met his aunt and cousins." She flushed with shame. "My family."

Was this a lesson? It was a revelation. Ariock felt rocked to his core. He had a long-lost family he had never known about.

A cousin, right in front of him!

The Dovanack mansion had been eerie and echoey with just Ariock and his mother. No wonder Jonathan Stead, aka Garrett Dovanack, felt such a strong urge to protect his family! He was half Alashani. It was probably a genetic instinct.

"Wow." Vy stared from Jinishta to Ariock and back again, no doubt measuring their size difference. "Actually, I can see it." She laughed. "You're both fearless and stubborn-as-hell overachievers!"

Ariock was grateful that Vy could share his joy. She'd been exposed to his lonely beginnings on Earth. She understood how much this meant to him.

Jinishta cleared her throat. Her cheeks remained pink. "I had not intended to tell you. My family…they do not live in paradise. They have an apartment in the scratch, next to a nussian wrestling pit."

Ariock grinned. "I go there all the time!"

"Oh." Jinishta offered a small smile. "Well, they would love to meet you. If you are willing, of course. They are, um—well, they are your family, too."

Ariock hardly knew what to say.

He had assumed that everyone in his family was dead. Jinishta—his cousin! —had no concept of how bleak it felt to be alone. Alashani took their big families for granted.

Jinishta looked braced for rejection.

Did she expect him to refuse because he was the supposed messiah, too good for common people? Or because he came from paradise, where birds sang and the sun shone?

"Yes!" Ariock assured her. "Of course I want to meet my cousins!"

Jinishta's smile was huge and completely uncharacteristic of her. "Then I shall tell my parents to prepare to meet you." She began to force away the beautiful expression. "We should get back to practicing—"

She squealed in surprise when Ariock wrapped her in a hug.

His human family members had been murdered by Torth or accidentally killed. He could not count any Torth as family members, even if he did have some unknown distant cousins who owned slaves. He doubted that he would ever marry and have children, the way his lucky hybrid great-grandfather had done. Yet he had discovered his Alashani cousins by sheer luck.

And they actually wanted to meet him!

Jinishta pulled away, laughing, when he let her go. She adjusted her Yeresunsa mantle. "Welcome to the family, Ariock."

# CHAPTER 13

# JUST ALIENS

Ariock eased his way down the narrow staircase, careful as he followed Vy. The underground city was composed of stairwells and steep alleyways, all cramped and too small for him.

"Goodbye," called a matronly woman, the one who'd baked the most delicious desserts. "You must come again! I will send you some gingerroot cake and you tell me what you think of it."

Ariock was delighted that he understood without translation. Vy was teaching him the slave tongue so quickly, he dreamed entire conversations that weren't in English.

Some of those dreams were more about touch than speech. It was a good thing Vy couldn't read minds.

"I can't believe they're related to Jinishta," Vy said, laughing. She unfurled the scarf that one of Jinishta's sisters had given her as a gift, admiring it.

"I know," Ariock agreed. Jinishta's family—all nine siblings, twenty-odd nieces and nephews, plus parents and various cousins—were plump and cheerful. They were neither rich nor poor but were a big, sprawling family, with roots in every facet of society. One cousin had married a gemstone dealer. Another was a factory overseer. One was a low-class brawler, much to their shame, but they talked about him anyway.

The family was immensely proud to have the messiah as well as the premier Yeresunsa in their midst. They'd showed off Jinishta at every opportunity, and they'd welcomed Ariock with more gusto than he'd expected. They had handed him steins of mushroom ale, and they'd begged him to try baked roasts from well-loved family recipes. Kids clamored for his attention, play-fighting and showing off their dolls. There was music and dancing, and old folks who shared gossip about who had married whom, and the talk of the neighborhood.

All in all, Ariock had stayed up too late, and he might have had too much ale and too much of everything. Jinishta had admonished him about that, saying that a warrior in training like himself should maintain dignity.

Jinishta had left before the dancing got started. Probably too much happiness for her to handle.

Kessa and Weptolyso had also made appearances, but they'd left hours ago. Only Vy had stayed with Ariock the whole time.

"That was more fun than I've had since…since my life on Earth." Vy hopped down the last step on her good leg. She did a cute dance move, hair fiery in the lamplight.

"*Aonswa!*" Footsteps ran down the stairs behind Ariock.

That wasn't enough to distract him from Vy dancing in the street. Her dress, laced with silver and studded with rubies, was cut to flatter a petite Alashani maiden. On buxom Vy, it was almost intimidating.

Ariock ducked out of the stairwell and straightened to his full height. His peaceful sleepiness vanished, replaced by something that felt like a basic need.

"*Aonswa*, this is yours!"

Vy stopped dancing, curious. So Ariock followed her gaze.

A maiden thrust a gift basket into his hands. At the same time, she bounced up from her position on the stairwell, grabbed Ariock by the cheeks, and kissed him.

Fervently.

On the lips.

Then she lost her balance, giggling and blushing, while Ariock straightened in shock. He narrowly avoided hitting his head on lintel.

"I can give you other gifts." Her tone was an insinuation. "Ask for Moesi. Me." She pointed to the tops of her snow-white breasts, exposed above a tight corset. "Your cousin Eishel would be happy to arrange…anything…for you."

Ariock studied Moesi's face, struggling to figure out if she actually liked him. Was that possible? Or had someone dared this maiden to pretend to seduce the freakish giant?

"And I don't mind sharing you," Moesi said. "You're a big man. Five or six chambermaids could really treat you well. I have friends." She licked her pink lips. "Think about it."

She flounced back the way she'd come, skirts rustling.

Ariock watched Moesi go, more shocked than ever.

This had to do with his status as the supposed messiah, he felt sure. High Councilor Chaniyelem kept swapping his chambermaids for new ones, and their sly smiles did not imply housekeeping.

Now that Ariock thought about it, he realized that he had missed a lot of context back when he couldn't understand the slave tongue.

Vy made a dejected sound. She was limping away.

Ariock caught up with her in a few strides. In normal times, he guessed these streets would be empty. The underground did have commonly shared sleep-wake cycles. But gawking pedestrians clogged the area, because the city was full of pilgrims. Lots of travelers from other underground cities had come to Hufti in order to see the prophet Migyatel—or to meet the messiah and his two angelic women from paradise.

"It looks like fungus balls," Ariock said, inspecting the contents of the gift basket. "Maybe they're infused with liquor?" He offered the basket to Vy. "Are these truffles?"

Vy didn't even look. "I don't want them."

Ariock had a guess about her sudden sadness. She probably regretted partying while her foster brother remained imprisoned in a dungeon pit. He felt the same guilt.

But he wasn't going to fish around and bring up a sore topic. Vy tended to be candid. If she wanted to share her worries, she would.

The palace district was uphill, making Vy's limp worse. Did she have too much to carry? His cousins had foisted so many trinkets upon her, she needed an extra satchel for all the gifts.

"Let me carry your gifts," Ariock offered.

"I'll just hire a rickshaw." Vy gave him a sad smile. "You don't need to keep to my slow pace. You might as well go ahead."

She said it nicely, but her giddy happiness was gone.

Nussians passed them, hauling families perched on oversize rickshaws. Every spare bedroom in the city was occupied. Vy searched for an empty ride.

"Then let me haul your rickshaw," Ariock offered.

Vy laughed with only a little bit of humor. "Oh? The great messiah is going to haul my rickshaw? That's sweet, but no. We get more than enough people staring at us."

The great messiah.

Did she think it was fun, to be praised for miracles he would never do? Ariock kept having nightmares about albino people dying in horrible ways. They cried for salvation while Torth collared them, or while they drowned in a flood, or they fell off precipices. He failed them.

It was a good thing dreams couldn't come true. Ariock had had a vague uneasiness about his dreams ever since a nightmare had shown him his mother's death before it happened. That had to be just a morbid coincidence.

"What's really wrong?" Ariock was sick of guesswork.

Vy searched his gaze. "Isn't it obvious? I don't belong here. I don't belong on this planet, or…" She turned and limped away. "Go home to your chambermaids."

Ariock stopped in the middle of the street. Vy couldn't be jealous. Could she?

That seemed unthinkable.

Vy never invited cuddling, even though it was socially acceptable here. The Alashani were a touch-friendly culture. After so many misadventures and losses, she must secretly detest Ariock. She had lost her leg because of him.

Besides, Vy had her choice of male attendants.

But what if his guesswork was wrong?

"Hold on," Ariock said, catching up to Vy. "Are you trying to get rid of me so you can hook up with an Alashani man?"

"Huh?" Vy studied him with the same lack of comprehension that he felt.

"I guess I can understand that," Ariock said. "Since I'm about ten times more awkward and weird-looking than you are."

She looked shocked.

"Feeling alien and weird is supposed to be my thing," he said. "Not yours."

Vy's face softened, and she chuckled. It sounded rueful, but laughter was a million times better than anguish.

"Neither one of us belongs here," Ariock assured her. "We're aliens."

Vy seemed happy to hear him say that. Perhaps she really did feel as uncomfortable in the Alashani underground as he did.

"But we're desirable aliens," Ariock said. "Not just me. You are, as well."

Vy laughed bitterly. "Because I'm from paradise. And I look like their Lady of Sorrow goddess."

Ariock nodded. He had seen statues of the goddess, and there was a resemblance to Vy. It was mostly in the flowing hairstyle.

"But trust me," Vy said, "the Alashani are not actually into a one-legged giantess."

Ariock realized that her unhappiness might have roots as messy as his own. Perhaps even worse. For Vy, being alien was an unwelcome new problem. Ariock had had a lot more time to get used to being different.

"If you've got men rejecting you," Ariock said, "then they're idiots. You're a million times more gorgeous than any Alashani."

She gave him a sidelong look of skepticism.

"They're too fragile-looking for me," Ariock admitted. He was pretty sure that he might accidentally break an albino maiden if he tried to do anything physical with her. Vy was small next to him, too—everyone was, unless they were nussians—but at least Vy had substance.

And at least Vy was brave enough to say what was on her mind. Alashani maidens tended to just giggle and pretend to be clueless.

Or worse, they pretended to like him. Ariock was mostly sure that the ones who threw themselves at him, like Moesi, were part of the bribery economy. They were spies. Everyone wanted to get to know the messiah.

Vy's smile was bittersweet.

She stopped in the street, and Ariock saw that she was struggling with emotion.

He knelt and enfolded her in his arms. Vy's shoulders shook with quiet sobs.

A buck-toothed adolescent boy tried to intrude. Ariock sent the boy away with a warning look. An elderly lady tried the same thing, holding up a comb for him to bless. Ariock glared. No one else dared to disrupt his intimate moment with Vy.

"I know I should be happy," Vy said. "Cherise moved on. I wish I could do that. I mean, we're safe. I'm grateful. But..."

But it wasn't Earth.

Ariock held her.

"I miss my mom," Vy said. "I miss Thomas."

Similar thoughts had weighed on Ariock's mind throughout the party. Being near a family stirred up those kinds of memories. The absence of loved ones was painful.

"I understand," he said.

"Thomas won't talk to me," Vy said. "He's going to die in that pit unless we do something."

Thomas weighed on Ariock's conscience more than anything. According to news from the dungeon, Thomas had not made any move to touch the light-weight puzzles he'd been given. He no longer moved at all. He would eat or drink when forced to do so, but he didn't respond to the voices of friends such as Vy.

"I'm worried," Ariock admitted.

"He's so fragile. And if we lose him...?" Vy trailed off, no doubt embarrassed to mention the importance of their one and only starship pilot.

No one else could calculate the entry and exit points for temporal streams. Nontelepaths could not access the Megacosm in order to fish out the necessary numbers. Without Thomas, they would be trapped on the Torth Homeworld forever.

"And my mom." Vy's voice was muffled against his chest. "I don't know if she's alive or enslaved or what. I don't know what the Torth are doing to Earth."

Ariock held Vy, glad for the feel of her encircled in his arms. If only he had the power to save Earth from the doom of conquest and enslavement.

"I can't stop missing sunlight." Vy leaned against him. "Every day. Every hour. Isn't that stupid?"

"Not at all," Ariock said. "I miss it, too." The ubiquitous lamplight had a thin, deficient feel. Darkness always lurked overhead.

But he felt like he was hugging daylight right now. Vy felt wholesome.

"I wish I could think of a way to protect Thomas." Ariock offered his Yeresunsa mantle so she could dry her tears. "I just don't know any place in the universe that would be safe for him. Not this underground world. Not Earth. Not anywhere."

"Well…" Vy peered up at him with her clear blue eyes. "I hear you're some kind of messiah?"

Ariock nearly faked a reassuring self-confidence. But he couldn't do that. Not to Vy.

"Can't you give a command or something? Tell them you heard a holy voice that said they should be nice to Thomas?" Vy sniffed and blotted her face. "Sorry about your mantle."

Whenever Ariock considered fully accepting the role of messiah—owning that lie—a knot tightened inside him. That knot had nothing to do with saving his friend Thomas, and everything to do with the thunderous expectations of millions of albino people.

"I'm not going to lie like that," he said. "It wouldn't help Thomas in the long run. I'd be found out."

And then the Alashani would want two heads on spikes, not just one.

"What if it's not a lie?" Vy asked.

Ariock waited for the punch line. She had to be joking.

"I mean…" Vy bit her lip, as if holding back an argument. Then she went ahead with it. "What if Migyatel says you're the real deal? Isn't that possible?"

Her eyes measured him.

Searching for a savior.

Ariock struggled against a tidal wave of emotion. Vy, of all people, should know that he was human. She was supposed to be immune to the Alashani religious madness.

"Do you…" Ariock paused, feeling more alone than he ever had. "Do you think I'm the chosen one?"

Vy hesitated.

It was intolerable. Ariock backed away from her. He needed just one person who could laugh at the messiah madness.

Maybe Thomas was the only person in the universe who could understand how absurd it all was. Ariock should visit the dungeon again.

"I don't think it matters what the Alashani believe," Vy said. "I know where you're from. I know you're a good guy."

Relief washed through Ariock, stronger than he could have imagined. Vy was on his side.

"It's wrong to mislead them." Ariock gestured at the gawking pedestrians, none of whom could understand his foreign language. "All these people expect me to lead them to light and glory. I don't want to bribe the prophet into saying I'm the real thing or anything like that. They're going to find out the truth sooner or later. And don't you think they'll be furious, once they know I'm not the chosen one?"

"You're really afraid," Vy said in a tone of realization.

"Of course I am!" Ariock said. "If I could actually defeat armies and slay the Torth Empire, don't you think I would have by now?"

She looked stunned.

"I wouldn't be hiding down here," Ariock said. "I would have marched out with Thomas a long time ago. I wouldn't be...well, terrified...to go back to the surface."

"You're terrified?" Vy studied him anew.

"Yes. Of course." Ariock figured that he might sound pathetic, but he no longer cared. It was a relief to be able to confess his fears. "My powers are not enough to defeat thirty-eight trillion Torth." He thumped his chest, indicating the knot of scar tissue hidden under his tunic and mantle. "You know that. Thomas knew that. I fell in battle. One well-placed nuke will destroy me. And anyone who's with me will die."

"Oh." Vy caught up with him, her artificial leg clicking against the stone tiles in a dainty way. "I never thought of it that way."

Ariock stopped her before she could get too apologetic or sympathetic. He didn't deserve much sympathy. He was, after all, a failure.

"I just want someone who understands." Ariock realized how dismissive that sounded and tried to backtrack. "I mean, I just...I just want you to remember that I'm human."

Vy took his gigantic hand in both of hers. She studied it.

Ariock had the familiar urge to withdraw, to hide his freakishness. Instead, he let her examine how her hand fit inside his.

"I keep thinking of you as unstoppable," Vy confessed. "I assumed you were fearless."

That was such a wrong assessment, Ariock laughed without humor. "Every time I've fought an army, innocent people die. You don't think that terrifies me?" He nodded toward her ivory-carved leg. "That was almost your life."

Vy's gaze softened. "That scared you?"

"I can't think of anything scarier," Ariock said. "Whenever we talk about rescuing Thomas and running up the Stratower, to try and break into some ultrahigh-security spaceport, all I can see is you in danger."

Vy looked thoughtful.

"And the worst thing is," Ariock admitted, "it's inevitable. The Alashani are going to find out that they're wrong about me. Either Migyatel will tell them or they'll figure it out eventually. And then what do you think they'll do?"

"I see." Vy had a tone of realization.

Ariock nodded. "They'll decapitate me. Or they'll hunt me. I'll have to leave this safe haven, like Eidelwen did. Like Jonathan Stead."

Vy gazed at him with sympathy.

"I'm going to have to fight an army," Ariock admitted. "Either a Torth army or an Alashani one. Or both."

She understood. He could see it in her eyes.

"And every time I do that," Ariock said, "people I love end up dead."

Vy swallowed.

"It's not worth it." Ariock felt sure about that. "So I'm trying to think of another way. Anything else. Anything at all."

"We need Thomas's advice," Vy said.

Ariock yearned for genius advice. But the jailers would not allow anyone to speak to Thomas in a foreign language. They insisted that his visitors stick to the slave tongue, so they could eavesdrop and understand every word that was said.

"Jinishta won't allow anyone to have a private conversation with Thomas," Ariock said. "She won't budge on that."

Vy gave Ariock's hand a squeeze. She tugged him, indicating that they should walk onward. "I've heard that she's going to have you swear the Warrior's Pact very soon."

"Really?"

"She was going to wait until after Migyatel's arrival," Vy said. "But I guess her warriors are impatient. They do want you as one of them. It sounds like there are rumors going around. People say that seers are predicting disasters."

Disasters. Like in his nightmares?

Ariock shivered and tried to dismiss his unease. His worries were manifesting in his subconscious. If other people were having nightmares, too, that was probably just a coincidence.

"So people in the underground want you on their side," Vy said. "Even if Jinishta decides to reject you for whatever reason, premiers from other cities will try to recruit you."

Ariock liked that idea. If enough Alashani accepted him, then surely he could convince them all that Thomas was a good guy?

He had to do something to save Thomas. Failure was unacceptable. After all, Thomas had given up his own promising future and nearly gotten himself killed in order to pull off a rescue that should have been impossible.

He was entitled to Ariock's protection.

If Ariock let go of that promise simply because it was convenient to do so—simply because he was comfortable underground and afraid to go to the surface—then he would be unfit to call himself a warrior, no matter what Jinishta had to say about it.

*"No one can save me,"* Thomas had said.

That might be a real prophecy. Who would have guessed that one lone child could incite hatred from so many people? The Torth. The Alashani. Any alien slave who met Thomas would probably hate him on sight. Humans had bullied and abused him. Wild zoved wanted to eat him alive. And his genetics saddled him with a deadly neuromuscular disease.

The entire universe seemed to be conspiring to kill the boy.

Ariock clenched his fists. He had made a promise. He was not going to let Thomas die before he did.

"I'll meet you back at Chaniyelem's," Vy said. She limped toward a rickshaw-rental kiosk, clearly exhausted from walking on her dainty peg leg.

Ariock walked past her, and past the vendor. He selected one of the light-weight single-rider carriages. "How much?" he asked the vendor.

"Hmm." The vendor smirked at him. "We don't make them for your size. Sorry."

Ariock carefully picked up the rickshaw. He set the flimsy contraption down in front of Vy, ignoring the admiring onlookers. "I'll be your hauler."

Even the vendor gawked in disbelief.

Vy studied Ariock as if trying to figure him out. "Are you serious?"

"I can't ride next to you," Ariock admitted. "Since I'm not a typical Alashani. But I'm not abandoning you to go home alone. We're doing this."

He pulled out the pouch of coins Chaniyelem had given to him and handed it to the astonished vendor.

Vy giggled. "You're a million times better than any Alashani man." She climbed onto the cushy seat.

"I was hoping you'd say that." Ariock finished the purchase, took back his coin pouch, then lifted the handlebars.

Stares and double takes followed them all the way uphill to the palace district.

# CHAPTER 14

# AN ANSWER

Ariock approached the waiting congregation of Yeresunsa. He felt massive and dark, looming like a thundercloud over the finely dressed albinos.

He had ignored Jinishta's request that he wear gemstones for his induction ceremony. He was never in the mood to go jewelry shopping. His only adornments were a few golden plates and the Yeresunsa mantle stretched across his shoulders. He doubted that anyone would chastise him on an occasion that was meant to honor him.

Sure enough, Jinishta barely showed her disapproval with a flick of her gaze. "Here is our most holy chamber," she said. "The heart of our monastery." She turned her back on Ariock and used her powers on the round wall.

The air gained a charged feeling, like weather before a thunderstorm.

The wall rumbled. It began to roll aside. The entire wall was a stone wheel, larger than Ariock, built to be moved by powers.

A light glowed from the chamber within.

Not torchlight.

Ariock shielded his eyes. This brilliant white glow looked like stadium lighting. This was not anything steam-powered. Either it was magic, or the Alashani had a power generator squirreled away in there.

"It is glowing already!" one of the Yeresunsa whispered.

Murmurs echoed off alabaster walls as others whispered. Judging by their hesitancy and awe, the power crystal shouldn't glow yet. Not when the candidate was so far away.

"What is a power crystal?" Ariock asked. He wanted to become a warrior just so he could be trusted to go aboveground. But what if they wanted him to touch a nuclear reactor or something equally insane?

"The crystal gauges your raw power," Jinishta answered. "Not every city has a power crystal. We are fortunate, in Hufti, to have one of the largest."

Ariock felt ignorant, having lived among the Alashani for nearly two months without learning whatever this was. "How does it work?" he asked.

"You merely walk to it," Jinishta said. "And touch it."

"That's it?"

"That's it," she confirmed.

Ariock looked doubtfully at the ultrabright chamber. He saw pedestals in there, and things displayed on each pedestal, like items in a museum.

"Do not touch any of the sacred relics," Jinishta warned him.

"What are the sacred relics?" Ariock asked.

The answer was probably something that every Alashani schoolchild learned. Jinishta looked pained, but she did try to explain without condescension. "They are holy items that we, the Yeresunsa, are entrusted with protecting."

"Why?"

"During the Age of Chaos, it is said, a wise prophet commanded Yeresunsa to honor the past in order to honor the future." Jinishta seemed aware that her answer was inadequate. "Many sacred remnants were lost or ruined. We guard these as best we can."

"Oh." Ariock knew that further questions would be a dead end. The Alashani rarely questioned matters of holiness.

They trusted their prophets. They trusted their gods. Statues and shrines throughout the city honored the Lady of Sorrow and other gods, such as the Maiden of Candlelight. Nussians sometimes prayed to a nussian aspect of the Lord of Thieves before a wrestling match. That god was said to bestow luck and wealth.

The other Yeresunsa glided into the well-lit chamber. Robes swished. With their white hair and ivory staffs and white or off-white robes, they looked like a group of somber wizards.

"Let's go," Jinishta told Ariock.

He steeled himself and followed Jinishta. Was it his imagination, or did the glow brighten as he entered?

Fluted walls stretched up to a fancy rotunda. The center of the room dropped in a spiraled ramp that led downward toward the glaring white light. Looking in that direction made Ariock squint.

The museum relics were interesting, though.

One appeared to be an upright loop, a Möbius strip of red metal. There was a marble statuette of a woman with feathered wings, and that was interesting because the Alashani hardly knew what feathers were. The alien Kemkorcans among them had wispy feathers like moth antennae.

A holograph flickered above another pedestal.

Ariock gasped when he saw the damaged recording. He walked closer to inspect the blurry, silent, flickering video of a woman who seemed to be giving a pleading speech. She looked human.

Was that a clean, beautiful version of the Stratower behind her?

"Do not touch the relics," Jinishta warned.

Ariock was getting really tired of Alashani rules and regulations. He yearned to show this ancient relic to Vy, but non-Yeresunsa were not allowed to set foot in the inner sanctum of the monastery. And he had to honor Jinishta as his premier, along with all the laws she enforced.

"How old is this holograph?" Ariock asked.

Jinishta shrugged. "The holy relics are said to come from the Age of Glory."

Oh, right. There were no seasons or months underground. Every day looked the same.

"How many lifetimes ago was that?" Ariock asked.

"No one knows," Jinishta admitted. "It was before the Age of Starvation, and before the Age of Chaos. These relics are said to be from the era before the Torth ruined everything."

Ariock shifted his attention to the winged statuette. "She doesn't look like an Alashani." She looked somewhat like Vy and Cherise—human, or Torth— but he did not mention that.

"That is how angels look," Jinishta explained. "I know that they look like somewhat like Torth." She regarded him with defiance, stating a fact that few of her people knew. "But the Torth themselves are twisted, evil versions of angels."

Demons. Ariock understood that was what *rekveh* meant.

Had the Torth once been like humans? Maybe they had been magic users. Maybe they had been more advanced, in terms of technology. But once upon a time, the inhabitants of the Torth Homeworld had walked in sunlight, and they had created these emotive holographs and statuettes.

Some calamity had changed them.

Now the Torth Empire wanted to obliterate humanity.

Someday, in the far distant future, aliens might handle the few relics that survived from the enslaved planet Earth and wonder about its long-dead Age of Glory.

"Ariock," Jinishta urged him, "you must go down the ramp."

No one else was going anywhere near the ramp. The other Yeresunsa had assembled into a loose audience, shielding their eyes from the fierce glow.

"You must go alone," Jinishta said. "The power crystal is already alight, and I have never seen it glow this brightly. It will glow more brightly as you approach."

"Will it blind me?" Ariock asked.

The question seemed to surprise Jinishta. She looked worried for a moment, but said, "Keep your eyes closed. Feel your way with your powers, if you must."

Ariock walked toward the ramp, full of misgivings. If every remnant in this chamber was preserved from the long-forgotten Age of Glory, the power crystal might also be ancient. Was it a functioning relic, like that flickering holographic recording?

If only he could share his questions with Thomas. The boy would surely have some useful speculations.

"When I touched the crystal," Jinishta said, "I saw a glowing reflection of myself. It was beautiful. That is how I knew—how everyone knew—I was powerful. The crystal does not flare bright for everyone. For most warrior candidates, it is dim. For you? It is glowing very bright."

"Is it dangerous?" Ariock asked.

"The crystal will not harm a Yeresunsa," Jinishta said. "But to be safe, I guess that you should keep your eyes closed."

Ariock descended the ramp. Light blazed through his closed eyelids.

*It's something nuclear*, he thought. *It has to be.*

When he sent his awareness downward, exploring the source of the light, he sensed a geodesic shape. It seemed solid and crystalline all the way through. Gemstones always seemed obvious to his Yeresunsa awareness. This one had an exceptionally weird structure, and it was quite large, like an ostrich egg.

He forced himself to take another step down the ramp. And another. Tears leaked from his closed eyes. Light flared through the arm he'd raised to shield himself.

Jinishta and the other warriors would surely sense if he quit walking.

If they could pass this test, so could he.

*Can you?* his inner self queried. *They aren't cowards and failures. They aren't letting a friend suffer in a dungeon pit. They did not get a village of ummins slaughtered.*

Light blazed through him, merciless. Even with his eyes squeezed shut, his world was white.

Another step.

Did he deserve the honor of being a warrior? He wasn't sure.

The crystal consumed his focus, as if pulling on his awareness. Ariock felt as if he was cascading into the thing, disembodied, swirling down the spiraled ramp.

He risked one more small step.

He needed to reevaluate why he was here, what he was trying to accomplish. He shouldn't risk going blind. Even if Jinishta welcomed him as an official member of her team, he still wouldn't be able to sneak around. He still couldn't help Thomas.

One tiny step, barely a shuffle…and something brittle exploded. It sounded like the sky room window shattering.

Ariock instantly cocooned himself in solidified air.

He was safe from shards of crystal or anything that might fly at him. But nothing did. His extended awareness told him that he was safe.

The light was dimming. The shattering sound continued, and as it grew fainter, the light receded.

Ariock dared to lower his shielding arm. He was afraid to open his eyes, in case the light flared again, so he extended his awareness instead.

The suctioning source was gone.

Instead of that tug on his power, Ariock only sensed normal air.

The shattering noise dwindled into the sound of tiny pebbles grinding underfoot. Ariock seemed to be in darkness, so he opened one eye with caution.

He saw utter blackness.

Both of his eyes fluttered open reflexively. Was he blind? Ariock forced away panic and used his powers to scoop nearby air into a crackling orb of electric light.

His orb illuminated the ramp he stood on. Ariock was tall enough to peer past the edge and see all the way down to the tiled floor below. Sparkles twinkled in the blackness there.

The last sparkles faded like dying fireflies.

Excited voices echoed in the darkness above him. Warriors leaned on the balustrade, staring down and all talking at once.

"It broke."

"He broke it!"

Ariock felt like a giant oaf. He should have known better than to try to explore the crystal, or whatever it was, with his awareness. The thing had probably existed for longer than the Torth Empire. Maybe it had gotten brittle with age. Maybe he hadn't been gentle enough.

"The messiah will break traditions." One of the Yeresunsa spoke like an orator, and everyone else quieted to hear. "There shall be darkness before the light."

The onlookers seemed to mull that over.

"It was foretold!" a woman squealed.

Sparks crackled as Yeresunsa lit torches or created orbs of light. They used the tops of their staffs as focal points.

A young man fell to his knees, peering at Ariock through the balustrade. "Messiah," he said feverishly.

Several old women and men debated the prophecy. Others clutched their mantles and gazed at Ariock with stunned awe.

If the crystal's brightness reflected the raw power of an individual, then it seemed Ariock might have caused it to overload. He hadn't even made it all the way down the ramp before it shattered into mini-crystals, each of them overloading and shattering still further.

Jinishta could have warned him.

Better yet, she should have put this test off indefinitely!

Ariock trudged up the ramp. He could have flown over their white-haired heads, but he wasn't in a mood to show off his powers. Prophecy, prophecy, prophecy. He was sick to death of their superstitious beliefs.

"You see this scar?" Ariock pulled aside his mantle and tunic collar and showed the scarred dent to Jinishta. "This is where Orla healed me."

Orla had not been invited to this gathering. She was too young, and she had yet to undergo the crystal test herself.

"I should be dead," Ariock went on. "Except I got healed. I was carried through the dead city by Weptolyso. I've been saved, multiple times, by other people. Including my friend Thomas, whom you've imprisoned."

Most of the Yeresunsa continued to gaze at him with adulation.

Ariock pushed up the sleeves of his tunic. His tunic had to be specially cut in order to accommodate the cruel iron thorns implanted in his forearms. "Do you see these disfigurations?" He rotated his arms, so the onlookers would see the spikes. "These used to be attached to heavy chains. I was a prisoner. Condemned to death."

The warriors watched him in fascination.

"Guess who saved me?"

Jinishta's gaze sharpened with a warning look.

"Thomas," Ariock said, answering his own question. "If not for him, I would be dead."

The warriors exchanged uneasy glances. Flen was on prison duty, but his buddy Haz stood in the audience. He was among the warriors who looked obstinate. No doubt they wanted the inconvenient *rekveh* to die.

Ariock breathed out his fury. "If you believe in prophets and power crystals," he said, "why won't you believe me about Thomas?"

Some of the warriors looked hesitantly agreeable. True believers?

"The *rekveh* is comfortable in the prison," one warrior dared to assure Ariock.

The others broke into arguments. The messiah had just proven himself without a prophet to confirm his status. Hadn't he?

Well, Migyatel was supposed to arrive any day now. She should be here tomorrow!

But she had taken so long. Was she afraid to meet the messiah? Was it possible she knew something sinister that she was afraid to speak in public?

Was it true that she dreamed of major disasters?

Well, any upcoming flood or Torth invasion would surely be caused by the *rekveh*. And if such an unthinkable calamity happened, the messiah must save everyone. Wouldn't he?

Jinishta sounded uncertain. "Breaking that crystal was a major sign, regardless of what you want to believe or disbelieve. It means something to all Alashani." Her pale eyes searched Ariock's face, looking for the savior.

Ariock reached the top of the ramp. He walked through the now-gloomy chamber, towering over his supposed peers. He had thought—hoped—that Jinishta was different from the other fools in this underworld. He wanted her as a friend. Was she going to turn into just another worshipper?

Ariock rolled his arm to show Jinishta his suicide scar. "I tried to kill myself," he said. "Is this a sign of your savior?"

Jinishta looked torn.

"These are not the marks of a messiah." Ariock tried to think how to explain how wrong she was. "I thought you knew better than to believe all this prophecy crap. I thought you…"

He gave up trying to explain. What was the point?

He strode past everyone in disgust. A sense of hurt lingered. He had truly believed that Jinishta was different.

He wanted her sour looks, her straightforward glares. Was she going to start bowing like the rest of them?

Except she commanded the supposed messiah. She wasn't going to let Ariock leave the underground. And the instant she decided that he was incapable of leading her people to light and glory? Never mind her friendship. She would stand in his way.

"Ariock, wait," Jinishta called.

The air began to feel like gel, slowing Ariock's powerful strides.

He turned, furious at Jinishta or whoever was attempting to trap him in place. Did they want to see a power display?

"If it helps," Jinishta said, "I will tell you a little-known fact about your father."

She meant his legendary great-grandfather. The Alashani had shortchanged the rest of his family.

"What?" Ariock demanded.

Jinishta drew a deep breath. "Jonathan Stead broke the power crystal in Bebeshar."

A few of the Yeresunsa looked astonished.

Ariock imagined Garrett Dovanack as a young man, walking down a spiraled ramp, goaded on by albino Yeresunsa. Had he rejected the undeserved worship, like Ariock was trying to do? Or had he welcomed it? Maybe old Garrett had secretly reached out with his powers while approaching the ancient crystal and shattered it on purpose.

Ariock laughed. There was irony in the Alashani desperation to believe.

"Your scars are proof that you can be wounded," Jinishta said. "Just like anyone. It is not my place to foretell your future, but whatever happens, you are still under my command."

Well, that was something. Jinishta was admitting that he might be an ordinary guy, at least.

"We still must wait for Migyatel to arrive and foretell your future," Jinishta said decisively. "She is supposed to arrive very soon."

Ariock did not want to meet the prophet. He didn't want to be announced as the messiah or decried as a fraud, one way or the other.

Why should it be so important to them? Why should it matter so much?

*"I went on a pilgrimage to meet Migyatel,"* Jinishta had told Ariock, when he'd asked her why she believed in the prophet. *"She told me I would be a leader of warriors. She even predicted that I would have a major crisis of faith. She foresees truly."*

Ariock faced the believers. "You're all so sure that you deserve light and glory," he said. "But you have glory here." He indicated the alabaster pillars and vaulted ceiling. "And light." He nodded toward soapstone lanterns. "You have plenty of everything." At least, they did when compared to all the enslaved people of the galaxy. "Why do you want more?"

They looked guilty and startled. Even Jinishta looked that way.

"Why do you want a messiah?" Ariock looked at the Yeresunsa, one by one. "I don't understand what you expect."

He walked away.

# CHAPTER 15

# AN OTHER MIND READER

Drip, drip. Drip.

Drip.

His primary sense was auditory. His jailers had removed the blindfold except during visits, but it didn't matter. The well shaft was utterly dark. He might as well be blind. He did not have a wristwatch or any possessions other than his filthy robes. His wildfire power was withered. It wasn't worth using.

Every echoing drip was so familiar, Thomas could envision the fluid dynamics of individual, distant stalactites.

His ears were attuned to the slightest whisper. He would hear the distant footfalls of his jailers if they deigned to approach. He estimated that their next visit was six hours away, with a thirty-eight-minute margin of error.

His nameless mother awaited him across the veil that separated life from death.

She welcomed him with a shredded throat and open, bleeding arms. *Join me, my son*, she urged without a voice, without a living mind.

Thomas suspected that she had been capable of love, despite being a Torth. Soon he would feel her love. All he needed to do was die.

Oh, and he needed to prove that he was worthy of love.

His mother had made immense sacrifices in order to give him a chance at having a life outside the Torth Empire. He must honor her sacrifices by avoiding the Megacosm, so that Cherise and Vy and Ariock would be safe, wherever they were.

He needed to remain alone and powerless until his time *(his life)* ran out.

To stave off the unending, gnawing siren song of thirty trillion minds, Thomas continuously struggled to keep his mind occupied. He did everything he could to distract himself. Weeks, days, hours, minutes, seconds, microseconds…the ticks and tocks blurred to meaningless numbers. Thomas averaged the time between service visits from his unknown jailers. He multiplied that number by the sum total of echoing drips during an interval. He collected numbers and made pointless equations with them.

Every few days, Kessa visited. Clicking toenails. Otherwise it was Vy and her ticking gait. It sounded like his foster sister was using a peg foot. Thomas could draw some conclusions from that hypothesis. The jailers were low-tech. They could not make prosthetic feet.

Or maybe the voices that sounded like Vy and Kessa were merely imitations.

Maybe this was all an elaborate illusion and he was dying in the Isolatorium.

Thomas had tried talking to them. He had pleaded for help. He had even tried threats. Nothing worked.

So nowadays, he no longer responded to their concern. He had better things to do.

Thomas ignored the blacksmith's puzzles. Neither flipper blocks nor interlocked rings could be dismantled and used for suicide, so they were useless to him.

The sketch materials held a lot more promise.

The jailers had put a few flimsy scraps of canvas on the filthy floor for Thomas to find, plus a soap-like charcoal stone. Crude materials. Thomas had etched and sketched like a madman, although he was weaker than an infant. The unseen jailers did force him to eat and drink, although they had grown lax.

Drawing must look like progress. The jailers were probably pleased to see him engage in an activity after he'd done nothing but sit for two months. Indeed, they had removed his finished masterpieces and replaced them with a few more canvas scraps.

Thusly, Thomas had whittled the charcoal stone to a sharp point.

It wasn't much. The stone piece was more brittle and breakable than metal or glass. Still, it was sharper than the slime and mold in his dungeon pit.

Thomas rolled the charcoal back and forth across stones, sharpening its pointy end. The faint scraping added to the monotonous, ambient dripping.

His unwashed skin crawled, infected by microscopic alien parasites. One of his earlobes was a mess. A wild zoved had bitten it off, and his jailers had never properly cleansed or bandaged that wound. He tried to scratch the itch by rubbing his head against the wall.

The most excitement Thomas had had during the past two months was when a cave slug inched into his pit.

Thomas had cupped the alien gastropod in his hand and let it slime all over his fingers, playing with it, examining its rudimentary brain. After he'd absorbed every trick the slug's instincts had to offer, he could have let the creature inch away. But he feared it would never return. So he had twisted its tiny little mind.

It turned out that a zombified slug was the same as a healthy slug, except it lacked any will to survive. Thomas had mentally commanded it to use scent signals in order to invite more of its kind down into the pit.

The broken-minded gastropod had wormed away. So far, no more slugs had entered Thomas's range of telepathy. He suspected the one he'd sent away had wriggled without purpose until it died.

The effort of brainwashing the slug had made Thomas feel dizzy and weaker than ever. He was so close to death, he doubted he could brainwash anything more complex than a slug. But if a person ever entered his range again…

Oh.

He was ready.

First, he would absorb the smorgasbord of fresh data. He would wring out every last thought and memory. Thomas trembled with yearning. Just a kiss of another mind. Just a brush.

He wedged the sharpened charcoal into a cleft at the base of the wall. He had devoted weeks to scraping several dozen clefts, each one a slightly different size, in preparation for this. The charcoal point fit snugly. It would not jiggle loose.

Probably not even when his exposed throat fell onto it.

The point might break off. Thomas had considered that. He was ready to erode a new point, but he would have to do it quickly. He could not afford a failed suicide with such canny jailers. By the time they showed up with the usual bowl of mushroom gruel and latrine bucket, he needed to be a corpse, beyond any chance for revival.

This time window now was his best chance.

Possibly his only chance.

Would Ariock be dismayed? For a while, Thomas had believed that Ariock would rescue him. There were promises. Ariock had visited him in the darkness above.

Twice.

"You don't deserve to be here," Ariock had said during his second, more recent visit, his deep voice echoing down the narrow shaft. "I know that."

Thomas, blindfolded, had said nothing.

"I've been where you are." Ariock had spoken gently. "Trapped and alone. When I thought I was going insane, I imagined your voice in my head. You were there for me even when you weren't really there. I knew you would come to rescue me. And I will do the same for you. I promise."

What could Thomas say in reply to that? Ariock had suffered as a prisoner for even longer than he had. If their mutual friends were safe and well treated, well, of course Ariock wasn't going to jeopardize their safety just for Thomas.

If they were safe, then Thomas was no longer useful. He knew that. They knew that.

"You're stronger than you know," Ariock had told him. "You can survive this. I know you can."

That was when Thomas knew the promises were empty.

As one of the strongest individuals alive in the galaxy, Ariock had no concept of how it felt to be too weak to move. He was all bluster. His words were meaningless.

"I'll do everything I can," Ariock had said. "You won't be in the dark forever. I promise."

Thomas heard limber sounds. Ariock must be standing up, preparing to walk away.

"Vy or Kessa will visit you next time," Ariock had said. "We are working on a way to keep you safe."

Thomas wanted to beg. Instead, he gritted his teeth and forced himself to sound uncaring. "You need to get me out of here," he said. "Or I don't know what I'll do."

Far above him, Ariock had paused. Stalactites dripped in the distance.

Other feet shuffled—one of the mysterious jailers.

Thomas could imagine Ariock's huge face, brows lowering. He wouldn't like to be threatened.

"You sound like a Torth," Ariock said after a moment. "But I know you're human."

Ultimately, it didn't matter if Ariock walked away, never to return. It didn't matter if Cherise decided to forget Thomas and move on with her life. Thomas had made a binding promise to bring his friends to safety or die trying. If his death bought them safety, then he must die.

And if he was truly safer inside this pit than out in the Torth-ruled universe, as their visits implied, then he supposed he was better off dead.

"I never apologized for having you crucified." Thomas spoke to dark, silent air. "I'm sorry." His voice was faint, like dripping stalactites. "I wanted you to know."

That was many days ago. Ariock had not returned.

Thomas adjusted his position, optimizing his chance to gouge his throat with the charcoal point. Force was key. If he did it right, he would choke to death on his own spurting blood within minutes instead of hours.

He leaned back. This was it.

He would free himself from his own superfast thought processes.

Never again would he have to remind himself, every second, to stay away from the Megacosm.

Sorrow deeper than a grave washed through him.

But it was not his own sorrow.

The overwhelming grief came from a mind nearby, impossibly close, close enough to touch. Somebody else was in the pitch-black pit with him.

Thomas could hear her breathing.

Her mind overflowed with hopelessness. Loneliness addled her thoughts, to the point where she didn't even know who she was, or how long she'd been imprisoned. Her memories were fragments. All she knew was unending isolation.

*You suffer*, her pain-twisted mind whispered without words. *I suffer.*

"Who are you?" Thomas whispered.

A moment later, he felt like a fool. No one else could fit inside this shaft without even touching him. His sense of reality was rotten and untrustworthy after so much isolation. He must be suffering a hallucination.

Pathetic.

Time to die. He angled for a throat piercing.

*No one can help Us.* The other prisoner's pain moaned across his mind, like wind howling across an empty chasm. Thomas craved another mind, but her mind was a raw wound, deteriorated beyond the point of madness.

Hands groped his twiglike arms.

Long, silky hair brushed his fevered skin.

Fingers explored his rags, desperate for touch, from what seemed like a dark void.

She was real.

Thomas didn't know how she could fit in this shaft with him, or where she had come from. He began to weep. How could he have written her off as a figment of his imagination? He was incapable of inventing a phantom like this, drowning in so much sorrow, racked by loss and guilt. He wished he could help her.

The other prisoner wept harder, pathetically grateful that he could hear her lonely mind.

She had enough perceptiveness for Thomas to determine that she was a mind reader, like himself. But her memories were as insubstantial as mist. If she had ever known about the Megacosm, she had forgotten its existence. An impossible eternity had passed since the last time she'd communicated with anyone else. The jailers must have forgotten that she existed.

She grasped his hands firmly.

Monstrous power jolted into Thomas, as vast and formidable as a tidal wave.

It kept surging, more power than he'd ever felt in his life. His awareness sprawled out, mapping the dungeon cave within nanoseconds, pinpointing stalagmites and empty shafts. There was a massive gate, operated by heavy gears and pulleys designed for giants.

Thomas was inundated with raw power in the way that Ariock had raw power. He could levitate out of this dungeon pit. He could crack the prison in half. With less effort than a sigh, he could obliterate the whole cave system and possibly the entire planet.

*Use My power*, the other prisoner urged in her mind. Her long hair tickled his arms, like cobwebs. *Free Us. Free Me.*

Thomas was a superconductor. A nuclear reactor. A bomb waiting to go off and destroy millions of lives.

He hesitated.

Hadn't he promised to keep his friends safe, even if it meant his own death? Hadn't he assured Kessa and Ariock that he would keep his powers hidden?

He had suffered for two months. He had sacrificed everything. If he obliterated everything within a thousand-mile radius, then Cherise and the rest of his friends would die, which wasn't fair to them. His suffering and sacrifices were for their freedom. That had to mean something.

Thomas tugged his hands out of the other prisoner's grip.

She let go, and all that terrifying power vanished.

The dungeon rumbled. Stalactites broke. Thomas collapsed against the slimy wall, teeth chattering, weak and dying.

*You don't want…?* The other prisoner wrenched away, grieving and hurt by his rejection. She had shared something dear, something that cost her effort. With her mind so incoherent, she could not direct her power; she could not figure out whom to use it against or where to apply it. All she could do was lend her power to someone more sane, a fellow prisoner who might wield it properly.

The lonely prisoner had no sense of the difference between reality and illusion. She did not know which way was down or up, or how to find freedom. She did not even know why she was existed.

She vanished.

Thomas was alone in the pitch blackness, weak and sick and dying.

There was no way for a person to enter or exit that fast, unless that person had mysterious powers. But she was gone. Thomas heard his own breathing, and faraway drips, and the skitter of pebbles in the aftermath of the dungeon quake.

That other prisoner, that lady of sorrow, had felt certain that Thomas was akin to her, even in her insanity.

She was an other mind reader.

Trapped in this awful dungeon.

Isolated.

Aching for death.

Would Thomas be isolated for eternity like her? If he pierced his throat and choked to death on his own blood, would he hover in a twilight state between life and death, suffering forever? Was that what had happened to the lady of sorrow?

The phantom of his mother whispered inside him, with her throat torn open and her eyes unseeing. *This is eternity, my son.*

Thomas's scream of despair echoed off rocks.

It yielded no effect on the dripping stalactites.

If the other mind reader, the sorrowful prisoner, heard him scream, she did not show up. She no longer trusted Thomas to help her.

No one could help. No one would. The jailers would not. Nor would Ariock. Not Vy. Not Kessa. Not Cherise. No one.

Thomas opened his mouth and screamed, and he did not stop, except to draw breath for more screams. He could no longer tell if he was alive or dead, but he needed someone, anyone, to hear him.

Even if that meant screaming for the rest of eternity.

# PART FOUR

*He will be your salvation. Only he can lead you into light and restore you to your former glory. Follow him or perish.*

—Preserved scrap from the lost Prophecies of Ah Jun

# CHAPTER 1

# REASONS TO LEAVE

The balcony trembled. Rock walls shifted and groaned, causing lanterns to sway on their chains.

The rowdy audience quieted and looked around with unease. Even the wrestlers paused. The nussian behemoth had been about to pick up Ariock and body-slam him, but they both looked uneasy.

So the quake was probably not Ariock's doing.

Yeresunsa powers were against the rules of the wrestling match, anyway.

Kessa exchanged a look with Vy. If it wasn't caused by Ariock…

The tremor died down. Soon the room was still and mostly quiet. There was no damage, aside from a few hairline cracks here and there.

"That was not me," Ariock assured the audience in his accented version of the slave tongue.

"Just a natural quake, then?" his opponent asked.

Ariock was disheveled from the wrestling match. His armor was scraped, his hair messed up. He had actually laid aside his Yeresunsa mantle, since it was valuable material and he didn't want it accidentally torn. Yet everyone on the stone bench seats surrounding the pit looked toward him for answers. He was the Yeresunsa here.

"Yeah." Ariock spoke with blustery confidence in a way that reminded Kessa of nussians. "I'm sure it was nothing. The aqueducts are still flowing. We're fine."

People took his word for it. They laughed in relief, slapping each other on the back.

Kessa wasn't as sanguine. She had seen Ariock act that confident right before a battle he had lost. He had a way of masking his worries, or anything that he considered to be weakness in himself. He would never admit, in public, to being afraid.

"Let's call it a draw?" he asked his opponent in a light, cheery tone.

That was enough of a clue for Kessa. Ariock's mind was no longer on wrestling. That meant he was worried.

Kessa didn't even know why he sparred and wrestled so often. He was risking a broken skull. Why not attend musical theater instead? Like Weptolyso. That nussian had surprisingly sensible taste in entertainment.

Vy had a theory. She thought that Ariock was working through the trauma of his arena fights as a gladiator, taking control and mastering the horrors that had previously made him feel so helpless. She said that reenactment was one way that traumatized people coped with life after the trauma.

And these activities did seem to help Ariock release some pent-up frustration. The city was full of pilgrims who wanted to meet the prophet and kill the *rekveh*.

"Come on," Vy whispered. "Let's beat the crowds before everyone starts to leave."

Kessa adjusted the beads of her skull-net as she strode next to Vy. They were both overdressed for this neighborhood, but it hardly mattered. Everyone knew who Vy was. The angel from paradise was unable to blend in with any crowd, due to her peg leg and height and red hair.

People glanced surreptitiously at Kessa, too.

Yenna had offered to hide Kessa's neck scar with a fancy bejeweled choker necklace. Kessa had recoiled in horror. Her reaction against having something wrapped around her neck was so strong, she worried that she had permanently offended High Councilor Deschuba and his family.

Kessa overheard low voices as she passed bystanders in the arena crowd.

"...quake was weird. It could be the start of doomsday."

"Oh, please. There is no such thing as doomsday."

"My upstairs neighbor is a seer, and he's having recurring nightmares. He is telling anyone who will listen that there is a flood coming."

"A flood? How is that possible? As long as we have aqueducts and Yeresunsa, the city is safe."

"Anyway, we have the messiah to protect us."

"He hasn't sworn the Warrior's Pact."

"So what? He seems like a nice guy. You can tell Jinishta trusts him."

"Have you heard? They're cousins!"

"The nightmares are because we have a *rekveh* in our city. I hear that they radiate evil."

"I have a seer in my neighborhood, too. She keeps dreaming that our whole world will collapse. Like, the ceiling will fall and crush us."

"That's horrific."

"At least it's not a flood."

"Oh, there are nightmares all over the city. One of the seers says there will be a plague!"

"I've heard of one who dreams that Torth will invade our homes and slaughter us."

"Ugh."

"You're joking, right?"

"Is anyone really certain that Ariock is the messiah?"

"I won't be sure until the prophet Migyatel says he is."

"As soon as that *rekveh* dies, we'll all be better off. Things will go back to normal."

Kessa sneaked a glance toward Vy to see what she thought of the gossip.

Vy ignored the uneasy chitchat. Both she and Ariock seemed good at ignoring implicit threats to Thomas's safety. Jinishta had tripled the guards in the dungeon. People were even beginning to openly doubt that Ariock was the messiah.

And hadn't Vy seen Thomas's drawings?

Kessa shuddered just thinking of those frantic charcoal sketches. One of the most haunting drawings showed a skeletal figure, its ruined mouth spewing darkness onto its shredded throat. Empty eye sockets and tangled hair hinted that it was Thomas's mother, the nameless Servant of All who had died from torture in the Isolatorium.

The most disturbing sketch was a monstrous rendition of Cherise fused with the Upward Governess. Each one devoured the other's entrails while shadow children rode seesaws in the background.

Thomas had smeared blood on the drawings. He'd scrawled barely legible pleas, using the human writing system of Earth. Kessa was taking writing lessons from Cherise, so she been able to decipher the words. MERCY. KILL ME.

Elite Alashani tittered uneasily about those drawings, wondering how the prisoner could draw so skillfully in an unlit cave. They whispered that his ability must be demonic and his mind must be depraved beyond any hope of redemption.

Ariock wasn't worried enough, in Kessa's opinion.

"Kessa?" someone called. "Vy?"

People pointed, and Kessa followed their gazes to one of the stone gateways that served as an entry and exit point for the small arena. Jinishta and two other warriors stood there. They wore black, which was a cause for alarm.

Black meant battle mode. Black meant they were going to decapitate mind readers.

"Kessa." Jinishta looked relieved to see her. "I was told you were here. We need your help."

Kessa blinked in surprise. If the warriors sought help, surely it would be from Ariock, not her? Ariock knew the slave tongue well enough to get along without help from an interpreter.

Jinishta did not even wait for Vy to limp closer. She plunged into the crowd, and people saw her purple mantle and backed away. Jinishta leaned close enough to whisper.

"The *rekveh* is screaming."

Vy looked shocked and sickened.

"We have tried to calm him with water and a cleansing," Jinishta whispered. "But I think the quake unsettled him. He is babbling in many languages, and he will not calm down." She shot a quick glance toward Ariock, probably wondering if he had caused the tremor.

"We have to go to Thomas!" Vy said in a low, urgent voice. "Leaving him alone in the dark like this is cruel."

"I came to ask just that," Jinishta agreed. "Will you hurry with me to the dungeon?"

Vy took a rocking step, her look of heroic frustration plain. She wanted to run.

"I will go," Kessa volunteered. "You tell Ariock."

"No," Jinishta cut in. "Please do not trouble my overgrown cousin with this news. I have just received word that the prophet Migyatel has arrived, so this is terrible timing."

"What?" Vy looked startled. "Now?"

"I am sure she will take time to freshen up," Jinishta said impatiently. "But I do not wish to make Ariock angry or upset before meeting her."

The other warriors glanced at Ariock with fidgety attitudes. He seemed to be having a friendly chat with a couple of nussian wrestlers, unaware of any problems. The wrestlers passed around an earthenware bucket to refresh themselves with drinking water.

"Just tell him, please," Jinishta said. "Kessa? The *rekveh* needs to hear a friendly voice, I think, and he calls your name. Will you come?"

"Of course." Kessa laid a hand on Vy's arm to show that she cared. "I will talk to Thomas, I promise."

Vy looked miserable. But she could not run, and rickshaws could not traverse the dungeon pathways.

She nodded and limped away, toward the wrestling pit.

Soon Kessa was speeding along behind Jinishta. Her thoughts turned to Thomas and his ultrafast mind. His secret brilliance. His dark drawings.

Kessa still longed to speak with him, to learn from him. She had never gotten enough answers about the universe. What untapped secrets did he hide?

She wondered if Thomas had somehow caused that minor earthquake.

# CHAPTER 2

# TOUCHED BY SORROW

"This is not our usual route," Kessa observed as she jogged after the premier Yeresunsa.

They raced through a cramped tunnel that was just wide enough for a single albino. Jinishta leaped over fallen rocks, carrying a swinging lantern. Kessa followed suit. If Ariock ever wanted to use this tunnel, he would have to crawl for quite a long ways. He would probably need to use his powers to widen parts of it.

"This is a secret route that leads into the lower dungeon," Jinishta admitted. "Please do not tell Ariock."

Overall, people trusted Kessa with secrets. Most Alashani believed that former slaves would obey all kinds of commands. Warriors like Jinishta could use their powers to bully anyone, so perhaps that was why they trusted Kessa as a natural subordinate.

So far, Kessa had not shown them any reason to think otherwise.

The tunnel ended at one of the dungeon checkpoints, a plain, rocky chamber with two Yeresunsa elders seated at a table. They played a game to pass the time.

"Finally!" one of the Yeresunsa elders exclaimed, seeing Jinishta. She stood and began to use her powers on an immense gear-and-pulley gate.

The gears churned. The gate cranked open.

"We had to tie up the *rekveh*," the other warrior whispered. Now that the gate was opening, they kept their voices low. They did not want the prisoner to catch any hint of what they said.

"Why?" Jinishta whispered.

"It was trying to inflict harm upon itself," the warrior replied.

Poor Thomas. Kessa clicked her beak, but no one paid attention to her dismay. She dared not say anything. She was aware of her lack of powers.

Jinishta pulled extra lanterns off the wall. Firelight danced in her luminous eyes. The glow softened her white skin and hair.

She handed one to Kessa. "Come on. Remember the visitation rules?"

"Of course, Premier Yeresunsa," Kessa said meekly.

They all behaved as if Thomas was dangerous. Ironically, they were oblivious to his powers and his intelligence. Kessa half wished Thomas would ignite a flame, just to see the shocked reaction from Jinishta and the other jailers.

Both of the elder warriors raced ahead. They would use their powers to blindfold Thomas and to listen in on this visit. They insisted that Kessa only speak the slave tongue here. They would not tolerate any sinister foreign languages.

Thomas's faraway voice was hoarse. "Kessa?"

He must hear the clicks of her toes as she approached.

"Yes." Kessa hurried to the edge of the pit. "I'm here."

She was relieved to hear him speak. At least his desultory silence had ended. He had not spoken for many weeks.

"There's another prisoner," Thomas said, his voice ragged and desperate. "They've forgotten about her. Another mind reader. In this hellhole. Tell them, please!"

The other dungeon pits were moldy and empty. Kessa had visited often enough to know that. She glanced around anyway.

Jinishta and the other jailers frowned. They had overheard Thomas, and they shook their heads. There was no one else imprisoned in this lowest level of the dungeon.

"I can see what's around here," Kessa called down. "I promise, there are no other prisoners."

"She has powers." Thomas had to pause to catch his breath between every sentence. "I don't know how long she's been trapped. But she needs help."

The flickering lamplight barely reached the distant bottom of the shaft. Thomas looked pitiable, with rags binding his skinny arms against his malformed body. His formerly pristine golden tunic was reduced to filthy rags. The usual blindfold wrapped around his head.

"Kessa?" he called. "If you can do anything at all, tell them to find her. Another mind reader. Like me. Trapped."

A chill crept up Kessa's spine. She could not predict what a mentally unstable supergenius might do.

Her friends dismissed the fact that Thomas had outwitted a Torth supergenius who was supposedly the smartest being in the known universe. Did they think that was luck? Kessa felt sure it was not. Thomas was a Yeresunsa, but his mind was more deadly than any Yeresunsa power.

And the Alashani had no clue. They feared the doorway inside his mind that connected him to the Torth Majority. They had never heard of the supergenius mutation.

"She has long, tangled hair," Thomas said, his voice raw and desperate. "She was crying. I read her mind. I felt her sorrow. Please help her!"

Jinishta's brow was furrowed, as if she was trying to solve a puzzle. The elder warriors looked suddenly outraged. They exchanged angry looks.

Lamps flickered. A shift in air pressure indicated that Yeresunsa powers were in use.

"How many are up there with you?" Thomas asked in the human language.

"Four," Kessa said.

Jinishta gave Kessa a forbidding look. She made a clamping motion, as if she wanted to shut Kessa's beak.

"They're wrapping my ears," Thomas said. "Kessa, look for that other prisoner. She held my hands. They're lying if they tell you I'm the only one. She doesn't deserve to suffer down here for eternity. No one does."

He was so frantic, Kessa tried to offer reassurance. "I will tell them."

"Please," he went on, unable to hear, rendered blind and deaf by the head wraps. "Help."

The warriors used their powers to gag Thomas with a cloth, reducing his words to pleading noises.

Kessa was done acting meek. She studied the Yeresunsa jailers, certain that they were hiding some monstrous secret. Why else would they look outraged? What had Thomas said to make them angry?

"Is there another prisoner?" Kessa demanded.

"Of course not," Jinishta said.

"The Lady of Sorrow would never appear to a *rekveh*," one of the elder warriors said in a sneering tone. He planted his fists on his hips and glared at Kessa. "It is clearly telling lies, trying to make us believe it is an Alashani. Who taught it about our religion? It should not know that we exist!"

Kessa gawked at the accusation in his tone.

Even Jinishta was glaring at her. All four warriors bristled with static electricity.

"You think Thomas saw the Lady of Sorrow?" Kessa hesitated, almost afraid to give offense. Street shrines all over the city displayed statues of the weeping goddess. The statues were often encircled by a shallow moat of water. Some of the statues were fountains.

But no one ever hinted that the goddess might be a prisoner. Or telepathic. Or any sort of a real person.

"I thought she is a myth?" Kessa said carefully.

The hotheaded elder drew a spear, as if ready to skewer Kessa.

Jinishta stopped him with a command gesture. She turned to Kessa with suspicion. "The Lady of Sorrow does not appear to everyone. Her appearances are very infrequent. And very selective."

"She would never choose a *rekveh*!" the elder reiterated.

"What do you mean?" Kessa hoped for an explanation. "Who does she appear to?"

Jinishta folded her arms, as if bracing herself to explain something difficult to a child. "Sometimes," she said, "a soul leaves a body before it is their time to die. They encounter the Lady of Sorrow weeping in the darkness at the watery boundary between life and death. Her hair flows like water." She made a combing gesture. "And if the Lady chooses them to be a hero? She will touch them and send them back to the realm of the living with her blessing."

Kessa gazed down at the gagged figure of Thomas, cocooned in rags. Had he experienced a holy vision?

"It's true," another warrior said, addressing Kessa's skepticism. "My great-aunt's brother-in-law survived a cave-in, and he saw the Lady of Sorrow. He said that when he was crushed and dying, unable to breathe, he heard her weeping in the darkness, right near him. She didn't touch him. But he swears that he could hear her."

"So Thomas was near death?" Kessa tried to rein in her anger. "Is that why you tied him up? He tried to kill himself? What you are doing here is cruel. It is no different from what Torth do to slaves they have a problem with."

The warriors gazed down at her as if she was nothing but a pesky child, making childish accusations.

"The *rekveh* must be lying," the hotheaded warrior said.

"Thomas never tells lies," Kessa snapped.

"Mind readers do not have souls," the warrior insisted. "They cannot be chosen by the gods to be heroes."

"Are you saying Thomas was chosen to be a hero?" Kessa asked.

A plump warrior exchanged looks with her peers. "He said he was touched. He said he held her hands in the darkness."

The others looked uneasy.

Another elder warrior glared down toward Thomas. "If it was truly touched, then wouldn't it be powerful right now? It would fly out of the dungeon and do heroic things."

Jinishta saw Kessa's curiosity and explained. "Only heroes get touched by the Lady of Sorrow. It is a common theme in legends about great warriors."

"Like Jonathan Stead," another warrior put in.

"Yes," Jinishta admitted. "Jonathan Stead was touched by the Lady of Sorrow. That is how he escaped the Torth, so it is said."

Kessa cocked her head, encouraging elaboration.

"When a hero is chosen," Jinishta said, "the Lady of Sorrow holds his hand or caresses his skin, and, through her touch, the hero gains her immense power."

"For a short while," a warrior amended.

"Yes." Jinishta seemed relieved to be done with the explanation. "That is what happened to Jonathan Stead. He suffered in the Isolatorium, but his valor was so great, the Lady of Sorrow touched him. She granted him the power to break free."

"And to save a thousand other prisoners," another warrior added.

Kessa studied Thomas anew, wondering if he was suffused with magical holy power. He looked weaker than a cave worm. If he had a heroic destiny, it was beyond her ability to guess.

"It is mocking our faith," an elder warrior said with disgust. "It said she is a mind reader. A *rekveh*. What a disgusting lie!"

The warriors went on arguing, troubled by unanswered questions. How could the imprisoned *rekveh* even understand what it meant to be touched by the Lady of Sorrow and live? How had it learned so much about Alashani lore? Why would it tell such a bold-faced lie? What was the benefit? Did it think they were credulous idiots, willing to believe anything?

"One thing is certain," Jinishta said, arms still folded. "That *rekveh* is no hero."

Distant footsteps echoed from the faraway open gate. Lanterns swung as two more warriors jogged closer.

Jinishta picked up her own lantern and raised it to identify the runners. "Anshi? Haz? What is it?"

Anshi and Haz doubled over, gasping for breath.

"The prophet," Anshi said, managing to get words out. "She ordered everyone in the city to gather in the grand plaza."

"Now?" Jinishta stared in disbelief.

"Yes!"

"And she wants to see the *rekveh*." Haz shot a dark look toward the pit. "Apologies, Jinishta, but the prophet Migyatel commands us to bring the *rekveh* to the grand plaza."

Kessa internally reevaluated Thomas's circumstances. Perhaps he had a future, after all.

A heroic future?

Jinishta grasped Haz by the shoulder. "You heard her say this? You saw her? With your own eyes?"

"Yes," Haz said simply.

The other warriors muttered in shocked outrage. But the runners had more to say.

"She told many warriors," Anshi said. "Chaniyelem is spreading the word. Migyatel will foretell the future of Ariock, but she wants to foretell the future of this *rekveh*, too. I don't know why."

The warriors exchanged looks.

"Maybe it has to do with the doomsday dreams?" one guessed.

"Do you think those dreams are going to come true?"

"But we have the messiah! Surely he will protect us?"

Jinishta looked as if she wanted to grab her spears and hurl them. Her white hair crackled with electricity.

She looked from the runners, then to Kessa, then down to Thomas.

Finally, she said, "Prepare a prison transportation cage." She seemed to reach an internal decision. "We will bring the *rekveh* to the grand plaza, as requested. But do not fear. The prophet would not put our people in danger. If the *rekveh* makes any threats…?" She tapped her quiver full of spears. "It can go straight back into that pit. I will make sure of that."

The warriors seemed heartened.

Jinishta began giving orders. "Efviam. Naru. Tchensi. Go find willing haulers and guards. Get a drape to hide the cage. Get Blind Lela, too. Haz? Anshi? Go prepare the audience in the grand plaza for the *rekveh*. And Gunsigtel? Find out why the prophet wants to see the *rekveh*, if you can. Report to me as soon as you have answers."

Kessa watched in amazement as the warriors jogged away. Jinishta was not ostentatious or proud, but that made her easy to underestimate. She had earned loyalty from her warriors. She got to know them and their families.

Ariock, in contrast, spent his free time with Vy rather than with his fellow warriors.

He had not even bothered to learn the names of most of the warriors. The messiah label hardly mattered. These warriors were loyal to Jinishta. If a crisis arose, they would follow her. Not Ariock.

Thomas might be on the brink of losing his sanity. And now the Alashani wanted to bring him into a massive and overwhelming crowd?

It seemed like a potential crisis situation.

"I would like to help," Kessa said. "Will you let me prepare Thomas? I think a friend should talk to him before he faces a crowd."

Jinishta paced as she thought. "We may all need help. There are a lot of bad dreams going around. The city is unsettled."

Kessa supposed she agreed.

"You will come with me," Jinishta decided. "We have to keep the *rekveh* safe. Many foreign Yeresunsa are visiting our city, and they may try to decapitate him on our way to the grand plaza. You can speak to them."

Kessa glanced down at Thomas, exasperated and worried.

At least he would get a chance for answers soon. The prophet needed proximity in order to foretell someone's future.

He would probably be grateful for a chance to read a fresh mind.

# CHAPTER 3

# JUST WORDS

Ariock gazed at the teeming city spread below him, with its lamplit bazaars and curiosity shops and hole-in-the-wall taverns. Stone houses, three to six stories tall, connected in seamless neighborhoods that were punctuated by stairs, bridges, and jagged alleyways.

People were on the move. Why were so many of them streaming toward the grand plaza? Surely the prophet needed more time to rest from her journey?

He could guess what she would say about him. She would probably scream, "Fraud!" in the voice of an orator, across the grand plaza for all to hear.

"So." Vy snuggled closer. "Am I the only person you ever bring to your fortress of solitude?"

She and Ariock were indeed alone, relaxing on the sloped surface of a rock that stuck out from the massive cavern's wall. No one had ever built a ladder to this perch because the slope looked so precarious.

"I'm surprised this isn't some kind of Yeresunsa hangout spot," Vy said. She was beautiful, her hair shining, curled and spread over stone.

"No one else can get up here," Ariock admitted.

Far below, a couple of albino maidens stood at the apex of a bridge, giggling and waving at him.

"Do you know those two?" Vy sounded like she was trying to force casualness.

"Nope," Ariock said.

One maiden made suggestive motions, clinging to the bridge balustrade. Her distant shouts were bawdy. Ariock looked elsewhere. The Alashani had a notable lack of shame when it came to sexual matters. If only his powers included invisibility.

Vy began to say something. She stopped, cut off by a piercing horn blast that echoed throughout the city cavern.

The pace of traffic changed. Pedestrians surged out of doorways and stairways. Rickshaws paused to take on extra passengers. The maidens on the bridge looked toward the immense outcrop at the heart of the city. That wall loomed over the grand plaza amphitheater, where Chaniyelem had introduced Ariock as the messiah months ago.

"Crap." Ariock couldn't hide his nerves.

The prophet Migyatel couldn't possibly want to meet him right now. Couldn't she give him another hour? Another day? Another week?

"Ready to go meet the prophet?" Vy asked.

Pedestrians pointed up at Ariock. They probably imagined rays of light and glory radiating from him. They all expected him to go to his destiny, to lead the Alashani people out of hiding. To vanquish the galactic Torth Empire.

"It will be okay." Vy caressed his arm. "This is the way to save Thomas."

Right.

Ariock scooped Vy into his arms and prepared to jump several hundred feet to the thoroughfare below.

First, he sent his awareness to his chosen landing spot, the way Jinishta had taught him to do. Distance and scope were obstacles for other Yeresunsa. Not for him. Even at this distance, Ariock was able to form barricades of pressurized air, preventing people from darting into his readied landing spot.

Jinishta was tireless about giving him useless warnings. According to her, power depletion was a common hazard. If a depleted Yeresunsa ignored the excruciating "warning headache" and kept forcing themselves to use their powers, they would either drop dead or else fall into a coma.

Ariock thought he might have experienced the warning headache once or twice, but he had doubts. He had tried to force himself to use his powers when he was critically injured, and although he had failed, he had not dropped dead or fallen into a coma.

Jinishta and the Alashani were wrong about a lot of things.

Vy clutched him as they plummeted fifteen or twenty stories. Perhaps he was too preoccupied for a graceful landing. He slammed into the intersection hard enough to crack a couple of polished stone tiles.

Vy looked exhilarated. She still gripped him tightly.

"You okay?" Ariock gently set her down.

"Oh yeah. I'm fine." She slid off his arms and onto the stony street.

People streamed past them now that Ariock had released his invisible barriers. More than a few stopped to cluster around him.

"*Aonswa.*" A nussian bowed her broad head to Ariock. Cuffs and rings bedecked her spikes. "May we escort you to the grand plaza?"

Before Ariock could refuse, the nussian shoved ahead through the crowd, thundering, "Make way!"

Albinos and other sapients leaped aside.

To Ariock's horror, two more nussians showed up with drums hung around their thick necks. They made an imperious drumbeat, calling attention. They must have been preparing for this.

"Dancers, too!" the nussian in front boomed. "We must make an entrance befitting the messiah!"

Vy gaped at the hubbub.

Ariock imagined himself at the center of a gaudy parade, towering, unable to hide. His fear would be obvious to anyone who looked. "I'm not ready."

Vy looked up at him.

Ariock glanced toward the palace district. Would he have time to gather some cave-sheep jerky and mushroom hardtack? What about canteens? And his giant-size clothes?

He could grab everything necessary for a rudimentary escape.

"I, uh, need to change my clothes," he told Vy and the loudmouthed nussian. "I can't go the grand plaza wearing this." He had already changed into clean woolens after his wrestling match, but he tugged the outfit as if ashamed of its perfect fit and silver needlework. "I need to go home first."

But from there, how would he break Thomas free from the dungeon?

Combat had costs, especially when innocent people were nearby. Ariock remembered his lifeless mother. If he tried to break Thomas free, someone else's mother and father would try to stop him. His cousin would try to stop him.

People might die if he started a battle, no matter how reasonable he tried to be.

There was a balance scale. On one side lay Thomas, alone. On the other side were Ariock's friends, including Vy, plus millions of free albinos and runaway slaves.

"Ariock." Vy spoke as if soothing a frightened animal. "It will be okay."

His vision blurred as he considered how to balance the scale of justice. He didn't know how to help Thomas. He didn't want to abandon Vy and lose her forever.

He blinked away tears. He needed to maintain self-control. Warriors did not lose control of their emotions, because that was dangerous to other people.

Vy looked perplexed.

It seemed she had no idea, absolutely none, that she was safer here, in the Alashani underworld, than anywhere else. Earth was off-limits and doomed. The distant reject planets were dangerous and lonely. Vy had to stay with the Alashani. Ariock simply had to make her stay, even though it would feel like amputating his own limbs. Every place else meant slavery and death.

He was going to have to wreck his way to the surface of the planet and leave everyone else behind, except for Thomas.

For Thomas.

Every fiber of his being screamed against making that enormous sacrifice. *Are you really going to abandon Vy?* a deeply honest part of his mind whispered.

*You're planning to get rid of sympathetic, friendly, beautiful Vy in exchange for Thomas? Are you really going to throw away all your friendships and make war against Jinishta?*

Ariock tried to squash his fears and doubts. He owed Thomas his best efforts at protection. That was final. Nonnegotiable. He wasn't going to break his promise just because it was convenient.

Was he?

Ariock yearned for extra time to weigh his options. He would rather face a Torth army than face this decision. A small army, at any rate.

He kept backing away. The nearby worshippers began to look concerned.

People packed the boulevards. Every street was flooded with albinos. They mobbed toward Ariock, blocking any possibility that he might walk away unnoticed. His rabid fans had all heard where he was, and now they offered—pleaded—to escort him to the grand plaza.

"Ariock." Vy spoke in a firm voice. "Put me over there, so I can face you at your height." She pointed to a grotto wall, too high for her to climb onto. "We need to talk."

Ariock obliged her. A conversation would buy him time to figure out what to do. The overeager mob respected anyone from paradise, and they would probably let Vy chat with the messiah, uninterrupted, for at least a couple of minutes.

Once Vy was at eye level with him, she reached for his face. She held him, forcing him to gaze into her sky-blue eyes, and giving him a look of deep sympathy.

"They're just words," she said.

Urgent decision factors crowded Ariock's mind. He couldn't make sense of what Vy had said.

"Whatever Migyatel says, they're just words." Vy continued to hold his gaze. "She can say you're the messiah, or she can claim you're a fraud, but it doesn't matter what she says. At all. Your future is what *you* decide. No one else gets to determine your fate."

As Ariock gazed into Vy's eyes, he saw trust. Vy trusted him to do good things, regardless of what other people wanted or insisted upon.

Vy pulled his head close. She leaned her forehead against his. "Your future is not up to Migyatel," she whispered. "Or anyone else. You're the one who makes it happen."

Then she waited with steadfast patience, ready to follow Ariock in whatever action he took.

He realized, then, that his biggest struggle might not be against Torth armies, or Jinishta's legion of Yeresunsa warriors, or how to keep Thomas alive.

His main challenge would be to figure out a future without the sympathetic force that was Vy.

He didn't think he had the strength to say no to her.

Onlookers lined up to give him an aisle. A marching band was bumping into place. Ariock knew the slave tongue well enough to translate what the worshippers kept eagerly repeating.

Messiah. Show us who you truly are.

Maybe Alashani society would collapse in shambles once they learned that their supposed savior was nothing but a clumsy, cowardly, useless man?

Well. Perhaps that recalibration would be healthy for them.

Ariock straightened his back. It felt unnatural to stretch like this, unashamed of his colossal height, but it felt like freedom.

Vy was right. He had been allowing Jinishta and Chaniyelem and the crowds to determine his fate. To constrain him.

His great-grandfather Jonathan Stead had done that. Jonathan had altered himself in order to fit other people's expectations and perceptions. Then he had fled toward cannibals and the Torth because he was terrified that the Alashani would learn how subpar he was. Jonathan had risked an entire civilization—risked the freedom of millions of Alashani—in order to preserve his reputation, such as it was.

Well, Ariock Dovanack was not Jonathan Stead.

Instead of fleeing, he would force the Alashani to confront their mistake, head-on.

Let them rile themselves into a slavering mob. Whatever Migyatel had to say, Ariock would endure it with stoicism. Then he would walk away. He would leave the Alashani populace stunned and sickened and rescue Thomas.

Let the Alashani learn that their prayers for light and glory were too vague to be answered. Let them ponder their wrong assumptions. Ariock could fend off their attacks in a mostly nonviolent manner, he felt sure. His Yeresunsa mastery had vastly improved since his first training sessions with Jinishta.

Ariock lifted Vy off the grotto wall and placed her beside him.

If the Alashani wanted a messiah, they ought to consider how worthy—or unworthy—they were for salvation.

It was time for them to reconsider their ancient beliefs and quit torturing a helpless, disabled child.

# CHAPTER 4

# CITYWIDE

"Yes, the *rekveh* is going to be brought here," an usher told a frightened elderly couple. "Yes," he said in response to a question. "But don't worry. Many warriors are keeping watch." He nodded toward the ramparts. "They are ready to handle any situation."

Albino faces peered down from the top of the outcrop, framed by somber black hats and uniforms. More stood at the edges of the plaza. The spears in their quivers were plain black iron, not frilly showpieces.

Kessa continued to push her way toward the prime seating area, trying not to show interest in the conversations around her. She surreptitiously studied the plaza and counted ninety warriors who were visible.

Ninety warriors. Some of them must be foreign pilgrims. That number was definitely more than adequate for safety.

"I understand why the prophet wants to foretell the *rekveh*'s future," a bejeweled woman said. "She will tell everyone what evil deeds it plans to do. And then our warriors can kill it before it has a chance."

Kessa hoped that wasn't the case.

"But really," another bejeweled woman leaned in. "Why bring it into a crowded plaza? Can't Migyatel just visit it alone in the dungeon?"

"It's a ploy," a bejeweled man said, joining their conversation. "This is probably Jinishta's idea to appease the messiah."

"How does this appease him?"

"The *rekveh* will reveal its evil nature, and then Ariock will have no choice but to admit it and to stand aside and allow good warriors to kill it."

Kessa's beak twisted in disgust. She was familiar with hatred, or so she believed. She hated the Red Ranks who had murdered her mate, Cozu. She hated her former owner. But how could so many people feel so certain about a person they had never met? They judged Thomas based on rumors and hearsay alone.

The Alashani as a people were just about as far from the Code of Gwat as it was possible to get.

"Jinishta doesn't fear Ariock," one of the ladies scoffed.

"Oh yeah?" The man replied in a patronizing tone. "Ask yourself why none of our warriors have dared to kill that *rekveh* after all this time. You know plenty who want to. Right? Like Shelda."

"I suppose," the lady replied. "But they must respect the holy prophecy."

"That's right," the other lady put in. "The messiah has 'a loyal mind reader.' That is written in holy scripture, whether we like it or not."

Kessa wondered how many warriors actually respected the prophecy to that degree. She suspected that a fear of Ariock did play a role in protecting Thomas. Lately, Jinishta had pitted Ariock against four opposing warriors in the sparring chambers. Ariock kept winning.

"The premier chose to personally mentor Ariock," one of the ladies said. "Why would she do that if she mistrusts him? And if you want to count the gills on a mushroom, I have personally heard that he's a kindhearted giant, from reliable people."

The argumentative man laughed dismissively. "All I'm saying is that if something happens that Ariock doesn't like, you can be sure he will throw a mighty tantrum. That's why there are so many warriors posted around here." He gestured. "We're going to see his true reaction. He will either prove that he is the savior—or our enemy."

Other listeners laughed nervously.

"We're safe," they assured each other.

Kessa inwardly wondered. She knew Ariock. He would not meekly step aside and allow himself or his friend to be executed.

He would fight, if it came to that.

Drumbeats thundered across the grand plaza, adding excitement to the already zealous crowd. Kessa saw refugees from Duin among the crowd, and they flinched. The percussion evoked something like battlefield explosions and thunderclaps.

Most of the people in this plaza had never experienced a war zone or a storm. They laughed. They joked. Secure in the knowledge that their warriors would protect them, they rocked to the music.

No matter what species they were, they had a sameness. Woolens in the hues of granite or marble. Tunics weighted by silver or gold pendants. The albinos had long necks and coiffed white hair; other sapients imitated that with wig-like hats or tightly coiled rosette decorations.

The crowd hushed as Kessa looked for a seat. There was a rock plateau, and up on that stage, several foreigners prepared an ivory chair with a seat cushion.

Kessa knew they were foreigners because their style of dress was different. They wore pastel colors and leggings instead of swishy pants.

"Hey!" A bejeweled albino pointed at Kessa, nudging his companions. "Isn't that the leader of those runaway slaves? Kessaw?"

"Kessa," she corrected, sliding past cushioned benches.

"You've traveled with Ariock, right?" The speaker twisted around to match her progress. He was probably a merchant, scented with oils and laden with jewelry. "I heard that you commanded the *rekveh* as well as your own ummins. Is that true? Does the *rekveh* obey commands, like a slave?"

"Thomas is at our mercy," Kessa said with care. "But I think it would be a mistake to treat him like a slave."

On the stage, one of the foreigners helped an ancient lady shuffle toward the chair. She was so wrinkled, her eyes looked permanently closed. They sat her down and propped her up with pillows and blankets.

"How old is she?" someone whispered.

"Prophets live unnaturally long lives," someone else explained. "They foresee everything in their own lives, so they can actually choose the manner and the hour in which they die."

Migyatel smiled at the audience. Her mouth was sunken and toothless, but she looked beneficent. Dramatic bonfires illuminated the stage at each end.

If the tales were true, this prophet had actually met Jonathan Stead. She had been a little girl at the time, too immature to be allowed to touch him and foretell his future, but she had seen the legend.

Kessa looked around for Ariock, hoping to measure his reaction. No sign of him yet.

But Cherise was recognizable in the front rows.

She sat between albinos in purple mantles.

Flen and Haz wore street clothes, but they still had quivers full of spears leaning against their bench seats. It seemed there were at least a dozen warriors in the audience. That was in addition to all the warriors who stood on the ramparts or around the plaza.

Kessa spotted a familiar thorny bulk, and she slid past benches to join Weptolyso. She had to wait to catch his attention, since he was listening to a chatty red female nussian on his other side. A few of his thorny spikes were cut down to nubs.

"Peace, Weptolyso," Kessa greeted him. "What happened to your spikes?"

"Oh. Peace, Kessa." Weptolyso passed a regretful hand over the missing spikes. "They will grow back. A fool down in the scratch called me a liar. He said I was making up stories when I described the desert on Umdalkdul."

The female nussian said gently, "That isn't why he attacked you." To Kessa, she said, "Some nussians don't like the things Weptolyso has to say about our people in Torth realms."

Kessa clicked her beak in understanding. She had encountered a lot of misconceptions about slaves. Sapients here did not want to hear about their enslaved brethren, some of whom would fight to protect their Torth owners.

"The nussians here are soft," Weptolyso grumbled. "They cannot imagine real hardships."

"I am Yuey, by the way," his companion said, introducing herself.

"Pleased to meet you, Yuey. I am Kessa."

"Kessa!" The female nussian looked astounded. "You are the one who led the messiah here?"

"This is Kessa the Wise," Weptolyso affirmed.

Yuey bowed her head in a nussian salute. "I have so much respect for you, Kessa. Please tell me—"

The audience surged and buzzed, distracting Yuey. Even the drummers stopped to gawk at the main boulevard where it fed into the plaza.

Kessa hopped up onto her stone seat for a better view. She expected to see Ariock duck under the triumphal post-and-lintel gate. Instead, nussians approached. They bore horizontal beams that supported a palanquin draped with black curtains.

"Thomas," she said in a low voice, to let Weptolyso know.

An extra guardianship of black-clad warriors strode ahead and behind the procession, proving that the prisoner was not to be trifled with. The audience recoiled as if they sensed danger.

"The *rekveh*," Yuey breathed with trepidation.

Thomas was undoubtedly gagged, blindfolded, and tied up. For all anyone knew, he could be dead in there. What melodrama! Yet not even foolhardy children dared to get close enough for a glimpse.

Weptolyso wrapped an arm around Yuey as if to shield her. But then he asked Kessa, "How is Thomas?"

"Not well," Kessa answered. "Weptolyso…" She hesitated, then lowered her voice, stretching up so he could hear her. "If things go awry today, Ariock may need to escape with Thomas. I plan to leave with them." She had already prepared a travel pack, waiting in her room in Deschuba's palace. "I expect you to stay here, where it is safe. But I wish—"

"I am not staying behind." Weptolyso swiveled his eyes to stare at her. "My path is with Ariock."

Kessa reassessed him. She had prepared to say farewell to her nussian friend. He had admirers among the Alashani nussians.

"I would come, too," Yuey said, having leaned close in order to overhear. "Ariock is the messiah. Our path must be to follow where he leads."

Kessa wondered how Yuey and all the other Alashani would react if Ariock turned out to not be their messiah.

The audience surged with extra excitement, and people tripped over each other in their haste to claim any spot, whether seated or standing. Distant drumbeats reverberated off stone buildings. Horns trumpeted the approach of someone important.

Kessa scanned the plaza, mapping the place in her head. She could not guess what might happen after Ariock made his entrance, but she wanted to be prepared for anything.

# CHAPTER 5

# REVELATIONS

Ariock felt conspicuous even without dancers, horn blowers, and drummers clearing the boulevard. As he entered the grand plaza, people stood for a better view of him. Albino women screamed in rapture. Other people gave joyous shouts of "Light and glory!"

"The messiah is here!"

"They say he can destroy Torth as easily as breathing!"

Albino hands strained to touch Ariock. He avoided looking at the worshippers, because he didn't want to study their eyes, trying to figure them out. He was tired of struggling to understand why these people yearned for a messiah. He had asked around. Everyone seemed to have a different personal reason. Maybe that woman wanted someone to free her from a heap of family obligations? Maybe that man wanted a purpose to fight for, so he wouldn't spend his days in taverns, slowly killing himself with mushroom ale?

No one was perfectly happy with their lives. Ariock supposed that was the human condition. But the Alashani made a habit of crying for someone powerful to fix their paltry problems instead of asking for help from councilors or spiritualists or friends. They wanted a savior. They wanted a guy to defeat the Torth Empire for them while they sat back and watched.

It was like relying on a hammer for every task in carpentry.

A coalition of Yeresunsa hurried to meet Ariock, resplendent in short capes. They ushered him toward the stage, where a very elderly woman awaited him on a throne, ready to judge him.

Migyatel wore a Yeresunsa mantle. *Of course* she was a member of the privileged warrior class. Ariock was learning that no matter how meek and humble the warriors acted, no matter how socially equal they were to the high councilors, their inherent powers gave them authority that no one but another Yeresunsa could challenge.

"Ariock, will you be okay on your own?" Vy asked. Several well-dressed Yeresunsa were tugging her toward the audience.

"You might as well enjoy the show," Ariock told her. He spotted Cherise and gave her a wave.

A couple of albino merchants leaped up, offering their seats to Vy. "Will you sit with us, lovely angel?"

She looked uncertain, but people slid aside to make room for her. She sat.

Chaniyelem hurried down one of the aisles, gesturing for Ariock to step onstage. There was nothing up there except for bonfires in urns, the prophet on her ivory chair, and a black-shrouded cage that was set apart from everything else.

Audience members shot furtive, fearful glances toward the cage.

"There you are." Jinishta strode toward Ariock, bedecked in an embroidered black and silver outfit. "It is time. You must—"

"Is that Thomas?" Ariock pointed toward the shrouded cage. He doubted the Alashani would dare to bring the dreaded *rekveh* here, but he had to ask, to make sure.

Jinishta looked offended at being cut off. In private lessons, she was informal and casual, but here in public, Ariock knew that he was expected to show deference to the premier Yeresunsa.

"Yes," Jinishta said with perfect composure. "Migyatel asked to see your mind reader."

Ariock reassessed the black-shrouded cage. Thomas was actually here?

"We must know whether you are the messiah or not." Jinishta stepped aside. "Go and meet the prophet Migyatel."

A drumroll signaled the audience to quiet down. Everyone waited and watched.

Jinishta's pale eyes were unyielding. The spears in her quiver looked functional, but her true weapons were the warriors who watched from the ramparts.

When Ariock extended his awareness, he sensed countless life sparks in the grand plaza. Some of those sparks shone with more intensity than others. He thought Jinishta was one of those.

Yeresunsa.

The albinos who wore quivers and mantles had more intense life sparks. And there were at least a hundred of them in the vicinity. Purple mantles dotted the front rows. They sat in the audience, in the box seats, and up above.

If Ariock disobeyed, this situation would get dangerous.

He ascended the marble steps to the stage, feeling a bit like a prisoner himself.

Inside that cage, Thomas might be suffering from prison maladies, like sores. Ariock considered ignoring Migyatel in favor of healing his friend.

But healing proximity would give Thomas an illegal glimpse inside his mind. That would unnecessarily provoke the crowd—and all the watching Yeresunsa.

It seemed best to respect the Alashani for a while longer. Honor their rules. Once Migyatel told everyone that Ariock was a fraud, they were going to feel like painfully stupid religious zealots. He should try to retain some goodwill so that he could placate the mob.

Migyatel worked her toothless gums. She said something in a wispy voice, and the whole audience quieted to listen.

Ariock forced himself to walk to Migyatel without showing fear. It was best to just get this over with.

*They're just words*, he reminded himself.

Migyatel was gnarled like a knotted pine tree. A thick blanket lay across her lap, and her hands were lumpy with arthritis. Ariock felt a grudging respect for her age. This woman had met his long-dead ancestor. She had been a little girl, but she had actually spoken to Jonathan Stead.

What had she told the legendary hero? Had she insinuated anything about getting married and raising a family on Earth?

"Give me your hand," the prophet whispered to Ariock in the slave tongue. "Prophecy requires touch."

Ariock barely understood her frail voice beneath the snap of bonfires. Murmurs and coughs echoed in the vast plaza.

He knelt. Even on one knee, he towered over the old woman on the ivory chair, but she did not stare at him or size him up. All she did was open one of her frail hands, urging touch.

Ariock realized that she was blind. She might not have any clue what he looked like.

And with her frail voice? Maybe no one would be able to hear her fortune-telling.

Maybe his fears were overblown.

His hand would not fit neatly in her grasp, so he gently touched two of his fingers to her palm.

The instant his skin contacted hers, Migyatel threw back her head and howled. "OHHHH!" she shouted in the slave tongue. Her suddenly powerful voice rebounded off the cliff-like wall. "HE IS THE ONE!"

Ariock jerked away as if burned.

"*AONSWA!*" Migyatel pointed at him.

Messiah.

The audience rose like an earthquake. They raised goblets, jumped, or hugged each other. "Salvation!" The proclamation rose like a storm, from many voices into one great roar.

"Light and glory!"

"ARIOCK!"

He backed away, not caring if it was rude or offensive. The Alashani were berserk. They were like an audience at a rock concert, jumping up and down and shrieking with emotion.

Migyatel smiled.

Was this a joke to her? Was she senile? Did she have any clue what she'd incited?

"You're wrong," Ariock said.

The frenzy drowned out his deep voice.

Disgusted, he began to walk away. He had better things to do than entertain a bunch of hyper fanatics. Thomas needed healing.

A wall of air shoved Ariock back.

Jinishta had jumped up onto the stage, and although she eyed him with wary respect, he knew that she was the one who had shoved him. "Your *rekveh* can wait," she said. "Migyatel is not finished. Let her tell your future."

Migyatel made papery sounds and held out her hand, as innocent as a baby begging for a pacifier.

*False prophet!* Ariock wanted to shout. *Liar!* His anger whipped out and coiled around nearby objects. "Too bad," he said. "I owe Thomas a healing."

Jinishta planted herself in his path, white hair puffed out. "Migyatel traveled all this way. Your future is the future for all of us, Messiah."

The audience hushed, punctuated by sporadic shouts of rapture.

Ariock forced himself to withdraw back into his body so he could think. Jinishta was just trying to do the right thing for her people. He could not blame her for being an Alashani.

The frenzied audience was unexpectedly on his side. His friends, such as Vy, seemed to believe that was a good thing. The supposed messiah could do whatever he wanted to do.

Except it was a sham.

Ariock wasn't fit to destroy the Torth Empire. He knew that, even if no one else did. And it was only a matter of time before the Alashani figured out the truth.

"The sooner you do this," Jinishta told him, "the sooner we can unveil your *rekveh* and have his future foretold."

Oh. They were going to let Thomas out of that cage?

Jinishta gave Ariock a look of sympathy. "What are you afraid of?"

Afraid?

Ariock glared down at Jinishta. He wasn't afraid of a little old lady. He just...well...

He just didn't want to hear another word out of the holy prophet. What she had said was damning enough. She had set him up for a colossal failure, a task he could not possibly measure up to. What else did she want to say? Was she going to outline his upcoming failures in painstaking detail?

Migyatel smiled blithely, apparently unaware that she had ruined his life.

Jinishta held herself with wary poise. At least a hundred warriors were ready to back her up, if it came to a fight.

"Fine." Ariock glared at Jinishta, to let her know that he did not appreciate feeling trapped and threatened. "But I am going to help Thomas after this."

He knelt next to Migyatel again, giving her a stern look which she could not see. She shouldn't smile. She ought to be ashamed.

"*Aonswa*," Migyatel whispered. "Your light scorched me. I am better prepared, now. Give me your hand."

Ariock fought an internal battle with himself, unsure if caving to this so-called prophet was wise.

But Migyatel seized his fingers like a vulture attacking a carcass.

"Oh!" she shouted. "I see the largest tower in existence thrown like a spear!"

Ariock rolled his eyes at her drama. Was she talking about the Stratower? That thing was older than the Torth Empire, and its roots probably went deep beyond bedrock. It was bigger than a city, bigger than a mountain. No one was going to pick it up and throw it.

Migyatel kept speaking in her high, gasping voice, trembling like a tea-kettle full of boiling water. "I see a terrible doom for the Alashani. It is almost upon us." Tears rolled down her wrinkled cheeks. "Many will not survive."

The audience rumbled uneasily.

"But you are the savior!" Migyatel declared. "You will lead the surviving Alashani to light and glory! Slaves run to you! I see their collars breaking off! Torth flee at the very sound of your name! You will shatter their evil empire, just as you shattered the power crystal!"

"Right." Ariock shot a glance toward Vy, down in the audience, so he could share his sarcasm with someone who understood reality. "Destroy the Torth Empire. Uh-huh. It's on my to-do list."

He tried to pull his hand away.

Migyatel held on with a surprisingly tenacious grip, no doubt enhanced by Yeresunsa power. Like her forceful voice.

"Two women tug you in different directions," Migyatel said. "Beware! They will break you, unless you can bend toward one without hurting the other."

Ariock wanted to laugh. Surely Migyatel felt the size of his hand? She must imagine that he was quite an attractive freak, to have women fight over him.

"Three mind readers will advise you," Migyatel went on. "One speaks truths. One speaks lies. One will tell you whatever you desire to hear."

That was imaginative. Ariock began to pull away again, but it seemed the crone wasn't finished.

"Oh, I see them! A weak child. An old man. And a beautiful woman."

Ariock guessed that the prophet must have heard a description of Thomas, to come up with an adviser who happened to be a truth-telling child telepath. But the other two? They were unlikely to exist anywhere in the universe, except in Migyatel's fevered imagination.

"I see your doom." Migyatel drew a sad, shuddering breath. "But you can avoid it if you heed my advice. Oh, great one, be wary of your advisers. You need them, but remember that they need you. Do not let them rule you. Heed your own counsel. You are of three bloods. You are descended from the new, the old, and the ancient. Heed the wisdom of each blood!"

That sounded like the end. Ariock withdrew, but Migyatel threw his hand away. Tears coursed down her wrinkled face. She quivered and sobbed, as if she had just survived a terrible ordeal.

"You have a heroic future." Her voice was a croak. "I wish I could be there to see it."

"You will, Grandmother." That came from one of the foreign warriors, a well-dressed woman seated in a box seat in the front row.

Ariock straightened to his full standing height, towering over Migyatel and her throne-like chair. "Are we done?" he demanded.

Jinishta gave him a solemn, reverential nod.

Ariock wanted to wrestle four nussians at once, or perhaps share a keg of mushroom ale with some friends. Migyatel's supposed prophecies twisted inside his heart. He assured himself that she was nothing but a senile lunatic. But beliefs had power, and he could see that the Alashani audience believed every word she'd said.

Even Jinishta gazed at him with shiny-eyed worship. Her last shreds of doubt were gone.

If Ariock asked her to share a drink with him, she would obey only out of worship. Nussians would revere him instead of sparring with him.

The prophet Migyatel had mortared a barrier between Ariock and everyone else. From now on, Ariock knew, he was doomed to be the messiah. Or else he would be nothing.

Migyatel spoke, now frail and elderly, no longer boosting her words with power. Her voice sounded like rustling papers. "Bring forth the *rekveh* prisoner. Let me see his future."

# CHAPTER 6

# TO SEE AGAIN

Sound returned to Thomas as the wrap unwound itself from his ears.

Distant murmurs.

Horrified whispers.

Rustles. Coughs.

A vast audience, upward of ten thousand people.

It was not the glorious immersion of the Megacosm, but it was a great improvement over the dripping silence of the pit. His unknown jailers had brought him someplace new. Thomas remained blindfolded and gagged, but now, instead of sitting in slimy filth, he lay on burlap.

He heard flames. Bonfires and torches in lieu of artificial lighting? More evidence that his jailers were low-tech.

Fear laced their breathing, their whispers, their voices.

For the first time in his imprisonment, Thomas heard his jailers. Their version of the slave tongue had a mushy, foreign cadence. When they spoke whatever their native language was, Thomas did not recognize a single word. Whoever they were, these people were unknown to the Torth Empire.

It was easy enough to put two and two together.

Thomas had long suspected that a free population of runaways must exist on the Torth Homeworld. Otherwise Jonathan Stead could not have hidden in the dead city for as long as he had. Sure enough, this unseen audience included wet snorts from nussians, and beak clicks, as well. They had ummins and other sapients among them.

An unseen force propped Thomas against the bars of his cage. Another force held his head upright. The gag loosened, then unraveled away from his dry, thirsty mouth.

"Can you hear me, *rekveh*?"

The female voice was unfamiliar to Thomas, marked by that mushy accent. She sounded like an orator.

"Prisoner," she said. "Answer me. Do you have a name?"

At last.

Thomas worked moisture into his mouth, aware that he needed to act meek and cooperative until he could get within telepathy range of someone. These jailers probably had no clue that he could twist minds.

Even so…they had retained their freedom in the Torth-ruled galaxy for centuries or even millennia. They must be Yeresunsa. It was the only plausible explanation for their secret existence and their power.

"My name is Thomas." His voice was a weak rasp.

"All right," the orator-jailer said. "We have questions for you, Thomas. Answer to our satisfaction, and we shall remove your blindfold. Perhaps you will be allowed to rejoin your friends. Is this understood?"

Thomas thought it was prudent to learn as much as possible about his jailers while revealing as little as possible about himself. So he said, "Sure," in a toneless way, hiding his desperation and eagerness for freedom.

Suppressing his emotions was easy. He had done it often enough as a Torth.

"If we catch you in a lie," the orator-jailer said in a more aggressive tone, "then you cannot expect freedom."

"Ask your questions," Thomas invited without emotion.

The vast audience quieted. They sounded more fearful than ever, and the orator-jailer hesitated, perhaps put off by his emotionless demeanor. Thomas began to reevaluate his strategy.

Then he heard Ariock's deep voice, resonant in the vast space. "Thomas? If you need healing right now, just say so."

Ariock sounded defiant, as if daring the jailers to attack. But the fact that Ariock had spoken to Thomas in the slave tongue—fluently!—meant that he was purposely forthright with the jailers. He had some kind of rapport with them. He trusted them to some degree, and since they did not silence him, they must trust him as well. Therefore, a fight would not be in Ariock's best interest.

"I can wait for healing," Thomas told him.

"All right. If you're sure." Ariock sounded concerned. "They just want to feel assured that you can be trusted."

The orator-jailer cut in. "Thomas, you claimed that you heard a woman who wept in the dungeon with you. What, exactly, did you experience?"

The audience seemed to hold its breath. Tens of thousands of people must be listening.

Thomas's throat tightened, but he rejected his urge to scream all his fury and frustration. He was not going to cry. He would not let anyone see him as a wreck, least of all these jailers.

"She appeared right next to me," he said with clinical detachment. "I felt her long hair. And I read her mind. She's been forgotten for I don't know how long. In her mind, it was eons. I think she came to me because she sensed that I was a prisoner, like her. And she's a mind reader as well. She seemed to believe we could help each other. She had no hope at all. But she did have, well, a lot of power."

That was an understatement. Thomas wondered if he should warn his listeners about how dangerous the other prisoner was. She was like a nuclear bomb waiting to go off.

Or worse. It might only be a matter of time before she made contact with another angry prisoner, someone who would channel her immense power without hesitancy. A duo like that might be as deadly as Ariock in full-blown berserker mode. And really, no one, not even Thomas, had any idea how deadly that was.

"I think it's important to find her," Thomas finished.

The vast audience murmured. Thomas couldn't guess why they sounded so derogatory, so offended. What had they expected him to say? If only he were close enough to scan some minds.

"You believe this apparition, this lady, was a mind reader." The orator-jailer sounded disgusted. "An imprisoned mind reader."

"She is," Thomas said stiffly, trying to discern their reasons for doubt. Did the jailers have a different story about the weeping prisoner? How many people—how many generations—had lied about who she was?

*No one can help me*, the weeping prisoner had told him without words.

If no one believed she existed, then maybe no one had ever properly tried to help her.

"How do you know that she has a lot of power?" the orator-jailer asked in a wary tone.

"She held my hands," Thomas said. "That was when I sensed her power. She offered it to me. But I…" He knew the truth would make him sound like a liar, but he went ahead anyway. "I refused. That much power isn't for me. I didn't feel worthy."

Murmurs. The audience was beyond Thomas's range of telepathy, but he understood a few words. "Quake."

They must have felt the tremor when the weeping prisoner offered her power to him. It was real.

"She vanished after I refused," Thomas went on. "I can't guess where she is. Maybe in one of your pits? But I think she is able to travel through stone, or project herself, sort of like a ghost."

Thomas could tell, by the embarrassed throat clearing, that the jailers did not quite trust his story.

"I know it sounds crazy," he said calmly. "But I read her mind, and I'm certain she's a real person. A Yeresunsa, I guess. She's been imprisoned for a long time. And she is not entirely sane."

If he ever became free, he would search for the weeping prisoner. No one deserved to suffer like that. No matter whom she used to be, no matter what she'd done, she had paid for it. She deserved at least one person who cared about the fact of her existence.

Thomas would rescue her.

Either that, or he would be the one to put her out of her misery.

"Let's move on," the orator-jailer said. "We have heard that you lived as a Torth. You have owned slaves. Is this true?"

"Yes." Thomas didn't hesitate. The refugees from Duin could be gregarious, and they must be here, welcomed as runaways. They would have told all they knew.

"It is said that you tortured slaves," the orator-jailer said with righteous judgment. "You harmed an ummin named Pung. And a human named Cherise Chavez. You also sentenced the…" She backtracked. "You sentenced Ariock to death. Are these things true?"

Here were his crimes. This interrogation was a trial.

"Yes," Thomas admitted. "I did those things."

"Why?" she asked.

Thomas hesitated for the first time. He could say he'd been coerced. But during his months of imprisonment, he had reexamined his faults a billion times over, and he had reached a few new conclusions. He would not offer stock excuses when he could articulate the truth.

"The Torth became my family," he said. "I wanted to please them."

The truth was more complicated than that, but Thomas doubted his jailers could envision the addictive power of being a cog in the galactic wheel of the Megacosm. Millions of other people's experiences, healthy or disabled, magnificent or enslaved, had sifted through his mind every waking second. From that godlike perspective, the fate of a few slaves had seemed insignificant.

The Torth Majority did not care about individuals, and so Yellow Thomas had not cared about individuals.

That was a toxic approach, he now figured. Slaves had healthier priorities. To slaves, large groups were abstract, whereas a single individual could seem to matter more than an entire city or planet. That strange but wonderful outlook made them superior to the Torth.

So during his imprisonment, Thomas had deconstructed who he was and pieced his identity back together from a human perspective.

He was smart. He was dying. He was a Torth hybrid, but he was also half-human. American. A friend. A foster brother. A prisoner. A target. A power to be reckoned with. A seeker of knowledge, and a teller of truths. He used to be a nameless Yellow Rank, equal to all other Yellow Ranks, but now that was only a fraction of his identity. He was a sapient being with a lot of unique complexities, and, like the mysterious magic of telepathy and Yeresunsa powers, the whole of who he was transcended the parts.

"The Torth are not my family anymore," he said.

The orator was quiet for a moment, perhaps mulling over his simple answer.

"Very well," she said. "Your answers are acceptable, Thomas. I have one final question. If you join us, will you give your assurance that you will not harm us?"

Thomas stiffened.

It would be easy to assure the jailers that he was meek and harmless, and that he would never cause problems…but lies caught in his throat. Honesty was a big part of his identity. It would be an internal betrayal. He would lose integrity.

"What we ask," the orator said, enunciating each word, "is your discretion. If we remove that blindfold, then you must never, ever convey your newly gained knowledge to the Torth. Or to any mind readers."

Thomas drew a breath to offer the indemnity they wanted.

Instead, uncertainty burned in his chest. Uncertainty, and misery. If he agreed to keep major secrets from the Torth Empire, that meant he could never ascend into the Megacosm again, even if the Torth welcomed him back—unless the Torth gleaned these secrets on their own, through other means.

It would be like swapping one form of blindness for another.

And without the galactic network, he'd have less of a chance to track down the forgotten prisoner who wept in the dark.

"I am wary," Thomas said, "of swearing vows to people with agendas that are unknown to me."

Thomas could hear angry intakes of breath, and movements as unseen people exchanged glances that were no doubt outraged.

"Swear it," the orator said in a steely tone. "Or you will never have freedom."

Thomas sagged. He wanted to see Cherise and Kessa and Vy again, to make sure they were all right. But to give up the Megacosm? Maybe he was better off dead.

"It's worth it," Ariock said. "Please, Thomas."

Somewhere farther away, Vy spoke. "Thomas, they're good people, mostly. This promise will be worth it. I swear."

Which meant Cherise had to be safe. Otherwise Vy would condemn the jailers instead of supporting them.

"Fine." His voice quavered.

So what if he had to pretend that the doorway in his mind was sealed shut—at least for as long as the Torth remained ignorant of this underground society? He was unwelcome among the gods, anyhow. He was not wholly Torth. He should probably embrace the human aspects of his identity.

"Let me have my vision back," Thomas said, "and I will keep your secrets. I promise."

The blindfold began to unravel. A golden glimmer reached Thomas's vision, and his eyes watered with the pain of being able to see again.

"We will trust you," the orator said in a mistrustful tone.

Thomas said nothing. The jailers could have demanded his fealty, but they had not. They could have enslaved him, or demanded that he take active measures against the Torth. They could have pumped him for information, the way the ummins of Duin had done, but they had let that opportunity slip away, as well.

It seemed the jailers believed he was useless. Harmless.

What a mistake.

# CHAPTER 7

# GHOSTS OF THE DEAD CITY

Uneasiness churned in Cherise as the blindfold unwrapped itself from Thomas's head.

The albinos boasted about their purple eyes. They might relax if they could see Thomas's original, natural eye color.

Instead? Thomas's yellow eyes reflected bonfires. The artificial iridescent color evoked searchlights and other technology utilized by Torth. It highlighted his alienness, along with his sunken cheeks.

"I don't like its evil look," Flen whispered.

Cherise placed her hand on Flen's embroidered sleeve. "I'm sure Thomas is finding it difficult to see. That's why he's squinting."

She doubted that anyone, except maybe Vy, recognized the glint of repressed rage in Thomas's bloodshot eyes. Residents of the Hollander home, and researchers at Rasa Biotech, had learned that it was a bad idea to obstruct him.

She hoped the Alashani would not have to learn that lesson the hard way.

Oblivious to her worries, Flen leaned close to her and whispered. "Why is the *rekveh* so unimpressed? Shouldn't it be shocked to see our underground realm?"

That was a good point. Cherise could not imagine how anyone, even a telepathic supergenius, could glean salient information about the Alashani while kept in the dark.

But he was Thomas. If anyone could think of a way out of ignorance, it would be him.

"He's good at making educated guesses," Cherise said.

A crease formed between Flen's brows. "Torth are supposed to be stupid. Aren't they?" He looked at Cherise for confirmation, aware that she had been enslaved.

"Many are." Cherise hesitated. "Thomas is not one of the stupid ones."

She really ought to explain about Thomas's mutation. But this seemed like the wrong time to reveal that she and her friends had been lying about Thomas's capabilities for months.

Thomas's bloodshot gaze swept the audience, no doubt collecting every detail of every tidy white hairdo and chinless face. The albino women favored weblike snoods and diadems to restrain their thick curls. High collars emphasized long necks, and scalloped necklines showed off jewelry.

For their part, the Alashani studied Thomas with frank fascination. Most of them had never seen a living mind reader. They'd only seen the decapitated skulls of long-dead Torth. To them, Thomas was a monster straight out of a fairy tale.

"So." Thomas spoke in a rasp. "You are the ghosts that haunt the dead city."

"You will never reveal us to the Torth." Chaniyelem had kept her aplomb throughout her questioning of Thomas, but now she spoke sharply, perhaps second-guessing her mercy toward the mind reader. She stood as far from his range of telepathy as she could get without falling off the stage.

Thomas's restless scan paused on Cherise. He blinked painfully and stared.

Cherise wished she could hide. She became hyperaware of the diamonds in her blue-tinted black hair, the platinum hoops dangling from her ears.

And the electric sparks crackling over her Yeresunsa boyfriend.

Cherise grabbed Flen's arm. "Stop!" she whispered.

"Why is it staring at us?" Flen's face was hard with fury.

"It's okay," Cherise breathed, terrified that Flen might hurl spears at Thomas. "You could kill him easily. He knows it." She squeezed Flen's arm, offering reassurance.

Flen relaxed a tiny bit. The air lost tension as Thomas's gaze roved onward.

"You look well," Thomas said without emotion. He seemed to be speaking to Kessa and Weptolyso. The nussian's spinal ridge poked above the crowd.

Kessa perched on cushions, richly garbed in a golden skull-net and an embroidered tunic. Thomas's wristwatch on her arm looked like an alien artifact. And so it was. Long ago, on another world, Cherise had given that wristwatch to Thomas as a gift for his birthday.

"*Rekveh,*" Chaniyelem said with impatience. "Are you ready to have your future foretold?"

The audience looked keyed up, not entirely serene about placing a mind reader near their beloved holy prophet. Flen tensed, ready for battle.

Thomas shifted his critical gaze toward Ariock.

The giant stood tall with his arms folded, looking as well-groomed as a high councilor. A purple mantle decked his shoulders. Golden plates cuffed his forearms and collar.

"Have they elected you their king?" Thomas asked in English, his tone dripping with irony.

Ariock gave a self-conscious shrug. "It's a little worse than that. Their prophet"—he pointed to Migyatel—"just convinced everyone that I'm the messiah, destined to lead them to light and glory."

His embarrassed laugh showed how ridiculous he thought that was.

"Messiah." Thomas tasted the word. There was no humor in it, but Cherise heard an undertone of scorn.

"They wouldn't let me near you." Ariock unfolded his arms and walked toward Thomas, shoulders slumped with regret. "I'll heal you now."

Cherise was secretly glad. She remembered sick and dying alien slaves hiding in sewage shafts, avoiding tyrannical owners. Thomas looked worse. He was skin and bones.

As Ariock approached, there was a shout. Chaniyelem and quite a few councilors and Yeresunsa had something to say about it.

"*Aonswa*, please wait!" Chaniyelem begged. "Let Migyatel tell us his future, first, before you allow him to feast on your mind!"

Jinishta blocked the cage. Such a petite person should not have obstructed Ariock, yet he stopped in his tracks, as if faced by a venomous snake ready to strike.

"Let us learn what his future holds," Jinishta said. "Then you may heal him."

The bonfires wavered, hit by a draft. The crowded cave air changed, like a storm on the way.

"You promised to keep Thomas in good health," Ariock told Jinishta. "I trusted you. Now, why does he look so malnourished?"

Next to Cherise, Flen tensed. His weapons quiver rested against his leg, and Cherise had no doubt that he would defend Jinishta if Ariock insulted her too much.

Cherise clutched his sleeve. She needed to figure out a way to give Flen pause, to prevent him from launching out of his seat and flipping over backrests, shooting lightning and throwing spears.

"The best care in the world would not make your *rekveh* friend any healthier," Jinishta said with defiance. "He was born feeble. Anyone can see this. You will have plenty of time to heal him, but healing will not make any difference. If you are wise, you will want to hear his future. If he is destined for an early death, or for ignominy, then better you should know now, rather than waste your efforts healing..."

She trailed off. The air felt stormy.

Thomas's weak voice took over as soon as she stopped. "It's okay, Ariock. I'll wait to be healed. This isn't worth a fight."

Ariock gave him a questioning look.

"I'm sure," Thomas said, answering an unspoken question that he could not possibly detect from such a distance. "I want to read one of their minds." He licked his lips and gave Migyatel a hungry look. "I can hardly wait."

The old prophet smiled blithely.

Perhaps Migyatel remained serene because she was blind. If she could see the way Thomas sized her up, as if she was a feast, she would probably not be smiling.

"I'm ready to have my future foretold." There was an overeager tremble in Thomas's voice.

Jinishta and Chaniyelem exchanged looks of trepidation. Even Ariock began to look concerned. "Are you sure?" he asked Thomas again. "Everyone else can wait."

Chaniyelem cleared her throat. "Thomas," she said, her orator voice faltering. "Before we place you near Migyatel, do you have questions which we might answer?" She searched his bright-yellow eyes. "I'm sure there are many things you wish to know about the Alashani?"

She kneaded her hands together, no doubt hoping for questions. She must wonder how much Thomas already knew about them, and what nefarious means he had used to soak up such forbidden knowledge.

Flen was alert, more tense than ever.

"Let's skip the tedium of questions and answers." Thomas paused for a wheezy intake of breath. "I'm a fast learner."

"*Rekveh*," Chaniyelem said. "You must appreciate how far we are trusting you, showing you secrets no mind reader has ever known." She searched him with a probing gaze. "You are the first person of Torth heritage to enter our realm."

Thomas gave her an unappreciative stare. "I doubt that."

Chaniyelem straightened, offended.

"No *rekveh* has ever seen us," Jinishta said hotly. "We are very careful."

"Except for Jonathan Stead," Thomas said.

He watched their outrage like a scientist studying the results of an experiment. Jinishta bristled, sparks zipping along her tunic and hair. The immense audience writhed and hissed with angry whispers. Chaniyelem glared at Thomas as if he'd turned into a cave worm.

"That's blasphemy," Ariock explained in a mild tone, in English, so the aliens would not understand. "We'd better apologize." He switched to the slave tongue and said in a placating tone, "Thomas is very sorry. I'm sure he's confused after his long imprisonment. He didn't mean to offend."

Thomas offered the albinos a tight smile. It bore no resemblance to an apology.

"This proves that Thomas needs healing," Ariock added. "After that, we can go ahead and have Migyatel foretell his fate."

Thomas yelped in surprise. Suddenly he was floating, cradled by the burlap rag. An invisible force—Ariock—lifted him out of the open-topped cage and flew him across the stage before Jinishta or anyone else could attack.

Most of the audience gaped in shock, or consternation, as Ariock used his powers to levitate Thomas, while simultaneously holding his hands in the healing posture.

"*Aonswa,*" Jinishta said in a seething tone. "You have no right!"

Flen glared with outrage. But Cherise inwardly cheered for Ariock. He understood the importance of giving Thomas a friendly mind to read first, before putting him in proximity of a revered Alashani like Migyatel. The healing was an excuse. A good one.

Shudders rippled through Thomas's fragile body. His legs and arms dangled like twigs while filth and scabs peeled off his skin. Even his hair looked cleaner, regaining a bit of sheen.

His eyes went wide and full of wonder. No doubt he was soaking up as much of Ariock's recent experiences as he could.

It was over within seconds. Ariock used his powers to cradle Thomas in the burlap cloth, then sent him toward Migyatel.

Jinishta clenched her fists, but it seemed she lacked the gumption to challenge the messiah on this matter. How far would she take a fight in a plaza full of innocent people?

The burlap slid to a stop at Migyatel's slippered feet.

Thomas lay there, close enough to read the mind of the prophet. His look of starvation vanished. He peered up at Migyatel with a sickened combination of dazed wonder, awe, and...

Was that panic?

Migyatel continued to look blindly ahead. "I am ready," she whispered in her papery voice. "Give me your hand, *rekveh.*"

"I don't want my future read." Thomas rolled his head to look at Ariock and the others on stage. "Can we skip this? Please?"

Electric rage rippled up Jinishta's arms.

"It's best to just get it over with," Ariock said with some sympathy. "She'll say a bunch of meaningless stuff." He rolled his eyes. "Then the audience will be appeased, and the show will be over. You'll be able to recuperate."

Thomas cringed away from Migyatel's fumbling hand. "Please?" he asked Ariock in a terrified squeak. "I don't want her to touch me."

Flen sat forward, alert. No doubt he was ready to defend the holy prophet from whatever insults the *rekveh* might cast at her.

Cherise leaned forward as well, because she had never seen Thomas this scared.

Did he find the prophet's memories too overwhelming? What was making him leery?

The Alashani watched without mercy. They would not allow Thomas to dodge the spectacle they'd all crowded together to witness. After all, he was already within range of Migyatel. He was already reading her mind and sucking up her secrets. Surely he had to bend to their rules in return.

"Sorry, Thomas." Ariock sounded less sympathetic. He switched to English. "Just ignore whatever she says. It's lies."

But Ariock began to look uneasy, despite his confident attitude. Thomas ought to know whether Migyatel was a charlatan or a genuine prophet. By now, he probably knew her favorite toys as a child. He'd probably soaked up every dream she'd ever had.

Thomas did look overwhelmed. He lay on his back, struggling unsuccessfully to crawl away. Tears streamed down his gaunt cheeks. "Keep her away from me," Thomas whimpered. He stared at Migyatel, transfixed by something terrible that only he could see.

"I will not harm you, *rekveh*," Migyatel said gently. She held out her hand, like she was coaxing a kitten. "The future can be scary. But futures intertwine and tangle together, like veins. Some are short. Some are long and affect many others. The messiah is at the center of many. He bends some, he ends some, and he ties others together. If you are part of his prophecy, then your future will have an impact on his, and his on yours. Come. Let us see what it is."

The audience was rapt, but Thomas looked miserable with dread.

Cherise felt her innards clench—not with anticipation, but with reluctant sympathy. Thomas should not need to go through another ordeal. He had suffered enough. In fact, he still looked sick, despite the healing Ariock had given him. Why couldn't the Alashani give him time to rest?

"Just get it over with already," Flen growled.

On the stage, Jinishta made a disgusted sound of impatience. She used her powers to manipulate the burlap into a ripple, which pushed Thomas within Migyatel's reach.

The prophet seized his small hand.

Her sightless eyes bulged. Thomas's eyes widened, as well. They were peculiar mirrors of each other, equally horror-struck.

An anguished wail tore out of Migyatel.

Her shriek bounced off stone walls and silenced everyone in the grand plaza—perhaps everyone in the city. Alashani sat on the edge of their seats, eager for prophetic predictions. Those standing clutched each other's shoulders. Everyone held their breath and listened.

But Migyatel's wail choked off in a strangled gargle.

The way she swayed to one side, she looked like she might be falling into a trance. But she was really falling.

As everyone in the grand plaza watched, Migyatel toppled sideways out of the ivory chair. She landed on the ground with a boneless clunk.

She had not braced herself.

She did not stir.

"I didn't kill her!" Thomas said in English. His pleading gaze locked on Ariock. "She died from an aneurysm or an embolism or something along those lines. I didn't do it!"

Silence.

Thunder seemed to fill the city as row after row of Yeresunsa warriors stood. Up on the rampart, warriors crackled with lightning and drew spears. More warriors looked ready to hurl their weapons with deadly precision.

Lightning snapped across Ariock's huge arms and massive chest, illuminating his Yeresunsa mantle.

The rest of the audience stirred like leaves swirling before a storm. Parents tried to hustle their children out of the plaza. Elderly couples attempted to sneak into the aisle. Teenagers whispered with panicked uncertainty.

"Don't." Cherise clutched Flen's arm.

He was standing, puffed up with fury.

Cherise stood, too. She forced Flen to see her. "Don't," she said again.

Nearby warriors remained furious, but Flen seemed to remember his duty to protect innocent people. He lowered the spear he was holding.

"You have nothing to fear," Cherise said, pleading for Flen to believe her.

Yet she had trouble believing it herself. Ariock radiated danger. Vy considered him safe and cuddly, but Cherise had seen Ariock pick up armored Servants of All and snap their spines. She doubted that his sparring sessions had taught him enough self-control.

If Ariock and the warriors attacked each other, it would be up to her—and maybe Vy—to stop the mayhem.

# CHAPTER 8
# PLACES TO GO

All pretense of kindness was gone. Everyone who wore a Yeresunsa mantle stood ready to hurl spears. There were even deadly students, children cloaked in Yeresunsa mantles, eager to kill the disabled boy who looked so small and alone on the vast stage.

Ariock shielded Thomas.

He didn't give the dead prophet much of his attention. Migyatel was beyond help. He sensed her lack of a life spark.

Thomas's life spark was weak. Too weak. His sores were cleaned up, thanks to Ariock's healing, so why was he still unwell?

Just how abusive had the jailers been?

Jinishta had promised to keep him healthy. She had looked Ariock in the face every day and assured him that the *rekveh* was fed regularly and that he was taking his medicine.

Was this what she considered to be adequate care for someone so fragile?

"I swear," Thomas said to the audience. "I didn't kill her."

"I believe you." Ariock felt pained that his friend needed to spout reassures that he wasn't a murderer.

But no one else believed Thomas. Yeresunsa crackled with sparks.

One of the foreign warriors vaulted out of a box seat. She landed on the stage and ran to the dead prophet, heedless of her proximity to Thomas. "Grandmother?" She made a hasty examination of the corpse.

Moments later, her grief-stricken cry echoed off the granite cliff. "Migyatel is dead!"

Albinos turned to each other in shock throughout the grand plaza. They had gathered to witness their beloved prophet announce prophecies. They had not come to see her die right in front of them.

"Die, *rekveh*!" The granddaughter of Migyatel hurled a spear at Thomas. She threw it with such power-enhanced force, the shaft actually broke off when it struck the invisible shield of air.

She blinked at the space Thomas had occupied a second ago. She was not yet aware that Ariock had used his powers to yank the boy into his protective arms.

"That *rekveh* is no friend of ours, *Aonswa*!" a warrior shouted.

"He murdered the prophet!" another warrior shouted.

Ariock cradled Thomas, shielding him. Nobody quite dared to try to skewer Thomas like this. They would not accidentally attack their messiah.

"It was a natural death," Ariock told the enraged warriors.

"Ariock." Jinishta spoke without mercy. "The *rekveh* needs to be in our custody." She pointed to the empty prison cage.

A sea of pale Alashani faces watched from the plaza. Their white hair shone like dust.

An army of warriors began to gather behind Jinishta. They all held spears, which Ariock knew they could hurl at nearly supersonic speeds. So many warriors could tear apart the grand plaza.

Ariock's awareness whipped outward, eager to encompass stone and air. Urns and goblets floated. The bonfires flared.

He ripped himself out of the environment, struggling to stay small and normal. Monstrousness wouldn't help this situation.

"I made a promise to protect Thomas with my life," Ariock told Jinishta. "I honor my promises. And I remember that you made a promise, as well. You promised to keep Thomas safe."

She actually had the temerity to look angry.

"No one will kill your precious *rekveh*," she said. "But we do need to question him. Migyatel died right before she could announce his future for all to hear. I do not believe that timing was an accident."

"The *rekveh* silenced her," another warrior said with certainty.

"It murdered her," the elderly granddaughter said.

"Torth have a power to give pain seizures," an elderly warrior proclaimed. "It gave her a pain seizure. I saw it!"

Ariock knew that was untrue. He had suffered enough pain seizures to know that they required intense focus, and during the confrontation with Migyatel, Thomas had looked too horrified to be that focused.

"The prophet died from natural causes," Ariock said, pleading for the Alashani to understand. "Maybe she had a…" He paused before he could finish saying "a vision." He didn't want to imply that Thomas's future was shocking enough to scare an old lady to death. He didn't want to implicate Thomas at all.

"Migyatel foresaw something," Jinishta seethed. She pointed at Thomas. "That *rekveh* knows what."

Ariock wished Thomas would volunteer some information about Migyatel's final vision. This must be a tragic misunderstanding.

Jinishta pointed up at Ariock. "You are still a guest in my city. You are under my command, Ariock, even if you are the messiah. Put the *rekveh* into my custody."

Thomas shook his head in refusal.

"I don't think so," Ariock told Jinishta.

"This is not a request." Jinishta held herself with catlike grace, the way she stood in sparring sessions. "I am your premier. You have not even sworn the Warrior's Pact. I am ordering you to do the right thing."

Sadness washed through Ariock. Jinishta was supposed to be on his side. She had embraced him as her cousin. To an Alashani, that was supposed to matter more than friendship.

And now? She was treating him like an enemy.

"Relinquish the *rekveh*." Jinishta watched Ariock as if he were a new and formidable monster. "He needs to tell us the future Migyatel foretold for him."

No one threw a spear—yet—but warriors blocked certain rows in the audience. Vy and Kessa would not be able to escape. They might as well be hostages.

Jinishta's gaze challenged Ariock. "Are you claiming yourself to be an enemy of the Alashani?"

Ariock understood the implication. Any Yeresunsa who flouted laws was considered to be a criminal, and a danger to the Alashani civilization. It meant immediate execution.

Vy watched him from the front row, surrounded by powerful warriors. Ariock felt trapped and helpless, despite his power.

Just as Thomas had been when the Torth had pushed him around as a Yellow Rank.

Ariock firmed up his shield. He was not going to let anyone bully him or push him around.

"I already put him in your care," he told Jinishta. "I'm sorry. But I don't trust you."

His words were like a spark dropped on kerosene. Jinishta didn't even have time to give an order or a signal. All at once, Yeresunsa hurled spears, and unseen forces tried to pry Thomas away in various directions. Lightning strobed, leaving the air sharp with ozone. Thunder echoed throughout the huge cavern.

Ariock reinforced his invisible shield of pressurized air.

The massive audience saw powers being used, and they swarmed toward the exits. No one wanted to be trapped with a lot of angry Yeresunsa.

"Calm down!" Chaniyelem yelled in her orator's voice. "Let's be reasonable!"

Attendants rushed to her, tugging her out of harm's way.

Councilors shoved each other in their haste to get away. Maidservants dropped trays and fled. Families shoved past doddering elders, and children shrieked as they got cut off from their parents.

Someone knocked over a lamp. Screams of terrified agony erupted as a man caught on fire.

The mob became a stampede toward the exit gates. Albinos screamed, punching and kicking each other in their haste to get away. A panicked nussian bulled through a crowded aisle, leaving bruised and battered people in his wake.

The chaos gave Ariock an unexpected moment of respite. While dozens of Yeresunsa warriors turned their attention toward their people, trying to quell the riot, Ariock dared to turn his back on the madness. He quit his protective shielding long enough to give Thomas another—more thorough—healing. He cradled the boy in the crook of his arm and poured all his energy into the too-weak life spark.

That ought to do it.

Except Thomas's life spark continued to gutter like a candle sinking into wax. He looked almost more like a bundle of sticks than a living person.

He was unwell.

"I healed you," Ariock said, frustrated.

Thomas offered a smile. "You did a good job."

Not good enough. Ariock glanced over his shoulder at the riot and decided to risk another round of healing. Maybe he'd gotten distracted the first two times?

Thomas wheezed as Ariock healed him. Afterward, he seemed just as sick.

This was unacceptable. It was technically Ariock's fault that Thomas had barely survived the dungeon pit. Therefore, it was his job to make sure Thomas had a future. He would not fail.

"Only an idiot tries the same thing over and over again," Thomas rasped, "expecting different results."

It occurred to Ariock that he could simply ask Thomas for a diagnosis. The boy had all sorts of medical knowledge stored in his brain. Maybe he just needed better nourishment?

"I'm as healthy as I can be," Thomas said. "All things considered."

"What does that mean?" Ariock said.

Thomas replied with a mysterious grin.

Ariock tamped down his frustration, realizing that his friend had lost many reasons to trust him.

Screams piled up, not just nearby, but throughout the whole plaza. The exits writhed with desperate people shoving past each other.

Someone fell off a balcony, pinwheeling their arms and screeching.

The fire was spreading fast, burning upholstery and leaping from chair to chair.

Yeresunsa encircled Ariock and Thomas, trying to batter down the invisible shield. Ariock became aware that electricity was crackling around him. It raised the hairs on his arms. Loose debris raised around him, like hackles.

They were going to tear him apart, shield or no.

Ariock strengthened his shield and gathered energy in one outstretched hand. He released it explosively, sending warriors toppling.

"Why are you attacking the messiah?" A young warrior planted herself in front of Ariock, facing her peers. "We must obey him!"

Spears meant for Thomas and Ariock slammed into the peacemaking warrior instead. Spears stuck out of her as she fell, her landing softened by her Yeresunsa mantle.

Ariock watched in horrified regret as her life spark guttered and died. What a wasteful death! Maybe she had assumed that the chosen one would protect her, but she'd been sadly wrong. Ariock was preoccupied with keeping a tight shield around himself and Thomas. He could not spare extra attention for a stranger.

Now she was as dead as Migyatel.

"Murderer!" one warrior screamed at another warrior.

"She got in the way!" another yelled.

"*Aonswa!*" That pleading cry came from Orla, the healer. "I will follow and obey you!"

A few other warriors fell to their knees, cowering in prayerful poses. One sobbed and begged for Ariock's mercy.

Jinishta shouted in the native Alashani tongue, probably calling for law and order, but the warriors had become a squabbling mass. Half of them wanted to kill Thomas. The other half were getting in the way, trying to worship Ariock.

"STOP."

Ariock's deep voice thundered like an avalanche, amplified by the extra air he inhabited.

Yeresunsa halted with their spears ready to throw, quivering. The rioters froze. Everyone in the grand plaza, and perhaps the city, stopped what they were doing, at least momentarily.

The huge urns floated in midair, their bonfires roaring. Ariock realized that he'd connected to them in his anger.

Rage seethed in him, a liquid danger that threatened to seize the world around him. His Yeresunsa awareness kept jumping out and connecting to walls, pillars, candelabra. He had to pull himself together every few seconds. If he didn't get his rage under control, he might accidentally tear down the cavern.

"Stop protecting that *rekveh!*" a warrior demanded. "Too many seers are having nightmares, Messiah! There is a doom coming! Migyatel herself said it!"

"Get rid of the *rekveh!*" someone else shouted in agreement.

Albinos lifted their chinless faces in defiance. They ignored the would-be peacemaker, who lay in a pool of her own blood. These Yeresunsa had accidentally killed one of their own in their mindless frenzy to murder Thomas.

Slaves would never be so reckless. So self-absorbed.

Countless quadrillions of slaves suffered injustices every day, while the Alashani had no concept of how lucky they were.

"You want light and glory?" Ariock said, glaring at the Yeresunsa warriors. "I don't see how any of you deserve it."

Snaps of electric anger coiled and uncoiled around him, reflecting his mood. He stepped over the dead warrior, Thomas in his arms.

"Ariock." Jinishta sounded uncertain. Was that a trace of fear? Ariock had never wanted anyone to fear him.

He needed to get away from the Alashani underground. He needed to leave this planet. Otherwise he was really going to start hating himself again, the way he used to.

He walked past the warriors.

Jinishta spoke in a cold tone behind him. "You may not leave the city. I have not deemed you fit for travel to the surface."

Ariock made a sweeping motion with his free hand, ripping away their quivers. Weapons hovered in midair, each as familiar to Ariock as his own fingers. When he moved his hand, the mass of quivers and spears flew across the plaza and clattered into a harmless heap.

He stepped off the stage.

He waded past overturned cushions, past stone benches, making his way toward Vy. Shards from broken goblets littered the ground.

Footsteps pattered up the cliffside steps. Jinishta shouted rallying words in the native Alashani tongue. When Ariock glanced at her, her return glare promised trouble. He wondered what commands she was giving.

Then he decided it didn't matter. She had her Alashani pride, and he had places to go.

CHAPTER 9
# AN END TO CHARITY

When Ariock approached the jam of people at an exit gate, there was no need for displays of his power. Albinos took one look at the sick child in his arms and fled in terror, screaming.

No one saw the irony in fearing a frail, undeveloped child, instead of the gigantic and massively powerful Yeresunsa who carried him. They reacted as though Thomas would eat their children. Never mind the fact that Ariock had killed slaves by accident, whereas Thomas had never killed any innocent bystanders.

"Someone has to make sure he gets his injections," Vy said. She kept pace with Ariock, concerned for her foster brother. "I'll go tell Cherise to tell Flen to get his medicine case. It's got to be in the dungeon."

"My medicine is not important," Thomas said.

He sounded certain. Yet he was wheezing slightly, his voice was weak, and his life spark continued to feel fragile.

Vy shot him a sisterly look of concern. Then she shifted her attention to Ariock. "Will you wait for me? You're not going to leave me behind when you leave this city, right?"

Ariock knew that he ought to tell her to stay underground. She was relatively safe in the Alashani underground.

Safer than anywhere else, anyway.

It was easy to imagine being bombed by Torth, or falling off the Stratower if he tried to climb it, or being thrown in the Isolatorium. The last thing Ariock wanted to do was expose Vy to constant danger.

Vy planted her hands on her hips. "I don't want you to be relaxing on some alien beach while I'm stuck in a cave for the rest of my life."

She seemed to have guessed the reason for his hesitancy.

"Someone has to take care of Thomas," Vy pointed out. "You can't trust anyone else. It has to be me."

Ariock felt his resolve crumble. Vy was right.

He nodded, inwardly kicking himself for letting his heart override his brain. He didn't know how to refuse her.

"Hey, Flen!" Vy shouted, seeing the warrior escorting Cherise up an aisle. "Will you get Thomas's NAI-12 case out of the dungeon, please?"

Flen glared at Thomas with murder in his eyes.

"Yes," Cherise assured Vy in English. "I'll ask him later. Where should we bring it?"

Flen took a step closer, spears ready to throw, although he was careful to stay out of telepathy range. "Tell me, *rekveh*," he said, "What did the prophet Migyatel foresee in your future?"

Thomas was barely audible. "Nothing that can happen."

Flen bristled with fury. "What did she see? Answer!"

Ariock pulled Thomas up higher, away from questions.

"Why are you hiding it?" Flen demanded.

Thomas turned away. He was clearly unwilling to explain what Migyatel had envisioned during the seconds before she had keeled over, dead.

Ariock remembered that the prophet had tried to make a proclamation. She had looked stricken, as if faced with something momentous. She must have seen something.

Or foreseen something?

Ariock felt a chill run up his spine. He didn't want to believe in prophecy, but of all the people on this dark planet, Thomas was the least likely to get suckered in by falsehoods or imaginative hallucinations. Why wasn't he joking about her final vision?

What had he soaked up from Migyatel?

Maybe it was some dark craziness that would trigger the Alashani even further.

Or it was an actual prophecy.

If Migyatel was authentic, that meant Ariock was, in fact, destined to lead the Alashani to some sort of light and glory. Except he could not possibly protect countless millions of people, along with Thomas and his friends. No one could.

If the fate of the Alashani civilization rested in his incompetent hands, then they were all doomed.

Jinishta and her big, welcoming family. Everyone in the underworld. Doomed.

"Migyatel was wrong about both of us." Thomas focused on Ariock, laboring to breathe. "She must have been."

Ah. She was a false prophet after all.

Ariock wanted to laugh at himself in disgust, even as he sagged in relief. Destroy the Torth Empire? Bring freedom to the galaxy? Ha. He felt like a self-absorbed idiot for believing the hype even for a second.

The messiah treatment was warping him. He needed to get away from worshippers and just be plain Ariock again.

"Let's meet at Chaniyelem's palace," Ariock told his friends. "I'm leaving the underground as soon as we get Thomas's medicine. I'd rather keep the departure group small. I don't know how likely we are to survive once we head back to Torth lands."

That should deter most people. Weptolyso and Yuey headed toward the exit. Kessa was hurrying away as well. Ariock hoped they weren't planning to pack bags and join him. They ought to stay underground.

Flen looked like he wanted to go on an angry tirade, but Cherise clasped his hand and whispered something that seemed to calm him. The flush faded from his albino complexion. He allowed Cherise to tug him toward an exit.

Good. Ariock would rather rely on someone else to retrieve the medicine case. He didn't want to face the dungeon traps and an army of angry Yeresunsa barring his way. Cherise truly was an angel.

"I need to pack a few things." Vy limped toward a boulevard. "I'll meet you at the palace?"

"See you there," Ariock promised.

He ducked under the nearest exit gateway. The boulevard was nearly devoid of people, although there was plenty of trash and debris.

The fountains weren't running. That was strange. Weren't there supposed to be Yeresunsa on duty at the aqueduct at all hours? It seemed no one was pumping water through the city.

Knots of albino people gossiped in alleyways, bathed in cozy lamplight. They fell silent and shied away when they saw Thomas.

The boy gazed at everything with hungry curiosity. Ariock could imagine the sights through fresh eyes. Shop fronts. Balconies. Shrines. Gargoyles and dramatic friezes. Balustrades. Most entryways were well lit, despite being in a cave. Narrow stairwells leading to secretive apartments. Nearly every surface was adorned in some way.

Ariock had never lived in a place where he truly felt at home, but the Alashani city of Hufti had become cozily familiar. It evoked a realm of dwarves or gnomes straight out of a fantasy novel. He suspected that he would miss this place more than anywhere else.

"I'm not worth leaving all this," Thomas said.

"Yes, you are." Ariock guessed that Thomas was responding to his thoughts. "Your life is worth more than anything I have here."

"But you're safe here." Thomas's voice was raspy from disuse, but he spoke with some force. He was arguing. "You need to stay underground."

Part of Ariock wondered if the supergenius was right. Thomas tended to have good judgment. But…

"If we stay, someone will kill you," Ariock said. He knew it with certainty. Jinishta and Chaniyelem might eventually be reasonable, and they had the authority to impose law and order, but they could not control everyone. Many warriors were out for blood. "We have to leave," Ariock said. "There's no choice."

"I'm dead anyway," Thomas said.

He sounded at peace. It was as if he wanted to die.

Again.

Ariock refused to accept that. Thomas had looked vengeful at first, when they'd first unwrapped his head. He must want something out of life. He was a survivor. He had survived spinal muscular atrophy, as well as bad foster parents and the Torth Empire. That dungeon pit could not be the final straw. He wasn't going to die.

"No." Ariock made it a simple statement of fact.

"No one can save me," Thomas said.

His fury had seemed to wither only once he went into close proximity of the prophet Migyatel. Ariock half wondered if Thomas had absorbed something terrible. Had he seen something that made him afraid of his own future?

"You're going to live." Ariock made it a promise.

A scent of fried food caught his attention. Perhaps Thomas just needed some decent nourishment?

Ariock followed his nose to a side alley where a street chef fried snails over a steaming griddle, mixing them with mushrooms. Escargot was a popular snack food, although Ariock personally preferred cave fish sashimi.

"Excuse me," Ariock said in the slave tongue, looming over the griddle. "I'd like to buy one order for my friend." He presented Thomas.

The chef's bland smile turned into a gape of terror. He backed against a stone wall, holding the spatula like a shield.

Ariock balanced Thomas in one arm while searching for his coin pouch.

"Take! Take!" The chef gestured at the pile of freshly fried snails.

Ariock considered telling the chef that Thomas was born to fulfill a prophecy. But no. He was done endorsing superstitious beliefs.

He used his powers to place a gold coin on the counter, which was enough to finance a feast. Then he carefully selected a bowl, scooped up some escargot, and offered it to Thomas.

"No, thanks," Thomas said. "I'm not hungry."

He looked starved.

Ariock studied the boy with frustration. Was he lying about his hunger?

Thomas's zest for life used to be all-consuming. Ariock had talked with Vy for hours every day, and she had told him about her family. She'd recounted Thomas's machinations with employees at Rasa Biotech, playing them off each other in order to direct research in the ways he wanted.

Thomas had wanted to live so badly, his sheer willpower had dragged an entire industry of medical research in his wake. Thomas had certainly dragged Ariock out of his own self-pity. He had made Ariock want to be a better person.

That version of Thomas seemed buried. This yellow-eyed prisoner was more like a Torth. Apathetic. Nihilistic. And self-absorbed.

Ariock knew all about that. He had spent far too much of his own life wallowing in unearned shame and self-hatred.

*If you really want to hate yourself,* Ariock thought to Thomas, *try decimating an entire spaceport with people inside.*

He held a piece of fried meat to Thomas's mouth. If the boy wasn't going to care for himself, then someone had to do it for him. Whatever Thomas was guilty about, he was wrong. He was human. They both were.

Thomas took a reluctant bite. "You're an idiot," he said, chewing weakly.

"Right," Ariock said.

The chef edged away, and Ariock thanked him before he could abandon his griddle. He hiked onward and uphill, toward the palace district.

The Alashani underworld was filled with temptations and beauty. But Ariock was always aware that he had not earned the coins he carried, or the worshippers who bowed to him. None of the luxuries of this hidden underworld belonged to him. It was all charity.

The Alashani and their messiah prophecy had shackled Ariock, in a way.

This underground prison was a lot more subtle than the Torth arena. It was like his growth disorder, which used to constrain every aspect of his life. It seemed he had always lived in caves. The idea that he could simply walk away and exit this place and travel to other worlds...it almost felt like too much freedom. But Ariock felt sure the universe was full of unexplored niches.

Somewhere, he would find a place where he and Thomas could truly fit in.

# CHAPTER 10

# RIVER OF TEARS

Activity surrounded Chaniyelem's palace. Nussians loaded industrial sacks or stoneware jugs onto wagons. Albinos wore hiking backpacks loaded with supplies, and couriers rushed between labor crews.

Ariock didn't like what he was seeing. It looked like preparation for a major exodus.

A familiar ummin emerged from the hubbub. Kessa wore her own hiking pack, and she looked relieved to see friends. "Thomas," she said. "How are you?"

Thomas's brows made a shrugging motion.

"I could not dissuade Chaniyelem," Kessa reported, shifting her attention to Ariock. "She insists on sending you off with worshippers and a lot of help. Plus, many people wish to follow you. Pilgrims. Spiritualists. Anyone who is looking for light and glory."

Ariock stared at the worshippers in stunned dismay. How was he supposed to sneak into Stratower City while being trailed by a baggage train?

It wouldn't work.

Like his famous great-grandfather, Ariock needed to forge a stealthy new identity and spend the rest of his life in hiding. If a single Torth learned about the Alashani…? Instead of light and glory, they'd get death and slavery.

"I'm not bringing them," Ariock said pointedly.

Kessa looked pained.

Ariock bent to address her. "Will you please find Chaniyelem? Tell her I appreciate all her help, but I don't want luggage or fanfare. Just some travel supplies. That's all."

Kessa studied him. "It is not a bad thing, to have help."

"It *is* bad," Ariock said, frustrated. How could Kessa be so wise and so obtuse at the same time? "I'm failing Chaniyelem and all her people," he tried to explain. "It isn't fair for me to take advantage of Alashani beliefs. Anyway, I can't get anywhere with so much stuff following me around."

Ariock gently set Thomas down atop a barrel, freeing up his hands so he could pull off his Yeresunsa mantle. It was a useless garment. He would use it as packaging.

"Ariock," Kessa said.

He looked at her, wondering why she hadn't gone to find the high councilor. Did she expect him to beg?

"Ariock," Kessa said, "I respect you. But..." She clicked her beak. "You are wrong to insult the Alashani."

"How am I insulting them?" Ariock asked, annoyed.

"You shook the Alashani when you arrived on this world," Kessa said. "You put them at great risk by breaking their laws."

Ariock used his powers to tear the golden cuffs off his wrists. He didn't need ornaments.

"Now you worsen that risk by leaving," Kessa went on. "Their doomsday might happen because of you. Chaniyelem knows this. Yet even so, she honors you, as much as she can."

Ariock let go of his Yeresunsa awareness in surprise. Kessa was right. He had been so angry at the mistreatment of Thomas, he'd completely forgotten that Thomas did actually pose a legitimate threat to Alashani civilization.

"Must you insist on kicking sand in their faces while they say goodbye?" Kessa said. "You can leave them with fears and uncertainties. Or you can leave them with peace." She folded her arms. "I think you should dismiss the luggage when you are near the Torth realm. Let them understand why."

Ariock's shoulders slumped. Kessa had very valid points.

And anyway, he didn't have time to argue about luggage. He had more important concerns, like Thomas's medicine. Flen had better be fetching the case out of the dungeon.

"All right," Ariock agreed with reluctance. "They can follow me for a while. But I'm not going to slow down."

"You should stay in Hufti," Thomas said with vehemence. He switched to English, so none of the eavesdropping worshippers could understand. "The Torth have death traps around Stratower City. You shouldn't even try to cross the border river. You don't have a prayer of getting into the spaceport. Not on foot."

"We'll figure out a way." Ariock suspected that Thomas could brainstorm ways to steal Torth vehicles, if he really put his mind to it.

And Thomas might not be aware of how much Ariock's skills had improved. Jinishta had taught him how to supercharge his own strength and agility by infusing his body with Yeresunsa power. He should be capable of leaping hundreds of feet or running up towers. Nighttime and rainfall should hide him from sight. He even had enough excess power to levitate platforms, if he needed a way to fly with his friends.

They should be fine. He would just avoid epic battles.

"You'll have people slowing you down," Thomas said with an edge to his voice. "Like Vy. And especially me. It's too much."

"We can't stay here," Ariock said. "There's no choice but to leave. We'll go to one of those reject planets."

"If we get caught," Thomas said, "the Alashani won't survive. Everyone here will be enslaved or murdered."

Did Thomas want Ariock to feel hopeless?

Well, too bad. Defeatism might have worked on Ariock a few months ago. He had grown since then.

"We won't get caught." Ariock tried to feel confident about that. Surely the Torth had relaxed their vigilance? After two months, they should have forgotten all about their escaped gladiator and renegade supergenius.

"The Torth regret having let Jonathan Stead get away," Thomas said. "They'll be keeping watch, guaranteed. The Torth Empire never makes the same mistake twice."

"So we'll be extra careful." Ariock scanned the wagons for a place to put Thomas. He didn't necessarily want the boy responding to his every thought.

He found a wagon with some extra room, and he began to make Thomas comfortable there, padding blankets around the boy.

"*Aonswa?*" a workman asked in a reverential tone. "Chaniyelem paid me to be your guide."

Ariock turned to assess the albino who wore drab woolens, like a common workman.

"I am Gav." The workman tipped his cap in a gesture of respect.

Thomas explained, rasping from the effort, "Gav is a long-distance courier. He can guide you to the final exit along the underground waterway, the River of Tears. That's the closest exit to Stratower City."

Gav backpedaled, watching Thomas with wary curiosity.

"He won't hurt you," Ariock assured the courier.

As he processed Thomas's explanation, he remembered that the Alashani realm included thirteen cities, plus smaller settlements, all of it underground. Yeresunsa must have done quite a lot of tunneling over countless generations.

Kessa leaned in. "I have heard that the route along the River of Tears is safer and faster than traveling aboveground through the dead city."

Ariock imagined a comfortable walkway with rest stops. That did sound a lot better than wading through pitch-black ruins full of sludge serpents and wild zoved.

"Thank you," he told Gav. "But I'll want to travel fast. Is that okay?"

Gav looked at the massive baggage train and laughed. "You set the pace, Messiah." He walked away, shaking his head.

Other friends began to show up. Pung. Weptolyso and Yuey. Ariock's albino cousins, each of whom wanted to hug him and weigh him down with gifts.

"I, uh, will not be traveling with you." Pung looked down in shame. "I am so sorry." He began to offer excuses—"I owe Councilor Karyum a great sum of money," and "I promised to teach Vodov and Naru how to shoot blaster gloves"—until Ariock stopped him with a gentle hug.

"You are wise to stay here," Ariock assured the smuggler. "I respect you for it, and I'm happy for you. There's absolutely no need to apologize."

Pung bent his knees, Alashani-style. He walked away with a lightness in his steps, as if a burden had been lifted.

There were refugees from Duin, and chambermaids, and councilors, including Chaniyelem. Vy joined the commotion, slowed down by her own parade of farewells. A male attendant carried her luggage.

As the departure got underway, Ariock became keenly aware of who had not showed up.

Where were Cherise and Flen?

Where was Jinishta?

Not a single warrior had shown up. Ariock really hoped Jinishta was relaxing somewhere and not holding an angry rally.

He found one of his matronly albino cousins. "The next time you see your sister Jinishta…" Ariock had to collect his thoughts. "Will you please tell her that I appreciate every lesson she gave me?"

If only he could apologize for the stress he'd brought to Jinishta and her people. It seemed wrong to burden a proxy with those sentiments, so he just said, "I wish we had been able to say goodbye to each other."

Jinishta's sister gave him a look of empathy and a promising nod.

"Ariock?" Vy made her way to him. "I just heard from a courier. Cherise will meet us on our way out, at the aqueduct."

Ariock didn't like that.

"I trust her," Vy said, reassuring. "I'm sure she'll have Thomas's medicine." She glanced toward Thomas, who was bundled up on a wagon. "Can I ride with him?"

"Of course." Ariock helped her climb aboard. "Mind if we get going?" He feared that Chaniyelem would arrange a banquet and a dance if he stayed for much longer.

"Sure." Vy seemed intent on inspecting her foster brother. She touched each of his ankles. "I'm seeing signs of kidney failure." She frowned at Ariock. "I thought you healed him?"

"I did," Ariock replied. "Several times." Just in case, he gave Thomas a refresher healing. Then he spread his awareness.

To his dismay, Thomas's life spark was still guttering.

Thomas laughed weakly. "You can play messiah, but you can't play God. You left me in that pit for too long."

Ariock exchanged a look with Vy. She looked almost as guilty as he felt.

"I think he needs to be on dialysis," Vy said in English.

"You mean, like, in a hospital?" Ariock asked.

Vy gave a solemn nod.

Ariock straightened, determined to hide his frustration. He would save Thomas. He just needed some tips from Orla, perhaps. He should have spent time learning from the Yeresunsa healer instead of training solely as a warrior.

"I'll send someone to find Orla," Ariock said. "And I'm sure Thomas will benefit from a dose of NAI-12."

Vy looked uncertain, but she nodded.

"We'll get going." Ariock picked up the wagon handles and began to haul it down the cobblestone street. That seemed to signal the entire baggage train. Dozens of wagons and rickshaws lurched into motion, hauled by nussians, following him.

"Let us take this burden, Ariock," Weptolyso said. It seemed that he and his girlfriend, Yuey, were offering to haul the lead wagon.

"Thank you." Ariock let the pair of nussians take over, although he felt a sense of shame, knowing that he would later ask these friends to stay underground.

He spoke to workers, asking them to find Orla. But only two followers seemed eager to obey. Everyone else wanted to stick with the messiah and follow him anywhere.

And the number of followers seemed larger every time Ariock glanced around.

There were starry-eyed adventurers, scholars, and spirituals. There were common laborers and their merchant employers. Ariock even saw children riding on wagons, accompanying their parents. Did they think the messiah was hiking toward a fun vacation instead of deadly danger?

"*Aonswa?*" a maidservant called. "I packed extra spears with your tunics. Would you like those to be readily accessible?"

Someone else yelled, "*Aonswa!* The city water isn't working, so I failed to obtain as many water casks as required. Would you sanction ale on this journey? We have plenty of that."

Beer? On a march toward a Torth-ruled city?

People kept shouting out, begging the messiah for his attention. They wanted his authority, his favors, or his blessings.

Ariock wished he could tell them to go home. Stay safe. But he could already tell that most of them would ignore that command. It would turn into an argument, which he didn't have time for.

Hopefully they would leave during the march to the surface. A few minor hardships should scare them away.

Or perhaps some lightning bolts?

He just didn't want to shepherd a bunch of religious fanatics.

"Kessa?" Ariock found her among a group of ummin refugees from Duin. "Will you do me a favor?"

Kessa gave him a questioning look.

"Will you lead these worshippers?" Ariock asked. "I mean, handle their questions and keep them from causing problems with each other?"

Kessa gave him a skeptical look of helplessness, and Ariock could have kicked himself. Why was he trying to burden a friend?

Well, he guessed he trusted Kessa with leadership. She had led their shipwrecked crew through the dead city. If not for her, Ariock suspected they would have lost a lot more lives along the way.

"Never mind," he said, apologetic. "Sorry."

"I am willing," Kessa said carefully. "But no one will obey a runaway slave." She pointed to the scar around her wrinkled neck, as if it was a mark of shame.

"Oh. Right." Ariock was fed up with Alashani snootiness toward slaves and former slaves. "Would you mind if I change that?"

"What do you mean?" Kessa asked.

Ariock augmented his voice with flows of air. "Everyone!" he announced. "Kessa the Wise is braver and wiser than most people, including me. If you have any more questions for me? Bring them to her. I would be pleased if you obey any request that Kessa has. She speaks on my behalf."

Kessa stared at him in shock. The refugees gawked, beaks open.

Ariock gave Kessa a nod of gratitude. He outpaced her, hoping that he hadn't given her a bigger task than she could handle.

Gav led the whole procession. The rush of an unseen river echoed in the distance, down a steep, winding street. A clean, watery scent misted the air.

Ariock paused for one last look back at the city of Hufti. Alleys spread out like a maze. The grotto fountains that should be burbling with water were dry, and Ariock tried not to ponder what that implied. No one was manning the aqueduct.

Were the Yeresunsa donning battle gear?

The procession marched downhill, and Ariock went with them, past door lintels of jade or onyx, past shrines to the Lady of Sorrow or the Lord of Thieves or the Maiden of Candlelight. The lamplit underworld glimmered like buried treasure. It was even more vibrant than electric human cities, or neon Torth metropolises, in its own way.

It was beautiful.

*My people*, Ariock thought with a little swell of pride. *Let the Alashani survive for all eternity.*

Twinned colonnades soared to a distant ceiling. Candelabra filled notches, so the misty air glowed with a flickering golden light. Far above, lost in shadows, Ariock could just make out hints of the ancient Alashani pretzel script.

The River of Tears flowed around a U-shaped bend, majestic and dark. Bioluminescent eels and cave fish wriggled in its depths. Ariock knew that this river was the most powerful force imaginable to Alashani denizens. It connected all life and all cities in their underworld. He had never visited this section of the river, but its gateway was imposing. It led to a stone bridge. And across that bridge, on the far side of the river...

A horde of black-clad albinos clogged the bridge.

These were not merchants or artisans. Quivers with spears bristled above their shoulders. Black gauntlets protected their arms, and black-wrapped leather padded their chests. Only Yeresunsa who had sworn the Warrior's Pact were deemed worthy of such gear. Even their lips and eyes were outlined with black makeup. Their lanterns reflected in the water, illuminating sharp stalactites that hung from the ceiling.

Jinishta stood at the head of the army.

"Your road ends here," Jinishta told Ariock, her voice amplified by power, loud enough to carry across the river. "The *rekveh* must be questioned. Put him into our custody. Or you will die."

# CHAPTER 11

# LIFE OR DEATH

Ariock met his cousin's angry glare. Was this the send-off that Jinishta wanted to give him?

It was a declaration of war. It was just as stupid and needless as the Torth Majority's decision to hunt and kill Ariock.

"I cannot allow you to destroy us." Jinishta planted her fists on her hips, defiant. Her mantle hung loose on her chest, black instead of purple. "We have shown you our faces and our homes. Our lanterns. Our laughter. If you get captured by Torth, they will destroy everything we love. They will murder us."

"I will not get caught by the Torth." Ariock had to raise his voice to be heard across the river.

Jinishta looked disparaging. "We had to rescue you from the Torth. Remember?"

Ariock was all too aware that he was backed up by soft civilians and disabled friends. Jinishta had an army of hardened warriors at her back.

"I saved you," Jinishta said. "Orla healed you." She gestured, and Ariock recognized the teenaged healer standing at the fringe of the army, her mantle purple because she had not yet sworn the Warrior's Pact. She looked embarrassed.

"Orla." Ariock wondered how he might persuade her to help Thomas.

"There is a reason why we do not allow irresponsible, half-trained children to run into danger," Jinishta admonished. "You are a threat to everyone who values freedom."

Her condemnation cut deep, perhaps because Ariock recognized truth in what she said.

He hiked to the foot of the bridge, so he could face Jinishta and her army more directly. "You swore an oath to protect the Alashani," he called. "I swore an oath to protect my friends. And I take my oaths as seriously as you do."

Jinishta's face hardened.

Ariock's own expression hardened as well. "Thomas saved my life several times over. I will not abandon him."

The warriors looked ready to attack. Vy and Kessa looked like they wanted to intervene. Weptolyso snorted a warning, spikes popping out.

"Isn't that—?"

"Make way!"

"Cherise?" Vy said.

Ariock turned to see Flen and Cherise hurrying under the immense gateway for the city. The NAI-12 case looked like an alien relic on this world, it was so obviously from Earth. Flen cradled the thing.

"Don't!" Cherise begged. "Give it to me, Flen? Please?"

"Send it to me, Flen," Jinishta called from across the river.

A look of misery came over Flen. He stopped at the stone-lipped embankment, clutching the briefcase. He looked from Cherise to his premier, back and forth.

"Come on." Cherise held out her hands to receive it.

"Throw it to me," Jinishta demanded. "Now, Flen."

Even with a Yeresunsa power boost, a throw across the river might fail. The rough water could break the delicate injection pen and glass vials.

"No," Ariock said.

Flen made the wrong choice.

Ariock could see his intentions even before he gathered his resolve and flung the briefcase. Jinishta stretched out her hand to catch it.

Ariock reached out with his awareness and seized the airborne medicine in an airy embrace.

Determined forces attempted to wrest the case out of his mental grasp. They yanked hard. Ariock shoved them away. Stalactites broke off from the ceiling, hit by tumultuous air.

"You have no right!" Jinishta said through gritted teeth.

She used to sound apologetic and kind, but now she was toying with Thomas's life.

So much for family and friendship and religious worship. Ariock knew that he would never earn Jinishta's respect.

But he had strength. The warriors had better respect that, if nothing else. He was done with gentle niceties.

He split his focus. Part of him held on to the briefcase while another part of him gathered water into a tidal wave.

The threat seemed to be enough. Some of the warriors got unnerved, and Ariock let the wave splash down, causing yells of distress. The briefcase hurtled into his gigantic grasp.

"Ariock." Jinishta sounded desperate. "You must let us take custody of the *rekveh!*"

"I don't want to hurt you," Ariock growled in her direction. He handed the NAI-12 case to Vy and immediately shielded her and Thomas with a wall of pressurized air, plus his own body.

Vy unlatched the lid. She did not hesitate, not even to share a look of triumph. Ariock loved her for that. She was devoted to saving the life of her foster brother, the same way Ariock could focus on constructing a suit of armor.

"Are you going to force us to fight you?" Jinishta demanded.

"Get out of my way," Ariock said. "Take your army and leave."

At least some of Jinishta's warriors looked unnerved. Perhaps they did not want to defy their messiah? They might love Jinishta, but some of them must be thinking that she was wrong.

"Ariock," Vy said softly.

Ariock glanced at her. He glimpsed the interior of the medicine case, full of glass vials, row after row, some right side up and some upside down. Every vial was empty or missing.

Vy ejected the cartridge from the injection pen. Empty. There was no vial inside.

She dug into cushy pockets to pull out fallen vials. They were all empty.

"There's no medicine." Vy held the case so he could see.

Jinishta continued to talk, alternately pleading for Ariock's attention and demanding it. He tuned her out. Seeing the empty vials, he understood. He should have suspected this weeks ago.

Months ago.

The "care" for Thomas had been pretense. A show. Jinishta and her warriors had faked concern for Thomas, just to keep the big, gullible giant happy.

"It's gone," Vy said.

Thomas had been getting sicker—for how many weeks?—and not a single one of the cowardly, puny Alashani warriors had mentioned the fact that his regular injections were no longer happening.

And Ariock had been stupid enough to believe their empty reassurances.

He seized the neck of the nearest Alashani, who happened to be Flen. When he slammed Flen against an ancient stone column, cracks formed from the impact. Rocks fell.

Ariock used his powers to cushion Flen, just enough to prevent his bones from snapping.

"When did his medicine run out?" Ariock was going to force these warriors to admit to what sort of jailers they were.

People were screaming for him to stop. Not Flen. The warrior couldn't breathe. He struggled in Ariock's one-handed grip, legs kicking, and unable to reach the floor.

"How did you really treat Thomas?" Ariock loosened his grip enough for Flen to draw a gasping breath. "How long as he been going without his medicine?"

"It was not Flen," Jinishta called. She had ventured onto the bridge. "Please let him go."

Her soothing tone, like a sister addressing a foolish brother, usually put Ariock at ease and made him feel normal. But she had no right to be so cavalier. The sight of Thomas looking so deathly ill filled Ariock with helpless rage.

Jinishta didn't care about anyone's suffering unless that person was Alashani. She had no concept of what it was like to hang from a metal cross in an alien desert, alone and dying. If she had ever valued Ariock, as a cousin and a friend, then she would have thanked Thomas and treated him like a human being.

More than anything else, Ariock was angry at himself. Thomas was dying, and it was ultimately his fault. He had made a promise.

And he had proven to be a colossal failure.

"Ariock." Vy sounded scared. "Calm down."

Ariock became aware of the sound of the river, more thunderous than it had been. Runnels of water cascaded over one another, responding to his taut nerves. Objects floated in his vicinity. Pots, blankets, lanterns, even carriages. Wheels spun, weightless.

Ariock's awareness had spread far beyond his body without him realizing it.

Everyone else had noticed. His followers muttered worriedly to each other. Weptolyso's spines retracted and expanded in a nussian sign of anxiety.

Ariock carefully withdrew his Yeresunsa connection from the rock walls and the water. The river surged. The bridge groaned, and cracks formed in the cavern ceiling as he let go.

"Explain." Ariock let out a slow, furious breath. "How long has Thomas been missing his medicine, while you told me lies?"

Jinishta pursed her tiny lips. No doubt she was concocting a false answer.

Ariock felt dangerously close to losing control. His attention kept lashing out, wanting to fill the cave and the river. Was Flen urinating in his pants? Liquid pattered down. Ariock had almost forgotten that the warrior still dangled from his grip.

Thomas's hoarse voice caught his attention. "…medicine ran out. Two months ago."

Two months?

Ariock's mind reeled from the betrayal of Jinishta. That was far too long for Thomas to go without his medicine.

"There wasn't much left to begin with," Thomas said.

"I'm sorry we didn't tell you," Jinishta said. "But you must realize that a serum cannot save his life. Surely you realize that?"

A serum? As if NAI-12 was just some herbal tea.

"You have no idea what you're talking about." Ariock's fury whipped into the river and spiked into rocks. It seemed the only person brave enough to offer truthful answers was Thomas.

Ariock let go of Flen and went to the boy. He barely noticed Flen crying out in pain as he dropped several feet to the floor.

"They did give me the last few injections." Thomas lay curled up and weak, packed in blankets. His chest sounded congested. "But Ariock? I was spacing out the doses even before…before they got me. The Upward Governess used up most of my supply. There was barely a week's worth left by the time…" Thomas closed his eyes from the effort of speaking. "By the time we were in the streamship."

"Why didn't anyone tell me?" Ariock begged to know.

Thomas drew another painstaking breath. "Well, look how you react." He opened his eyes long enough to meet Ariock's gaze. Unbelievably, there was humor in his yellow eyes.

He actually thought his own death was funny.

Ariock gripped the wagon's guardrails. The iron bent in his massive fists. Thomas possessed the knowledge to pilot an interstellar ship—to take them anywhere in the galaxy—but instead, he wanted to bend his intelligence toward suicide. What a monstrous waste.

Well, Ariock would keep his promise, no matter what.

They were not going to be stranded on this primitive world. He had to get Thomas to a spaceship, fast. Then they would make a quick, furtive stopover on Earth to get a resupply of NAI-12. It was feasible. Ariock would find a way to make Thomas live. He would force it to happen.

"How long will you survive?" Ariock asked.

Thomas tried to answer and coughed weakly.

Ariock used his powers to gently work air into Thomas's lungs. He healed the boy again.

Then he realized that Thomas was actually laughing.

"A week at most," Thomas said. "Probably less? My internal organs are shutting down. Everything is atrophied. Lungs can't expand. Digestion is off." He gave Ariock a smug grin. "And there is absolutely nothing you can do to save me."

Ariock didn't know if it was possible to get to Earth in under a week, but it was worth the effort.

He couldn't waste a second. He wouldn't sleep until he had ransacked the Rasa Biotech vault and taken all the medicine.

"You failed, Messiah," Thomas said.

"You will live," Ariock said.

Thomas closed his eyes, still grinning like a triumphant corpse. "Migyatel was wrong about me. There's no way I'll… Never mind. It's impossible." He chuckled. "Not going to live." His tone became regretful. "Wish I could have rescued the Lady of Sorrow, though. I hope someone saves her."

Ariock turned away from the suicidal boy. He faced the army that blocked the bridge and the road beyond.

"We should have told you," Jinishta admitted. "But I was asked to deceive you. I am very sorry."

Yeah, right. Asked by who? Jinishta was the ultimate authority in the city of Hufti, unless one counted Chaniyelem. And Ariock knew that the high councilor who had hosted him would not have gone behind his back in such an underhanded way.

He expanded his awareness upward. Up and up and up. He sampled the stormy surface of the planet, where shrieking winds and sleet pummeled the skeletal ruins of skyscrapers.

He could join that wind, even from this distance. He could become a tornado of epic proportions. Maybe he could even expand larger. He could probably wreck a path of destruction through Stratower City. Maybe he could bring Thomas to the spaceport ultrafast?

Only he did not want to hurt innocent slaves.

Also, a storm would warn his enemies of his impending arrival and give them time to prepare. Bad idea. Sneakiness was the best approach to exiting this miserable planet.

Ariock snapped back to his body.

"Get out of my way," he told Jinishta and her warriors.

His tone echoed through the cavern like thunder. He had fought armies tougher than the Yeresunsa who blocked his path.

# CHAPTER 12

# AN ARMY AT HIS HEELS

Ariock was done wasting time on stubborn Alashani and their stupid beliefs. He picked up the wagon handles and strode across the bridge.

The warriors seemed to decide that fighting him wasn't worthwhile. They scrambled to get out of his way.

"This isn't over," Jinishta said in a challenging tone. She spoke to her warriors in the mushy Alashani language, and Ariock recognized quotes from the messiah prophecy. He had heard it enough times.

The warriors picked up travel packs. It seemed they had come prepared for a trek.

Or a pursuit.

Ariock realized what was happening. Jinishta would ensure that their messiah would leave "with an army at his heels," thus fulfilling that line of the prophecy. What nonsense.

"Where is Gav?" Ariock demanded.

The courier raced to catch up to him. "Messiah?"

"How quickly can you lead me to the edge of the Torth city?" Ariock asked.

Gav was reliable, because he did not even hesitate. He seemed respectful rather than afraid. "I have made that journey in three pendulum orbits, *Aonswa*," he said. "But for a group this large? It may take six."

Six days. Thomas could be dead by then.

"I'll do it in one." Ariock sped up. "Lead the way." If the families and slow travelers fell behind, that was for the best.

As Gav loped ahead, Weptolyso drew close. "Will you allow me and Yuey to haul the wagon?" he offered.

"I've got it," Ariock told his nussian friend. Whoever hauled the wagon would set the pace, and he could haul faster than anyone. "You would be better off staying behind. Anyone who follows me to the surface of his planet will likely die."

Weptolyso let out a wet snort of determination. "I have seen far too many nussians who are puppets at the whims of Torth. If you are destined to defeat many Torth, then I can show my kindred a better way of living. Some truths are worth the risk of death."

"I'm not the messiah," Ariock said.

The nussian swiveled his reddish eyes with a doubtful look. "Certainty," he said, "is not the same as truth."

That was Kessa's favorite catchphrase. As an adherent of the Code of Gwat, Kessa tried not to make presumptions or jump to conclusions. She avoided certainty on esoteric matters. Ariock gritted his teeth, but he wasn't going to debate slave ideology.

Instead, he amplified his voice so that everyone could hear. "I cannot guarantee anyone's safety. If you've traveled with me before, then you understand the dangers I'm heading into. Please turn around and go home if you value your lives."

No one heeded his warning. The hangers-on kept on marching behind him. Even with the thunderous river, Ariock heard a great many footsteps and creaking wagons in his wake.

"Cherise is coming," Vy said, twisting around to look behind them.

"She should stay behind, too," Ariock said. He inwardly had to admit that he wasn't sure he wanted company from someone with loyalties to the Alashani warriors, even if she was originally from Earth. Cherise might just try to sabotage him or slow him down.

"This is needless," Thomas said in his raspy, weak voice. "You should stay underground. I promised to bring you to a place of safety or die trying. You promised to protect me no matter what. Which one of us kept his promise?"

Ouch.

Ariock was humiliated, but he assured himself that Thomas was only partly right. It wasn't over. Thomas might be dying, but he had a secondary medical supply in Boston, on Earth. Also…

"Where is Orla?" Ariock looked at the worshippers keeping pace with him. "Will someone find her and ask her to come here?"

An albino stepped into view, hurrying to keep pace with his strides. But it wasn't Orla.

Jinishta managed to glare at him even while she walked rapidly. "Orla cannot heal your *rekveh*," she said. "No one can. Mortals like us cannot stand in the way of the Lady of Sorrow when she calls for a soul."

"I thought you believe that *rekvehs* don't have souls?" Vy asked from the wagon.

"I am uncertain about your Thomas." Jinishta shrugged, looking ashamed. "Maybe he saw the Lady of Sorrow. But whether she touched him or not, anyone can see that he is near death. There is no serum, no ointment, that can possibly outdo what the best healers in the world can do."

"Thomas invented it." Ariock wasn't going explain medical science to a cave dweller. He barely understood the medicine himself.

The River of Tears rushed past the walkway, its waters as pure as snowmelt. Ariock had to duck his head every so often to dodge stalactites.

"I wish I had told you." Jinishta strode fast to keep his pace, although she avoided going near the wagon with Thomas in it. "I am very sorry." Her tone softened. "I could not say a word without betraying Migyatel."

Ariock's grip on the wagon handles tightened, making indents in the soft corkwood. He wished Jinishta would stop making excuses. He wasn't as gullible as she assumed him to be.

"Migyatel sent me a missive, soon after you arrived," Jinishta said. "She begged me not to let you discover that your *rekveh* friend had run out of medicine."

So she was blaming the dead prophet? How noble.

"It's true," another warrior called from behind the wagon.

How many of Jinishta's loyal warriors had known that the NAI-12 medicine was depleted? Probably all of them. It was probably common knowledge among Thomas's jailers.

And not a single one had communicated the problem to the people who cared.

"I don't believe you." Ariock's voice came out heavy and cold, insulated from the shards of glass that seemed to be grinding up his heart.

Jinishta looked ready to defend her poor excuse.

Let her try. Ariock was ready to shove her and her whole army into the water. He slowed, then stopped in the middle of the walkway.

"I don't want your company," he told Jinishta. "I'm not your messiah, and I'm not feeling friendly. You pretended to care about my friend. I can't trust you."

Kessa's unassuming voice broke through the tension. "Ariock? There is way we can find out, for certain, how trustworthy Jinishta is."

It took Ariock a moment to catch on to what she meant.

When the idea hit him, it felt like a refreshing drink. "Of course," he realized. "We have a mind reader."

What little color was in Jinishta's face drained away. Her albino skin became as chalky as her hair. She backed away.

Ariock had no sympathy. "Come on," he invited. "Stand close to Thomas. I trust him. Let him tell me whether you're telling the truth or not."

Thomas was propped up, encircled by blankets and pillows so he wouldn't topple over. Despite his illness, he looked eager. "That's right," he said to Jinishta. "Come a little bit closer."

Other warriors hurried away.

Jinishta stopped herself, frozen with what looked like uncertainty. She dared not take her gaze off the threat posed by Thomas, but she looked at

Ariock from the corner of her vision. "You trust that *rekveh*?" she asked him in a pained tone. "Over me?"

"He's never lied to me," Ariock pointed out. "You have."

Jinishta studied her former prisoner, no doubt recalling every horror story about the fearsome monsters known as Torth. Torth could paralyze their victims with pain seizures. Torth could eat souls.

"I won't torture you," Thomas said. "At least, not without Ariock's permission."

"He won't hurt you," Ariock said, impatient. Maybe he should ask Jinishta to become the first Alashani to hug a *rekveh*? Ha. That would show true bravery.

Instead, he said, "You claim that you weren't intentionally trying to kill my friend. If that's true, then let Thomas judge your mind. That will be all the proof I need."

He expected more excuses. Jinishta wouldn't have the guts to own up to her lies, or to face her superstitious fears about mind readers.

To his surprise, though, she took a fortifying breath and walked timidly to the wagon. She stopped once she was within the outer limit of Thomas's range.

"Tell him," Jinishta snarled. "And you had better not tell lies, *rekveh*."

Thomas did not respond right away. He watched Jinishta with hungry fascination, like the most attentive student in the universe. He was likely collating knowledge, learning everything Jinishta knew about the Alashani culture. Maybe he could compare it with whatever he'd soaked up from Migyatel in the seconds before she died.

"Well?" Jinishta clenched her fists. "Hurry up and tell him what Migyatel told me."

Thomas leaned back, languid and satisfied. "Hmm… Interesting."

Jinishta's eyes widened with outrage.

She was probably playing an imagined scenario in her mind, trying to prove her innocence, but Thomas wasn't cooperating. He kept on absorbing her thoughts.

Just as Ariock considered how he might hurry things along, Thomas spoke.

"Yeah," Thomas said at a leisurely pace. "Three pendulum orbits after we arrived, a courier showed up at the Yeresunsa monastery. Apparently the prophet Migyatel sent him. She did warn Jinishta and other local Yeresunsa to keep quiet about my medicine running out."

Jinishta leaped backward with acrobatic agility, putting herself beyond Thomas's telepathy range. She gave Ariock a look of wounded triumph. "I did not know you well at that time, Ariock," she explained. "The prophet implied that you would be angry—and very dangerous to all of Alashani civilization— if you found out."

So it was true.

"I am sorry." Jinishta sounded sincere. "I just did not know how to trust you. And once I did? It seemed far too late to mention it."

Ariock's shoulders slumped. He supposed the prophet had been correct about his angry reaction, even if she'd just been guessing blindly.

Thomas went on. "Jinishta invited that courier into her cozy private office, and they shared a few cups of blue-pepper tea. The courier brought other news. For instance, Migyatel sent well wishes to Jinishta's great-uncle Fayut. I gathered that he's a distant cousin of Migyatel's family."

Jinishta backed farther away, and farther still, staring at the mind reader with newfound terror. She had no way to know that he'd already soaked up her memories. She must fear that she was still within his range.

"Migyatel predicted that Fayut would recover from his cough," Thomas said.

"That's enough," Jinishta interrupted.

"Also," Thomas said, "Migyatel did actually direct Jinishta to protect and care for the *rekveh*. I find that remarkably strange. I don't know what induced her to say that."

Ariock folded his arms. He still felt duped and betrayed, but maybe it wasn't as extreme as he'd guessed. The prophet had wielded huge influence. Jinishta was more skeptical than most of her people, but she was, after all, an Alashani.

"Well." Ariock picked up the wagon handles. "Thank you for telling me, Jinishta." He began to haul the wagon, slow at first. It would be nice to part with his cousin as a friend, rather than as enemies.

"You have not sworn the Warrior's Pact." Jinishta's contrition turned to determination. "Your stubborn foolishness is likely to condemn us all."

His stubborn foolishness? Ariock glanced at the massive army behind him, cluelessly marching toward dangers which they could scarcely imagine. These people had never seen transports or missiles or kamikaze nussian slaves. Most of them had never even experienced the rain-soaked night.

"You might as well turn around and go home." Ariock picked up his pace. "Will you please send Orla up here? I want her advice."

"You are the messiah," Jinishta said. "People will follow you no matter what. There will be more from other cities who join your army. It is my duty to protect the Alashani realm. So I cannot let you go aboveground without swearing the Pact."

The suicide pact.

Ariock thought of arguments. He could tell Jinishta how stupid their prophecy was. He could explain that the best way for Jinishta to protect her people was to go home and prevent any more from following him.

But Thomas needed medicine, fast. Ariock sensed his life spark wavering.

"I don't have time for Alashani ceremonies." Ariock sped up, his long legs carrying him at a natural speed that was difficult for anyone else to maintain, even though he was hauling a wagon. "Go away."

He marched upstream. The river roared out of some unknown source beneath Stratower City. Perhaps it really was composed of tears? No one knew for certain. But it was pure, and it hosted life. Bioluminescent alien fish and creatures played in its depths.

"You cannot change the course of prophecy," Jinishta said. "It is like the River of Tears." She gestured. "More powerful than any of us. You say you are not the messiah, but a true prophet has foretold your future. It will happen."

# CHAPTER 13

# WORTH IT

Cherise wended past creaking wagons. She jogged past albino hikers, some of whom were so exhausted, they resembled ghouls. People took turns sleeping in wagons, but Ariock himself never slowed down. None of the overburdened wagons would hold him, anyway.

Flen was more haggard than most. He said the whole messianic army was crazy. Cherise had told him about the inhibitor serum, and he said that if the Torth could truly disable Yeresunsa powers, then no one should go aboveground ever again.

He had a good point.

Flen's feelings were sour and getting worse. Cherise hadn't realized how much he was complaining until she'd run ahead to catch up with her friends from Earth.

She wasn't exactly sure why she wanted to visit Thomas. Perhaps to say farewell?

When she caught up with the lead wagon, she found Thomas, Kessa, and Vy all sound asleep. Cherise hiked alongside them and tried to collect her thoughts.

The Torth Empire had not invaded the Alashani underworld. That meant Thomas had not alerted his Torth brethren in the Megacosm. He was purposely protecting people like Flen—his jailers—from enslavement and disaster.

Why?

Maybe Thomas really did respect the so-called slave species. The Alashani had a secret world. A way of loving. They were superior to the Torth in many ways, and maybe Thomas recognized that.

After a while, Thomas opened his yellow eyes. He regarded Cherise.

"You're protecting us," Cherise acknowledged.

"Always," Thomas said, his voice weak.

He wasn't a monster. Cherise felt torn, after months of hearing propaganda that painted him as evil. Her rescuer did exist. Her friend. Her protector.

"I can't protect you," Thomas said, "if Ariock brings a bunch of clueless Alashani into the Torth realm. That will doom everyone here. He should stay underground."

"Isn't doom a part of the prophecy?" Cherise wondered. She was certain that Migyatel had mentioned an upcoming doom.

"It's common sense," Thomas said. "Never mind prophecy."

Ariock marched onward, focused on the road.

"Tell him," Thomas said. "I'm not worth it."

Cherise felt very small compared with Ariock, and that was not just due to their size difference. There was a power difference.

Nevertheless, she sprinted to catch up with him. "Ariock?"

Ariock looked down at her, heavy brows hooding his brooding eyes.

"You'll attract Torth attention if you go aboveground," Cherise said. "Thomas doesn't want that."

Ariock contemplated her for a while. Behind them, wagon axles creaked. Lamps bobbed like distant fireflies, their glow reflected by the underground river.

Not many people spoke to the *aonswa* this way. Flen certainly wouldn't. The way Flen told it, Ariock had strangled him and nearly suffocated him. It was only by sheer accident that Ariock had gotten distracted and let go. Flen had needed to change into a spare pair of trousers afterward.

But Cherise didn't think Ariock was all that cruel. Or all that stupid.

She straightened with more certainty. "You would endanger everyone. The Alashani. And Earth. All for Thomas?"

Ariock gave it some thought. He offered a helpless shrug, and a nod, and he never stopped walking. "I made a promise."

There was more to it, Cherise saw. Guilt. Ariock felt responsible for the way Thomas had suffered, and he was trying to make up for months of negligence.

And maybe Ariock believed that he could fix any problem, or rescue anyone in need. He seemed to have infinite endurance. Whenever Jinishta had predicted that her pupil would fail at something, he'd outshone her expectations. According to Vy, normal limitations did not apply to Ariock. He was different.

So perhaps a part of Ariock really believed that he was a savior?

Beyond all that, Cherise recognized grim determination when she saw it.

No one had been able to talk Thomas out of inventing NAI-12. Cherise used to bring him food or whatever he needed. She had helped him to succeed in spite of the naysayers.

She fell back, letting the giant outpace her. If prophecy was real, if Ariock had a heroic future, then Thomas was certainly going to be part of it. Cherise was sure of that. Hadn't she seen a spark of determination in him after the Alashani had removed his blindfold? It had been brief. But it had been there.

"Your life is worth the risks," she told Thomas.

# AFTERWORD

Thank you so much for reading *Colossus Rising*. Your support means more to me than I can admit without being blasted to death!

The next book, *World of Wreckage*, is a turning point in this series. Torth supergeniuses and Alashani prophets cannot predict what destructive mayhem is about to sweep the galaxy. Thomas and Ariock are on a path to destroy the Torth Empire.

If you liked what you read, please leave an honest review wherever you bought this book. Your feedback will ripple across the internet and make me feel as if I have an inner audience, and I will love it.

The Torth series:

Torth Book 1: *Majority*

Torth Book 2: *Colossus Rising*

Torth Book 3: *World of Wreckage*

Torth Book 4: *Megacosmic Rift*

Torth Book 5: *Greater Than All*

Torth Book 6: *Empire Ender*

# ACKNOWLEDGMENTS

Special thanks to my readers on Royal Road and Wattpad. You know who you are! I only know you by your usernames, but I've learned to recognize those names. I appreciate you very much!

I particularly want to thank readers who supported me on Patreon. That means a lot, and it's hugely helpful to my crazy writer lifestyle. You help me feel legit!

I'm also grateful for Rebecca Roland, a physical therapist who helped me to get a handle on caretaking for Thomas, and Kayla Whaley, who answered my questions about spinal muscular atrophy. Additionally, I learned a lot about living with SMA from Shane Burcaw's videos and books.

I want to thank the Bat City Novelocracy group who read the early draft of this novel, and then critiqued it for like three hours in person, Odyssey Workshop style. Ellen Van Hensbergen, Leigh Berggren, Marshall Ryan Maresca, Kevin Jewell, and Nicky Drayden: Thank you!

There were other beta readers who offered constructive advice on the first draft: Brian Rappatta, Sarah Kelderman, Ethan Reid, Michael Ceranko, Geoffrey Jacoby, Rebecca Shelley, Susan Shell Winston, Laurie Lemieux, Jennifer Weiderman, Marc Geddes, Jose Gustavo Costa Jr., Mike McCauley, Colleen Robbins, Vidya Gopalakrishna, Marissa Engel, and my mom. Thank you!

And especially, as always, my wonderful alpha reader and husband, Adam Robert Thompson. You really are Thomas and Ariock combined! (Uh, a lot less brooding, though.)

# ABOUT THE AUTHOR

Abby Goldsmith is a member of SFWA and attended the Odyssey Fantasy Writing Workshop with George R. R. Martin as the writer-in-residence. She has directed video games for LeapFrog and Nintendo, and her Torth series gained an audience on Wattpad and Royal Road. Goldsmith has lived on all three coasts of the United States and currently resides in Texas, where she is married to her favorite reader.

If you'd like to hang out in the Megacosm, join the Torth Discord server at: Discord.gg/gDYVXdS2qz.

Or subscribe to Abby Updates at: AbbyGoldsmith.com/subscribe.